CW01499060

There was a fingerprint on a page. The fat indentation of a thumb. It had brushed against carbon paper and smudged itself, intricate as an aerial view of an island in the Pacific. There looked to be walls on this island, a maze leading ever inwards until the whirl swung round and you found yourself, as mysteriously, on the way out.

An island of no escape.

It was on a document marked 'CONFIDENTIAL. The Execution of 15 Allied Prisoners of War on Ballale Island 1944.'

The document had to be locked away inside a safe. And there his fingerprint was.

For ever.

Eric Keeling listened.

In the next office, through the glass partition, he could hear the steady drone of the typewriter keys – the tinkle of the bell, the almost comforting percussion of the shaft being pushed along. There was, for whatever reason, a moment's pause.

The undersole of his right foot prickled, as did his scalp. He felt guilty. Even as his hands, of their own accord, separated the two sheets of paper and he placed the bottom sheet down inside his briefcase.

'I'm taking them back to the hotel for homework,' he was already saying in a jocular, teasing voice. 'I'm a swot, always have been. A mother's fucking little boy.'

He could hear the other boys, what they'd say, how they'd say it with a little curl of irony on their tongue.

He clicked his briefcase to. He slipped the case down by the legs of his desk. He was sweating. Partly it was the heat. It was Tokyo at its most oppressive. The rains were yet to come, and the air felt stagnant.

He listened to the voices through the glass partitions: two typists talking about a movie.

'He's an absolute dreamboat.'

'He can park his slippers under my bed any old time!'

The second voice was that of an older woman. Australian. There was a small titter of laughter, then the sporadic sounds of typing took up.

Everyone was waiting for lunch.

Eric looked at the second hand of the clock. It seemed stationary for a second. Then it flicked into life.

He was still living on Tokyo time. Which was a bit of a joke if you let yourself think about it.

That had been one of the first things they did in the camps. Forced you to live according to whatever time it was in Tokyo, regardless of local time, whether it was morning or night.

Tokyo time.

He knew it well. It was as if the second hand ticked inside his being, his hollow self. Which was ridiculous, given that the mirror returned to him this mocking image. An apparently hale and hearty Kiwi bloke with flesh on his bones, a little Ronald Colman moustache trimmed above his lips. A slightly suspicious look in his eyes.

That was his physical being. But inside his skin he was haunted. Not at home.

He was blistering with anger, blank with it. He bore the relation to his old self of an actor impersonating himself. He could act as Eric Keeling, the highly decorated soldier who had received his gong from General Freyberg. But he sensed himself, at odd times, to be someone fraudulent, suspect, as if all over him hung an aroma of inauthenticity.

Just at that moment, the door opened.

'Captain Keeling, sir, any more evidence for me to type up?'

Janice had put on fresh lipstick, a bright Hollywood red. She was a plain-looking girl with an awkward nose. But there was something about her, a determination to be more than her looks. She came from Iowa, she had said to Eric when he asked her.

'Originally . . .' she had said, then left a pause as she had busied herself with the war crimes documents. He didn't say anything but had concentrated on the nape of her neck, which was oily, ivory, with two distinct creases. Her blonde hair was done up in a bravura roll, anchored by pins. It announced her ambition.

'How long have you been out here?'

'I've been out here so long I don't know rightly where's home,' she had said later, in the hotel room.

It had been a mistake, both of them realised that. But it was a time of mistakes.

'No thanks, Janice,' he said to her now. He had the feeling they were speaking in a double tongue. Her clear pale blue eyes had looked into him. He felt himself flushing.

'I'm engaged,' he'd said to her that night. 'Back home, I'm engaged.'

He had said it as though he were talking about someone else. She was dressing. He was naked. She didn't say anything, but patiently went through the retrieval of her undergarments as if she were reassembling a self. Her hair was down, and from the bed, in the half light as she bent over, she had a sturdy Norwegian back. Short legs, with a tan line from a tennis frock up the back of her calf muscles.

'Back home, I'm engaged too,' she had said, with a faint click of sarcasm in her voice. 'Or I was.'

This lingered in the air.

He suddenly felt cold. His sweat felt cold.

'Lost at Iwo Jima. Not officially. Just not listed or anything. Maybe he's alive somewhere . . .'

She was dressed now.

'It's a long time ago,' she added. 'Now.'

There was that indefinite pause, the fraction of it. He struggled to sit up. But he was exhausted, he realised that. He wanted to sleep.

'Don't worry,' she had said. She was putting her roll back up. Anchoring it with pins. 'Don't you worry about a thing, sir,' she said, with just that same hint of sarcasm in her voice.

It was a time of mistakes, it was true.

Eric Keeling set out across 'Little America', back to his hotel. Everyone connected to the war crimes unit lived nearby. It was the administrative heart of the occupation, a network of streets and European-style buildings that had escaped the carpet bombing. Far beyond it were the blocks where nothing had survived. Square miles of ash and greyness.

He'd have a bath – well, not a bath entirely, since 'the Ritz' didn't run to that. But he'd cleanse himself. Shake the miasma off himself momentarily, as he crouched down, douching himself with warm soapy water from the wooden pail.

He bathed two times daily. This was something new. Or rather it had started when he got out of the camps.

It was one of the things his mother had commented on, that first week back home in New Zealand. First of all, as a joke. Then, silence. Finally his mother said to him, 'Son, we don't run to two baths a day in this house. You're using up all the hot water.' Keeling could remember the shock of his mother saying this. He'd felt a moment of complete insanity. He wanted to say, But it's not me using the water. Then the obsessive smallness of everything attacked him. He got angry.

His mother, looking into his face, seemed frightened. Her mouth fell ajar; her false teeth clicked down from her upper gum.

He'd had to walk out. He'd gone for a long, long walk. It got worse when he came back. Mother crying. She kept trying to catch his arm. She kept saying, 'I'm sorry, son. I'm sorry.' Which made it worse.

He'd shifted out to a boarding house in Symonds Street, in town.

He felt absurdly betrayed. By his own mood swings,

which he sensed in some part were unreasonable, even unfathomable. Then he started finding it hard sitting on trams, looking at all the fat, self-satisfied faces nodding in rhythm with the vehicle. He kept waiting for something.

Then he realised he was 'free', he'd been released. It was over.

But it didn't feel like it.

He'd got off the tram, and found himself standing trembling in the middle of the footpath in a place he didn't recognise.

He'd gone back to the boarding house, packed his bags and shifted out.

He went to Rotorua and stayed at De Bretts. He'd gone bathing in the hot pools with a morbid abandon. He had the intensity of someone who had been through extreme experiences. He seemed to frighten people. He also ate with a passion, as though he could never get enough food. He felt a stranger to himself, as if all his previous life was a dream.

Then he had got the call to Wellington, the medal. They'd sprung the trap. How about getting away, going to Tokyo? Work as an investigator in the Second Australian War Crimes Section.

Escape.

Now he wandered through what they all called, sardonically, 'Little America'. An American soldier was on point duty, directing the traffic. A Japanese traffic warden, a little further away, watched the American's gestures carefully and a second later imitated them with beautiful precision. American jeeps were parked everywhere and Eric, like everyone else, had to show his security pass to get in and out of the zone. By now, after two years in the place, it was like a phantom act: it didn't mean much.

It had taken him a while to realise this. Then he began to feel the possibilities.

Some Nip kids were running alongside him, calling out for chewing gum. Even though he was wearing an Australian uniform, the fact he came from the American HQ indicated wealth. He ignored them. Suddenly a really skinny kid, wearing a men's pair of shoes without laces, sores running up his shinbones, snot hanging out his nose, was standing in front of Eric. There was something so aged and lost in the kid's face, his eyes. He said a few words in Japanese in an absurdly high, almost girlish voice. The other kids burst into screels of laughter. Faces were looking at him, into him. The kids disappeared as quickly as they'd appeared.

'Oh, mistake!' said the boy.

Keeling walked on, past the old granny squatting on the ground with a few wares of despair displayed in front of her – a battered tin teapot, cracked doll face, bundle of what looked like rags. The skin on her face, he noted, looked charred. Beneath was her new skin, a livid pink. She raised a hand up, in a begging gesture.

As he walked along, his shadow slid over the objects, then detached itself and disappeared.

He entered 'the Ritz', as they called the inn. It took a moment for his eyes to adjust to the dimness. There was that immediate sense of beer-soaked carpets, old cigarette smoke: the bitter tang of an all-male atmosphere. Through in the Anzac Bar he could already hear the pock of billiard balls, leisurely, assured. A soft mat of conversation hung in the air, though there was nobody to be seen.

Eric nodded lightly to the receptionist, an Australian sergeant called Shaw. Shaw saluted, but a little slackly. He was smoking and sorting mail. The fume from his smoke ran up, urbanely, over the downcast plane of his face. Shaw was heavy-set, with powerful shoulders and a weak face: he was an alcoholic perhaps. Eric knew there was almost nothing Shaw could not get: he operated an unofficial black market. In his own small world he was a man of power. So, when meeting a superior officer, there seemed to be some internal struggle going on within him: usually it was expressed through a fawning attitude which held within it something implicit – contempt.

Shaw said to him, without removing his cigarette, 'Hot afternoon for it, sir.'

'Yes, Shaw.'

Eric was waiting to see if he had any mail. But he knew Shaw knew this – hence he would not answer. Shaw's lugubrious eyes gazed back at him, so he walked on. Dismissed. There was a bray of male laughter coming from the billiard room. It sounded like a dirty joke. Keeling felt himself flushing for some reason. He began to climb the stairs.

'Oh sir?' Shaw's voice came from behind him. 'I almost forgot. Someone came in earlier, looking for you, sir.'

Keeling gazed back across the surf of 'sirs'.

'A Yank, he was, sir.'

Shaw was already looking down, continuing to sort the mail. A hint of a smile.

'I told him you'd be back soon but he left.'

Keeling felt suddenly exhausted. These attacks of utter tiredness still overcame him. He had trouble even walking along the dark carpeted corridor. The whole building still stank of smoke. It was as if the bombing all around the hotel had entered the place by stealth, taken refuge there. A stench, a scorched smell, dry, high up in the top of the nostrils. He fitted his room key shakily in the lock, pushed the door back. Something like a sense of despair opened up before him.

He walked inside. Kicked the door shut behind him. Fell down on the bed like a dead man. He sank into an abrupt and deep sleep.

2

They called him Tiny. He had grown up in New Zealand in the 1920s and he was tall, so it was natural he was called Tiny. It was either that or Lofty. His birth name was Eric Harald Keeling, but he kept quiet about that. He was tall and thin as a piece of paper, as slender as the page of a book when it stands on its own, away from the rest, before it falls. This is what he was like when he was twelve. As he got older, he began to 'fill out'. This is what his mother, Alice, said. It made him feel as if he were an ideogram that wasn't all there. As if he were one of those drawings made up of dots but nobody had quite connected all the lines yet.

His father Arthur, a draper, had died not long after Tiny was born. So Eric was a widow's son – with all this meant in terms of protection, and obligation, of growing up fast and not growing up at all.

His mother was anxious that he do well. She had been left with barely enough to live on. They owned a bungalow in a not very good street in Ellerslie, round the back of the racecourse. On warm days there was a distinct smell of horse manure drifting on the breeze. There was also the frailer echo of a yell coming from the members' stand on race days. Tiny grew up in what seemed a paddock of perfumed women in fox furs and slouch hats, walking towards photographers who snapped them with a just perceptible click. They arched their backs. Tiny never went in through the gates. He loitered outside, breathing in the excitement, all the louche smells of chance, success and sex.

He picked up tickets and the odd threepence.

His mother, finding these, demanded an explanation. He kept silent. He wanted his own secrets. He was developing his sense of self. She strapped him. Hard.

His mother was a Methodist, a teetotaller, and her proximity to the racecourse, for her, had biblical overtones. She talked of sin, deliverance – frivolity and being saved. Tiny would drowsily awaken to the sound of horses' hooves thundering across the turf, a hectoring voice rising to a climax. In his dark room, it seemed he had awoken into a life other than his own, a possible being who was free to experience excitement and risk.

He was forced to take a nap every day after lunch on the weekends, as if he had to catch up with growing. He delivered the morning paper during the week, and after school he worked delivering groceries. This kept him tired, so that life to him seemed a matter of drowsiness, awakening, of never quite catching up. His life seemed made up of dawns in various shades. His mother always moved around the kitchen like a mute. She insisted on getting up. She never spoke beyond Good Morning (which she had told him came from God, from banishing the spirits of the night). He rode off into rain, to frost, to the startling stillness of what could seem like the first morning.

But if this was at one end of his day, the other end was more soiled, more like a glimpse into some kind of arrested drama. The back doors of houses, a woman emerging out of the gloom in which she had hitherto seemed invisible, the illicit pleasures of the purse opening and shutting, the glance down at him, sometimes assessing, sometimes completely blank. He was not himself here, he was 'Mrs K's boy'. He felt himself embedded in this being, as though he had no surplus existence.

Only once, when Mrs Herring asked him in to put down the groceries on the kitchen table, did she ask him how old he was. He noticed several rings of water on the table top, as if a glass had hurriedly been withdrawn. Mrs Herring looked flushed; her eyes were sparkling unnaturally. There was an air of excitement about her, as of a race drawing to its climax. Tiny had the sense of someone else being in the house. Mrs Herring had felt for her purse, which was hanging off the back of a kitchen chair. She turned her back to him and counted. He heard the beautiful purr of notes. These were hard times, so this sound was amplified by longing. In the end she said she had no change, she'd catch up with the grocer next time round.

The following delivery Eric had come across a short man dressed in a sharp suit, his hat at a tilted angle. He was walking up the path around the side of the house. This was shrouded by tall hydrangeas and led to the back door. It was that flat time of mid-afternoon when the streets were empty of everyone apart from widows. Or a mother with a pram, looking as if she were escaping.

The man had been startled to see Tiny, who already towered over him. There was an immediate granite sense of competition. Tiny didn't know this at the time. He felt a little at sea. Then the manikin had relaxed and swept his hat off like someone in the movies.

'Calling in to see the Mrs myself,' he said with a joviality which struck Tiny as out-sized. As the man spoke, Tiny saw gold in his teeth. It glittered, then disappeared.

They had arrived at the back door simultaneously. It stood wide open. There was a lambent square of light upon the lino floor. Tiny's eyes wandered. A marmalade cat lay on its back, legs in the air. From upside down, topaz eyes interrogated both of them.

The man with gold teeth rapped his fingernails on the glass of the door and called out: 'Toodle-oo!'

A woman's voice, from inside, came back – lazily. 'Oodle-too!'

Tiny heard a noise which sounded like a squirt, and then Mrs Herring came down the hall, smelling of something overpowering. She looked momentarily startled to see Tiny there; her hazel eyes moved from Tiny to the manikin. She was smoking, he noticed. Tailor-mades. A ring of lipstick round the stem.

The manikin said, 'The lad'n I have come a-courtin'.'

She laughed a little. Her clothes were loose and golden. A string of Bakelite beads swung low as she leaned forward for the groceries. As she did so, Tiny had a glimpse of lacy camisole, the crease between her breasts, and sensed some denser, more private perfume. He felt drunk, disoriented.

The manikin was offering him a florin.

'Treat yourself to the flicks, sonny-me-lad.'

And then he flicked the coin up in the air. It rose, twirling, glinting, head over head until Tiny, his instincts aroused, leapt forward to catch the coin which fell with a *plupt!* into the small of his palm.

It was warm, as if it had rested against the man's leg.

There was something so extraordinary about all this that Tiny, who would have instinctively refused an offered coin, took it silently.

He suffered all through that night and the following week. The coin hid at the back of his drawer. He would slide it open, feel for the coin under his ironed handkerchiefs. Finding its faint metallic knock, the afternoon flooded back, except now he saw the manikin and Mrs Herring disappearing up the hall from the kitchen door. They vanished into the silence, which gnawed hungrily on them, an unspoken, unnamed delicacy.

He asked his mother who Mrs Herring was.

'A widow like me,' said his mother, after an appreciable, suggestive silence. 'Why?'

He just wondered.

He felt his mother's eyes boring into the top of his head. He had deliberately waited till she'd turned her back, the enamel teapot in her hand. (She herself only added boiling water to cold tea, preferring the economy.)

He had a sense of widows being possibly different.

Every Sunday his mother disappeared after church to visit an elderly woman friend, an invalid even more indigent than herself. He said he'd go to the museum. He'd use his bike.

His mother stood there listening, wide eyed, as if she could hear the wing of his sin. Then she took his face, holding it under the chin, and pulled it into the light. He felt the light on his cheekbones, his lips. The lids of his eyes.

'Don't disappoint me, Eric,' she said.

He felt the old familiar sense of something being beyond him, some mystery, some equation he could not quite comprehend, but one which weighed downwards, tilting towards never being good enough. There was only the photo in the hall of his father, retouched so he never seemed quite real. The long thin nose, the eyes lifting up to another horizon, beyond the camera.

His mother never talked about his father, except to say, 'He was a good man.' She always said this a little belligerently, as if people doubted her word.

He had died in the Influenza Epidemic.

'Why would I disappoint you, Mum?' he managed to say huskily, though his voice was breaking so the sentence slid out of control.

She gazed down into the freckled face, staring as if to make sense of what lay behind or beneath the pattern of his freckling.

'Wear your sun hat, son. Don't speak to strangers. I'll be home by the four o'clock tram.'

This was his mother's sole moment of pleasure a week, visiting an invalid, the daughter of a mayor who had fallen on difficult times. Perhaps his mother felt her own life was, on reflection, better.

It was this afternoon his life changed.

He discovered the tin box in which his father had kept all his treasures.

The box was hidden on the top shelf of the hall cupboard. If he considered it carefully, his father's eyes led him directly to the spot. Perhaps, after all, this was what his father had been looking at all those years. Yearningly, each eyelash individually combed, as if with the flick of a penknife.

Eric had occasionally seen the tin box up there, but because the house was full of shoeboxes, hatboxes, boxes of all sorts, he had paid little attention to it.

His mother made cloth animals. She did this as a genteel addition to her widow's pension from the South British. She sat in the front room, as though by this very act acknowledging that her life as a social woman was over. She put up the leaves of the big oak table, placed her Singer machine upon it.

His view of his mother: crunched down by the little bulb, forehead pincered as she stared downwards, pins in her mouth. She refused to put the overhead light on if she could save a penny. The little faces of the Japanese dolls, camels, Sambos, elephants, penguins lay about, their bodies as blank as his own – genderless, bare patches of cotton handstitched into generic trunks.

Gradually his mother's enterprise crept out from the table and covered the carpet square, the sofa and two chairs until finally the sitting room was no longer itself but an unofficial toy factory.

So Eric was used to boxes.

But this tin box was different. It never moved. Never opened. It stayed there, the one fixed pivot of the house.

For whatever reason, that afternoon, with his florin thrust into the deepest recess of his shorts pocket, Eric found himself getting out the kitchen chair, standing on it, edging the tin box down.

First of all dust fell into his eyes, blinding him.

He coughed. Held still, to see if anyone had overheard him.

It was one of those cool grey days when a chill wind fingers down your spine.

Nothing moved, except far away, on the main road, he heard a tram screeching to a halt: metal on metal.

The tin box was made for tea, decorated to look like a pirate's chest. Green and orange. He lifted the lid back and saw inside an ocean floor of objects.

Eric tiptoed to the front door, turned the key. He went to the kitchen door and closed it. He went back into his room and sat on his bed, facing the door.

He opened the chest and began unloading the contents.

3

He had a memory of wallpaper. Autumn leaves seemed to be floating on a tide. He could remember the smell, too, a faint whiff of camphor, Sunlight soap – the indefinable scent of his father's tin box . . . Inside the box there was something metal, a leather strop, a strap, buckles, military buttons, an old unused dressing, some nail implements . . . He was opening the tin box and putting the objects into order. He was trying to work out the order. He thought if he could only put them into an order . . . his father would come back . . . like a photo negative slowly turning into an image . . . so, in a certain light, if it was held just so, you could see all the details, the eyes smiling looking straight at you . . . if he could only put the objects in order . . .

When Eric awoke, he was back in Japan.

There was a note under his door. It was on thick paper. Eric saw it when his eyes had opened and he had reasserted his primacy over his room. It was like this each time he woke: there was a battle between what was memory and actual. Dream had more authority than reality.

Lying on his side, stinking hot, he could feel his own body heat, the jut of an erection. The mouldy paper walls seemed to undulate, breathing in time with his own lungs. The watching eye of a single lightbulb peered down at him.

He remembered back to when he was alone in his cell. He had arrived at that moment of horror. He could no longer find anything to think about.

He had, over the three years of his captivity, eaten into the precious store of memory of his previous life in Auckland. He had unknowingly lived his earlier life in a spendthrift way. He realised that now. He had hardly registered anything much at all. But in prison, in a cell, he had been thrown back on to the pittance of his memory. And like a pauper he spread his past out around him. Night by night, as day followed day, he inspected his poverty – his wealth. He catalogued, he put away. Then there was the day of unquiet horror: there was no more.

He had walked as far as he could go into the interior of his past. He had been relying on door after door opening before him. Until, in the end, he had hit this wall. He wasn't in a cell with a small peephole and bucket for shit. He wasn't even that skinny carcass whose brittle flesh, with its rising welts of scabies, distended stomach, rickety limbs, he inspected.

He was in a dark tunnel, and there was a kind of eternal silence. He could remember quite clearly calling out: *I haven't got anything to think about.*

And the strange thing was, ever since that moment, he

had not been able to think of his past any more. It was as if, at that second, he had frozen. An internal clock had stopped.

Tokyo time.

He'd been living in the single room at the Ritz for over a year. He had asked for a room with a window. His window looked out on a wall. He had shifted when the man in the room beside him had taken to having a different woman in his room every night. It began around 11 p.m. and got worse through the early hours of the morning. The sounds of the man and various women drove Eric almost wild with despair.

This was when he had slept with Janice. It had been a brutal animal fuck, as if he wanted to find something in her, or assault her. Yet she had managed to meet him on the same grounds. Whatever had been in her was as forlorn and passionate as his own need. She would never say to him he had cried out like a child, like a lost child, at the moment of climax. He had cried out, Oh Jesus! Jesus! Jesus! in an ever-descending note of imploring.

She had asked him a few weeks later if he was religious. 'No,' he had said, surprised. She said, 'I thought you might have been brought up a Catholic.' He laughed then.

She thought at that moment, he has the face of a disappointed boy. But his laugh disappeared and he took up his war crimes documents as though he were running late, and he said, walking out of the room, 'I was brought up a Methodist.'

There was a snarl in the undertone in the way he said 'brought up' which intimated to her that he might no longer be a believer.

A believer in what, she herself wanted to know.

She sort of believed, for the sake of belief, but in her heart she no longer knew what to believe: the headlines? the death lists? the peace? Or the Cold War, as it was now being called? She hardly knew what to believe, especially as there was so much pressure again, to believe.

It was the same old shit, she wanted to say to herself, but this half-formulated view she kept to her private moments, to inspect when she was alone, trying to work out what she'd do with the rest of her life. Already it was a dangerous thing for a girl like her to be in the Armed Forces. By 1948, anyone half-pie decent, with what could be considered any looks, had a husband. The only women left in the army were the ugly, the bereft, and those, like the lesbians, who regarded the turf as their own.

She semi-wondered, while she curled her hair up on the top of her head and looked for a pin, which camp she belonged in, and laughed bleakly.

It was time to get out – in fact, the time to get out had passed.

She found herself in Tokyo because, ever since Iwo Jima, she had lacked the spirit to move. Or she told herself this. She said things to herself that sounded like they came from a slangy Hollywood movie: things like, 'My heart's been shot to bits.'

But those kind of films had gone out of fashion. Everyone was sick of the war, sick of death, sick of everything to do with it.

That was why she hadn't got out of the army.

She hadn't moved fast enough.

Something in her was slow and faintly dead. Or in suspension, as they used to say once upon a time, in those suddenly far-off days – 'for the duration'.

Eric recognised the handwriting of Lieut. Randolph Bayton. US Intelligence. It was Janice who had introduced them in the bar of the Press Club. Everybody drank a lot, drank as if they were hoping to discover, down the bottom of the tunnel of drink, why they drank. There was something so concentrated about it.

The thought had crossed Eric's mind that Janice and Bayton had possibly slept together. Their meeting seemed pre-arranged. He had watched the way the two Americans sparred and laughed as they talked; but Bayton — call me Randy — was perhaps like that with all women. Rising up when a woman entered a room, pushing a chair under the seat with just the right deferential intimacy.

He was an American gentleman.

Randy was not exactly good-looking. His forehead was not quite right, it was too broad and high. It looked like he might have been burned in an aeroplane accident. He wore his nutmeg hair in a sweeping fringe, which was unusual among the Americans, most of whom favoured a shaven brutality. This sweeping fringe gave to Randy's face an oddly boyish look, startled.

Women plainly felt it enticing, though Eric wasn't sure if this was because they wanted to mother him.

He thought this until he met Randy's wife, Anita, who was small, compact and smart. She crackled with sexual electricity. Randy had asked Eric back to his quarters after their first game of golf. They lived in a palatial house in what everyone called, mockingly, 'Washington Heights' — a slightly hilly suburb of Tokyo that had escaped all evidence of napalm.

It had all happened artlessly, or at least this was what Eric had thought back then. He thought his life might be finally falling into place. Randy had been saying to Janice that his old golfing partner had been sequestered to Korea. This really let him down. Randy depended on his golf for a little bit of relaxation – 'away from all the sickoes and crims' was what he said.

Eric had overheard this. He had felt Janice's pale blue eyes straying to his face, and she was saying to him, 'Eric? Don't you play golf?'

It had all seemed so accidental, and the truth was Eric was so relieved to get out of his claustrophobic room, to escape the sounds of those people through the wall, the parade-ground thump of his thoughts.

Randy asked him incredulously, as if he'd just discovered the most wonderful thing. He practically pleaded with Eric to play golf with him as a favour. And Eric had accepted with pathetic gratefulness, like a child being offered a holiday away from loneliness.

Randy said he would call round for Eric the following Sunday. He had been as good as his word.

Eric had borrowed some clubs from Shaw, who folded the note away into his inside shirt pocket with a smooth, magician-like action. Then he and Randy had driven away, out through the burnt-out wastelands of Tokyo until they came to the strange oasis of the Koganei Golf Club.

At one time this contrast would have startled him, caused him to think afresh of all that had happened. Now he had become a creature of habit; he inhabited the lunar landscape of destruction, just as all the others did: the old picking their way through the ash, the burnt tin; the kids on the street begging; the young women offering their bodies. Through some sort of lottery, he, Eric Keeling, was driving past them in a jeep. It could so easily have been the other way round. He no longer inspected the nature of chance: he had lived through chance and all its variables. He was lucky: he was a survivor.

The clubhouse was an elegant building, entirely art decoratif in its detailing. Beautifully laminated pale woods, gleaming chrome and ziggurat lights. The greens were like dense velvet. The only other people playing were high-ranking American officers, all of whom Randy knew as friends. He introduced Eric as 'my young friend from Maoriland'. Eric found himself shaking the hands of people he normally only saw from a distance and saluted.

Now they accepted him immediately as one of themselves, and Eric felt bathed in some kind of acceptance that was healing – or partially healing, since Eric at the same time felt divorced from whatever role he played as a human. Since he was no longer sure of himself, he was no longer sure of anything he felt. Except one feeling, which was that pure memory.

They had kept playing golf there all through the autumn. One day, seemingly accidentally, while they sat in the beautiful lounge bar, enjoying a scotch and a cigar, Randy had told Eric that this was where the Axis diplomats and Japanese aristocrats had come at the very end of the war, when the Japanese were beaten. Here they waited for the conquerors, drinking expensive alcohol, smoking cigars, looking out at the too perfect green.

Eric looked at the place with different eyes after that.

Randy's handwriting in the note slanted to the left; was written, rather oddly, in a heavy lead pencil, in capitals. Increasingly Eric had come to see Randy's handwriting as a kind of ransom note. It was implausibly impersonal, as if trying to disguise any personality that might be revealed in smaller lettering. Eric told himself all this was ridiculous, but some other part of him said: *Listen to your instincts.*

Randy's note announced that Anita was unexpectedly going home. They were having a cocktail party. Eric was to bring a lady. 'If you can find one!' He'd underlined this, and jabbed a deep dot at the end. 'Anita would love to see you.'

'We've hardly seen you at all lately, darling,' Anita had said the last time he'd been to see them. 'Are you avoiding us? I know we're frightfully dull and old for a youngster like you.'

It was her joke with him, her way of handling him. He was thirty-two. Anita was in her early forties but dressed and acted with the dynamism of someone much younger. Her hair was black, shorn off in a pageboy cut; before that she had had deep curls which Eric had thought looked sensuous and womanly. Her new haircut made her look younger, and somehow surprised. Randy and Anita seemed a deeply affectionate couple, and Eric had, for quite a time, pictured them as how he might, in an ideal future, like to be: sophisticated, as if all of life were a rueful joke, and everything would be all right so long as you could make fun out of it.

Anita was a New Yorker. Randy was from the Mid-West. Without knowing precisely what this meant, Eric understood it was part of the routine of their humour. Randy played at being a hayseed farm boy and she played at being a Broadway vamp, doing imitations of Ethel Merman grinding out 'There's No Business like Show Business'. There seemed a lot of joy in Randy and Anita's life, and Eric hung around them with the melancholy of a circling satellite.

One night he'd gone out to a party at their house. It was a poker night. He had got there late. He'd gone back to his room after a day of investigations at Sugamo Prison. There was always a backlash every time he went there. It was to do with locks. Darkness. Stillness. The black crease of trapped humans. In some senses it didn't matter that they were Japs now, locked up in cages. Or that they deserved to be. It was something larger than that. It was the stillness of time. The stoppedness of time. The unforgiving minute. Its dye had leaked into Eric's soul. He had come back to his room and fallen into an uneasy, dream-fuelled sleep.

When he woke up, it was eleven o'clock. It occurred to him it might be too late to go to the party. But he also felt it would be impolite not to go, and at least a part of his soul was still frozen forever in that earlier incarnation – a Methodist boy trying to do his best.

Doing what is right.

Outside their house he could hear the driving rhythm of Glenn Miller's 'Gal from Kalamazoo'. There was laughter and, closer to hand, the voices of people in intimate conversation on a front balcony.

'Eric baby, come on up,' Randy called out. 'We thought you wouldn't make it.'

A shadow dislodged itself from the others grouped on the top balcony, and various voices, blotted with drink, called out greetings to him. Eric, whose idea of sophistication until recently had been a chromium tea wagon laden with sponge cakes accompanied by a cut-crystal thimble of sherry, felt exhilarated by the changed condition of his life. He still felt, at this stage, that he could be loved, or just liked — it didn't matter really. He was still trying, like an apprentice, to see where he fitted in, and in some senses it didn't matter too much to him where it might be. Anywhere was okay, and essentially the same.

A drunk woman, someone's wife, had opened the door for him and begun talking to him as if they were in the middle of a conversation. The woman had bright yellow hair and a big smile. Her dress was long, reminiscent of a sarong, and had a strident pattern of flowers on it. Out the corner of his eye, Eric could see a Japanese servant, a man, bowing away from them. He had come to the door at the same time. A door closed quietly, like a hatch.

'You don't really think that, do you, sweetheart?' the woman was saying to him. She turned back to him and, taking his hand, pulled him through the door.

The living room was set out in poker tables. There was a low fug of cigarette smoke lying across the room. Various players were staring down at their cards. There was an odd, taut atmosphere of concentration while a Japanese manservant worked the room with a tray. He worked with professional discretion, not precisely engaging anyone in conversation, but with small murmurs and carefully choreographed actions he freshened up drinks, emptied ashtrays. Faces like masks were buried in the smoke.

Various players momentarily moved their gaze to take in Eric, the newcomer. Perhaps a draught of fresh air had come in with him, because the cigarette smoke in the room fractured, wavered and then slithered away from him. Faces became more defined and he recognised men from the golf course. Those turned towards him nodded, or simply gazed. Then the game took up again.

'Darling!'

It was Anita. She had backed into the room, holding a large silver tray on which there were American hotdogs and sauce.

'You look famished. A growing boy like you. You need to eat.' She came closer, then edged her head round so Eric could kiss her. His lips passed down the tensile slide of her neck, where a long elastic muscle seemed to ride. He had a sense of the smell of her hair, its cleanliness, and some other perfume, probably sprayed on much earlier in the evening and just at the final perimeter of its scent. It was mixed in with something earthier and more pleasant: her body smell.

She swung the tray round to him.

'Eat! Eat! You look so thin!'

She was saying this in a mock-Jewish grandmother's voice. It was a shtick she kept up with Eric, pretending to be his solicitous mother, looking after a forlorn and lonely bachelor boy in the Forces.

He took a hotdog, but she insisted he have another.

As she turned away, she murmured to him, 'Doll, this is the funeral parlour part of the party. The fun part is out on the balcony.' And she leaned her body into his momentarily before she pushed him, slightly, in the direction of some heavy glass and wooden doors, in the Frank Lloyd Wright prairie style, at the end of the room. Eric felt her body heat.

He badly needed a drink.

An American general, Jason K. McDougal III, glanced up at Eric, then slid his cards away from Eric's glance. He had a huge cigar clamped in his mouth, and a stream of smoke unfurled. He nodded to Eric in a dismissing yet friendly acknowledgement.

'Hori,' he growled.

It was what they had come to call him on the golf course. Eric had tried to tell them one evening it was what Maori men were called back home. They had looked at him as if they expected a further explanation.

Behind the doors, the music swelled, and there was a crush of bodies. It was late in the history of the party, and Eric received a vivid imprint of patterns of desire and boredom. Various groups of people were talking with a highly animated, hysterical vacuity, a drunk nearly always at the centre of hilarity.

Randy came towards him holding a crystal glass that had clearly just been rinsed in cold water. In his other hand he held up a bottle of scotch. It was a third full.

He handed these over to Eric, then massaged his back muscles in a gesture of greeting.

'You old dog, trust you to arrive when the party's warmed up.' Randy was yelling. 'Earlier it was like a fucking morgue in there. Too much brass and not enough kitten.'

Kitten was his word for women. It nicely circumvented the more pungent usual word. And in fact 'kitten' was what he most often called Anita.

Eric poured a long deep scotch. He threw it back in one draught, then poured another decent finger.

'Attaboy,' murmured Randy drowsily. He pinched the muscle on Eric's arm. 'You go at it hard, baby.'

He often called Eric baby. Randy and Anita had no children. It wasn't really talked about at all. Some people assumed they were waiting till they were both out of the Service. Other people left a painfully tactful silence. Anita herself, as if she couldn't stop bringing it up, was always calling men 'baby', 'babydoll' and other terms that, in the military, seemed extraordinarily loose. But Anita and Randy were recognised as being *sui generis*. She was the daughter of fabulously rich people who had made their money on the West Coast, then gone to New York to get some 'class', as Randy said ironically. They both seemed too conspicuously well educated and rackety to be in Intelligence. They were showy, always badly behaved at parties and a huge relief to have around.

Eric had got vertiginously drunk. It was as if there was a backlog of drunkenness he needed to explore. As if the three years of captivity, in which he had not been able to lose consciousness, now greedily demanded back payment. He drank that night, exploring again that tunnel down which he had walked in prison. That tunnel through remembrance to the locked-off room. He drank, finally, to escape himself.

He had various dissolving and discombobulated memories of that night in the days and weeks later. Voices throatily roaring out about a wind sweeping down the Oklahoma plains. A large man wiping his spectacles as tears ran down his face. Someone dropping a crystal glass and its shattering on the floor. The crowd standing back, looking down. A woman laughing as in pain. Lipstick kisses on the side of Randy's cheek that made him look clownish. Eric longed to tell him about the kisses but some immense muted silence had fallen on him. Nobody talked about intelligence, prison, war crimes.

He had a memory of the kitchen door swinging back at one moment and seeing inside a woman who looked like Janice. She was kissing someone. Her arms were awkwardly placed across the man's back, and for a second Eric saw a woman drowning.

The door swung shut. Then he found himself in a jeep, with Lantern, a British Intelligence officer, sitting squashed in beside him. He knew Lantern by sight. In a joint meeting of British and Australian Intelligence, Lantern had been a sardonic presence. At a precise moment of deadlock, he had cleared his throat and unblocked the impasse.

Eric had been standing back to back with him at the party, until finally their backs came to rest against each other in alcoholic stupor. Lantern had a huge and ludicrous laugh. This is what attracted Eric to him.

Lantern had pulled Eric away with him. 'Do you want to escape?' were Lantern's precise words. 'Do you want to escape?'

They were tipped out deep in Shinjuku. The place was noisy, glistening, busy. Possibly Eric's extremely drunk state gave him a sense of dawning calm. He felt like he was on the brink of some great clarification. He had only to follow on alongside his new pal – they were arm in arm – and he would arrive at a point which would solve his great perplexity.

Eric began to realise he was in a part of the city he no longer knew. They went down under an underpass, into a small betting shop, out the back, then down a lane. This lane was curiously quiet. Lit squares of paper indicated windows. Lantern told Eric to put a sock in it. They had been singing, he came to realise later, the song 'I've Got My Eye on You . . .'

Lantern's accent wasn't precisely upper class. It had a softer burr. Lantern later told Eric he wasn't English at all, he was Welsh. But he had been to English schools, and later went down to Cambridge. Then he had 'got mixed up in Spain', as he said it.

They had reached that moment when both sketched in an inevitable history. But as was the case with everyone at that time – unless you were a braggart – the details were brief, elliptical; the briefer the comment, the more explosive.

They were in a drinking den. They were drinking whisky – black-market whisky necessarily, since they were the only gaijin there. There had been an almost total silence when they walked in. But the woman behind the counter had recognised Lantern and they performed brief bows of recognition.

Eric noted that Lantern spoke to her in what sounded reasonably confident Japanese.

Eric looked at the woman. Height five foot two inches, possibly in her early thirties, though it was also possible she was prematurely aged. She wore men's trousers, an apron, canvas shoes, and jade earrings, her sole feminising ornament. She had the prominent cheekbones of a Korean, and puffy eye sockets. Her face was singularly devoid of all make-up or artifice. She spoke an excitable, explosive Japanese that made her seem slightly dangerous. She enjoyed the banter of the other men in the tavern, which soon enough took up and crashed down over the two gaijin, returning them to anonymity. Eric noted she was helped by another woman, who looked like her but was a subtly different edition.

When Lantern came back from the counter, he said very quietly to Eric two words: 'Unit 731.'

Another British officer rolled in. He was a red-faced man walking with the careful calibration of a drunk. His face beamed out a celestial form of happiness, and like a fool he was elaborately greeting the tavern occupants to the left and to the right – in perfect English.

''Scuse me. Terr'bly sorry. Terr'bly terr'bly sorry . . .'

Luttrell and Lantern greeted each other like long-lost friends, saluting each other and working on what looked like a comedy routine. Men in the tavern were laughing, nudging each other. Luttrell and Lantern kept it up, the whole elaborate charade of two English officers greeting each other in a foreign land.

'This is my friend from Maoriland.'

It crossed Eric's mind that it was odd he was always called this; Maoriland glamorising the sparse utilitarian words 'New Zealand'. It also occurred to him it was a coincidence a Pom used the same term as the Yanks.

'He's happily joined us . . .' Lantern's voice sounded as if it were going up hill, then had run out of steam. 'He's joined us . . . got away from those ruddy Yanks.'

'The lovebirds?' Luttrell said as he swung down on to the bench. 'Baby?' It was a stunningly malicious rendition of Anita's voice.

'What is it, kitten?' Lantern replied.

Eric found himself saying like a prig, 'They're friends of mine. I like them.'

'Of course, of course,' murmured Lantern, smiling.

Luttrell offered a hand of cold cooked flounder. 'O lucky escape, young chap. Lucky escape.' He was beaming at Eric beatifically. Then he stood upright, almost tipping over the trestle table. 'Let's get a drink,' he said, as though it were the most terrific and novel idea.

Much much later, Eric remembered, he heard Luttrell

saying to Lantern, 'When do we pull out exactly?'

Eric was aware of a peculiar silence. Instantly, even through the density of his drunkenness, he came awake. He thought, perhaps this is what I have been waiting for. Perhaps this is the moment of clarification?

Lantern turned in seemingly slow motion, his pale grey eyes looking up into Eric's face, and then into his eyes. The look was a coolly considering one.

Eric said nothing.

Luttrell had filled his lungs with air and was bellowing now.

'Kitten! When did you say you were leaving?'

'I didn't.' Lantern's voice was spectacularly sober. And cold.

Luttrell reacted as if he had been slapped. But his reaction was a moment too late, and then he tried to fumble it.

'It is getting late, isn't it, baby?' He pronounced the word with an American inflection. His voice was contrite.

Lantern stood up, stretched.

'I feel like a fuck,' he said. 'Do either of you fairies want to join me?'

Later still, chaotically, Eric could remember washing up with Lantern. Luttrell was lying on his back, in a pool of vomit. He was unconscious. Lantern had his pants down round his knees. He was washing his penis, which he was inspecting carefully. As with all males, Eric shared a speculative interest in other males' sexual organs. Lantern's, he noticed, was uncircumcised. It had the reddened tumescence of a man who has just come away from sex. It was a long, thin, wandering, lonely-looking penis.

Eric was still trying to catch his breath. They had shared the same woman. This had come about seemingly accidentally, as though they had both chosen the smiling girl simultaneously. She had what looked like an air of freshness. In the clear light of the stairwell, Eric had been shocked to see how old she really was. She wasn't a teenager, more like someone whose age had prematurely been stalled at a certain point. Then she had moved away from the light and, as if by magic, she had changed back into a fresh, smiling teenager.

During the act, Eric noticed she kept her eyes wanly open, looking at an abstract somewhere over his left shoulder. Her mouth had gaped open at one point and she had one black tooth in the front. She also seemed unnaturally hot, though Eric put this down to Lantern, who had been upstairs with her for only a few minutes.

'I'm strictly an in-out man, myself,' Lantern had said with the faint trace of a blush on his face. 'Over to you, Kiwi,' he said, for the first time acknowledging Eric's identity.

Eric had found the sex almost unbearably erotic. Too soon he reached his epiphany, and he groaned out loud and swore. The eyelids of the young woman beneath him widened – Eric thought it was like the shutters of a shop opening again for business. They looked at each other for a second of complete impersonality. Then he slid out of her wetness and lay there panting. She slid away from him, and went to wash.

It was later, as Eric washed himself, shamefully, because he was still a Methodist boy at heart, Lantern said, pulling on a cigarette thoughtfully, 'We're going, old man. Got the word from high up. Today. We're all going home.'

Eric had taken a moment to comprehend what he meant.

Lantern pushed the toe of his shoe into Luttrell's vomit-soaked body. Luttrell groaned and tried to push Lantern away.

'. . . You mean?'

Eric felt at that moment the perfect ping of clarity. This was what the whole obfuscation of the evening had been driving towards, then. This moment now. He must be still and receive it.

'We're shutting up shop. Saying sorry Japs, old chaps, it was all a big mistake – no hard feelings, eh? We're scarpering. See you some time.'

Eric said nothing. He felt that great angry deafness descend on him.

Lantern looked deep into Eric's eyes. He seemed to be taunting him.

'We're releasing,' he said very casually, 'all our class As charged with murder. Tonight. Three of the cunts who were up on cannibalism charges. Farewell new-found friends.'

He turned away.

'Luttrell, you useless piece of shit.' Lantern was bending over and talking to Luttrell quite fondly. 'It's all over now, kitten. It's time baby took you home.'

4

Eric got back to his office after his snooze at the Ritz. It was ten past two in the afternoon. The bathing had been no good. His brief sleep had, if anything, disoriented him further.

The phone was ringing. He tried to ignore it but instead found himself picking it up.

'Baby, why are you avoiding me?' It was Randy. 'Does my breath smell bad or something? You know Anita'll be sore as hell if you don't come along to her farewell. We miss you, baby, we do. Both of us. We'd both love you to come early. Just the three of us. Cocktails. At six. Agreed?'

Eric felt his breath make a sound of subsidence. He felt his breathing become flecked, hesitant.

Beside him the door opened. Janice held a pile of documents.

'I got to go,' Eric said. As he put the phone down he

could hear Randy's voice continuing to speak, to seduce, to argue, to harry, to bring him back to heel.

Janice looked at him for a moment interrogatively.

'You look like you could do with a day off,' she said in a light, conversational voice.

It was always a little difficult between them.

He picked the papers up, ignoring her. He turned his back to her.

'Thanks.'

He thought it had been a dream. The conversation with the Pom. He'd woken the next morning with a hangover of hallucinatory intensity. The light coming in the window attacked him brutally. But it was a working day. He'd washed, dressed, all the time seeming not to be present in his body. Yet since this was an echo of a deeper psychological state, oddly enough he felt at home. In homelessness. Internal chaos.

He had managed to get inside the Dai Ichi building before vomiting in the ground-floor toilet. He vomited until bile came out. Then he dry-vomited some more. When he came out, he realised something was up. A passer-by told him General MacArthur had just entered the lifts. There was the usual sense of power having passed by — a kind of tidal wash. Even the guards looked pleased with themselves, touched by a greater significance.

AJ, a boy with the face of a farm boy atop a brutishly muscular body, winked at Eric and grinned.

'You look kinda green, sir,' he said, saluting.

Eric managed a sloppy salute.

Eric wanted to say, 'Something's up, isn't it, AJ? The Brits are pulling out. They've been told to open the prison doors.'

But AJ's healthy American features rendered Eric's question impossible.

Pulling out. The British were going home. It was as if whatever withdrawal had started at Singapore was continuing on. And on, and on, until the British were a world power no more.

Eric went up in the lift, feeling at the same time the motion was too much for him. It was an old lift and rickety. He grabbed hold of the side, as if he were on a rollicking ship, all the time thinking, I dreamt it. What Lantern said.

He got into his office.

Janice floated in with a large glass of cold water. It had ice in it. He looked up at her, stricken with an abject sense of gratitude. Her eyes touched his for a moment, then she moved towards the door.

'An English Intelligence officer.' His head pounded. 'Welsh, actually. L . . . L . . . I can't remember his name?'

'Caryl Lantern?' she said. 'Ex-Guards officer. Son of a diplomat. Tall thin streak? With a laugh to wake the dead?'

He nodded. At the same time he looked into Janice's face to see if there was any knowledge there, any pre-knowledge. Eric had the crazy idea he might be the last to know. About the pull-out.

It was like the camps. Where rumour was truth. Amelia Earhart was Tokyo Rose. There was a new car and fridge for everyone who made it back home. London was a suburb of Berlin.

'Yeah,' Eric said, taking the glass to his lips nervously, letting the silvern liquid spill down his gullet. 'We sort of went out on the razzle a little bit last night.' He took another sip. 'He seems a decent joker.'

'. . . Joker?' Janice said, as if she were rolling the meaning of the word over in her mind. 'I don't know if that's a word I'd use.'

It was on the tip of Eric's tongue to say, Do you know him? But then he thought, What business of mine is it if Janice fucks everyone in the whole British Intelligence Service?

He was irrationally randy. Maybe his face gave him away, because suddenly a wise look slid over Janice's, and without another word, she turned and walked out. She was whistling an indecipherable tune as she went. After a moment Eric realised it was 'I've Got My Eye on You'.

Through the glass partition, a few moments later, there was the sound of women whispering, then laughter.

His phone rang.

'Look, I need to meet up with you.'

Without him saying his name, Eric sensed, knew, it was Lantern.

'I think I was bloody indiscreet last night.'

There was a pause.

'Eric?'

'Yes?'

'You with me?'

Pause.

'Yes. I think so.'

'I thought so.'

There was the sound of Lantern breathing out regretfully.

'Fuck,' he said. Then there was the sound of what seemed like a hand being placed over the receiver and Lantern's odd patrician-sounding voice talking to someone irritably. 'I won't be long. Tell him I won't be long. For

God's sake, woman, tell him I'm busy. Sorry.' Lantern's voice came back into his ear. 'Let's meet for a drink after work? Hair of the dog and all that.'

'Okay.'

'Great! Great!' Pause. 'Can you come to our HQ? No, no, that's not quite right.' A small pause. 'I know. Let's meet in the East Gardens by the palace. Around eight. Is that all right?'

'Yes,' Eric said.

There was an appreciable silence.

'Oh by the way. Last night. That girl. I enjoyed that.'

Eric laughed. 'Mate, I did too.'

'Cheerio.'

He'd rung off.

Eric had got there on the spot of eight. He couldn't help himself – he had always been someone who arrived on time. Perhaps there wasn't enough happening in his life. Or maybe it was a symptom of how he took things too seriously, too literally. He asked himself this as he began his third cigarette.

He had bathed a little too carefully, dressed consciously, as if, he thought wanly, he were going on a date. It was pathetic really. He needed friends, friendship: he was a young man who had lost three years of his youth. The wound was still there. He felt he hardly knew how to behave any more – not with people who weren't trying to humiliate him, threaten him, abuse him. And yet this new world was open ended, exciting, even nerve wracking. He was aware he was sweating lightly.

He glanced down at his watch again. It was 8.17 p.m.

His mother had given the watch to him for his twenty-first. A Buren, gold plated, as stylised as a '40s automobile. On the back she'd had engraved his initials, the date: 1938.

Sometimes it seemed the only part of his personality intact.

To the left of him, in the dim night, were the vast walls of the old palace. The park outside was cut into prim Victorian-seeming paths. And beside him a cuckoo-clock-like gardener's cottage. Eric moved past it carefully, because there was often an Alsatian, aggressive and slathering, tethered on the porch. A GI had taken up residence there, shifting his Japanese whore in with him. Eric could see dim shades in the dark, a white tee-shirt, shorts hanging on a line: an unsubtle declaration of American power.

Inside there was a flicker as someone moved past a light.

Gradually, over the gravel, he heard a faint crunching sound. Eric glanced at his watch. It was now 8.26 p.m.

A Japanese woman holding a drunk-looking GI round the waist disappeared into the dark. She turned her pale disc of a face towards Eric.

Eric breathed out. He threw his cigarette away from him, the sparks flaring up, then dying down.

He'd wait another moment, then go.

It's a long way from Ellerslie in Auckland, he thought.

A discreet cough in the dark.

Lantern was standing on the grass. He had a coat over his uniform. He stood a distance away, and waited for Eric to come to him. As he came closer, Lantern's elegant Gothic features ruffled and he smiled.

'Kitty, kitty, kitty,' he said, and made a small movement with his fingers as if he were lulling along a little cat.

Eric laughed.

Lantern made no apology for being late, slipped his arm companionably through Eric's, and together they walked off into the depths of the park.

Later Eric would wonder how it happened. The seduction was so effortless, so transparently easy. He had wanted to be taken out of his shell, and given a new identity, a purpose.

They had found a long grassy knoll and lain down. They were looking up at the stars. This struck Eric as so peculiar that he didn't know what to do, except go with it, thinking maybe this was how upper-class Englishmen acted. Lantern at the same time acted as if it were the most normal thing in the world, and this park was simply another version of a park on a great estate in England.

'Christ I feel crook,' Eric said.

Lantern laughed and offered him a cigarette. And then he'd begun talking, telling Eric odd things about his childhood. His father, he said, was 'nothing very much at all' – a second secretary in the Tokyo embassy in the '20s. Lantern, or Caryl as he insisted on Eric calling him, had been a kid there. Just young enough to pick up the language easily. Which had been fortunate, as things turned out. Caryl touched on being in Singapore on the day of the surrender. His voice here was dry, ironical, light. He sketched in the panic, the fear and also the odd sense of time coming to an end. Stopping while they waited for the Japanese to enter the city.

He talked then of a brace coming undone. Whatever had been held together up to that point had come undone for ever.

It was over, Caryl said, it was all finished.

Eric wanted to ask, What was all over? What was finished?

As if answering his silent question, Caryl said: 'Us. The British. It's over now for us. At least in this part of the world. Your part of the world.'

Eric was about to say this wasn't his part of the world. Yet the past five years or so had changed all that. It was his part of the world. Whether he wanted it or not.

'I've heard about you, Keeling. I've been following your reports.'

Eric sat up. Lantern sat up too. There seemed to be a different energy suddenly, the earlier, strangely philosophical talk merely a preliminary.

'I know what you're thinking. How you think about all this.'

Pause.

'Once you've been in the bag, maybe you see things a little differently.' This was Caryl again. 'The fact is we're going. Throwing our cards in. Washing our hands. Making a run for it. "A dignified exit". You could say, in Singapore, we got a bit of practice.' His voice was bitter.

'Why?'

Eric tried to stop his voice from sounding all his grief and outrage, but the word had been nestled all day in his windpipe so that it came out faintly whining, as if from a child. He coughed and repeated the word, this time with a flatter, more manly emphasis.

He wanted to say, What about the war criminals who killed so many people . . . ? What about justice?

Caryl's pale grey eyes scrutinised Eric's face.

'The Yanks want to shut down all Australian

investigations too. Did you know that? Release all prisoners. As soon as possible. Different priorities. Cold War. Japs our new friends.'

There was a moment of brooding silence. Only the soft impact of Eric's drawing in on his cigarette showed his emotion.

'It makes me sick.' This was Lantern. 'It makes me want to puke. To tell the truth.'

Neither man spoke for a moment, then Eric said, blowing out a big cloud of smoke, 'I know.'

It was like a confession and a contract.

Lantern turned and looked across at Eric. Eric had an odd sense of loss of perspective. Lantern kept encroaching on his personal space: he wondered for a moment if Lantern was a queer. But then he remembered the night before; worse, his penis spontaneously experienced a spasm of pure pleasure at the memory of it and he felt a slickness of wet trickling down his belly. He felt lost here, but allowed himself to experience the moment of sweet bewilderment.

There could be no forgetting.

That was right.

'You understand what I'm saying, Eric?'

Caryl had lain back, was lying there, looking at him attentively.

'. . . I . . . I think so,' Eric said, with difficulty, because he was frightened of emotional things. He instinctively retreated. But there was something here, something he wanted to know.

Caryl, in the dark, held his hand out.

Eric, for a moment, lay still, looking at the shape of Caryl's hand. He could see it was part of Caryl, the same as his Gothic-shield face: angular, white, ancient, peculiar – strong.

Then Caryl was pulling him up, making him stand.

Caryl said to him, looking away in the dark towards the shrouded dimness of the Emperor's palace, 'Come with me.'

They were inside the labyrinth. Eric was relying entirely on Caryl's knowledge of where he was going. Even so, Caryl paused every so often, looked about as though searching for a landmark, then he launched off again. Like many wiry men, he walked extraordinarily fast. Eric didn't like this. He began to feel a headache pounding in his temples. His hangover threatened to come back with renewed intensity. His skin felt hot and clammy.

Caryl had turned over his shoulder, looked at him intensely and said with a wild laugh, 'Is baby finding it hard to keep up?'

'Don't fucking call me that.'

Caryl said nothing, but let out a silvery laugh, which Eric decided he resented.

As they walked on, he said to Caryl's back, 'I like them. That's all.'

Caryl said nothing, kept walking.

'He's in G-2, you know that?'

G-2 was a special area of American Intelligence, a kind of inner circle which worked beyond the ordinary confines and legal restraints. Eric had often observed that Randy kept very floating hours and seemed to have a freedom quite different from the donkey hours worked by all the other men in that branch.

'His speciality is Unit 731.'

Silence plummeted.

Unit 731: the Japanese biological warfare unit which had been situated in Ping Fan in Manchuria. It had a staff of over four thousand, its own cinema, tennis courts, library and brothel. But there were two buildings in Ping Fan that were out of bounds, linked to the rest by an internal corridor. This was where they did human experiments. Nobody who went into the buildings for an experiment came out. Its head, Colonel Ishii, had disappeared towards the end of the war.

'You know the Yanks are desperate to bag the scientists. Especially Ishii. Biological warfare's the new thing. And of course the Japs were the only lucky bastards to have humans to experiment on – apart from the Nazis.'

'That's fucking sick.'

When they came to a diverging path, Caryl halted. He turned to Eric, glanced into his face and said, 'That woman. In the bar last night. Did you notice her?'

'The woman out the back?'

'Yes.'

'Why?'

'She worked at 731 as a scientist. I can give you the file.'

Caryl turned his back then. 'I can give you quite a few files.' There was something tentative in his voice.

Eric heard the silence.

It was the key. Into that room. Again.

He stepped inside.

'Now we're leaving. Someone ought . . .'

He didn't finish the sentence.

Eric said nothing, but he nodded slightly and he knew Caryl had understood.

Now they walked alongside each other.

Finally they came to an area so dark it was difficult to see. There seemed to be people sleeping under pieces of burnt tin. If you stood very still, you saw movement: rats. Rats moved over and round the sleeping figures, scurrying, not even hurrying. Their high little telegraphic peeps splintered the air. There was a stench of excrement and rot.

Eric felt a moment of pure disgust. He suspected the Englishman was unhinged. They walked through this circle of hell, and came to a smaller side alley that led unexpectedly to a gate. Caryl felt in the dark for a moment, glanced at Eric and undid a latch. He led Eric towards a small house. There was a door.

Caryl knocked, and after a moment a man came out. Eric noted his feet were bound with rags. On seeing Caryl his face, which seemed powdered with age and worries, changed. It became luminous. There was much bowing, and much smiling. Eric was introduced. He too was smiled at and bowed upon. They were eagerly welcomed in.

The room was poor in the extreme, but tidy. A woman, possibly the mother of the man, was tidying away some mats. On seeing the newcomers and after bowing to them, the elderly woman began to animate the embers under an iron pot.

They all sat on the floor.

Eric could not catch the accent of these people. His understanding of Japanese was rudimentary. Caryl, however, talked with ease. Eric listened and observed. He thought both the man and the woman looked strained. They were clearly pleased to see Caryl; their voices sounded affectionate. The elderly woman's eyes filled with tears at one point, and she rocked backwards and forwards, holding herself.

'Tsukasa's mother and father were servants in the embassy,' Caryl said to Eric, in translation. The couple smiled and nodded. Eric nodded.

'Tsukasa's wife died in the Tokyo fires,' Caryl said, but in an animated voice perhaps aimed at disguising what he was saying. 'As did their children.'

Eric said nothing.

Caryl was looking at him intently. He turned to Tsukasa and said a few words to him.

There was a long moment of silence.

Then Tsukasa began talking. He spoke in a low voice at first.

'This is something I must talk about. Please excuse the inhumanity of what I am about to say.' He coughed and cleared his throat.

He told the story of searching for his wife and children. And finding them. They had all been burnt by the napalm.

The elderly woman poured the tea.

'This is something I can never forget. Things I wish I had never seen. I wish to stop thinking about this but I cannot. I am both lucky to be alive but unlucky to be alive, living as I do with these memories.'

Silence held there. An ember sparked. The old woman refreshed their tea. Eric tasted the bitter brew, and as he did so the conversation picked up a little between Caryl and the mother and prematurely aged son. Eric thought he could catch them talking about Caryl's father, and a different version of the past, and gradually the feeling of horror faded a little, and was replaced by the delicacy of old friends joined together by grief and the effort of living with sorrow.

Much later Caryl led Eric out of the labyrinth. He said, 'I'm going to a bathhouse. Do you want to come?' His face was in the shadow, silvery, pale. 'I feel filthy. Inside, I feel filthy,' he said. There was a sad note in his voice.

Eric did not go to Japanese bathhouses. He obeyed the injunction 'Do Not Fraternise with Indigenous Personnel'. He had kept to an odd life while he'd been in Tokyo, staying among the expatriates, hardly ever venturing out into the floating world. Normally he would have refused.

He found himself nodding.

Caryl took him to a neighbourhood bath. Once again, conversation stopped. But whatever Caryl said worked, because there was laughter, and then more laughter through the room. Caryl and he stripped. Men were so often naked together in the army; undressing meant nothing. The men bundled their clothes into the baskets, cleansed themselves, in silence.

Caryl was first in the water. He lay there, relaxed. Talking in a quiet, steady voice, he said the word was that the Americans were negotiating to get hold of the records of the medical experiments from Unit 731. The old war was dead but there was this new war – the Cold War, he said, laughing a little, perhaps because where they were was hot, steaming, crepuscular.

'They want to rule the world, poor bastards,' he said. 'So it's important to them to find out what happens when humans are injected with anthrax or plague or typhoid.'

Eric didn't know what to say.

Caryl went to cool off in a shower. Suddenly he seemed

to recognise someone he knew, a young man, Japanese — a contact maybe? He disappeared in the steam, looking for him. Eric waited, but Caryl didn't come back, so Eric dressed, nodded to the woman who had taken their money and went back to his hotel.

When he came in the door, it was past 3 a.m. Shaw looked at him. Eric was aware his face was flushed still, his hair wet. Shaw said nothing, but on his elliptical face was the ghost of a condescending smile.

The following day Shaw quietly handed over to Eric, as if it were mail, the card of a bathhouse. On one side was a drawing of a beautiful, naked Japanese girl. On the other side was a slim, smiling Japanese boy.

5

Eric took the stairs two at a time. He was a little late for that afternoon's interrogation. But then it never hurt for a suspect to wait. He could remember waiting. He could still feel, as in a slow drip, the deterioration, the collapse of a personality under the duress, the hard emptiness of time.

As he came down the corridor, Eric felt the momentary rush of claustrophobia. It was a corridor lined with doors, all equidistant. There were two fluorescent lights baking everything in a harsh, even light.

His interrogation room was the third door along to the right. All the rooms were the same. Inside there was a wooden table, a dry inkwell. There was a wooden foldout chair of an improvised nature. This was placed at one side of the table. At the other side was a heavier wooden dining-room chair, ornate and Victorian. The seat was covered with a greasy acidic green plush that had worn away into rubbed patches of black by the legs. A fan on the ceiling turned. The very tip of the blade passed the fluorescent tube, so the room had a queasy, constantly fluctuating motion of shadow into extreme light.

Eric was used to it, and used it to his advantage.

He opened the door and Isamu, his interpreter, jumped up. Isamu Morozumi was a puffily overweight young man. His hair was smoothed back, in the style of a 1930s matinee idol. Time had rendered this look obsolete, but he persisted in it. His hair was heavily oiled. It gave him a strangely aged look, although he was only twenty-five. His clothes were the same shabby suit he wore day in, day out. It had begun to smell. It was a pin-striped suit of heavy material, cut in the English fashion of before the war. Isamu's attempt at smartness of appearance – of upholding a 'professional status' – was concentrated on his white shirt, which was religiously laundered. He had two white shirts, Eric had worked out, and one tie, a black silky one that appeared to be plain. Only when you looked more closely did you see that the darkness broke apart into the finest and most delicate pattern. Eric noticed that he also kept the polish of his shoes up, though they clearly needed re-heeling. Eric suspected they leaked. He had watched Isamu one day walking round puddles after a torrential downpour. Isamu's usually emotionless face was rippled, like a wind over a lake, by a pincered look of distress.

Eric had given Isamu an old pair of his own shoes he no longer wore. Isamu, the following day, had given Eric a paper rose. This had embarrassed both of them, and neither ever referred to the matter again. Isamu never wore the new shoes to work.

Isamu said, 'Good afternoon, Captain Keeling, sir.' He

smiled quite happily.

Eric threw the papers down on the desk.

Isamu hurried out the door, attempting to move away backwards as a sign of respect for the captain.

Eric knew he would return with a cup of tea, badly made and overpoweringly sweet. Usually there would be tea-leaves floating on the surface. But it was a gesture, or a statement.

Eric knew that Isamu's people were from Tokyo. His mother had died in the last weeks of the war. His father was old and had come to live with him. Isamu was unmarried. It had taken a long time for Eric to get this story out of him.

Isamu now slid the breakfast cup of tea across the desk.

Simultaneously there was a sharp knock on the door. It swung back, and Persill, an Australian guard, marched into the room.

Eric and Persill saluted. Beside Persill was a small, badly dressed and clearly frightened man.

'It's Matsumoto, sir!' Persill said.

Matsumoto was a soldier at a massacre. He had witnessed the execution of Allied prisoners of war.

Persill saluted again, then, his eyes for a moment catching Eric's with a glint of malevolent pleasure, he stamped out of the room.

Eric knew Persill would be waiting just outside the door. He also knew the guards hated this duty. They weren't allowed to smoke in the corridor, and the long hours of interrogation became for them a conflict between duty, boredom and the desire for a leak and a fag. Only very rarely did anything exciting happen.

Eric indicated Matsumoto should sit.

This brought out in him an apoplexy of nerves. He settled himself down, then jumped up, tested the chair, then sat down again.

Isamu stood to the side. He said to Matsumoto in Japanese (which Eric understood): Relax. This is like the dentist. It always seems worst at the start.

Matsumoto turned a face of panic to Isamu, then looked over at Eric with fear in his eyes.

Eric flicked through the papers on his desk. He began to feel weary. He had a second sense about whether an interview would go anywhere. Or he thought he did. Yet sometimes there was a small, contradictory detail. You had to stay alert for this. Because the whole arranged edifice of 'truth' could come tumbling down if you yanked on this seemingly minute contradiction. You needed terrier teeth, but you also needed alligator patience.

Eric went through the preliminaries, which were the same for every interviewee. Their basic history, length of service. Gradually the focus tightened into a year, then a month, a week – a day. This day then broke down into hours of the day, and what happened at particular moments.

This tightening of focus usually went with a perceptible rising in tension. Eric sometimes thought he could sense a liar by the absence of this tension. A good liar is always relaxed. A good liar is like a gambler, full of dissemblance. Sometimes, however, he was mistaken. Sometimes the trail went cold, and the interviewee left the room, and it was only later that night, in bed, when Eric reviewed the evidence of the day, that some small inconsistency popped into his head.

It was not unusual for Eric to take files home with him. (He was well known, in the war crimes unit, for his workload.) But he'd started doing something illegal: building a stash of documents, which he kept in a separate box in his room. He'd started doing this almost without noticing it. It just happened, or rather it gathered momentum after 'the business with Lantern', as he called it, converting the slipperiness of emotion into something hard, impersonal, manly.

Eric blinked. He'd need to catch up. His understanding of Japanese was basic, so he had to rely on Isamu whose translations were always swift, following on the end of the Japanese speaker's last words with only the smallest of pauses. Sometimes Eric conceptualised this as a game of shuttlecock, and there was the momentary silence as the bat was raised back in the air. Then the shuttlecock of language came flying towards him.

This afternoon Eric felt a great tiredness overtake him. Matsumoto had witnessed the execution of some Allied airmen on Ballale Island. After the defeat, the airmen's bones were dug up, pulverised and scattered in a lagoon.

'You dug up the bones?'

'Yes,' Matsumoto said, his face miserable but eager. 'I wished to give them spiritual peace, that is all.'

Eric, without looking at Isamu, said very casually, 'You took part in the killings?'

Matsumoto began speaking quickly, volubly. 'I thought it was futile murder, but that was the situation. I took up the sword like the others. Besides, I wished to punish the Caucasians for taking up arms against our Emperor.'

'You found it necessary to bayonet the airmen first?'

'I wished them to understand suffering.'

'Which is why you cut off the feet of one of the airmen? And then forced him to kneel, even though he was fainting from loss of blood?'

Matsumoto spurted out excuses.

Isamu held his hand up, and said to Matsumoto, 'Slow down. I have to translate.'

Matsumoto went on speaking as quickly again. Eric rapped his hand hard on the desk. Matsumoto jumped. Eric could sense Persill through the door suddenly paying attention. He might even be smiling.

Isamu said, 'I told you to speak more slowly!'

Eric said, 'You must speak slowly, otherwise I will mistake what you are saying. And mistakes can be bad for you.'

Isamu translated this.

Matsumoto nodded, looked dazed.

Eric let Matsumoto keep talking, nodding every so often as his fountain pen scratched over paper. The strange stop-start nature of translation allowed Eric to keep up.

It was all like a dance, or a machine. Suspect, translator, and the ink pouring out of the split nib of Eric's fountain pen. At times the line of ink looked like a rope that might feel its way round the neck of the speaker and snare and hook him up.

Matsumoto's frightened eyes were following the trail of the ink on the page. It was like blood flowing, he felt. It was like his veins had been opened up. The oppressive room, the strange steady stare of the gaijin. He wondered about what he was saying, the implications. But he made it clear that those responsible were people higher up. People he knew were no longer around. It meant nothing really, what he was saying. But he was still worried.

Then it was over, the gaijin was putting his cap back on his pen, and the blade of the pen, the nib, was sheathed.

'I'll read back to you what I have written.'

Eric read, Isamu translated.

'Is there anything more you want to add?'

Matsumoto shook his head.

'This will be typed up. You must come back tomorrow and sign. But in the meantime, if you sign here, on this piece of paper.'

In making this statement I acknowledge that it was made freely and voluntarily and that no threats were used or promises made to influence my statement.

Too many suspects had disappeared after a night's thinking through the implications of their testimony.

Eric had become aware, during Matsumoto's testimony, of a smell. This wasn't unusual in cases of extreme fear. Both he and Isamu had worked through the smell. A small blush of humiliation had coloured Matsumoto's cheeks. In fact the only moment of eye contact between Eric and Matsumoto had come when the smell became unbearable. But the room had no windows. Matsumoto had looked down, then away. Eric thought he caught a glint of malice in Matsumoto's features.

Later when Eric was standing outside having a smoke with Persill, Persill said to him he couldn't wait to get back to Australia.

He'd had a gutsful, he said quite passionately, of standing round waiting for something to happen. When nothing bloody did.

Eric took this to mean the amount of time it was taking to convict war criminals.

'It isn't bloody proper, sir,' Persill said with his flat-vowelled voice from Sydney's inner west. 'Not when I've got mates who didn't make it back. I'm carrying every one of those buggers on my back, sir, and I just can't stand it.'

6

Eric walked through the typing pool. He was aware that his presence there always created some sort of flutter. It was absurd really, the ordinary flirtatiousness of women, heightened by their isolation in a foreign place. Of course there were GIs, too many GIs. Eric was an officer, a tall, good-looking young man from the outside. Fresh faced. Fucked up, as he himself knew. But then there's always something enticing about a handsome man or beautiful woman with a complex past. He or she seems to cry out to be saved. Soothed.

Eric was partially aware of all this as he neared Janice's desk. Her desk was unoccupied. The rat-tat-tat of typewriters rose up all around him.

'Oh, Captain Keeling, sir.' It was Olwyn, the New Zealand girl. 'The boys want to know if you'll be going to our Anzac Day drinks. At the Commonwealth Club.'

He was caught off guard. He looked down at her – she was a dumpy little thing.

As if aware she were being appraised, she blushed painfully, and Eric was alarmed to see a veil of moisture pass over her eyes.

'I'd love to,' he said quickly.

'Good' she said crisply, perhaps to make up for her earlier, and transparent, moment of vulnerability. She resented him. His beauty.

He looked away.

'I'll write down the details. The boys'll be thrilled. They will.'

'Can you tell me where Janice is?'

A small, caught pause. 'She's out at lunch.'

Eric frowned. He trusted Janice to type up the interrogations immediately. It wasn't policy to leave documents lying around. He'd have to take them back to his office and lock them up in the wall safe. Security was mandatory around every document. Even his briefcase was double-locked, and then stored inside an old safe.

Eric walked back through the glass partition to his office.

Inside, Anita was sitting smoking. She looked pensive and the long single plume from the end of her cigarette rose in the air mink-blue, fluted. She was sitting with her legs crossed, a bright green high heel hanging off her toe. She was massaging the back of her foot.

'Fucking shoes,' she said. 'Fucking black market.'

Olwyn walked past, looking in.

'I mean "wretched" black market.' She laughed.

Eric swung the door shut. He felt angry.

'Don't be angry, darling. I can see that Randy and I have

fallen out of favour with yours truly and you don't . . .'

'I'm busy,' he said.

'Too busy for your oldest and dearest friends?'

Eric said nothing. He took his briefcase over to the safe, unlocked it, and placed the briefcase inside. He locked the safe again, blocking Anita's view with his body.

'What can I do for you, Anita?'

He looked into her eyes, which stared straight back at his. She was smiling at him, 'Oh come on now, baby, don't be like that. It's not our fault. It isn't! It isn't! Whatever's come up between you and Randy. Well, it's to do with your work. Not us, not us personally. Surely?'

She was standing up, fitting her foot back into her shoe. She was wearing an expensive perfume.

'You'll be glad to see the back of me, huh?'

Eric felt conflicted. He rose.

'No,' he said. 'Of course not, Anita.'

'Baby.'

A second too late, and as if a no longer willing part of the game, he said, somewhat moodily, 'Anita. Baby.'

She came and kissed him lightly on the cheek.

'That's better.'

Then she got a handkerchief out of her purse, a small unrealistically lacy one, and wiped the lipstick off his cheek. He flinched.

'We can't have you coming out to cocktails with lippy all over your face, can we?'

'I'm not coming out to . . .'

'I've cleared it all the way to the top. They say Captain Eric Keeling is working too hard. The Allied Command says that he must relax. The Great MacArthur himself was heard to say, That young Keeling needs to take things less seriously. Medicine recommended: one strong martini, followed by another.'

'I can't . . .'

'You can.'

'I don't . . .'

'You do.'

She was coming closer to him.

Then she said in a little plain voice, a dismal voice, the voice of a woman who knows unhappiness, 'Don't disappoint me, Eric. Don't make this any harder than it has to be. Please.'

And she stood there, looking up at him. He had a sudden perception that behind all the bag of tricks, the make-up, the repartee, she was perhaps not exactly a fulfilled woman. It struck him that he had no idea why she was going home. That perhaps Randy and she might not be getting along so well any more.

This saddened him. Like all young men, he held to one couple as an example of all the happiness he might one day share.

He sighed, picked up his hat, put it on his head.

'That's a good boy, Eric.'

She had a big American limousine waiting outside. There was a military driver. He took off at speed.

The files from British Intelligence had begun arriving in his room. There was no sign of who had sent them. Or how they had got there. His room was normally locked. Shaw downstairs would have a key, but it was unlikely he would have opened the room. Not without saying something to Eric. Shaw had said nothing when Eric came in. For once his face showed neither expression, nor interest. Perhaps this was because he was negotiating with a shady-looking Japanese man, a man who looked like a bookie, a small hat on the back of his head, a man who smelt of cigarette smoke and something more acrid.

The files were in a paper folder. On the top was a stamp reading 'Top Secret'. Standing there, in his room, Eric had flicked through the papers in one file.

```
The Ping Fan Biological Germ
Warfare Unit in Manchuria is to be
neither discussed, investigated nor
entered into War Crimes Files.
   All agents entrusted with
handling this material should be
cautioned that any information has
international implications. It is
of a highly sensitive nature and
every precaution must be taken
to maintain its secrecy. The
numbers of persons dealing with
this subject should be kept to a
minimum.
```

He glimpsed a name: Bayton, Randolph. His eyes sprinted down the print. It was a report from Randy: he was a contact point between the scientists at Unit 731 and US Intelligence. It articled another whole life from the one Eric had known about – golf, louche parties, gin, laughter. Of course. Randy's report was succinct, acute: he was offering indemnity against prosecution if the scientists headed by Colonel Ishii would leave Japan and go straight to America. Taking all their information with them.

Randy had been travelling all over Japan. The scientists were dotted away in small provincial towns, living under false identities – biding their time.

Eric felt an eagerness overtake him, a sense of anticipation. He sensed that Caryl was at the heart of things. In Intelligence he had the highest reputation of anyone in either British or American camps. He had an empathetic understanding of the interconnections between various acts and the structures from which the orders had come. His understanding of Japanese society was supple. Any day now he was going to land a major prize: one of the top Japanese commanders in South East Asia.

Eric responded to Caryl's almost incandescent desire to find justice – a desire that illuminated all the byways of the mazes, the labyrinth that was Japanese society.

Eric threw his hat on to his bed, turned the light on – locked the door. He took the papers and laid them out on the carpet. He took out a cigarette and he began to read.

There were slide samples inside a box. They were made of glass, and when Eric held them up to the light he couldn't make sense of them: they seemed like aerial views of valleys, hills, cleats of landscape. Others looked like anemones drifting in murky water. Each of the slides was identified by Japanese characters.

Eric checked the documentation: they related to testing pathogens on humans. The list was long – typhoid A and B; tetanus; cholera; tuberculosis; salmonella; plague; typhus. As many as four million doses were prepared.

'Death at one month occurred following a stormy course with fever immediately post-injection.'

Victims had been Korean, Manchurian children,

captured American and Australian prisoners of war.

Waves of plague epidemics periodically broke out near the Ping Fan laboratory and spread through the province.

Plague and typhoid were used with particular 'effect' during the Japanese occupation of China. Spores of plague were dropped by plane. Water sources were infected.

```
I can say that the number of
prisoners of Detachment 731 who
died from the effects of experiments
in infecting them with severe
infectional diseases was not less
than about 600 per annum.
```

Colonel Ishii, his scientists and what was described as a 'bulky cargo' were last seen in Changchun at the Kwantung Army headquarters, preparing to evacuate from Manchuria to Korea.

He had not been seen since.

Eric's phone rang.

'I've got to see you.'

It was Caryl.

'I'm busy.'

'Please. I'm at the British Club. I have to be here. It's the King's Birthday. Come and rescue me. Please.'

It was that final 'please', its intimacy.

They were together in this.

An hour later, Eric walked into the British Club. He saw Caryl in the distance, surrounded by brass. The men were all laughing heartily till a woman walked by and the mood changed into one of exaggerated respect. Caryl made eye contact with Eric but did not come towards him. Eric went and got himself a drink.

A band was playing country airs. The club was second rate with its fake panelling and tinted photograph of the stammering King–Emperor. The drink was lukewarm beer. Eric couldn't help comparing it with the American outfit: the depth of the comfortable chairs, the cut of the crystal, the quantity of spirits. The band changed its tune to a quick rendition of 'Londonderry Air'.

Caryl appeared beside him.

Abruptly, but in a voice of disconcerting intimacy, he said, 'Let's get out of here, Kiwi. I can't stand this place.'

Eric said as they walked along, 'I got the files.'

Caryl looked at him and a smile played across his lips. 'What files?'

Eric glanced hard into his eyes.

Caryl looked away. He began whistling that tune ... that tune ... what was it? 'I've Got My Eye on You, Sweetie-pie ...'

Caryl lived not far from British HQ. His room, like Eric's, was down a long corridor. But Caryl's room was larger. Space was power in Tokyo.

On a table was a photo of a beautiful woman in a silver frame. She had a long thin nose like Caryl's, brunette hair and an air of wealth, breeding. Her pale lips were twitched up into a strange smile. On her plastered hair was a small art-deco tiara in what looked like diamonds and sapphires.

'Who's that?' Eric asked.

'My wife,' Caryl said. 'She's someone else's now. But I'm fond of her.'

There was a series of elegant Japanese woodprints on the wall. When Caryl caught Eric looking at them, he said,

'Utamaro. Nanshoku.' This meant nothing to Eric. They were a series of courtesans, and some seemed beautiful, others grotesque. Eric also noticed Caryl's room had a table lamp with a yellow silk shade. Against the wall was what looked like a Japanese antique table. It looked civilised, domestic.

Caryl came back from the bathroom with two crystal glasses. The air was heavy. Eric kept watching Caryl as he moved around the room. He had become overpoweringly conscious of a line of hairs on Caryl's neck and the fine hairs on his wrist. His fingers, long and supple, shook slightly as he poured out the drink.

'There's no ice, I'm sorry,' Caryl was saying. Then he looked up and said, 'You're fond of Randy, aren't you?'

Eric nodded. How could he say: Randy and Anita offered me something I'd never known before. They were sophisticated, enchanting. Life around them was easy.

They had whirled him out of his old world, had picked him up like he was a lovely little mascot. Their 'baby'. Besides, he was lost anyway. He was floating.

As if sensing all these thoughts Caryl looked at him, smiled a little.

Eric said, stiffening – he wanted, needed to put some barriers between himself and this strange, glinting man: 'Why me? Why did you choose me?'

Silence. Eric had the sense of it being late at night, and of other lives moving round them; of only certain people being awake; and of a complex trail of lives and how they interlocked – those who could not sleep.

'I don't know. I knew about you . . . your time in the camps.' He shrugged. Turned his back on Eric. 'Sometimes you have to trust . . . your instinct.'

Eric nodded. It occurred to him his throat was really dry. He felt a great yearning to touch Caryl. To feel his warmth. This was so surprising to Eric as to cripple him with embarrassment. He flushed, sweated.

Caryl, looking into his face, laughed. 'Don't worry, Eric,' he said. 'I'd only sleep with you if you wanted.'

'I don't.'

'I know you don't.'

Caryl looked at him. His face was naked, yearning, brave, yet ready for anything.

'I'm sorry, Caryl.'

'Don't worry, Hori. This town is full of people, men and women, longing for company, a shoulder to sleep on.'

A shoulder to sleep on. The simplicity of the statement drove Eric mad. He longed, he wanted. But he couldn't bring himself. To that nakedness. Not with another man.

Caryl came towards him, a little wryly, a little sadly.

He said, 'You've never kissed a man before.'

Eric's instinct was to move back. Instead, he stayed there.

'I've never kissed a man before.'

Caryl came closer. He was smiling.

Eric leaned forward. He didn't know why he was doing it.

'Goodbye,' he said. And leaned further forward. Caryl's lips touched his. There was an immediate and brazen discharge of electricity between the two men. The surface of Caryl's lips, which were cool, smooth, leaned against Eric's, which were motionless. Caryl kissed him lightly, then, when Eric didn't withdraw, he kissed him more lingeringly. When the kiss finished, Eric said, 'I'm sorry Caryl, but I . . .'

'I know,' Caryl said, 'that's why I'm kissing you goodbye, Eric. You don't sleep with men.'

Caryl opened the door into the hall.

It was dark out there.

'You should go now,' Caryl said. 'I know it's late and I know . . .'

Eric came closer. Caryl was saying, nervously for him, because he wasn't a man to be nervous, 'The papers're dynamite, don't you think? You make sure they don't get buried or lost. I'm relying on you, Hori, to . . .'

It was at this point Eric in a fit of insanity decided the only way to stop Caryl talking, to quieten him down, was to place his own lips on Caryl's mouth. This happened so spontaneously that Eric felt he were inhabiting the body of a stranger – yet it was, he suddenly realised, a stranger he had always wanted to be. He thought he was discovering if not himself then at least some form of himself. He found he was kissing Caryl.

At first there was a disconcerting clash of teeth. Caryl let out a little gasp. Eric found himself grasping Caryl hard around the shoulders. He was uncertain how you kissed a man, how one man kissed another, whether one led and the other followed. He drove his tongue hard into Caryl's face. Caryl resisted for a moment, then something happened. His body had sagged into Eric's.

They parted briefly. Caryl kicked the door shut so it slammed, and in that second he looked into Eric's face, speed-reading everything, as if everything up till that moment had been a misreading. Eric found he was smiling.

'I feel randy as hell,' he said in explanation, and Caryl, laughing at him, took a step back.

'We don't have to do this,' Caryl said. His face was pale, glistening. He picked up his glass, and took a quick, deep slug. Eric grabbed his own glass, threw the scotch down and moved towards Caryl again. He wanted to penetrate right into the mystery of this man. He wanted, if it was possible, to fix him in one spot, to drink out all of his mystery.

He began to kiss Caryl hard. During the kiss, he squirted as much scotch from his mouth as he could into Caryl's. The alcohol poured down out of Caryl's mouth, down his neck. Eric licked it off, kissing the bristles, the strange maleness of his Adam's apple, working his way back up to Caryl's mouth, which was oddly slack, open.

Eric was tense with desire. He seemed to have changed in a nanosecond, and become agile, alive.

Caryl began undoing Eric's belt. Eric had not anticipated this. Or rather, the logical sequence of it suddenly frightened him. Was this what they were doing? He pulled away from Caryl, and they were silent a moment. Then Caryl surprised him. He stood a distance away from Eric and began loosening his own tie. He bent down and undid his laces. Eric made a move – he didn't know what he was going to do: to turn and flee was one possibility, a very strong urge, but the other was to stand there, on the spot. He had the sense of time becoming contemporary. Of living in the moment, not the past – that past which claimed nearly every moment of his life now.

The present flowered all round him.

He realised he must accept the gift.

Another voice said cynically, What have you got to lose? You who are lost.

Standing apart from him, and not implicating Eric in

what he was doing – not threatening him – Caryl stripped naked.

Eric looked at Caryl's body. He had a sense of power, of looking, of being able to look. He noticed the tan mark on his arms, legs, a scar further up on his shoulder, and a greedy suture mark, deep on his chest, running up to his nipples. He had long gilded hairs round his nipples, and a soft field in the concave part of his chest. His cock was swollen, urgent – slightly pathetic in its need.

This made Eric laugh. It was a cry of delight. Caryl laughed too.

'What is it, Hori?' he said, coming closer. He reached over to Eric's belt, undid it. He did this standing as far away from Eric as he practically could, all the while looking intently into Eric's eyes. There was the heavy thud of Eric's trousers as they fell to the floor.

Caryl came closer.

Smiling slowly – was it even with a hint of sadness? – he folded to his knees and took Eric's cock inside his mouth. First of all he kissed, tenderly, the hood of Eric's cock, then he ran his tongue along a vein on the shaft.

Eric shivered all over his body. He was aware of his buttocks shuddering, or spasming. He raised himself up on his toes and drove in, hard, to Caryl's face. There was a momentary gasp, down below, then Caryl reached behind Eric; holding his buttocks in each of his hands, he pulled Eric into him, then away.

They rocked like this, an engine of pleasure. Rapt.

Eric let out a low, slow groan.

At that precise moment, voices could be heard in the corridor outside. They were two officers walking back to their respective rooms. They halted exactly outside Caryl's door and began a long conversation about empire trade tariffs.

Caryl looked up at Eric and grinned. At the same moment Eric had an acute sense, an image, of fiery golden sap surging out up through his penis and exploding inside Caryl. He couldn't stop himself groaning out loud. It was an undeniable groan of male pleasure, imploring, guttural, animal.

There was a startled silence outside the door, then acute listening. Perhaps they were awaiting a female component. When it didn't come, the conversation took up in a carefully artificial way. The two officers walked away down the corridor and wished each other a somewhat terse goodnight.

Eric felt some elemental panic overtake him. Was he trying to reinvent himself? Become another person simply because his old self was so dead – so used up? He wanted something more than this. For this first time in his life, he actively wanted a man. He had never wanted anyone as much as he wanted – to be inside – Caryl. And wanted Caryl, for that matter, to be inside him. He wanted to be possessed, to be taken. He wanted an end to his aching loneliness, his utter isolation. How could this be considered disgusting beside what he had suffered?

So he gave himself up. It felt good, at that moment, to be losing his old self. He felt for the first time he was alive again. He had come back to life.

7

He waited to hear from Caryl, but there was nothing. He felt the freshness of memory haunt him. He kept being revisited by images, as if he had been another person in the room, some distant viewer. His view of Caryl, Caryl the man, the Intelligence officer, was set beside this other naked creature, a tender hungry animal. Stooped in compliance. Making small animal sounds. Of capitulation. Coming, Eric realised, from his own lips. To give up. To cede power. Control. To give over.

The long silence from Caryl seemed to delete all this, challenge its primacy, its importance. Eric had no idea how men behaved in a situation like this. Was he turning into a woman? Hanging around, waiting for the phone.

Then the phone rang, and it was Caryl.

'Can you "disappear" tomorrow?'

These were Caryl's first words, spoken without preliminary.

There was no recognition that anything had happened between them. Eric instantly decided this was better. Yet the sound of Caryl's voice inside his ear – his head – did something to him. He longed, instantly, to lose himself, divest himself of his personality again by merging with this – strange – man.

Instead Caryl was cool, all business, distant.

Eric could hear other voices on the end of the phone. Caryl was at work. As was Eric.

'Can you?'

The intonation in Caryl's voice rose. He sounded pissed off, or under pressure.

'Yes,' Eric said, though without checking anything. It didn't matter. Or did it? But he felt, in that instant, he would disappear, no matter what the repercussions.

They had met at the train station. Caryl, waiting for him, had allowed a single, wintery smile to mobilise his face.

'Hori,' he had murmured lightly, and nodded.

Eric's ears were filled with the soft reiteration of Caryl saying the name again and again during a crucial moment of their lovemaking. This was the sole sign that Caryl allowed him.

Eric nodded back. He too could be a stranger.

'I've got the tickets,' Caryl had said, and walked off into the crowd. It was the usual crowd of that time – a mixture of impoverished country people shifting about, carrying as much as they could. Women with children, humans as pack animals carrying whatever had survived the catastrophe. There was a sense of loss, of people trying to find, locate, search. Noise. Smell. Intimacy and yet alienation. A child without a leg on a crutch. Old beggars who slept in the station by night and moved outside the doors by day. Young women with taut watching faces. Men with worn faces, missing limbs. Younger men, who might have been kamikaze pilots but who now seemed at a loose end. People with skin disorders, people who seemed dipped in dust. All of them discreetly and not so discreetly pushing and shoving, trying to solve the vast mystery of how they might fit in again.

Through the crowd, a tall arrow of a man in an English uniform, darting and pulsing, followed obdurately by an equally tall man, his face overcast, in an Australian uniform.

'I'm off to Hong Kong next week,' Caryl said when they were on the train to Atami.

Eric said nothing.

'On business. Tying things up. Before we ship out.'

Eric didn't know what to say, so he still said nothing.

'You don't miss me, do you?' Caryl said mockingly.

Eric turned his face away. Then Caryl had said, in a low voice, 'I'm sorry, Hori, I'm a bastard. Don't forget that.'

They got on a train going to Atami. Caryl had said nothing about what was happening, where they were going. Eric felt impoverished by a lack of knowledge. He didn't know where he was being taken, or for what purpose.

The carriage was crowded, packed. The stench was almost unbearable. Immediately Eric felt overcome with an irrational fear. Faces, Japanese faces, looking at them both. As if all the eyes and faces belonged to a single stem-head. No emotion, no sensation of what they might be thinking. A child started bawling. There were no seats. They had to stand. Bodies crushed in round them.

Eric was pushed into Caryl's body. He waited to feel something, but Caryl turned his body sideways so Eric felt only his hipbone. Caryl showed no sign of any previous intimacy and Eric fought what he began to suspect were unreasonable emotions – expectations even. But he felt unexpectedly downcast. At the same time he worked, actively, to reject these mutinous feelings. He told himself what he had learned at such cost: feelings are a luxury.

He could not afford them.

The train lurched through its journey.

Stooping, looking out the windows, Eric saw the startling green of paddy fields. They had left Yokohama. He was entering a part of Japan he had never been to before. In fact, in his three years in Japan, he had stayed almost exclusively within a certain small area of Tokyo, going only to certain familiar places. He stayed within the bound foot of the occupation, he realised, with only occasional, necessary forays into that vast, overpopulated world in which resided, as the occupation saw it, the unarrested – those hiding, those on the run.

Nothing was as it seemed.

Now the roofs outside were thatched, not tiled. There were forests, hills. And the sea, shimmeringly hot in the sun.

They got off at a small station in Atami. From the platform, Eric saw the carriage saved for imperial courtiers. It was empty apart from two elderly gentlemen, wearing striped trousers, cut-aways, old top hats. They were sitting there, looking less at the people than through them with infinite *sang-froid*. They were playing some form of cards, and A was waiting for B to place his card down, which he did, after a long, considering pause. Nobody in the station showed any sense that this was unusual.

Eric said, belligerently, 'Those fuckers have a whole carriage, while we sit out the back with this stinking lot. We're sitting in there on the way back.'

Caryl had a ghostly smile floating over his face. 'Whatever you say, *mein lieber Herr.*'

Eric didn't like being played with. He resented it. He decided he hated Caryl. It had all been a mistake.

They had gone to an inn, taken a room. Caryl told him Atami was a honeymoon town, that was why he had brought Eric there. His eyes twinkled. Eric didn't know how to react.

Caryl ordered tea and food. They sat there. There was a smell of mildew, mice, old paper, about the place. Eric waited, and just when he was about to say, What the fuck is this all about, Caryl raised a hand.

'I want you to witness a curious local custom.'

There was a distant droning sound, then the beat of drums. It sounded festive at first, then the drumbeat announced its tempo – slow and processional. Through the window, a procession began to pass. Everyone was dressed in white. Shinto priests. Mourners. Banners. Whining instruments. Elderly women crying in a monotonous, endless wire of sound, not exactly weeping so much as emitting a sound that was a calligraphy of grief. The procession passed.

Caryl jumped up.

'Jump to, Eric. Chop, chop. One, two.'

They began to follow the procession, but at a distance.

They came to a temple-like building. From a distance they watched the coffin being carried inside and, through the open doors, its being placed before an altar. There was a wooden tablet beside it, covered in Japanese characters.

Caryl and Eric observed the obsequies – the hierarchies of mourning, the playful gauze of incense smoke, the nodding of heads, the half bows, the rituals of death and acceptance. Someone who looked like a widow was freely weeping, surrounded by a small clutch of family, a knot of grief.

People spoke – eulogies.

Sometimes the wind blew their way and Eric thought he could understand some of the words . . . 'hardworking . . . professional . . . dedicated above all'. But it was too hard to decipher. Eric had no idea what they were doing there.

The service was completed. The coffin was carried out to an elaborate wooden wagon, a sort of temple on wheels, which served as a hearse. Everyone stood to attention, then, as the temple on wheels lurched off, the family arranged themselves and began to walk behind the coffin. Some of the women wept. The men in dark suits looked downwards. Children dawdled and talked. Only one elderly man looked at – and appeared startled to see – the two gaijin. Caryl quickly stood back into a porchway, pulling Eric back.

The people dispersed.

There was the usual sound of near merriment which follows a funeral as people intuitively seek the life impulse in the face of the great dampness of death.

Caryl offered Eric a cigarette. Both men smoked in silence. Eric never once looked at Caryl. His face was closed, hurt, empty. Only once did he raise his eyes in one swift burst of appraisal. Caryl was looking at him fondly, smiling.

'What?' Eric asked brusquely.

Caryl leaned forward and placed a cool, almost cold finger on Eric's lips. He looked out into the street.

Everybody had gone.

They walked towards two men closing the doors of the temple. One of the men was old, with the closed face of a verger intent on practising his religion in silence. The other was a younger man, extremely thin. He appeared to be telling a joke. As the two gaijin approached he paused, nudged the older man.

The older man's face, on spotting the gaijin, underwent many emotions: surprise, fear, abject panic. He leapt back, a jump surprisingly athletic in one so old.

Caryl came forward. He spoke in Japanese.

'Whose funeral was that?'

The old man said nothing. He might have been deaf.

Caryl reached into his pocket and got out a note — a small note. Eric looked at the old man's face rippling. The younger man stirred.

'Whose sad passing have we missed? We would like to make an offering.'

The old man went back to the business of locking the doors, ignoring Caryl. He spoke to the thin man quickly: 'Ignore the foreign devils.'

The young man's face, however, showed a sudden and great yearning for talk. How did they come to be there? Had they been to Atami before? What part of the world did they come from?

'I am showing my young friend some of the rich traditions of old Japan,' Caryl said.

The old man's eyes for a moment glanced deeply into Eric's. Eric smiled idiotically — he didn't know why. He nodded. The old man ignored him.

Caryl got out three notes. He attached the notes to a leafless tree nearby.

'In honour of the illustrious dead,' Caryl said. 'So deeply mourned.'

The young man's eyes did not leave the notes.

'Father,' he said. 'Do you see what gifts are being offered?'

Caryl got out a fourth note and attached it to the tree. The young man's mouth was wide open. Eric could hear his breathing – laboured, excited.

The old man looked at him for a moment, then spoke up.

'It is the sad passing of Colonel Ishii,' he said, his eyes looking down at the earth. 'Lost in combat in Manchuria and only now has his body been found and buried. A most sad loss. Noble warrior.'

'I am sorry to hear it,' Caryl said. He turned to the young man and, in the full sight of the old man, gave him some notes of his own. The young man smiled with surprisingly childlike glee.

They walked away. The day was overcast, suddenly cool.

'What's all this about?'

'I thought you might like to see a local ceremony,' Caryl said.

'Fuck you too.'

Caryl stopped and looked at him, said, 'I'm sorry. This is hard for me too. I don't know whether to trust . . . not you, but . . . what I feel for you.'

Eric said nothing.

They returned to the train station. There was the usual mêlée. Eric was feeling inexplicably angry. He made a scene about the empty carriage for the imperial courtiers. All his anger and uncertainties surfaced, and he found himself yelling. He insisted that he and Caryl, as members of the occupying powers, had a right to sit in an empty carriage. The man he was dealing with was very short, a middle-aged man whose entire life had been spent in the railways service. He was apologetic but adamant.

Caryl stood to the side, smoking a cigarette, seemingly turned to wood. The short man went away. Inside the carriage, there were three imperial functionaries. The railway man bowed profoundly several times and began to petition. The face of one functionary turned and looked their way. A long conversation took place. Eventually the railway man came back and said, 'You are welcome to join the imperial carriage.'

Eric walked on first, followed by Caryl. The three functionaries bowed stiffly, showing no emotion whatsoever. Then they scrupulously ignored Eric and Caryl for the rest of the trip back to Tokyo.

Eric and Caryl didn't speak to each other, though when Eric's eyes for one moment glanced Caryl's way he was surprised to see the Englishman's face was animated by something like fond amusement.

'What?' Eric said to him. '*What*!'

Caryl shrugged, said nothing, but his body relaxed and his leg, as if accidentally, came to rest against Eric's thigh. Eric went to lift his leg away, but instead he let it stay there. They leaned into each other's bodies, in an exhaustion of emotion, for the rest of the trip back into Tokyo.

They were outside a house in the suburbs of Tokyo. It was an elegant, large mansion, walled off. It was dusk.

Caryl had insisted Eric come along with him.

'It'll all make sense when we get there,' he promised.

Eric, mute, rebellious but lulled into some strange state, followed Caryl.

Caryl looked at his watch. There was silence a while, then a side door in the mansion slid open. A woman servant feathered forward in the gathering dark, opened back the gates to the compound. She looked out into the street, retreated.

After a while an old-fashioned car, gleaming and black, came out. It was driving at speed. There was an elderly chauffeur in pre-war livery at the wheel. In the back, a man of about sixty. He was straight backed, with a drab moustache. There was something about him, not of the warrior but of the civilian. He wore old-fashioned tortoiseshell glasses and he had the curiously vulnerable look of a man who can see only close up – not into the distance. He seemed not to register the chauffeur, nor even the two men who now stood out of the shadows, on the footpath. But for a moment his eyes passed over Caryl and Eric, and there was a flicker, a startled register, which was instantly deleted, so the mask-like face returned to its dour, set countenance.

The car passed.

'That's Colonel Ishii.'

Eric looked at Caryl, not understanding.

'The chap we saw cremated today. Miraculously come back to life. And hopefully . . . in a moment . . . we'll see the magician himself . . .'

An American car sped out of the compound in a slither of gravel. Caryl grabbed Eric and pulled him back into the shadows.

'Alley-oop,' he murmured.

In the dark, Eric had an overpowering awareness of Caryl's body: he smelt Caryl's skin, its metallic scent. But there was also a rankness, like an animal aroused – to danger.

Eric brushed his body close.

'Look,' Caryl murmured, bunting back into Eric's body and his hand, hard, taut, masculine, grabbing hold of Eric's arm.

The two men held on.

As the car swept by Eric saw through the window a man looking down, a fringe of nutmeg hair hiding his face. He raised his face, seeming to sigh deeply. It was Randy.

That night Caryl and Eric slept together again. It was a more passionate exploration this time – Eric knew Caryl was going away. They made love with a quiet desperation, an abandon. So they spent the night as young men will, pursuing pleasure till they were completely drained and could make love no more. They lay together, limbs interlaced, each waking to the surprise of the stranger with whom he had slept.

Caryl went towards the window, pulled the blind back. In the grey morning light, he looked all over Eric's body, as if committing him to memory. He looked in particular at the wounds: the corrugation of the stab marks where bayonets had plunged in. He leaned down and kissed them gently. He rolled Eric over on to his front and his breath played warm over Eric's shoulders.

Eric lay there, arms akimbo, head nestled in the crook of his arms. He closed his eyes.

Caryl wasn't touching him; he was squatting over him. His breath fanned across Eric's back as he inspected him.

Eric's shoulder muscles spasmed.

'What happened here?'

'Rifle butts.'

Caryl kissed lightly where rifle butts had smashed down on the top of Eric's spine. With his tongue he traced the line up towards the base of the skull, where the rifle butts had concentrated: on bad days, this was the source of piercing headaches. The pain could drive him demented.

'And here?'

'Same. If you made the mistake of falling over.'

Caryl kissed this spot, this ache. He did this gently in the early morning light. He traced with his lips further down the knobs on Eric's twisted spine.

'Turn over.'

Eric did so.

'Why you, Eric?'

'I was tall. Too tall. They picked me out. An example, I guess. Made them look bigger.'

'No. Why you. Why me.'

They were face to face. Caryl looking down.

'Dunno, mate. Does to fill in a spare hour.'

They lay there, sharing a last cigarette.

Caryl was looking up at the ceiling. He was in a different mood now.

'The happy camper's on his way to America today, Kiwi. Being shipped out. America or bust for Colonel Ishii.' He gave a short laugh. 'Good to escape scot free, eh?'

Eric was silent. He was enjoying the smoke. As he stubbed the cigarette out and turned to Caryl, he murmured: 'Lucky bastard.'

8

Anita's car was not driving where Eric thought it would. Eric was tapping his hat on his knee, looking out the window. They had been silent since he got in. Anita seemed nervous for some reason. When her eyes touched his, they jerked away.

'Where are we going?' he asked at last, when the car turned away from the usual places: the Ritz, one or two restaurants — the few places that demarcated the limited lives of expatriates.

'Somewhere else,' she said.

He looked at her profile. 'You're not happy about going home?'

She glanced at him quickly, assessing something he couldn't quite work out.

'I always make do, Eric. That's the story of my life with Randy. Making do.'

She placed her hand down on the car seat. Her fingers touched his. She laced her fingers through and she said, in a low voice, a voice of misery, 'Hold my hand, darling.'

There was such an abject note about it, his fingers interlaced with hers. Her hand was moist, hot.

The car was waiting at some lights.

He looked out at the passing crowds. He thought he saw Janice coming out of the door of a hotel . . . the hotel he and she normally went to. She was with Luttrell. There was a shamefaced air about them. Eric was going to say something to Anita – something funny and smart – but when he glanced at her profile he saw it wouldn't be right.

The lights changed and the car took off. It was a powerful limousine and it moved out into a fast lane. They seemed to be going in the direction of the golf club. That made sense, in one way. But it was a long way to go.

Eric began to feel uneasy.

'How many people will be there?'

He wanted to work out his chances of getting an early lift home. He needed to see Caryl. To sort things out. He wanted to make it clear to Caryl it had all been a mistake. It had happened, it was even undeniable that he had enjoyed it – certain images from it were still minted fresh in his brain, ready to betray him with their relentless erotic power – but, all in all, it was a one-off kind of accident. He had found himself randy, alone and uptight. That was all. It was an accident.

The fact of the matter was he had gone straight back to Janice. He had asked her out the following night. She was going out, she said – but, seeing his face cloud over, she succumbed. Told him she could only spare him half an hour.

She met him in the hall of her hostel, ran upstairs to park the flowers he had brought.

'Let's go out,' she said. 'This place gives me the creeps.'

They were watched by Olwyn, upside down, drying her hair by a heater while another woman looked up from her crochet.

They had gone to their usual hotel. This happened almost wordlessly. Eric said to Janice something he'd never said before: they could maybe go on holiday somewhere together, take some time to really get to know each other.

The sex they had was swift, utilitarian and wordless. As she dressed, however, Janice said she had something to tell him. She turned around. There was a particular light coming in the hotel window. It was pale, washed out.

'I'm getting married,' she said.

'Who to?' he said, arrested not so much by what she said as by its coincidence with what they had just done.

'Colonel Luttrell has asked me.'

Eric stopped dressing. 'Why?' he said. 'Why Luttrell?'

'Why not?' she said, sitting down on the dirty armchair, pulling her stockings up and attaching them to her suspenders. She lifted her leg out and smoothed the nylons down. He watched her.

'It's not perfect,' she said, as though she were talking about her legs, or her stockings, 'but what is?' She looked up directly at him.

He felt himself flush.

'You're blushing,' she said in an emotionless, purely observational voice. Then she said, standing up, picking up her hat and going to the mirror, 'We'll leave the Service.

He'll get a posting. I'll serve tea and cakes. We'll have children, I suppose.' And she turned a suddenly tired face towards him.

He realised how beautiful she was. Not beautiful in a magazine way, but in a purely womanly way, with her instinct for survival, her strength. Even when she was tired like this, and seemingly defeated.

Eric felt at that moment a sense of forlorn grief, but whether it was for her or for him he didn't know. This is another fuck-up, he thought. Just like the night with Caryl.

'Good luck, I guess is what I should say.'

She said, 'It won't happen for a while. And when it does, you can send a silver salver.'

He laughed. He was straightening his tie.

They didn't kiss. They didn't even say goodbye.

He just said, before he went out the door, 'Thanks.'

'Randy's organised it,' Anita was saying, taking her hand away from Eric's, as if she sensed he wasn't paying attention. She looked out the side window, so he could see only the side of her face.

He began singing softly, for no particular reason, 'I've Got My Eye on You, Sweetie-pie'. He was surprised at the melancholy tone of his voice. She turned towards him. A single tear spilled out of her left eye and cascaded down her cheek.

'Why is everything such a fucking awful mess, Hori?'

Eric assumed Anita's sophisticated New York past had finally made her life here unsatisfactory. She didn't seem to belong in dreary post-war Tokyo.

'It's not that bad, is it?'

She squeezed his hand hard and looked away.

The car went up the long luxurious road that led to the main steps.

Eric was surprised there were no other cars there, except an American jeep.

'I guess we're early, huh?' Eric said, adopting an American accent.

She didn't smile. They got out of the car, went up the steps, and when they entered the vestibule Anita said to him, a little tensely, he thought, 'Darling, you go into the Jockey Bar. I'll join you after I've visited the powder room.'

He listened to the clack of her heels over marble. Then they hit the thick carpet, and the green baize door of the Ladies' swished shut.

He strolled towards the Jockey Bar. He pushed back the heavy wooden door.

Inside, the curtains had been pulled. A single billiard light was on, and under it sat General Bantock, a line of smoke rising from his cigar. Beside him was a pile of folders.

Bantock glanced up at him and growled, not taking his cigar out of his mouth, 'Come in, young Keeling. Come in.'

Eric came forward over the obscenely thick carpet, and saluted. Bantock waved his cigar, indicating the chair opposite. Eric sat down. For some reason, he thought of Caryl, and he thought of that moment, just before he kissed him, and Caryl's face had been turned to his, his lips open. Eric had the feeling he mightn't now make it to see Caryl that evening. To explain it was all over, and that it had never meant anything. He desperately wanted to see Caryl, to explain that.

Instead he sank down in the deep armchair which was so low to the ground his legs sprawled out awkwardly. He felt the shock of his exhaustion. He tried to take on a military pose. Bantock looked at him inscrutably, or was it with a slow, bitter smile?

Eric's eyes moved to the folders. He recognised them. They were the folders Caryl had given him. Unit 731.

He tried not to change his expression, but Bantock had clearly observed his glance. The general worked the cigar along in his teeth and nodded.

'There's an easy way of doing this,' he said.

'Yes sir,' Eric said mechanically. He couldn't stop himself turning to look over his shoulder. Improbably he expected Anita to come into the room, to rescue him. To call the general 'baby' and say it was all a misunderstanding. At the same time Eric understood this would not happen.

'The easy way is for you to tell me two things. The first is: who gave you these files? The second is: what were you going to do with them?'

'I . . .'

Eric's voice was thick. He felt deeply implicated.

'Let's start off with where you got them from.'

'They appeared in my room, sir.'

'. . . in your room.'

'I came back one night about a month ago and they were sitting in my room, sir.'

'Let's drop the sir stuff, Keeling. How did they get there? A fairy drop them off?'

Eric was aware of a stain of a blush over his features. He felt the heat in his neck, under his arms. He was sweating. Bantock was looking at him closely.

'No sir,' Eric said. 'I have no idea how the files got in my room.'

There was an assessing pause.

'Are you a fairy, Keeling?'

'No, sir!' Eric answered in a parade-ground shout.

The general said nothing. Then laughed. 'It's a joke, Keeling. A joke.' Then: 'Did you read the documents?'

'I . . . I glanced at them, sir, to see what they were.'

'Even though it says, very clearly, on the front, classified.'

'I was trying to work out how they got there, sir. I often take documents home from work, sir, and work on them in my room. I thought perhaps they were documents I'd got mixed up –'

'I know you're a good worker, Keeling. I have reports on you from your superior. By all accounts you are a model worker. If anything, you work too hard.'

Eric said nothing.

'Listen, Keeling. The material in these files is extremely confidential and if anything – so much as a word or sentence from these – was leaked to anyone – so much as a whisper to the press – it would give a distinct advantage to America's enemies. You know who I mean, don't you, Keeling?'

Eric obligingly said, 'I think so, sir.'

'Who?'

There was an assessing pause here.

'You mean the Soviets, sir?'

'The communists,' Bantock said, nodding.

Eric wanted to say, You mean our old allies? Instead he kept silent. He kept thinking, irrationally, of Caryl. He wanted to warn him, speak to him. Shockingly, and from the outside, as an eye witness looking into the room, he saw Caryl and himself involved in a single graphic image of fucking. This happened in such a powerful flash he jerked perceptibly in his chair.

Bantock noticed.

'There's a Cold War on – it just hasn't been announced yet. We're at war again and we have to be extremely careful . . . about who our enemies are and who are our friends.'

Eric hoped his eyes did not betray him. He felt a deep anger. He thought of all his years in the camps. Of fighting. And now he was on trial for being a possible enemy. A lost friend.

'You say you have no idea how the papers got there.'

'Yes, sir.'

'Who were you with before you got in? Can anyone verify for you?'

'I was out,' Eric said, thinking quickly. 'I quite often go for walks, sir. To clear my head.'

'To clear your head,' Bantock echoed, making the sentence seem as arid an excuse as it was.

'And what were you going to do with these papers?' Bantock's voice was silky.

'I was going to take them into the Australian Division and hand them in to a superior officer.'

'But you didn't.'

'I . . . I forgot, sir.'

'You forgot.'

'Something else came up, sir.'

Bantock's growl was deep, visceral. 'What do you think I am, you big ape?'

He leaned forward in the chair and his cigar came very close to Eric's face. The smoke streamed up directly into

Eric's eyes, making them water; the cigar was beginning to burn his eyebrows. The acrid smell of singed hair filled the room.

'You smartarse jumped-up little cunt from a no-account country that nobody'd even notice if it was pissed down the fucking drain.'

A vein on the general's forehead bulged. He reached down and took a swig of bourbon from a heavy cut-crystal glass.

Eric blinked.

The general ashed his cigar on the carpet.

'Now suppose we play it this way.' Bantock had sunk back in his chair. He was speaking more moderately now. 'Suppose you tell me how you came about getting this information which, in case you didn't notice, has abso-fucking-lutely nothing whatever to do with you.'

Eric was silent for a moment.

'Well, sir . . .'

'Let's start off with where you got it from first.'

'I . . . it was, as I said, sir, in my room.'

The general sighed.

'I only glanced at the contents, to see who I should return them to.'

'But you didn't, did you?' The general's voice was very soft.

'Didn't what, sir?'

'You didn't return them.'

'. . . I . . .'

Eric had a vivid imprint here, like an explosion, of Caryl's eyes looking up at him from down below. He saw the tiny lines of amusement and the wry, wicked glance in his grey-blue eyes. At the same time, Eric shifted in his seat, as if the surface of the chair was burning him. He put his finger in his collar and tried to get some air. The general's eyes were staring into him.

'Never forget, Keeling, we have our own intelligence. There isn't much we don't know.'

Eric looked back at him, daring him to speak. He decided, instantly, he did not care. He no longer cared. This was considerably freeing. And, he decided, yes, once he was out of that room he would go back to Caryl. First of all, to tell him what had happened, but then . . . to see him, to speak to him. To find some kind of truth or reality in him.

The general sighed. It had not gone quite the way he hoped.

'Fuck off, Keeling. But don't forget this. I'm watching you. I'm after your balls, and believe me, when I'm after the balls of any of my men they start to panic.'

'Yes, sir.'

Eric stood up, saluted.

As he walked towards the door, the general called out, in a completely different voice, 'Hey buddy! Aren't you waiting round for Anita's drinks?'

Eric walked out through the vestibule. There was no sign of Anita. A Jap manservant in a white jacket was polishing the outside of the plate-glass doors, as if his life depended on it. He looked through the glass at Eric.

Eric walked outside. There was the jeep. An MP was slouched at its side, smoking.

'I need a ride back to town, soldier,' Eric said to him.

The MP looked all over Eric's Australian uniform. He flicked his cigarette on to the manicured lawn.

'I bet you do, buddy,' the MP said to him.

Eric went in to the vestibule, phoned back to HQ.

There was a delay and he had to wait for someone to come out and pick him up. He sat down in the vestibule, where the only sound was that of a cloth being wiped over plate glass. He looked out at the green links and thought about the clubhouse at the end of the war. He listened to see if he could hear Anita's voice, or the general's. But there was silence. Finally a jeep arrived. Eric got in and went back to HQ.

He never saw Anita again.

9

He tried to call Caryl but he was in a meeting. He left a message for Caryl to call him, but had the feeling the call might get lost in the barrage of messages going in to British HQ. It was public knowledge the British were pulling out. The papers were full of it.

Eric went back to his room, bathed and hung about, waiting for a phone call. In the end, he couldn't stay in his room any longer; he got dressed and went round to Caryl's quarters. The sergeant there told him he had just missed Colonel Lantern. He was on his way to the airport. Was it anything important?

Eric said no.

The sergeant said, 'Not to worry, sir, he'll be back inside a week.'

They saluted and Eric walked back to his hotel in a daze. It got colder that night; it was the first intimation that the summer might be breaking. Eric wasn't wearing enough clothes, and he seemed to catch a fever. It attacked him with great suddenness, like a return of his malaria, and it was all he could do to get back to his hotel. When he did, Shaw saw him coming and, with an imperious click of his fingers, ordered one of the Japanese staff to help Eric up to his room.

Eric gave him his key, and as he opened the door the young man said, 'Parcel for Captain Keeling.' He pointed to a brown paper parcel on the bed. It was tied with white string.

'Are there any messages for me?' Eric asked.

'Messages?'

'Yes,' Eric said, angry suddenly at the obtuseness of the young man.

'No message,' he said. Then, bowing at the gaijin, he let himself out.

Without looking at the parcel, Eric threw himself down on the bed, and, not bothering to take his clothes off, he pulled up the covers.

He dropped into the black.

He dreamt about a girl he'd been engaged to back in Auckland.

They'd got engaged before he went away to war. Big mistake. Irene said she would wait. Then he came back, or part of him came back. Only part. Nobody seemed to notice this – or if they did, they were nervous, uncertain how to treat him.

Irene and he were going off on a picnic. It was June 1946.

Irene's mother, as she handed over a Thermos and the

ham sandwiches wrapped in greaseproof paper, the tin with the freshly made Madeira cake inside, murmured, 'Well, it's all behind you now, Eric.'

He knew it wasn't all behind him even as he cracked on tough, and said, 'You bet.' He remembered he'd even winked at the old girl. Meanwhile he was aware of Irene's glance, the depth of her perception, the way she kept looking – looking at him.

'There's not much to look at it, is there?' he said when they were lying on the picnic blanket, above the cliffs on Point Chev beach. Under the pine trees. The tide was out. There was a faint smell of mud on the wind.

He was very aware of the other lovers, all curved into each other like netsuke. Irene seemed on the point of saying something. He was overpoweringly aware of her clean, pink fingers with the nails that had been polished on an emery board. Her fingers were threading and rethreading the tassels on the border of the rug. He had never seen anything – anyone – so clean. She smelled of soap. Her hair smelled of rosemary. She was so understanding, and he held it against her.

There's fuck-all left of me, of all there used to be.

If only he could say it. Explain it.

Instead he'd turned nasty, and asked if she couldn't keep her hands still. Why was she fiddling all the time? Was she nervous being around him or what?

She had cried. He had felt wretched. In the end they had packed the rug, the Thermos back in the boot of the car (which Irene's father had lent them for the occasion – a Morris all hoovered clean, smelling of car polish). On the way home neither of them said a word, except when he pulled up before Irene's parents' place and he'd said,

'I'm sorry, Irene, I'm not much use for anyone at the moment.'

And unable to do anything better to explain it, he held his hands out in front of her. They both looked at them shaking. Small tremors shivered out across his palms, then towards his fingertips which vibrated – mercilessly – like a rabbit terrified before its own demise.

She had impulsively grabbed his hands. When he tried to pull them away, she begged him not to – not in words, not in language, but in small, animal-like gasps, grunts and sighs. He sat very still then. She turned his hands over, palms facing up, and she had kissed very slowly – licking more like it – the inside of one palm. He knew what she was saying. He felt the slight roughness of her tongue, like a cat's tongue.

But there was this fatal block between him and his feelings, and he didn't know what to say to her when he pulled his hand away from her, and said, 'Thanks. I know. You're a good girl, Irene. Too good for me.'

He had been surprised when she had cried out with pain. 'I'm not, Eric. Give me a chance. You keep pushing me away. You won't let me get close.'

That's what I want, he wanted to say to her. I can't bear anybody too close. I'm like an animal that needs to be left on its own.

She was crying again by then. He sensed the holland blinds move in the parents' front room. He was no returning hero. It was not how it was meant to be.

She got out and ran up the drive. Went inside. It was left for him to back the car up the drive and park it neatly, then take the keys inside.

Her old man was sitting on the back steps, cleaning

his boots. Eric felt a sense of defeat that he recognised from the war – the retreat. Her father held out a hand for the keys, not standing up as he might have done in different circumstances, man to man. Instead, as if it were understood between them that certain civilities were over, her old man just held out a hand, and when Eric slung the keys across to him, he growled, not even taking the pipe out of his mouth: 'Good-o.'

When Eric said, for some stupid reason, 'I put some gas in her,' her father said, with the faint hint of sardonic emphasis, 'Thanks, mate.'

That was the end of it so much as the engagement was concerned. Irene had written several letters to him in Tokyo that he had never got round to opening. That was how she got the news there was fuck-all left of Eric Keeling.

He dreamt of her unopened letters.

Then he began to dream about wallpaper. Autumn leaves that seemed to be floating on a tide. He could remember a smell too, a faint whiff of camphor, of Sunlight soap – the indefinable scent of his father's tin box . . . In the dream he was opening a tin box and putting the objects in order . . . he was trying to work out the order . . . if only he could put them in order . . .

10

He was delirious for several days. He was looked after by Isamu who was discreet, attentive, almost feminine in his solicitude. Eric had only a vestigial awareness of him. Really he was a pair of hands applying a damp cool cloth; he was someone who leaned over him and stared at him. The doctor came, looked at Eric and went. There was an anti-malarial pill to be taken. But Eric's consciousness was rising and ebbing; he was stalked all over again by the past, which presented itself as startlingly present.

The past was paying a call. Reminding him. That he could not forget. That his body, which he had begun to think might be his own, was really only a blank state which the past had the eternal right to reoccupy at any moment.

During his fever he was overpoweringly aware of the brown paper parcel, which he had not opened. Its importance loomed. He was convinced it was something from Caryl. He implored Isamu to hide the parcel in his wardrobe. Isamu had done this, but with a certain degree of scepticism. Only when it was not visible could Eric relax a little, but then he was haunted by the fact it might be stolen. Every time Isamu came into his room he had to open the cupboard and hold up the brown parcel for Eric to inspect. On seeing it, Eric would lose consciousness.

Once Eric awoke to find a stranger in his room. He was sure of this. It was a grey time of early evening, or perhaps it was dawn, or even the middle of a dull day. Eric was no longer sure of time. The figure in the room had his back turned to him and appeared to be frozen, aware that Eric had awakened. Eric tried to speak to this stranger, this darkened shape, but the shape made no movement. It became a contest: who would move first. Eric lost consciousness, and when he came to, and Isamu came in for his twice-daily visit (on the way in to work, on his way home) Eric asked if he had had any visitors. Isamu had gone downstairs and asked Shaw.

Shaw said, 'Not to my knowledge.'

Eric asked to be shown the parcel. Isamu obliged. It was still there. Eric noticed that Isamu was wearing the 'new' shoes for the first time. He sank back into what felt like a more peaceful sleep.

Now he seemed to be mending. When he awoke next, the room looked different, tidied, cleaned. And Isamu walked in the door, smiling at him gravely.

'I think the fever has turned,' he said. 'I have brought you some special broth. My father prepare it.'

He held Eric's head up carefully and helped him drink. Eric felt a pathetic form of gratitude.

'You been very sick, Captain Keeling, sir.'

Eric finished the broth down to the last drop. It was strange-tasting, slightly bitter, very clear. He was aware, at that moment, how sick he had been. He needed to sleep.

Isamu reached forward and patted his hand. 'I look after you, Captain Keeling, sir. I do whatever you want.'

Eric said, 'Are there any messages for me?'

Isamu said, 'Messages? No sir. Only from Ozzie mates. "Get well soon please."'

Eric went to sleep with the shape of Isamu sitting in his room, on a chair, not reading, not doing anything – just sitting looking out at the block of light.

He made it downstairs finally, to the dining room. He had been sick a week. Deliberately he had not opened the parcel. He would leave it till that evening. He was greeted by other officers and men.

'Had a rough time, young Eric?'

'Been playing rookie, eh lad?'

'You work too hard, chappie, better to take it slowly.'

Eric took this calmly. He had seen the stranger in the mirror; he had seen how the past had effortlessly reached out and claimed him again, returning him to that ghostly shadow of the man from the camps. He was thinner, and older.

He sat on his own.

The waiter, an elderly, apologetic man with perfect manners, came and said, 'Very pleased see you back, sir. We worried.'

Eric nodded and said thanks.

'The usual, sir?' asked the waiter.

Eric nodded, putting the menu away untouched. 'I'll give it a go.'

The waiter came back with Eric's usual dinner. It was a form of spam with dried peas and powdered potato, followed by a tapioca and jam pudding. This already faint echo of a European meal had changed under Japanese hands into something strange: the taste of each thing had subtly, even unsubtly, slipped.

Eric was overtaken by a sudden nausea, and he pushed the plate away. The man came back with some plain rice.

'You eat, sir, what you can. Very good for you.'

Eric began to eat slowly. He managed, over ten minutes, to finish half the bowl.

He felt drowsy. He walked into the main lounge. Over to the left were two officers, Pettigrew and Marchmont, playing ping-pong noisily. There was someone sitting nodding off over a spread-out newspaper that, as he fell asleep, slipped from his knees and drifted on to the floor.

Eerily, one page came sailing straight towards Eric.

At that moment Shaw came forward. He had a letter on a plate.

'This came for you, sir. Today.'

Eric saw it was an internal memo. His instinct was not to open it. Aware of Shaw looking at him intently, he took the letter, thanking him. While Eric slit the flap open – even a small action like this sapped his energy – Shaw tidied up the newspaper, folding it into a sheet with quick, almost brutal slaps and putting it on the arm of the chair.

It was an invitation to Janice's wedding. Silver printing in a Gothic typeface on cream paper. He felt a dangerous welling of emotion in himself, of tears. Then he told himself to stop being sentimental. He tucked the invitation in his inside pocket carefully as if it were a valuable bank note.

He would go to the wedding. He had an urge, as potent as thirst, to be back among his own kind. He had drifted away, that was what it was – he had drifted away from some core, some centre. Perhaps being with his own kind would remind him of who he was, not what he had lost.

His focus shifted to the newsprint.

He thought to himself he should, pretty soon, start reading newspapers again. Find out what was happening in the world. He guessed there was a whole backlog of work for him at HQ. And what would be the implications of the Unit 731 documents? He sensed, oddly, there might be none. It was a very delicate area, and the Americans could not afford any publicity about what was, at best, an illegal and highly dubious action. The less said about it the better. Still, Eric was aware he would have to tread carefully.

He also wondered whether Caryl was back.

At this precise moment his hands, probably as a diversionary tactic, reached for the paper. He smoothed the half sheet out on his skinny knees. He noted it was several days old. But even as he noted this he saw Caryl's face staring up at him.

It was a formal photo, taken in a studio. Eric saw the elliptical cat's smile on Caryl's lips. His eyes drifted up to the headline: 'Plane Crashes into Hill'. Under Caryl's photo was a sentence. 'Among the dead, eminent . . .'

Eric found himself compulsively reading the article. The flight from Tokyo to Hong Kong had crashed on hills just before landing.

'There were no suspicious circumstances.'

There was a small paragraph outlining the career of

Colonel Caryl Lantern, 34. It noted his promising war record, then talked briefly about his Intelligence work. General Bantock said, 'Nobody held Colonel Lantern in higher regard than myself. I speak for all in the United States SCAP when I say that we have all suffered an irreparable loss in Colonel Lantern's death.' The item ended by stating, 'Colonel Lantern was married to The Honourable Sarah Hadley-Ward of Hare's Chase, Shropshire. The couple, divorced, had no children. Colonel Lantern's parents both predeceased him.'

Eric's whole being locked up. He could not move. Then he had the absurd idea that so long as he did not move, the news would prove false. So he held still for a long time, realising quite consciously, however, that he would have to draw in a breath. He considered not drawing in a breath. But his body would not listen. It went into revolt and a strange sound, not unlike a sob, came out of his mouth. He stifled it, terrified that someone might overhear. Then he realised nobody was paying the slightest attention to him. He tried to relax.

A ping-pong ball came bouncing towards him. The ball dribbled down by Eric's shoes and Pettigrew, sweating and furious at losing the game, bent down with his silly little bat, scooped up the ball. Seeing Eric sitting so still, and not being matey by chucking the ball back, he glanced at the newspaper headline and said, 'Oh, bad bloody business that,' and walked away.

Eric sat there as the pat-pock-clack of the table-tennis game took up again, and he thought, Just as well I didn't get involved with him. He thought, I'm tough, I'm still alive at least. He thought, I'm not dead. At least I am not dead.

He was opening the wardrobe. He was feverish again, he was sure of it. He was positive the parcel was gone. But it was there, sitting where Isamu had last put it. It was from Caryl, Eric knew. It was some message he had sent on to Eric. Eric knew this even as he picked up the parcel and the evidence was quite clear for him to see. But he didn't want to see it.

There was a row of New Zealand stamps – mercurochrome red, startling orange, purple: a fantail, a king's head, a tuatara. Stamped over the images was a black intaglio that read: AUCKLAND NZ. Someone had handwritten, then underlined, 'By Air.'

Eric pulled the brown paper apart under the string. He could see bright scarlet knitting, rather uneven. He got his knife out, slit the string. A scarlet pullover flopped out.

Eric picked it up. It was the work of an amateur. The neck wasn't quite right. A little Croxley letter, earnestly covered with inked handwriting, fell to the floor. He picked it up and ripped open the pages. It was from Irene, the girl he had been engaged to. The girl who gave up on him when he came back so strange.

The letter said she had got married to Ben Tapin, the local electrician. Ben had been in Eric's class at Ellerslie. She was pregnant and she hoped to name the boy – it was going to be a boy, she was sure of it – Eric.

Eric made his way downstairs. Shaw was behind the desk. There was something in Shaw's face, something unreadable, when he looked up.

'Were there any messages?' Eric asked.

Shaw said he had delivered all the messages to Eric. Beside him, the old waiter bowed with an air of infinite regret.

Eric made his way back to the room.

The pullover was on the floor where he'd dropped it.

He picked it up, raised the sweater to his lips. He drank in the smell of lanolin, of fresh scoured wool. What am I doing here? he thought. Why can't I go home? he thought. But then he realised with the same clairvoyance that in some senses he no longer had a home. Caryl's words came back to him: *It's all over. Finished. Gone.*

He knew it was true but the scent of the wool's cleanliness and freshness made him think of a place called home. He found he was crying. He was sobbing, actually. He checked whether the door was locked and whether anyone could see him through the window. This felt deeply covert, as if he were involved in some secret and personal obscenity. He dragged his jacket off and slipped the pullover on over his shirt. He wrapped himself in it and felt enveloped. He went to the bed and lay down. He curled up in a foetal position in the gathering darkness, and for the first time since it all began so long ago, when he had left home as a brave young man, he cried.

Later that night, much later, he came to a decision. He opened the box that held the papers he'd removed from HQ. He had locked the door of his room. He had even taken the precaution of saying to Shaw downstairs he didn't want to be disturbed. When Shaw glanced at him, deep into his eyes, Eric ran a hand down his face and succumbed to a look of exhaustion.

'Still need to catch up on my sleep, mate,' he said. 'That malaria can knock you bad.'

Shaw didn't say anything. He didn't need to.

Eric got the papers out and looked through the evidence

of various Japanese soldiers he'd interviewed. He retained a vivid image of each man – his ability to look you straight in the eye, his eye never leaving yours, daring you to notice he wasn't telling the truth. Or more specifically, since it was culturally acceptable, that he told the truth about something parallel, which took your attention away from what you really wanted to know. Eric heard his own voice, at times raised in anger. He listened to the profound silence that fell.

It was all very simple.

He had to select a case that was watertight.

He owed it to Caryl.

Eric laid the papers on top of the tea chest. He worked hard. He selected. He found the case. He put the other papers back inside.

He sat down and let the blackness inside himself settle.

11

Eric arrived at the Combined Services Club later than he'd intended. The wedding party was in full swing. He had missed the church service, which he didn't mind at all. He had never had much time for religion, not since his childhood. Besides, the thought of Luttrell and Janice promising eternal faith to each other depressed him a little. So it suited him to leap up the stairs, two at a time, to a room reserved on the third floor.

It was a bleak-looking room, lined with cheap panelling. The girls had tried as much as possible to make it festive. They had hung crêpe-paper streamers and blown up balloons. There were large vases of paper flowers, faintly dusty, on either side of the door.

There was a shout of acclamation when he came in.

Eric passed down the narrow crowded table towards Luttrell. Luttrell was in full dress uniform, grinning like an idiot. His face was sweaty, flushed. Janice was in her bridal outfit, smiling tightly. She looked a little uncomfortable. She was wearing a surprisingly home-made bridal dress that looked like someone had skimped on the amount of fabric. Even her bridal veil lacked panache, and the cloth flower that was anchored to her head showed a hairpin very clearly.

The intimacy of the hairpin dislodged a swift wave of emotion in Eric, which raced through him. He reached down for her hand and, kissing the back of it swiftly, glimpsed her face as he rose. It was a private moment of vision, and she appeared to be warning him not to take it too far. She was holding back. Then she winked at him, deliberately. It's all play, she seemed to say to him. So play along, darling. Help me.

'Thanks, Eric,' she said to him a little drily, 'for the silver salver.'

'It was a token I thought you might remember me by,' he said to her. He was aware of Luttrell's vehement blue eyes looking at him. But as always he and Janice seemed to be talking about two things at once. He found her desirable and he decided on the spur of the moment he would like to fuck – fuck anyone really, but preferably one of the women at the wedding.

It was the usual erotic freefall of weddings, when the basic rationale for marriage stood exposed. Fructifying was its polite camouflage.

He glanced quickly down the table for a spare seat, and saw there was a space beside the little New Zealand woman – Olwyn. He squeezed in beside her and said hello. They formally shook hands. He felt a vivid spasm of desire at the moist touch of her hand. Their eyes met and a slow powerful blush moved down her neck and settled, in a vivid spot, on her upper chest by the neckline of her blue silk dress.

She was wearing pearls.

'It's snowing outside,' he said to her inconsequentially.

She said, 'Yes, I noticed some flakes on your hair when you came in.'

'A white wedding,' he said, and laughed.

She turned her head away from him. He had a vivid sense of the back of her neck. Her hair had come unpinned beneath the back of her hat, and some luxuriant, glossy brunette hairs had fallen free.

He longed to touch them. To tidy them away. He longed for the intimacy of being in a relationship with a woman. The casual symmetry of it. The salve of flesh. Of touch.

There are few things in life as important as human touch.

He suddenly saw it.

He became quickly drunk, as seemed necessary to the occasion. Through the serving of the mediocre food (pork, roast vegetables, beans, trifle, jelly, wedding cake), he and Olwyn talked.

Olwyn drank hardly anything.

He was surprised by Olwyn's essential decency and ashamed by the brutal nature of his lust. He was thinking of one thing only, acting like a sheepdog anxiously shepherding a startled sheep into the fold. But she was elusive.

She kept sipping at her glass of water. Looking at him squarely in the eye.

And while they talked about nothing much, Eric had a moment of understanding about himself: he had unmanned himself with Caryl. He had deliberately, he saw that now, taken away the armour of his masculinity. He had tried to turn himself into a woman, hoping in his womanliness he might find something, a feeling – something untouched, a spring of being left to him. But it hadn't worked. He had ended up only being wounded again. This was what he thought to himself as he sat there.

It had not worked out. He would probably never be intimate with another man again. Not in that way. He had ended up being wounded as badly as it was possible to be. A woman was easier like that. She didn't ask so much, or rather, he didn't ask so much of himself. It was easier, more natural, he supposed, the roles more laid out, more defined. He could keep being himself in a way he hadn't been able to be with Caryl. He had exposed himself there. He had laid himself out, naked. He had literally welcomed another man into his body.

That would never happen again.

He knew that, sitting there at this strange, hybrid wedding.

When the reception had run its course, he surprised himself by saying to Olwyn, 'Why don't I walk you home?' He meant metaphorically, since they would all be driven home, drunk, at this late hour. She had laughed and said why not.

When they got to the hostel Olwyn awkwardly asked him in 'for a cuppa'. He realised he needed to sober up. Besides, he had worked it out in his mind, during the wedding. He did this in a curious parallel, his subconscious mind needing to be freed by company, alcohol, mindless chat.

He would go for the case he'd selected. It was a case that

he could get a prosecution out of. He'd make sure of that. If the Yanks were wanting to close down investigations, he would ensure that someone somewhere was found guilty. Otherwise it was true: it was all a bloody sick joke.

For some reason, as Olwyn, in an embarrassed, schoolgirlish way, showed him into the visitors' lounge, he thought of something Caryl had said to him. He hadn't taken it in at the time, but it lingered. It had to do with what was involved in being a world power – or rather the supreme world power. About how it was always a poisoned cup. There was so much pride involved in it, so little real humility. It would always end badly.

What had Caryl said: it was over, finished? That world. But if it was over and finished, what was there now?

This world, a scummy hotel room in a bombed-out city, trying to locate people who had done unspeakable things during a war that had finished. Yes, the war was finished but peace had not come.

So they sat in that large and chill room before a two-bar heater. The furniture was battered, moved from place to place, as homeless as they were themselves. On the wall there was a photo cut out of a magazine of Princess Elizabeth at her wedding. Elizabeth was turned towards her husband and there was such adoration in her glance it seemed to Eric quite humbling.

Marriage was the thing. Normality. Getting back to it.

Getting out.

Down a corridor Eric could hear two women playing ping-pong, their subdued 'Damn!' 'Drat!' 'Blast!' childishly vehement. The pipes overhead indicated someone had just flushed a toilet. It was time for him to go. But he lingered, bathing in the ordinary decency of Olwyn's small talk.

It was refreshing, he decided, just to sit there. She had a woman's discreet ability to listen. Or be silent.

And as he sat there Eric Keeling conceived of an enormous, cavernous desire: to go home. He only recognised it at that moment. He would make this case happen. Then he'd resign.

He needed to go home.

That night he had a dream . . . it was about some wallpaper he remembered . . . and a box . . . he was opening the box and he was putting the objects in order. If only he could put the objects in order . . .

Old Bastard

1

I remember when he first appeared. The Interrogator. It was the beginning of it all. The fuss. I had no idea at the time.

I had just told Dad that Elsie, his partner, wasn't coming home. She'd died that night in Auckland Hospital. He was weeping, tears coursing down his cheeks. This appalled me – I can't tell you how much it appalled me, partly because it revealed how dependent on me he'd become.

'Dad,' I said to him, 'have you got a clean hankie?'

'In my second drawer; Elsie . . .' and he broke down again.

'*Where's Alison?*' he asked me when I came back. The look on his face was accusing.

'Dad, she's in London.'

There was a small pause.

'What's she doing there?'

'She works in finance, you know that.'

The way his eyes went to my face and clung there told me he was buying time.

'When's she coming, son?' he asked when I handed the hankie over.

I was beginning to feel frayed. Acting the saint isn't my natural posture. Yet I have to admit I felt strange. Was it corrupt to feel wanted, to feel that at long last, and at this most desperate moment — when I was fifty-four and Dad was nearing ninety — we'd worked out a way to be?

'*Who*?'

I thought it best to challenge him.

He had the TV on, playing quietly. His eyes strayed to the screen and I sensed he was calmer. He was even sitting at the table in his usual position where Elsie served him dinner. (He had placed his knife and fork down experimentally. I noted the fork and knife were reversed.)

'Alison,' he barked. 'When's she coming?'

'I haven't told her yet, Dad.'

'Told her what?'

There was cunning in his eyes and the ghost of a contemptuous smile on his lips. I couldn't tell if it was contemptuous of me or himself. Myself of course.

'That you . . . that we need her at the moment.'

'Don't go running like a sook to your sister, son. Have some pride in yourself as a bloke.'

He looked pleased with himself, sitting there with his knife and fork upended on the table, waiting for his meal.

'Don't expect me to cook for you, Dad,' I spat at him. I couldn't help myself. 'I've got my own life now. I've got Gary.'

Dad made a catarrhal sound at the back of his throat:

the sort of sound I recognised from childhood. It's a specifically male sound and it's meant to signify gorge rising.

I fought the heat rising throughout my body – my own sinking sense of who I was. It was like shrinking back into being the little sissy I used to be, frightened of him taking the belt to me. But rising in the other direction was a flare of anger. I wanted to hit him.

He looked frightened. He quailed back against the faded wallpaper. I felt appalled. I thought: *He thinks I'm going to hit him*.

Emotions were raw.

I went to the cupboard, and just as I'd seen Mum do many years ago I opened the door and hid my face within.

'Let's see what you've got,' I said. 'I might be able to run you up some tea.'

'You always were a good cook, Ross.'

Dad was peacefully loading instant peas on to the stainless steel tine of his fork and conveying them to his mouth.

He'd taken his teeth out. 'The buggers never fit,' he'd said to me when he came back into the room without them.

Gay men are famous for their predilection, even obsession, with aesthetics. This, at least, is what I've read. All I know is I felt an unquiet horror at the sight of Dad's toothless mouth. Its 'welcome to my world' was just a little too close for comfort. Was this me in thirty years?

The horrible thing is, the absence of his teeth changed his face entirely. He had been a handsome man in his youth: the photos proved it. My mother, even when bitterly disillusioned with the man, sang praises to his beauty. Now he presented himself with the full male shamelessness of not caring how he looked. There were no women around. He was not trying to attract anyone. Perhaps it was his dubious compliment to me as a male. I did not matter or care. Yet I did. I hated the way the removal of his teeth concertinaed his face down into a weird perspective. His nose, reddened and coarsened by a lifetime's addiction to alcohol, met the earthquake up-thrust of his jaw. His mouth was a contortionist's wriggle of constant motion. Even when nothing was in his mouth, he chewed his gums, making the occasional repulsive sucking sound.

He turned to me and — this was worse — rolled an affectionate eye at me. I felt the full force of his love — or, alternatively, if I steeled my heart, his need.

'You're a good cook, Ross. I hope all your . . .' And here he paused for just a moment, dangerously. I looked at him closely. Was he going to say 'girlfriends'? '. . . mates recognise it. Elsie always said –' he went on, turning away from me and gazing back at the flittering images on the screen – 'Elsie always said you'll make someone a wonderful wife.'

I looked at him briefly and took his plate away. Sensing my glance, Dad looked up at me, his eyes once again crafty and assessing.

'A bloke wants to come and see me.'

I was stacking the dishes. I would wash and dry them. I didn't mind this wifely duty. I preferred it to the length of time it took Dad to do anything. The more basic fact was I couldn't bear him chomping and chewing away right by my ear. At the same time I chastised myself for such a pathetic objection.

'Dad. *Can't you put your teeth back in?*' I found myself saying.

A shade of embarrassment, even humiliation crossed his face. I could see he was trying to work out why I would object.

'The old gnashers cause me pain, Ross. I've had enough pain in my life already. I'm jack of it.'

It was pretty unanswerable.

And I didn't pick up his lead about his visitor.

Hours later, as it felt – actually forty-five minutes, at the end of a sports programme – I rose to my feet with premeditated speed and said, 'I've got to go, Dad. Gary's expecting me home and then we're going out to the pictures.' It was a needless lie, with a shameless efflorescence of detail.

In fact I was going up to a night class at the university. I was studying creative writing. But I didn't let on to Dad. Something so 'nancy' would only unleash eviscerating scorn. He'd change creative writing to cooking and then to pinny-making. Better to keep silent. Better to hug your secrets. You could say it was our family motto – if we had one.

'His name's by the phone.'

'Who?'

'You don't have much of a memory, do you, lad?' Toothless mouth grinning at me.

'The man who rang you,' I echoed, already halfway to the door. I had my bag in my hand and a list of instructions to go over later with Dad: I would come out tomorrow night; we would go shopping for his meals for the rest of the week. My phone number at work. I'd ring him during the day.

Seamlessly, in the fortnight since Elsie had gone into hospital, I had slipped into being Dad's guardian.

I went out into the corridor. I turned on the light.

There, on the back of an envelope, Dad had written in large capital letters: HAZELDEAN. FRANK. TUES. 2 PM.

'What does he want?' I called out.

'Dunno exactly.' Dad's reply was muffled. He coughed. 'Wallah wants to talk to me about the war.'

Dad was up and polished when I called round during my lunch hour on the Tuesday. He had his regimental tie on. Jacket. And teeth in. He'd even brushed his hair in the old way (two brushes held on either side of the head, oil applied, then the brushes work away to give an ideal 1940s sleekness). It didn't matter that Dad was now by and large bald.

He had showered, shaved and was very clean.

'Ross, don't hang about,' he said to me. 'I'm busy.'

The surprise was in the kitchen. He had bought a packet of wine biscuits and a block of cheese. Inside the fridge stood a half dozen of beer. Up on the shelf, as added artillery, was a half of whisky. He must have walked to the local shops to buy it.

I whistled. 'Hell, Dad. How long is this geezer going to stay?'

'A bloke has to be hospitable.'

'Well, give me a ring when he's gone. I'll be at Gary's. We're going out to the five o'clocks, so ring before then.'

Sometimes it got complicated, the lies and actual truth.

'Okay, Captain.' He mock-saluted.

I couldn't help feel a sluice of improbable, almost overwhelming happiness. This was what he had always called Alison. I glanced at him fondly. But he wasn't looking at me. He was frowning, looking at something out the window.

'The garden bag's being collected today.'

'Thought it wasn't due till next week.'

'No, it's today.'

I waited.

'It's not full.'

I felt tired.

It was starting to rain. The cat next door stood in the dry, looking out at the dismal scene.

'You want me to go out and fill it up now?'

'I'm just saying the bag should be filled up. Otherwise it's wasting money.'

I threw a raincoat on and filled the green sack with garden waste. I did this angrily, thrusting the old twigs and garden rubbish down into the sack. I knew Dad was watching. At one point he rapped on the window, pointed to some weeds by the neighbours'.

You fucking miserable old cunt, I said out loud, knowing he couldn't hear me.

While I was in the wash-house, running cold water over my hands, I called out, 'Where's this bloke from, anyway?'

Dad came in with a towel. The sort of towel an old person uses, bald and inconceivably tiny. A 'hand towel'. I took it from him and ran my hands through it.

'The varsity. He's a historian,' Dad said, watching my hands with disgust. 'Here, don't do it like that. You're putting water all over the floor.'

He took the towel off me and, with surprising agility, bent over and mopped up the few drops of water that had fallen on the linoleum. He did this in big side-to-side gestures of sublimated anger.

'Why's he talking to you, Dad?'

I heard a small grunt of pain. He had locked down there, bending over. He straightened up slowly, only at the last moment and unwillingly taking hold of my arm. But the intensity of his grip shocked me. He glanced into my eyes warningly.

My hand dropped away as soon as it could.

He threw the towel into the tub and walked out. 'Something . . . I don't know – dictionary, he called it. Dictionary of National Biography.'

I stopped still.

'Are you going to be in it, Dad?'

I felt a piercing shaft of pride. Was it all going to be made worthwhile? Was someone, at long last, going to validate the wreck of Dad's life? Thank him?

'Didn't say.'

I went through to the kitchen where Dad kept opening up the cupboard and peering in. The repetition of this action made me feel bleak. I knew I wasn't facing up to something that my father, by his actions, was forcing me to recognise.

Dad closed the cupboard door, then opened it again quickly and peered inside.

'What you looking for, Dad?'

'Do you think he might be allergic to cheese? People are these days.'

I wondered where he'd picked up this nugget: either

the *Herald* or television, his two sources of paranoid information.

I was so relieved he'd come back online I smiled.

'It's not an afternoon tea party, is it, Dad?' I said with just the faintest hint of campness. Dad stood very still and looked at me. He grinned.

'Well, I'll be buggered.'

Dad hadn't rung by the time Gary and I went to the pictures. We were going to see a remastered print of *The Third Man*. Maybe halfway through the film I receded from the screen. Gary and I always end up holding hands in the dark. I know this is deeply embarrassing to admit. But it pleases me on an unspoken level. We glanced at each other swiftly in the dark – the kind of glance long-term partners exchange: briskly informational but based on an entire encyclopaedia of looks. I sighed.

The film was less involving than I'd hoped. Or perhaps I was just being nagged by the fact Dad hadn't rung. Maybe his visitor had stayed later than we thought he would? Undoubtedly Dad, once he started up on the war, would have a lot to say. It was equally probable that Dad would welcome a stranger as an ideal person on whom to unload his burdens. He had never told me much about the war. But then I suppose I wasn't all that interested. You tend to have a distanced view of someone who takes a belt to you.

Yet his silence worried me. There was the question of all that alcohol. Wasn't it a potent – too potent – mix: alcohol and memories of war?

I rang Dad when I got home but there was no answer. I tried again after dinner, then decided it was too late to go out there.

As it was, when I went to check up on Dad the next day I found the door unlocked, the beer and whisky bottle untouched. They were never to be opened.

Dad himself was nowhere to be seen. On the couch, however, was the shape of a man's behind. And there was an ashtray. In it lay a series of cigarillo butts, clearly stubbed out energetically, as if in mid-conversation. But on the very edge of the ashtray was a stranger sight: a cigarillo which had been lit but left unattended. It had burnt all the way down to the filter. Its ghostly shape, undisturbed, seemed to point to a long rendition – uninterrupted.

Its ash was brittle.

As I stood there, the cigarillo of its own volition crumbled.

2

The Otahuhu police phoned to say that Dad had been found wandering the streets, confused. They'd picked him up in the middle of the road, shouting at Japanese cars. He didn't know his address. They'd found my phone number on a scrap of paper in his back pocket.

When I got there, Dad was sitting in the public area. I was shocked to see how unkempt he looked. He looked like he'd slept rough.

'Here's the lad!' he called, the moment he saw me. He wavered to his feet. 'Told you he wouldn't be long. How'd you be, son?'

I felt myself shrivel. His pathos attacked me, but I also resented his booming voice – it brought back all my old phobias, misrepresenting me, our relationship.

A policeman looked up from behind a counter.

He glanced at me – the negligent son.

'Dad,' I said in a nettled sort of voice. I could feel a shit-eating grin on my face, I wasn't sure why. (To offset aggression? To protect my rage – in silence? I was as confused as Dad.) 'Dad, that's not like you, to get lost.'

I grasped hold of the bone of his upper arm and squeezed it, I could see, painfully. He turned to me and peered into my face. My eyes. I had the horrible feeling he was going to say he didn't recognise me.

'Dad tracked through the jungles of Borneo during the war,' I said to a noncommittal face behind the counter. 'He's not the kind of man to go AWOL. Not in Panmure at any rate!'

I croaked out a laugh. It was a dry sawdust laugh. Pathetic.

The man behind the counter was too busy for this.

'Gave him a cuppa. You take him home now?'

'You get lost when you went out shopping, Dad?'

He was having trouble getting the tongue of the seatbelt into the slot. I waited for a moment, looking ahead. I tried to keep my cool. Then, before I could control myself, I snatched hold of his belt and shot it together. There was a definite reprimand in the click.

He looked frightened.

I tried to drive off smoothly.

'Dad?'

He made a small sound. It could have been assent.

We passed the local supermarket. It was on two levels, and I knew from experience how easy it was to come out of a door and find yourself disoriented.

'I thought I told you to ring me.'

He was silent, chewing his gums.

'Dad?'

'Didn't want to bother you.'

'Dad, you won't be able to stay at home much longer if you . . .'

'I was looking for something,' he said in the small voice of a chastened child.

'What?'

I brought my car to a halt in the drive. Elsie and he had bought a little unit in the back of Panmure. It was the kind of place called 'easy maintenance' in real-estate speak. Pre-death is another way of looking at it. I noticed the lawns needed mowing.

The next door neighbour's cat lifted up off the drive and began to stalk down towards us.

'Oh look, there's Blackie.'

'No, Dad,' I said, leaving a nanosecond to debate with myself about whether it was worthwhile correcting him. Instantly I decided it was. 'That was our cat at Kiwitea Street. This is Gringo.'

'Gringo,' he echoed, but his voice sounded unconvinced.

I felt a moment's abandonment, eerie and spectacular, as his old face softened into intimacy. He got out and called the cat to him.

Gringo, stomach swinging, flopped down on his side, then eased over on his back.

Dad bent over him.

'Dad – you know that historian bloke?'

'Bloke,' he echoed.

'The one who came to see you.'

'Never turned up,' Dad said, losing interest in Gringo and heading inside.

'Bring the box in, Ross,' he called out as he went in the door. 'There's a lad.'

We were sitting having a cup of tea (my hands shaking, breath shallow, I felt a sense of a crisis all around me — I was in deepening denial).

'Ross, have you seen the papers?'

'The *Herald*?'

'No, the papers.'

I looked at him.

'Dad. You know that historian chap. Hazeldean.'

'Oh, he isn't doing me,' Dad said. 'He's doing Northcroft.'

I looked at Dad interrogatively, teaspoon in hand.

'Major wallah in the war trials, son. He was high chief judge and executioner.' Dad cackled. 'Well, not executioner exactly. That was an Australian bloke. Stood a good six foot four, he did . . . Had to bring him over from Darwin. None of the locals'd do it. Curious when you think what they'd been through. You'd think the buggers'd be lining up . . .'

I waited, listening.

'What execution's that, Dad?'

My voice was duplicitously casual. Dad had never talked of anything like this before. Such weighty matters in a kitchen.

Dad looked at me sideways. 'Pour the tea, son, don't let it get cold.'

I poured the tea and waited.

And waited.

'Dad,' I said, 'you were talking about an executioner.'

The look on his face was one of genuine surprise. He

brushed some imaginary specks of sugar off the laminate surface. He picked up his tea and breathed on the surface.

'Never could stand hot tea.'

3

It started with a car backfiring. I can't quite date when it first happened. But Dad hit the floor. He did this in our back yard, at Westmere, so it must have been around 1957. I would have been four. He gestured for us to get down.

Alison, my sister, was older than me by three years. She hit the ground. But she did this joyfully as if it were a game. I followed suit, making sure I didn't hurt myself as I sank. I was a sissy even then.

When Dad got up, and brushed himself down, there was the tiniest flicker of shame on his face. He looked suddenly old – or as he came to look when he knew he was defeated. He was about forty.

For a long time Alison let me think it was Dad's game. This helped. We did it together, an unlikely team. But I remember very clearly the day it all went wrong.

We were in Khyber Pass, collecting beer from a

wholesaler. It was like a collection point. I knew I was on foreign turf: every male there seemed to possess a way of standing – arms akimbo, legs wide apart. I also knew I didn't possess this body language naturally. I didn't want to get out of the car.

Alison nagged me to do it. She was already calling me 'girlie'. She thought she was helping me get over some impediment, just as someone finishes the sentence of a stutterer. In the end I had no choice. Dad strode over, mid-bark – he was in conversation with one of his mates; he wrenched back the car door, as though I had forgotten how to get out.

The men looked at the unlikely freak Eric Keeling had for a son. The men, I noted, all used a tone of voice when they were together. Nobody could exchange a sentence in less than a bark. And everything they said seemed to refer back to some code. It was, I realise now, the war, if you were old enough. Or it was rugby. All these men seemed locked in some eternal game, the rules of which I couldn't grasp. But I knew enough to know I had to get out of the car.

It was then a car backfired.

Dad hit the concrete, mid-comment. He did this with almost athletic gusto. Alison followed, as was our wont. I was the betrayer. I was too embarrassed. I stood there, solitary. I was the one who read the expressions on the faces of the men looking on. There was pity there, and shock.

A long silence seemed to follow as the backfire faded away. Then Jock – he had been in my father's camp during the war – came forward, talking loudly.

'You blokes keep loading the van.'

'All clear, Tiny,' he said to Dad, to make it into a joke. The other men, averting their faces, as if at a natural tragedy, went back to what they were doing, their voices just that little bit louder, laminating over what they had seen.

Dad's face when I could bear to look at it was taut. He went through the act of buying his beer. He wouldn't be defeated, I knew that also. In his place, I would have run. But he was a man. And I knew it was part of his understanding of being a man that you went on with things, even when things turned out wrong.

You could say this was his code in life. For his marriage, and me, his son.

For a war hero to have a homosexual for a son is a dilemma of sorts, I suppose you could say. If you are an only son, the stakes are raised again. Perhaps for this reason all my father's expectations devolved to Alison. I see this now. For a long time I saw her only as nauseatingly accomplished. She did everything right just as, in some strange answering symmetry, I did everything wrong. I disappointed my father in every way I could. Was this because I felt I had disappointed him on some fundamental level I could never redress? Perhaps. It is not easy having a war hero for a father. As for him having a homosexual for an only son, I see this was a burden too.

We drove back to Westmere in silence. Nobody said anything about what had happened in Khyber Pass. Or rather Alison's few attempts at conversation were ignored. And Dad had reverted to his prickly silence. We knew enough as children not to try to disturb him. We knew to creep around our house on tiptoes, our mother mouthing, 'Your father isn't feeling too hot today.'

He could suddenly snap and an arm would fly out. He hit Alison only once. The look of shame on his face was so terrible, I couldn't take my eyes away. It was in moments like this my father grew to hate me. He saw me looking into his soul. He could read in my face what he had become. So our mother would shoo us out of the house and close the door behind us. We knew we were excluded. And we looked back up at the silent, locked-up house. The only house in the neighbourhood that did not have a single item with 'Made in Japan' in it.

Alison and I pooled our information. After all, what was happening to us appeared a mystery. Our sources were the playground, war comics. The Japanese during the war were cruel. 'Unspeakably cruel' is what other kids' parents said, their eyes lifted over our heads, as if to glimpse something we could not – should not – see.

Perhaps this was why the news about the Japanese had to be whispered. It wasn't like the Germans. When we played Goodies and Baddies in the playground, it went without saying that if you were a Baddie you were a German. But nobody made you play 'Japanese'. Even then, there was a core of silence – of something unsayable – surrounding the Japanese.

And by implication, around what had happened to our father.

Dad had nightmares. I can still recall the terror I felt when I heard his screams. He seemed to be fighting someone, or pushing someone away. This is my adult mind making logical what seemed at the time an efflorescence of anarchy. It terrified me. Sometimes he even attacked Mum.

Lights went on; I heard Mum's voice saying, 'Eric. Wake up. Wake up!' And I heard him answer, 'What? What!' He sounded surprised to be back in the world of the little bungalow in Westmere with the cream dappled wallpaper and chromium three-branch lights.

Gradually the voices calmed down. My mother padded down the passageway, her feet cushioned by the carpet, then sounding sharper as she walked across the lino floor. (I slept in the bedroom just by the kitchen.) The seal of the fridge slurped open.

'Go back to sleep, dear.'

I could hear her pouring some milk into a glass from the big quart bottle. I listened to all these sounds, one following the other, because in themselves they gave me surety.

'Mu-uuuum,' I whined.

She came to the door quickly. 'Dear, go back to sleep.' She came in and kissed me once, twice on the forehead. Her lips were pleasingly cold. 'It's your poor old Dad,' she murmured, probably no more awake than I was. 'He's having one of his nightmares. Don't worry, darling, go back to sleep.'

But sometimes I couldn't get back to sleep. And I lay there seeming to hear the desperation of his yell. In my mind's eye I imagined all the things he had been through. I knew nothing of the realities of war, only what I had heard in the playground, seen on films and in comics. I knew he was a hero. But I also had this other consciousness of him. I wasn't sure how to match them up.

Dad in the daylight hours was like another man. He never made any allusion to his nightmares. I think he felt ashamed of them. His way of coping was to pretend nothing had happened. We all pretended nothing had happened. It seemed kinder that way. And if I happened to sleep in, because I hadn't been able to go back to sleep for a long time, Alison would barge into my room, pull up the venetians and tug the top covers off my bed.

'Get up,' she'd tell me in her prefect's voice. It seemed like on these mornings she was even more emphatic.

I pulled the covers over my head. I felt like I had just got to sleep.

'Get out of bed, lazybones,' she'd say. 'It's your turn to put out the rubbish.'

Dad in the mornings covered over any feelings he had about the night by being brusque, busy. None of us quite dared to get in his way. He was either showering, in which case you couldn't turn on a tap in the kitchen because he risked scalding himself, or he was shaving, or he was hurriedly throwing down some strong sweet tea before running out the door. His haste dared you to intercept it with a comment. His eyes never really focused on any of us on these mornings. I tried not to look at him. He tried not to look at us. So we existed, none of us quite looking at one another, all of us hearing his shrieks in the night.

What you cannot see is always more powerful than what you can identify. His nightmares gradually became my own. I was a master of the stratagem of the interrupted nightmare. The strange thing was Dad had no sympathy for my plight. I needed toughening up. Perhaps if I had understood what he had been through as a young man I might have understood better the brusqueness with which he armed himself, his cutting humour, his sardonic way of thinking I was some sort of joke – not a funny joke, but an absurdist joke willed on him.

All I felt was his contempt. I didn't understand this contempt was also partly for himself, for what he saw as his own weaknesses. He kept everything in. And we kept the secret of his nightmares to ourselves. We never went to stay with other relatives. In fact we hardly ever went away at all in the holidays, except to places that were isolated and where we stayed on our own. It was a kind of portable hell, when I think of it. Then, it just seemed an ordinary childhood.

Mum kept Dad's war medals to the last. They were pinned to an old hankie when I cleared out her unit. I learnt later Dad gave her the medals to look after. Not that he said that, of course. Dad could never say anything straightforward, not in the emotional department.

Mum told me he threw them into her lap. She was shelling peas at the time. She felt a sharp point and opened the handkerchief. The Pacific Star, the DSO. I know. I have them now. They are as close as I can ever physically get to Dad. Medals he was deeply ambiguous about.

Those, and the photo Mum kept, right to the last. I discovered it in her stocking drawer after she died. (It fell to me to tidy out Mum's little unit. Alison was 'unavailable'. She sent the most magnificent bouquet of flowers though. In the church, they had the look of having arrived at the wrong funeral, not that of my modest little mother whose favourite catchphrase was, 'It all comes out in the wash.'

There's a touching awkwardness in the photo. It shows Dad getting his gong from General Freyberg at Government House. Dad's in his demob suit, the shoulders too big, or rather his body isn't the right shape for civilian clothing. There's the rawness of Dad's face, his blunt haircut – the tension in his shoulders. He's a soldier on a parade ground when there isn't a parade ground any more.

For us as kids the religiosity of the clipping was what attracted us. We understood it was somehow sacred.

And there was the writing at the bottom of the photo:

```
'Captain Keeling has returned to
the Dominion from Tokyo. He is to
take up a senior position with
Dominion Breweries, Head Office. He
was recently engaged to Miss Olywn
Browning of Hastings.
```

That's as far as Mum ever entered Dad's public life. A footnote.

There was also another cutting that I never really understood. It was of a plane that had come down in Hong Kong, and dated 1949. There seemed no explanation for why Dad had it. When I asked Mum about it she said, 'One of your father's best friends was on that flight.' Attached to the clipping there was a photo of a man with the unusual Christian name of Caryl. It registered because it was my middle name.

The moment it was read out in a roll call at primary school I knew my life was finished.

I never really knew much about Dad's war. In fact I knew so very little I found I couldn't answer even the most basic questions – like what prison camps he'd been in, even what he'd done in Tokyo. Perhaps I kept away from it all because

I was subconsciously aware of how it had fucked up his life or, more importantly, Mum's, my own and my sister's lives. I didn't want to know. And Dad certainly didn't want to tell us.

But then he didn't need to. When I think of my childhood with Dad I see it as a form of photographic negative. There's a kind of darkness to it, and everything is subtly reversed. Dad lived in the daylight workaday world of the positive image, the presentable image. But we lived with his sudden switches into incandescent anger, his strange untouchability: if there were times of tenderness — and there were, in the earlier days — we also knew his deep and abiding anger, his sense of injustice. We lived with the hidden truth of an unquiet psyche. We lived with the negative.

Then it got messy. Dad had always been fond of the booze, but when it got too much my mother asked him to make a decision between her and the booze. He chose her of course, but continued to drink. Dad descended through a number of jobs — the same pretences, the same conclusion. He had a raw temper. He fought with his bosses. He seemed to have a huge chip on his shoulder.

I, with the pure vision of the inexperienced, despised him for it.

In the end Mum forced Dad out of the family home. He would have stayed if he could. But she couldn't stand it any longer. Besides, she'd found out about 'Mrs Thomson' by then. Elsie. Dad's lady friend.

After Dad had separated from Mum he'd call round for me every second Sunday. Take me for a drive. This was how I met Mrs Thomson. At first she seemed a distinct disappointment. Instead of a wicked Elizabeth Taylor type, she was a blowsy little woman with a short attention span. I always think of her sitting in the front seat of Dad's Vauxhall. It was a bench seat and I would be hanging on to the back of it.

When Dad was returning me home, he'd always stop the car round the corner before we got to our street. Mrs Thomson – *Call me Elsie, love* – would have to get out. As Dad drove away, with me now sitting on the warm leatherette, I would feel through the skin of my legs the heat from her body. More particularly, that part of her body which probably connected most intimately with my father. My father, while he waited for me to close the door, always tapped the steering wheel with small raps of impatience. He was already looking ahead, as if he could see the windows of my mother's front room – as if he could see, standing towards the back of the room, a sentinel.

I knew my mother always stood there. It was like a poem of her irresolution. She would not stoop to looking out through the net. But she found herself incapable of not standing there, hoping to catch sight of my father – her husband.

In the rear-vision mirror on my side of the car I would see Mrs Thomson – Elsie – looking down at the pavement. I always associate her with this look, just as I remember another habit that is associated with our Sunday afternoon drives. She used to get out a small lacy handkerchief, then, turning down the flap of the sun shield in the Vauxhall, she would examine her teeth in the mirror, spitting on the handkerchief and rubbing lipstick off her teeth. Her teeth were small pearly ones, a very neat row whose collective acceptability was dimmed by a single black tooth in the lower front. I often found myself staring at this tooth, wondering about its history. In many ways, I see looking back, I was trying to absent myself. It was an excruciatingly awkward situation for all of us.

My father, as he leaned across to open my door so that I could get out, engulfed me in his smell – clean, showered, the tang of Brylcreem: I could smell the hair on his body, the essence of his masculinity. He always leaned across me to open my door, letting it fall back on its own weight, as if expelling me; but this same act was also caught up in something else, a courteous gesture, perhaps, a feint of apology.

'Okay Ross lad,' he'd say to me. 'Spot you next time.'

I had long ago stopped kissing my father. But sitting there the taste of these kisses was still fresh on my lips. I longed for him to stroke my arm perhaps, or run his fingers through my hair. I had always loved it when he laid the flat of his palm on the very nut of my head. I would stand down below him, as within the shade of a tree, and I would rise up on the pads of my feet to feel the force of his body bearing down through the roof of my skull.

I would have liked to hop inside him. He would have protected me.

But, judging me to be a young man at eleven, he no longer really touched me. And I had disappointed him by being an ally of my mother.

Besides, all this was happening in a second. My real job, or perhaps the nature of my contemporary relationship with my father, was expressed through the fact that I had to catch the car door before its edge scraped down on the gravel and so damaged the paint work – a tragedy so immense I could hardly think of what it might mean. (Probably poverty for my mother, since my father might have to cut back 'the maintenance'.) The door was heavy; it swung away from me in a wide arc, full of its own momentum. I would startle myself out of my characteristic longing – the sadness of a boy farewelling his father for another two weeks – by grabbing hold of the handle. This I always did.

My father's reward was to say to me, 'Good man,' with such fullness and richness I found myself lingering by the door, hoping he might say more.

But then, when I checked inside the car, he was looking in the rear-vision mirror. He wanted to be back with Mrs Thomson. Already the door was closed, the deep maroon of the car winking away in the sunlight. He parped the horn once, twice, but this ebullient sound was full of melancholy for me.

Soon I knew my mother would be holding the door open for me. I knew she would say nothing. She never asked. But then she didn't have to. I always told her everything. Or nearly everything. The things of perhaps utmost importance I kept to myself.

Perhaps this started me off on my lifelong custodial keeping of secrets. It seemed to me, at that age, if I kept certain information to myself, then I might survive.

Alison handled it better than I did. She got out. She got an education, a good education, won a scholarship. Immaculately she withdrew herself from the mess of our family life. She was no help to Mum. I don't blame her for it now. She'd seen Mum be a doormat to Dad for so long. What young woman wants to model herself on that? And by the time Mum pushed Dad out, Alison wasn't really around any more. Not emotionally. She'd withdrawn. Dad of course worshipped her. Alison could do no wrong. And practically speaking, as far as I could see, she never did. Not that I didn't sniff round. It would have been much more companionable if my sister had fallen a few times.

4

Ross will try and say things about Dad. Honestly, I never noticed all that much. Besides, what parent is perfect? You have to take the good with the bad. I know I'm talking clichés here, but sometimes there's truth in commonly accepted sayings. Besides, I don't believe in looking back. What's the point? They did the best they could.

I know as a mother I'm not perfect myself, though I consciously try not to hamper my daughter by my own example. I'm not criticising Mum: she made the decision not to go out to work. She should have divorced Dad much sooner. She thought she was holding all the cards by keeping him on a string, but it wasn't like that at all. She just showed she was hoping he would come back. Then, irony of ironies, of course, when Dad did want to come back, she'd got used to being on her own. He was no gift by that time, anyway. His drinking had got out of hand.

Or so Ross told me. He'd ring me every so often, more times than not in some strange state which I suspected was either chemically induced or caused by pot. He was as bad as Dad in that way: neither of them wanted to look at reality.

Maybe being at a distance gives you clearer vision. The few times I thought of them all back in New Zealand their lives seemed so . . . compromised. I was fond of them, of course, as a daughter and sister is. But I didn't particularly miss them – the atmosphere. But of course memory isn't like that. It doesn't let you escape scot free. It gets its pincers on you, and before you know it you come to a terrible realisation. You are your memories. That's all you are – or were.

I prefer to live in the present, myself. Look to the future, is what I say. I have been a successful merchant banker for over twenty years now. I enjoy myself. I could do better. Who couldn't.

My brother was always spoilt. He never had to do the things I did, like a weekend job selling ice creams at the local dairy. But then the truth is I wanted to get out of that silent house with its accusations and atmospheres. I enjoyed the freedom of earning my own money. I also wanted to see how the world worked. Ross was always younger than me in more than years. He wanted to believe in fairy stories when I was already old enough to know there were no fairies – well, only the kind that appear in books.

I dodged old Mr Tamworthy who took me out the back of the dairy and unbuttoned himself. Initially I was quite interested, in an anthropological kind of way. I had never seen Dad naked. He covered himself up in front of us, and never, as far as I know, even swam in public.

I was an early developer. Ross was some kind of stalled little boy, wanting to believe his father was a war hero. I used to hear him boasting of it in the school playground. Till he got bashed up for it. I came across him once being bent into a puddle by Paul Tamworthy. I hit him hard on the back of the head with my bag, giving it a good swing to make sure he was so shocked by the pain he wouldn't retaliate. Ross was whingeing, crying, snot coming out of his nose.

'Don't you know enough not to skite about Dad?' I said to him when he finally stopped crying and we were walking home. (A rarity in itself, thanks to our age difference.)

'I don't understand,' he said, between stifled sobs.

I thought to myself, *No, you don't.*

I knew Dad had a girlfriend even before Mum did.

I joined the Brownies and then Girl Guides. I sang in the choir. Then I discovered tennis. There was a club up the road and my mother especially was enthusiastic about this. Perhaps she saw it as a world she might have glimpsed as a young woman or, more probably, read about in women's magazines. But it wasn't like that. Westmere verged on Grey Lynn, a tough working-class suburb where the kids played like they really meant it. I didn't care.

The moment I got out on that tennis court, I lost everything – Dad with his nightmares, my clinging brother and Mum always trying to make things better but only, poor woman, making it worse. I played until the sky seemed to seep into my eyes. I played till I saw nothing but white lines on asphalt. I played till my body hummed and my wrists strained and the muscles at the back of my legs burnt. I didn't know at the time that I wanted to lose something – I was too intent on winning. I got so that if I didn't win, I felt bitter. Not that I ever let anything show. I held it all in. It only meant the following week I played with more determination. I played anyone too. I was in training, I thought, to become as good a tennis player as anyone. But really I was training myself – preparing myself – for the art of escape.

I'd seen Dad and his moll one day when I was in Queen Street with Cheryl, my girlfriend. They were sitting in a car together, smoking cigarettes. Both of them looked stonkered. At first I felt shocked. What was Dad doing there? His car parked up in Queen Street, Mrs Thomson tracing small patterns in the steam on the windows. She was a fellow drinker. I see that now. At that stage I didn't understand about codependent alcoholics. They'd made this tidy, rather pathetic little world for themselves in a hotel room and, most of all, inside the protection of Dad's car. So long as he had that car, he was immune. It didn't matter what his job was, the car conferred an executive air.

I can remember when he had to sell the car.

He came round to pick me up. He'd rung first, as Mum insisted that he do – she said she was sick of him turning up drunk. To tell you the truth, it embarrassed me when Dad turned up on the doorstep. He was nearly always in some emotional state. Often he just wanted to talk to me or to touch me. I don't mean in the way people go on about these days. He just wanted a hug. Sometimes he smelt of loneliness so much it hurt. But I also, in some part of me, resented it.

I was doing what Mum should have done. The strange

thing was I made her the focus of my anger. I didn't understand this at the time. Anyway the phone rang and, as per usual, I got there first.

'Want to go for a drive?' Dad's voice was already slurred. I couldn't turn him down. 'I'll meet you on the corner in ten.'

This is what he always said, his form of code. 'Ten' never meant ten minutes, though; he was always late. One afternoon he never turned up at all. But I sensed he'd be round this time.

It was a quarter to five, a difficult time to slip out of the house. Mum was in the kitchen, making our dinner. Ross was in his bedroom. (He'd come to the door when I answered the phone. I knew he was listening in. For his sake I pretended it was Cheryl – I needed privacy at this stage, I was still growing.) He came out of his room and looked after me as I walked out the front door.

'Where you going?' he called out. The little spy.

'Mind your own beeswax,' I replied.

Mum came to the kitchen door and glanced at me.

'I need some fresh air,' I said,

'Well,' she said. 'Don't be too late getting back. I'm making your favourite tonight. Luncheon sausage and tomato sauce.'

I didn't have the heart to tell Mum that was a meal I'd loved when I was six or seven. There were some things she just didn't get. Besides, I was enjoying the deceit. I thought I understood Dad. I was on his side.

We drove off, Dad putting his foot down so the car seemed to leap away from the dull streets of Westmere. We tooled round Herne Bay. Dad liked to point out the grand old houses, hidden behind palms and hedges. Sometimes he parked up in Bella Vista Road and we just looked at the sea while he talked.

'I'm sorry I'm not around enough,' he said, glancing at me nervously.

I could smell drink on him. I don't mean fresh drink, though there was that. I mean when someone drinks habitually, heavily, day after day, it reaches a point when their skin perspires a strange, chemical smell. He was saturated, stewed in it. He was losing his looks too. He was collapsing inwards.

The sea was a gorgeous jade green that day. Over Henderson, in blue smudges, you could see it was raining. But on our side of the harbour, it was warm, still. The sun was running along all the power lines, glittering.

'Doesn't worry me, Dad,' I said, lowering myself in my seat so my knees rested against the glove pocket. He glanced at me.

'You're too old to sit like that,' he growled. But it was a tender growl. He lit a cigarette, shakily. 'I'm getting rid of the Vauxhall,' he said.

I sat up. Involuntarily I ran my hands over the leatherette.

'Why?' I said, then instantly wished I'd not pried.

'It's got too many miles on the clock,' he said, looking straight ahead.

'What will you get?'

There was a moment's silence in which, once again, but too late, I wished I could withdraw what I'd just said. I was too old to touch him. I couldn't do anything.

'Dad,' I said, 'can I've a cigarette?'

'You're not smoking now, are you?'

The moral tone of his voice caught us both off guard. We couldn't help but laugh, both of us, at the comedy.

'It's not good for a young girl like you,' he said, offering me a smoke out of his packet. As he leaned forward to press in the cigarette lighter, I smelt again, very freshly, his stained smell.

Catching me registering it, he stretched back and nudged the wheel of the window-winder down a bit.

The cigarette lighter pinged out.

I leaned down, very confidently, and placed it against the end of the cigarette. He watched me in silence. I breathed in and, as Cheryl had taught me, I fanned out the smoke down my nose. I felt tremendously adult, ready for anything. Except for the look on Dad's face.

'Don't grow up too quick, Captain,' he said to me suddenly. 'There's a lot of time to be adult – too much if the truth be known. Don't rush your fences.'

I glanced at him. *Who are you to tell me anything?* must have been written on my face.

He flicked on the ignition key. But the car gave only a strange gurgle. There was such a look of panic written on his face. He turned the ignition again and thankfully (I felt prickles of sweat stick into my body) the engine roared into life.

He sat up in his seat, as if he were riding the beast.

'Would you like to come round and see me this weekend at the hotel?'

'Will *she* be there?'

There was a slight pause.

He looked at me. I felt the disappointment, even grief, in his features. But I was only fourteen. I was pulsing with life. I wanted to go out with Cheryl that weekend. I felt that old age was faintly toxic and certainly contagious. I feared that if I met up with old Mrs Thomson (as I called her in my head, no doubt a little maliciously) I'd end up like them. A pair of losers. Sitting in a back room somewhere, getting quietly drunk.

That won't be me, I thought. I knew that even then.

Maybe I should have thanked Dad for this gift.

He showed me what not to be.

But I also felt the warmth of his approval. He'd catch hold of me at moments and say (the smell of alcohol so strong I wanted to turn my face away, but I knew I couldn't − I didn't want to harm his dignity like that), 'You go ahead, lass, and get what you want. I can see you're going places, Alison.'

He no longer kissed me. This had stopped a long time ago, about the time I got breasts. But what he did was even better. He held out his hand for me to shake, like I was a mate.

I feel the honour still.

— • —

On one of those interminable Sundays when Dad called for me (Alison was never asked out on these jaunts) I knew something was up immediately he pushed open the car door. His face was ashen. He said he was dropping me off at the art gallery. I was to meet Mrs Thomson there.

'She'll look after you, lad.'

I knew by now never to question Dad. Once he was in one of his moods, he was best left alone.

It took me many years to understand these moods had nothing to do with me. I can remember quite clearly the moment I discovered this remarkable fact. The discovery alone seemed to mark a maturing of my consciousness: in a streak of pure rationality, I saw my father's moods had nothing to do with my being a girlish sort of boy who had disappointed him in every way, he being such a man's man, a war hero to boot.

When I was a child, though, awareness of my father's moods brought with it a feeling of dread on my skin, a metallic sort of heat that had nothing to do with warmth but everything to do with embarrassment. I wished to stop breathing. I think I probably even altered my breathing to make it as low as possible. I knew I could do nothing quickly, or in a way which would startle my father. If I did this, I risked all his irascibility descending on me.

All too often, before he left Mum, this ended in the strap. The sheer irrationality of this act, as well as my mystification about its cause, always made the physical pain more unendurable. Then, gradually, over time I learned a mysterious and rather odd lesson: if I separated myself from my body, even as it registered the pain of the strap, I would not feel it so severely. It really didn't seem to make sense, because my body still felt the pain (and I was such a sissy that I dreaded the pain more than I felt it). But I also found I could separate myself from this abject boy, screaming with fear and that stranger wielding the strap, his face fixed, as if he were seeking to locate a solution to some abstract mathematical problem.

Our love was fused with hate – and an additional, probably more difficult emotion for a child to carry: pity. I actually pitied Dad. He was so wretched afterwards.

'She'll be inside,' Dad said to me when he dropped me

off before the grey château of the art gallery. All the shops were shut, and the gallery was the only thing open, apart from churches.

Dad sped off. It was the first time I had ever been on my own in the city before. Some childish invention sparked in my head. I could run away. I knew the wharves were down the end of Queen Street. I could get a job on a ship. I could become a Robert Louis Stevenson boy, full of pluck, working my way to another kind of life. But even as I entertained myself with these bookish deceits I saw Mrs Thomson come out the main doors. She was in need of a fag. She saw me, it seemed, with relief.

'This way, pet,' she called out to me in her catarrhal, malt-whisky voice. 'You don't want to leave a lady alone in the big smoke, do you?'

We were sitting in a milkbar. She had cut short the educational part of the afternoon. She had led me in with imperturbable élan, calling out to the owner as we came in, 'Hi there, Kev, I've brought my secret love child in with me!'

Normally I would have found this excruciatingly embarrassing but even I understood I was entering some kind of new moral universe where embarrassment was not considered a virtue.

Later, draining her milkshake, Mrs Thomson said to me, 'You're wondering where your pop is, I bet.' She raised her eyebrows and glanced at me complacently.

The fact was I didn't mind not being around Dad. But I felt it was probably not politic to reveal this to Mrs Thomson. She seemed fixated on fitting me into the model of a red-blooded boy scout of a lad – probably like all the boys she knew. The fact she so speedily overlooked all my failures in this direction was part of her idea of being kind. It only made me feel more inadequate. So I nodded vaguely.

'The devil on his back's bad today. He didn't want to come at all. I told him, you can't disappoint the poor little tyke. He's waiting for you. But he's got it bad all right . . .'

She was silent a moment, looking down into her milkshake.

'He suffered some terrible things in the war, Ross. You know that. I only hope that you never have to go to one.'

'Oh I'm never going to war,' I said brightly.

She looked at me a little startled.

'Well,' she said, her eyes going to the light out on the street, 'some of the things your father saw – and did, most likely – play on his mind.'

I was alive to the difference between 'saw' and 'did'. I looked at Mrs Thomson closely. Her eyes were liquid, shining. Obviously she adored my father. She was being his ambassador, explaining something to me.

'What did he do?'

'Well –' She looked alarmed. 'I'm sure I don't know the ins and outs of everything but in war, you know, terrible things happen.'

This didn't make it any clearer.

'What terrible things?'

'Well –' and here Mrs Thomson lowered her voice and glanced about the milkbar – 'things you would never believe the human mind was capable of. Only a devil could conceive of it.'

I nodded. This was better.

'Your Dad when he gets low keeps running the same thing through his head. It's like he can't escape it. That's when he has a drink too many. He's haunted, see. Haunted.'

She began scrabbling in her purse. The Craven A came out. But she laid the packet on the table.

I decided to be cheeky.

'What does Dad keep running over in his mind?'

She looked down the end of the room and the light played over her aging features. 'There are things you don't ever want to know, son. Take my word for it.'

She lit up, blew out a contemplative fan of smoke. I felt she knew more than I did.

'Is it something to do with eating humans?'

She looked at me sharply. Then her face creased into amusement. She ashed the sagging end of her cigarette, brought it to her mouth, sucked in with a thorough sense of enjoyment. As she breathed out a warm fug of smoke, she said, half laughing, 'You've been reading too many war comics, love!'

I flushed, as if caught out. But it was another emotion I felt.

She wasn't looking at me. She was looking back out to that source of light at the end of the milkbar. She shook her head slightly.

'So you see, Ross, when your Dad . . . he doesn't mean to bark at you as he does . . . but he's got a lot on his back. He carries a lot, you might say. You have to be good to him, Ross.'

I felt the full weight of responsibility even as it oppressed me. But I also knew this was not a situation in which I could declare my feelings.

I sighed, as though I empathised.

I was learning the art of deceit, a parallel survival technique to secrecy.

Where was Alison, you ask? She never came with us on these Sunday drives. No doubt because of the 'unhealthy' influence of Mrs Thomson. As a boy I was supposed to be immune. Or perhaps my mother was worried even then about my being without a father and what this might imply about my learning to be a male. Not that Dad offered much in this direction. He was normally closed, diffident, at times actively hostile. Like many men suffering an almost perpetual hangover he was often irritable.

But I would not like you to think we were separated from one another. Silence can be a pleasant thing between two people, and there were times with Dad and me when we felt bound together by a companionable lack of words – their non-necessity. Sometimes on our aimless drives around an empty city we would not say a single word between our initial greeting – 'How'd you be Ross?' – and our parting, 'Spot you next week, son.' Into this silence he would sometimes introduce a tuneless hum – a kind of vocal doodle that I later learnt was an old war tune: 'I've Got My Eye on You, Sweetie-pie'.

It's hard now, from this vantage point, to say how much I implicitly understood about Dad's war experiences. There were the small glimmers of understanding from instances like the one in the milkbar with Mrs Thomson. There were our 'mutual games' when Dad hit the floor or ground, when a car misfired. Perhaps another way of putting this is that, as a child, you derive your understanding of the world from your mother, your father: how much is implicitly understood is difficult to work out after a while. Suffice it to say, it was as vast as the sky.

5

I knew Ross would never get away. I left as soon as I could. I got a job in Sydney, working in a bar, then I flew to London. I disappeared. We wrote to each other fitfully, in the forced way of children on some kind of perpetual holiday. They were always postcards, all our news contained on one publicly viewed piece of cardboard. I used a lot of exclamation marks, as you do, to distract attention from what was not being said. (Experimentation, growth, ideas – and money. I got into advertising. Became an acolyte of Thatcher. I got serious about getting ahead.)

Ross then made a complete fool of himself by sending me an eight-page letter telling me he wasn't being true to himself if he didn't tell me he was gay.

The letter was handwritten and had a hectic note to it, the lines running up and down the page. I wondered if he were on drugs. I had to smile at his naïveté. Did he really think he had to inform me, his big sister, that he was queer? I'd known all along, from the soles of my feet, up the inside of my nostrils, from beneath the shelter of my eyelashes. I had been protecting him all along. He never realised how much he rode on my coat-tails. Never heard how often I discouraged all the other kids from ridiculing him. Of course when he tried to be heterosexual a little later, and got girlfriends, the girlfriends were all so weird and flawed it only drew attention to his nanciness.

Mostly, though, I had the luxury of entire months never once thinking of my family. Dad, it was true, sent me the odd note. It got to the point I didn't open them. In truth, every time I opened one of Dad's notes a feeling so plangent leapt out at me I ended up howling. The first time it happened I was so surprised I thought it was my time of the month. Instead, it happened each time, ritually, as if I were undergoing some kind of mourning. For my past, I now see, or a past I didn't have. So I learnt to leave those letters unopened.

The fact is I tried not to think. I cut those little intaglio islands out of the map. It wasn't hard; after all, they hardly registered anywhere else. Most places you went placed Australia at the very edge of the known world. When your eyes went to locate New Zealand, which they always did, you found we'd slipped off the map. We simply weren't there.

Then, out of the blue, my world imploded. It would be about eighteen months ago now. Just when I thought at long last I'd got away. But there it was. Prosaic. Clawing me back, in that insistently banal New Zealand kind of way. ('You owe me.') It was ordinary enough on the surface. A largish brown manila envelope. Stamps from New Zealand. I didn't recognise the handwriting – oddly mawkish, as if a schoolgirl were concentrating on her twirls, a lip pressed up as she invented 'joined together' words. There was no return address. But I intuited it must be to do with Dad.

Something went quiet inside.

But I was also running out the door, late for my appointment, a make-or-break meeting. I had spent three solid days preparing my report, and had got up early and looked through my notes. I felt cool, prepared. The last thing I needed was the detonation of my family life. I tucked it quickly in the inside pocket of my briefcase where it was safe but, I realise now, I wouldn't see it without searching.

As it was, that meeting took off and led into one of the coups of my career. I worked seven days a week on the rejigging of foreign debt of a certain African nation. I worked eighteen-hour days, adrenalised by the risks I was taking. I hardly ate; I closed myself off from the daily world. It probably helped that I was separating from my husband, Alec. I didn't want to go there. It was only when I gave myself a congratulatory break, three days in Madrid, staying at the Petit Palace Embassy Hotel, that I emptied out my briefcase – I do this ritually before each break; it helps to come back to a clean sweep – and I found the strange letter. I threw it into the bottom of my suitcase. On top I loaded the Jil Sander dress I'd wear to the opera and my Nike running shoes. (I also put in my guide books. I was a serious, well-informed traveller.)

I was sitting in the Buen Retiro Park when I opened the envelope. All around me was beauty of an airy continental sort – the crunch of gravel, and a soignée teenage girl walking by, her head held high. I felt for one second a kind of envy for the way young people float by in a self-sufficient daze, as though they've invented it all – love, beauty, intrigue, the future.

Then I thought of Juliette. My feelings darkened, though I'd learnt the painful way to proof myself against this sort of longing. There was nothing I could do about my daughter. She had left me. More than left me, she had abandoned everything I had worked to give her – the private education at St Paul's, the finishing school in Switzerland to improve her French; the expensive orthodontic work; riding lessons – all of it lost, abandoned. It was eighteen months since she'd rung me, then come round and visited me in Islington. I knew she was high. There was that bright over-vivacity, an emphatic sincerity that had in it an eerie attempt at control: she didn't want me to see the ragged shape of her nails, or the loose threads hanging off the bottom of her jeans, the slight tremor in her young hands – or the needle prick of her pupil, alternating with a glossy, tawny black.

'Tell me,' I kept saying to her, pleading with her. 'I'll do anything – anything – to help you. Where are you living? What are you doing? How do you live?'

She just looked at me with that sneer of the very young.

'Dad's helping me,' she said. Then she reformulated it in a way she knew would hurt. 'He helps me, Dad does.'

She'd picked up, I don't know where from, this appalling affectation of a South London accent. She used it on me experimentally, played me with it.

When I couldn't help but say to her, 'Why are you

speaking in that ridiculous assumed accent?' she said, 'Yeah Mum, just like your accent's so real.'

'It's different,' I said.

'How?'

'At least my accent got better.'

'In your opinion maybe.'

I was cooking her a meal with shaky hands. I felt uneasy about having my back turned to her. I didn't know what she'd do. I even eyed the Sabatier knives that stood to her elbow. Her eyes followed my panicky glance and she picked one up, gloating. She stood there with it – a sharp vegetable knife – and pricked the end of it into her second finger. A bright globe of scarlet. She smiled at me as she wiped it across each cheek, painting herself to look like some sort of tribal squaw.

'Just like you'll help me, Mum.'

I knew it was blackmail. I wanted her out of the house. But I was terrified, too, about what would happen to her if she went. I felt if she slipped out the front door I might never see her again. All the dark forces out there would pounce on her, infuse her with their evil powers. What happened later would be anyone's guess. (A body in a doorway down by the Embankment?)

'I need five hundred quid,' she said to me, laying down the veggie knife on the butcher's block but giving it a spin so it whirred around like some kind of fortune-telling device. And in the weird way of chance, the knife slowed as it came towards me, then pointed straight at me.

I reached down instinctively to take it away, but caught the side of my finger on the blade. (I always liked to have my knives scalpel sharp: if you are going to cut, cut deep and clean, I say.)

'No,' I said. 'I won't. It'll only go up your arm. You think I'm a fool. You only come here when you want money.'

Juliette did a strange thing then, one I'll always remember.

She smiled. That is, the muscles on her cheek involuntarily twitched back, so the corners of her mouth rose up and her teeth were revealed. I saw how little she was caring for herself – those expensive teeth, which had been straightened, cleaned and checked at six-monthly intervals in Holland Park Avenue, had a weird dimness, even a faint sheen of green. One tooth, to the left, had been knocked out. This shocked me profoundly.

'Oh Juliette,' I said to her. 'Come home, leave all that world behind you. Can't you see you're ruining yourself, everything I've given –'

This was a mistake.

The smile changed, became satiric. Even under her London pallor she flushed.

'Everything I've worked hard to give you –' I said, losing my nerve but also getting angry. Why am I having to explain myself, I rationalised. I've not done anything wrong. Alec and I, when we were together, spoiled her with too much money, making up for not enough – loathsome expression – 'quality time'.

She was throwing things into her bag – silver from the flatware drawer.

'What are you doing?' I cried out.

'Taking what I want.'

'Darling –' I said.

She just looked at me.

'See you, Mum,' she said as she went out the door. And from the front path, in the dark, her voice reached up to me, cool and challenging. 'And thanks for all your help. Everything you've *worked so hard to give me.*'

Did I imagine it, or did I hear someone else outside, either female or male, break into snuffling laughter?

I sat there in the park for a long while composing myself. I held the letter unopened in my hand. I wondered if there was a note from Dad inside. He had stopped writing to me many years before, when it became apparent I wasn't coming home. He probably felt abandoned. My Christmas gifts, so carefully chosen, so beautifully wrapped – so expensive – always went unacknowledged, and in the end I stopped even them. I thought the least he could do was drop me a line.

I opened the envelope when I was fully relaxed. In fact my fingers, of their own volition, slit it open. I looked down at them as at the hands of someone else, one of those people I've read about who supply beautifully shaped hands for television advertisements. And it was true I made of my hands something of a cult. I always had the nails manicured. Call it my vanity, if you will.

Now these hands independently were opening the cheap envelope. But instantly I leapt back into my body. I felt the smallness of a minor electric shock. I looked up quickly. Everything around me had become sharper, made up of oscillating atoms. The bronze lampposts. The flowers in the bed, geraniums a red of hallucinatory brilliance.

It wasn't a letter. It was a document. Or rather part of a document. I glanced at it only for a moment, but I could see it was old. (I went back to the garage at Kiwitea Street. Plunged in: vertigo. There was that bottom-of-the-creek smell.)

Perhaps I was buying time. I upended the envelope, expecting a small note from Dad. (I thought of half a page of Croxley. In that economical manner of the older generation, he might have ripped a page in half, then embossed each line with minute handwriting.)

Nothing. Nothing at all.

Instinctively I didn't open the document, which was folded. My eyes for a moment played on the back of the page. The paper was the grey-blue of officialdom, and I could see already something I'd seen once before – Dad's scrawled signature – along with a date – October 1949 – and, below it, an inversed scarlet stamp reading CONFIDENTIAL.

I opened my purse, carefully placed the detonator inside.

I went off to the Prado and looked very intently at their collection. For some unknown reason, or for reasons patently obvious, I hesitated for a long time before Goya's 'The Shootings of May Third 1808'. It was only after a while that I realised another person was standing there gazing at the same painting. I glanced at him – early middle aged, well dressed, presentable. He was trying to pick me up. I nodded to him briskly, intimating that the painting was indeed remarkable. I used my guide as a way of getting away. But for a long time, as I traipsed through the echoing galleries, I thought I heard the stranger's footsteps following me, drawing closer.

6

I lost the stranger. I stumbled back to my hotel room in the dazzling heat, the light outside intrusive even though I was wearing my sunglasses. It was only four o'clock in the afternoon, but I pulled along the curtains (heavy-weight Florentine damask). I felt I needed the shelter of darkness. In the gloom I opened the fridge, artfully disguised as a pillar. Light spilled across the carpet. Instinctively I chose Black Label. Only later I recognised it as Dad's tipple of choice for ultimate celebration. It was like he was trailing me, trying to tap me on the shoulder, speak.

I took the document with me, unread, and sank back into the feather cushions of the four-seater couch. I kicked off my heels and unpinned my pearls. I slid some whisky down my throat. I needed an anaesthetic.

I thought for a moment of Dad 'self-medicating', as

they call it these hokum days. A coarse laugh, almost a sneer, broke out. I looked around the gloom, in search of something. And spied myself in the elegant framing of a gilt-edged mirror. *Sister, what are you doing with your life?*, this simulacrum had the nerve to ask. All my success deserted me: the house fully paid for in Islington, the executive job with chauffeured car awaiting me outside the door every morning. Instead I saw divorce, abandonment, the daughter who loathed me and everything I had given her.

I felt like weeping. Oh God, it's the alcohol, I said to myself with distaste, plonking down the glass . . .

I reached for the document as an antidote.

It certainly sobered me fast. It broke in midway through.

(g) After about half an hour I heard shouts. One of the prisoners tried to escape by running into the grass. He was shot in the back. The two officers stopped arguing. The prisoners were ordered to stand. They did so in total silence. Nobody said a word. An order was given and the prisoners were shot. This happened in relays. They did not all die, however. I heard groans and cries. The guards began to bayonet them and hack at them with the native parangs. I was terrified and stayed up the tree.

(h) After a while the killing

seemed to stop and all became
silent. It had only taken about
fifteen minutes. It was dark by
this time. I saw a flame. I saw
Japanese soldiers silhouetted round
the bodies. After a while I smelt
human flesh.

(i) I heard the soldiers in the
distance. They sounded drunk.
I could hear all sorts of evil
sounds. I climbed down the tree. I
was terrified and walked the long
way home, avoiding the field. I
hid.

(j) The following morning 19
August 1945 I went back and looked
at the field. I wanted to make sure
that I had not dreamed what I saw.
There was nobody alive there. The
grass was beaten down and smeared
with blood.

(k) I saw seven bodies without
heads. I could not count the
number of bodies as many had been
dismembered.

(l) Things were scattered
all over the ground — broken
spectacles, false teeth, papers,
photos. There were hats and buttons
of Australian soldiers. I did not
touch anything. I was frightened.
I left the field. I told nobody

about what I had seen. I hid in the
jungle for three days.

<u>In making this statement I</u>
<u>acknowledge that it was made freely</u>
<u>and voluntarily and that no threats</u>
<u>were used nor promises made to</u>
<u>influence my statement.</u>
SWORN before me, 93256 Captain
Eric Harald KEELING, an officer
of the New Zealand Military Forces
and now attached to 2 Australian
War Crimes Section SCAP at TOKYO
this Eighteenth day of October One
thousand nine hundred and forty nine.

Signature of Interrogator

. . . .

It was Dad's signature.

I washed my hands very carefully. I did this for perhaps
too long, gaining time. When I looked up, the mirror
above the basin questioned me. It showed a woman the
wrong side of fifty, well assembled, holding it together.
I checked my parting: still another few weeks before a
touch-up. When I looked into my eyes, I don't know
what I saw — someone assured? I was challenged by my
own glance, I have to say. Why was I always so on the
case? What was I frightened of?

I turned the hot water off. My hands, my porcelain hands, were ruddy. I had been washing them for too long. I put the soap back, dried my hands in the depth of a luxury hotel towel. All the while I was thinking of those – disgusting – details and, more to the point, wondering who was sending them to me. What were they trying to say? Or do? Yet no letter could have been more eloquent.

Dad was in some sort of trouble.

The fact was I had been getting documents of this sort for quite some time. No name attached. My address handwritten in that mawkish way. No note inside. Sometimes they were about implanting anthrax into humans. Mass enforced prostitution. Beheadings. Always uncomfortable, horrorful things.

I had put the papers in a pile.

After a while I got to recognise the envelopes, and left them unopened.

I was good at demarcating areas in my life.

I turned the light off in the bathroom. Immediately the room, which could have been used efficiently for a slaughter, sank into a pelt of darkness: I retreated to the bedroom.

The strange thing was, for once in my life, I was unsure of what to do. In this situation perhaps the best thing was simply to sit and wait.

The hunter always does.

I had another whisky, but then, sensing it was dangerous to get drunk, I cut it out. I wanted to stay in control. I had too many memories of Dad as a lachrymose drunk to want to go there. Especially now. I ordered room service.

I didn't want to go out or, most of all, be that strange sight, a reasonable-looking woman eating on her own. I would go for a long walk after I had eaten. I would try and think it all through. Surely it would make sense if I thought about it long enough, coolly enough, with enough incisive analysis.

Failing that, there was my morning run: fifteen kilometres should do it – a ritual bath in ice-cold reason by another name.

7

The phone rang. Gary got to it first and I listened in while I folded the washing.

'Yes. He is. Hold the line.' Gary's voice was more than usually clipped.

He came towards me, looking at me intently. 'Ross, it's some bloke,' he said in a casual voice, which didn't manage to mask its enquiry.

'I don't know who it is,' I mimicked back to Gary, as if a trick had phoned in to Domesticity Central. Yet some vestigial guilt made me weirdly furtive. I felt a beat of excitement: perhaps it was some enticing stranger ringing me, offering me that change in my life which I perhaps subconsciously hungered for.

Being a gardener at fifty-four leaves left you oddly vulnerable to chance.

'Hello?'

'Good afternoon,' said a voice with a pleasingly deep timbre. It was the voice of a top; authoritative, but here curved into a stoop of politeness. 'Is that Ross Keeling?'

'. . . Yes?'

I heard the anticipation in my own voice.

'My name is Hazeldean and I spoke to your father.'

'Yes.'

I said the word as a doorstop. Quickly I redressed myself mentally. Pushed up my shoulder-strap, did up my fly.

'I'm putting together a bio of your father . . .'

I didn't listen to what he said next. I couldn't help myself. Small rockets of excitement were fanning open in Dad's night sky. I watched them for a moment, my face speckled, dazzled by the light display. At last. My feelings were so complicated, I realised that. On one hand I saw Dad as an A-grade bastard who'd done his best to hobble me, yet the human in me, as I'd got older, saw his own wounds. His pathos haunted me. And, here, was a stranger, a kind stranger, offering to palpitate Dad's heart.

I glimpsed that cigarillo, its ghostly shape – full yet empty – an expression of something enjoyed, yet holding its shape.

This digression happened in a split second in my head, and had physical side-effects: I began to breathe more quickly, as if I were sexually excited. I swung my body round and glanced at Gary, standing in the middle of the living room, looking at me intently.

Hand over receiver: 'Historian. Dad,' I whisper-mimicked. With my other hand I did a wank gesture.

Why I did this, I don't know. It was childish, self-defensive, the quiver of an embarrassed soul.

'Why Dad?' I said in a voice lacking – I prayed – any avenue into my real feelings. But I could hear myself, as though I were down the other end of the receiver: over-eager, thrilled to the last atom of my being.

'Your father was one of the few New Zealanders who ended up as a war crimes investigator.'

'That was a long time ago.'

I kept wanting to supply reasons for why Dad should be left alone; at the same time I wanted those reasons to be struck out, bypassed, blown away by an atomic-force wind.

Please forgive him and make his life worthwhile. Validate whatever experiences he had. Forgive him.

'I'm interested in that particular area of your father's war,' Hazeldean said. 'It's good and meaty.'

'What do you want of me?' I realised the minute I spoke it was scented with Blanche DuBois.

'I'd like you to look over a bio I'm putting together on your father. Tell me if you think it's off track anywhere. If I've got anything wrong.'

'I'll do my best,' I said, freed into a spasm of confidentiality. 'But you have to understand Dad told my sister and me practically nothing. He never said a word.'

There was a small pause – or a thunderous silence if you will. I sensed a lift descending fast, past many floors.

'Look –' Hazeldean's voice was cautious. 'I can see your Dad's not in too good a shape at the moment.'

'So you did see him! He said you'd never turned up.'

'I've been reading up about the physical effects of

the camps. Long term too. Terrible.'

I stayed silent.

'Will you come round?' he said. 'I feel I owe it to you . . .'

'When?'

'I have lectures . . . what about Friday? At five.'

I left a small pause, as if I was still indecisive.

'All right.'

His house was barely visible. The street, anyway, was one of those rare streets in Auckland that isn't a thoroughfare. At its end was a dog-leg, short, a dead-end.

The drive was in poor condition. I debated taking my car down, then decided to walk. It was a lowering winter evening; it would be dark, I knew, when I retraced my steps.

What I could see of the house was a curious affair two storeys in height; the front door at the top level had pieces of four-by-two placed over it to bar your way. The garden, or what passed for a garden, was overgrown. A westerly wind shivered the tops of the trees. The lawns, or what had been lawns, had succumbed to a riot of kikuyu. This sea of green, in abrupt waves and troughs, had been cut very sharply by a motor mower blade, so a car could get right up to the house.

The car was a late-model stationwagon, Japanese. I peered inside: it was chaotic, filthy. The windows were down. I smelt rain.

I searched for a door. On the bottom level of the house, under a deck, there were two sliding doors covered with a polythene curtain that had rotted into a distorted position. There appeared to be some sort of animal hair attached to the damp of the windows, as well as a lot of grease and smear at dog height.

It was just the sort of place to belong to a crazed, aggressive dog. I listened, but could hear nothing.

Just at that moment, on the top level, a light popped on and a toilet flushed.

I crossed the four-by-two laid over a pool of mud, and knocked on the door.

A long silence was followed by lights going on progressively, until the curtain was wrenched aside.

The associate-professor, deeply bearded, gut pressing against a faded Harvard tee-shirt, looked out.

'Ross?' he asked as he slid the door back.

An olfactory storm embraced me – dog, maleness, staleness, like white bread turned into fungi. He was wearing, I noticed, sandals. I glanced down at the socks – tramping club thick. He scratched himself under his armpit, then put his hand out.

'Could I have a glass of water?'

We were up on the second level. My nervousness made me dry mouthed. Hazeldean was safely anti-aphrodisiac as a male. But the room, lino floored, with a few Mexican rugs scattered about in scurfs of dirt, made me uncomfortable. The overhead light was a bulb covered in an aureole of cobwebs. One wall was entirely made up of books. Beside a sagging couch was a series of cardboard boxes. Everywhere you looked was a still-life of stasis, or perhaps, of the life of a thinker. I shuddered. There was a persistent underlying smell, a compound of dog piss, of something going off.

'Sure you wouldn't like a beer?'

'No. Thanks.' I wanted to remain sober. Stone cold sober.

In the kitchenette, I heard the hiss of a beer cap being wrenched off.

'Did you have much trouble finding the place?'

'No. I had a map.' I was being cautious in the face of his doggy matiness. Miss Priss.

I heard him rummaging through cupboards.

Not food, please. Not food.

I walked into the kitchenette. There was no sign of a woman, or rather every sign of a woman departed. A stack of takeaway plastic indicated the scale of the tragedy – there must have been at least twenty. The Kleensak, bleeding to the side, as if within it lay a dismembered body, revealed itself as the source of the smell.

I longed to open a window.

'Sorry, mate, not exactly set up for visitors here. Should have treated you to some grub at the Uni Club.'

I said nothing. He turned to me and grinned.

For one tragic second I looked at him as a sexual being. Probably one of those short-dicked men who plug away without finesse, no technique. The added bonus of cold spittle on your back.

No thanks.

He glanced at me for a moment, startled – did he see what I was thinking?

'Can I use the loo?'

He looked nonplussed. 'Oh. Bog's down the hall. Second door on the right.

In the stench of urine, I inspected a lonely toothbrush, its plastic splayed and worn. A toothpick, its end bloodied, had been flicked into the basin.

I let the flush die away, went out.

Hazeldean was standing looking out the picture window. It was dark now, and the window was a masterpiece of smeared grease. It could have been done by Rothko on diazepam.

He had one of the cardboard boxes open. In his hand was a series of pages, stapled together.

'What does Sugihara mean to you?'

I paused.

'Some kind of noodle dish?'

He burst out with a bark of a laugh, then grew quickly serious.

'Not exactly. What about Hinokuma?'

I frowned. *Hinokuma.* It stirred some faint memory. But I couldn't bring the name into focus. It irritated me, though, because I knew I had heard it.

'I'm . . . not sure. Maybe. Why? Where is it?'

'They're the names of Japanese officers. Sugihara was hanged for a massacre.'

'Oh.'

I didn't know what to say. Hanged and massacre were big words for me – for anyone.

'What's it to do with Dad?

I suddenly wanted to sit down. A strange wave of exhaustion swept through me, as if I had just glimpsed a long road ahead.

'Your father was the investigating officer.'

I nodded, slowly.

'I see,' I said, although I didn't. 'And?'

'And, well –' Hazeldean began scurrying through documents, papers, inside one of the yellowing cardboard boxes – 'I know I've got it in here somewhere.'

I sat in silence.

'It was the last case – almost the very last case the Allies tried –'

The sound of Hazeldean's fingers on the paper was beginning to annoy me enormously. '*And*?' I said, this time with a distinctly peeved note in my voice.

He kept scurrying, not answering me.

'What are you saying?'

'I'm saying –' He stopped for a moment and looked up at me. 'I'm saying it's an interesting case. That's all.'

He put the box aside. One part of me longed to casually pick the box up, look through it myself. Hazeldean followed my gaze, and then he smiled at me.

'Did your father ever talk about it?'

I looked at him. I looked down at the box. He kept his eye trained on me. With his sandalled foot, he nudged the top of the box closed.

'I think I'll have that beer.'

He turned to me, and said, 'I s'pose this is all news to you?'

'What?'

'Well, if, as you say, your father never said anything –'

I tried to think of how I could say it – express the immensely complicated business involved in 'not speaking': how this was both a passive-aggressive act that managed to say an enormous amount, but how this also acted as a kind of primitive taboo mechanism, forbidding you from knowing any details.

The name Hinokuma kept echoing in my head, however. I thought if only I could think more clearly I might remember.

'Did your father ever have any documents?'

'Documents?'

'I'm trying to build up a picture, you see. There seem to be some missing documents.'

'What sort of documents?

'Eye-witness accounts of the massacre.'

'What are you saying?'

'Nothing. At the moment.'

This sounded ominous. I looked at him.

He took a long slug of his beer. I watched his Adam's apple bob. His neck was hairy, right down into his tee-shirt. His man-breasts pressed against the material. He was completely out of condition: had that kind of unconsciousness of body that only a male like him could aspire to.

His eyes, crafty, intelligent, speared into mine.

'So – no documents?'

'I thought this was all about some of kind of biographical entry on Dad?'

He shrugged. 'Among other things.'

He leaned forward, and, from the pile of papers beside him, fished out a document.

He threw it over to me. It felt light as it landed on my knees. But my fingers were trembling when I picked it up.

When I glanced up, ten or fifteen minutes later, he was sitting there in a halo of smoke, the cigarillo on his bottom lip. I suddenly saw him completely differently. He was assessing me astutely, his eyes boring into my frontal lobe. He had reassembled and become the very image, I intuited, of the Interrogator.

I ran up the drive under icy rain. The spittle of drops

landed on my thinning scalp, acidulous. Shivers ran down my spine. Next door there was the yapping of some sort of miniature dog locked indoors. I heard the frantic scratching of claws on a wooden door or floor. I got into the car just as there was a cloudburst. The rain drummed on the roof. As I turned and backed away, I saw the lights being turned off in the associate-professor's house. Perhaps he was going out for the evening.

I watched the windscreen wipers take up their hypnotic trance. Streetlights smeared into darkness, light. Auckland streets seemed abandoned, everyone inside, safely behind lit windows.

The documents were revoltingly explicit accounts of torture. More powerful perhaps for being expressed in routine, mechanical language. All emotion had drained out of them. I had felt shudders pass down my spine just as, utterly fascinated and appalled, I kept on reading.

Hazeldean sat there, glugging and smoking, looking at me, a small smile carved into the corner of his lips.

'This isn't the worst of it, not by a long chalk,' he said. 'But you have to understand by 1943 the Allies usually killed all Japanese prisoners too. It descended into a cauldron of barbarism. On both sides.'

I shivered. There was something compulsive about the material: the moment you allowed yourself to look you were trapped. The material then read you. You became the picture frame through which the horrors looked. Wasn't it human nature to want to look at road accidents? Maybe even the desire to look was stronger than the moral implant that dictated that you should look away.

I was shaken, enticed, appalled. And beguiled. There was no doubt about it. It was like being plunged into a very good horror film. Or murder story, based on something that actually happened. Yet the worst of it was you understood with a sickening consciousness that you were no longer watching a horror film.

It was a snuff movie. And you were participating by the act of watching – reading – imagining.

No wonder Dad didn't want to talk about it.

It was like smearing horror on the world.

That Dad had had some small part in it all, in judging the outcome of these terrible and inhuman acts, seemed strange, inexplicable, yet also entirely explicable in terms of his corrugated strangeness – the corrugations of his soul.

But he was a broken man. He suffered increasing memory problems, had been medicalised heavily for over fifty years. His aches and pains, the result of the beatings he had taken in prison camp, and of starvation, were only now being harvested.

He was a wreck.

One part of me, hurt, cramped, trampled on by him, wanted to feed him to the wolves.

But I also knew I wouldn't.

I couldn't. I needed to protect him.

I woke up with Gary shaking me.

'You were crying out. What were you dreaming about?'

I grabbed hold of his body in the dark and fitted myself into his shape. I took comfort in the feel of his hand and I kissed him.

'Darling, thank God I've got you,' I murmured.

Gary placed a hand very lightly on my back. He squeezed his fingers around the ball of my shoulder. I knew them as well as I knew anything about anyone. We had been living together for fifteen years. We'd gone from being lovers in a dogknot to a close and old couple. We knew each other. That is, we knew each other insofar as couples move further apart the closer they come into close-up. I felt a spasm of love for the parts of him I knew – his strength and dependability and balance: why was I being so hysterical?

'I don't know what to do, Gary, about any of it. Dad's losing the plot. He can't remember to turn the lights off. He keeps going down to the shops, then forgetting what he's there for. He can't even remember who he is some of the time . . .'

Gary grunted, half asleep, 'Chill.'

I felt an unexpected spasm of bitterness.

During the night, later, as we scissored over, I felt the insistence of his hard-on pressed against the small of my back. Sometimes we'd fuck in a sort of dream-sleep.

That night I eased my body away and lay there, separated, looking into the dark.

8

Thought you might be interested in this.

A yellow stick-it note.

I recognised the handwriting this time. My brother. I felt a spasm of antagonism pass from him to me in that brief sentence.

Thought you might be interested (but knowing you, you cold bitch from hell, you won't.)

This time I glanced at the document quickly. It was some kind of biography of my father. But it wouldn't let me put it down. I felt myself sinking to my seat in the kitchen. I would be late. The car was coming to collect me in five minutes. An ideal time, I thought, to scan – pick the bones out of – this strange little potted bio.

There was no explanation of what it was part of, where it came from.

Thanks, Ross.

But as I read it, its content chilled me. I felt my body grow cold. Old. I aged in that instant. My hands were shaking. I was back. There. In that garage in Kiwitea Street. I closed my eyes for a moment. When I opened them again, I picked up the document, turned the pages over, as if expecting that on the back, in invisible ink (lemon juice on paper), there might be some other explanation.

There wasn't.

Keeling, Eric Harald 1917–
Prisoner of war, war crimes investigator

Eric Keeling was a war crimes investigator in Tokyo at the end of World War Two. He himself had suffered physical abuse and torture in a Japanese prison camp. He was instrumental in the controversial conviction and execution of a Japanese officer in one of the very last trials for war crimes in Tokyo. Doubts have subsequently surfaced as to the legitimacy of Keeling's actions.

I stopped here and looked out the kitchen window. The brick wall of the house next door, crenulated and faux-Georgian, pressed itself into the silty sky, then reformatted itself into something extraordinarily one-dimensional. What did this sentence mean: *Doubts have subsequently surfaced?*

Eric Harald Keeling was born at Eltham, near New Plymouth, on 15 December 1917. He was the only child of Arthur Sindley Keeling, a draper, and his wife, Annie Beatrice Harald.

Arthur Keeling allegedly died in the Influenza Epidemic that followed World War One. Yet no death certificate exists. A rumour persisted that he recovered from influenza and took advantage of the confused situation to disappear. Rumours continued to circulate that he was living in a Sydney suburb with a woman considerably older than himself.

Mrs Keeling relocated to Ellerslie, in Auckland. By all accounts, Eric grew up in straitened circumstances, attending Ellerslie School. It was at Dilworth School (for sons of Christians facing financial difficulty) that he first showed promise. He became a school champion in shooting, and eventually became *victor ludorum* and a school prefect. Academic subjects were not to his taste, although he scored surprisingly high marks in matriculation Latin exams. He left school at fifteen.

It was difficult for him to find work. It was 1932, the depth of the Great Depression and he sold stuffed toy animals, which his mother made at home, door-to-door. Then he disappeared for a year. This period of his life remains unaccounted for, to this day.

I was astonished. I knew only the barest rudiments, out of which the writer – who? – why? – had been able to plait a story. The Influenza Epidemic – Dad had talked of his father dying of the 'Spanish flu'. He'd talked of his mother making cloth animals. I had a favourite giraffe with a pearly button for an eye. I remember the hand-stitching to this day – fiendishly tight, close.

It is of interest that when World War Two was declared Keeling was in Sydney. He signed on for the Australian Air Force on 18 March 1940. He quickly rose through the ranks to the position of group captain. He was sent to

Singapore with the 448 Squadron of the RAAF. This was a desperate attempt to forestall the Japanese advance. However, the planes lacked rudimentary equipment like radar. He was captured after the collapse in February 1942.

He was imprisoned initially in Changi, then shipped to Borneo where he was imprisoned in the notorious Sandakan prison camp. He was part of a small group of prisoners who smuggled radio parts into the camp. When the radio was discovered, Keeling, along with five others, was tortured by the Japanese. He witnessed a close comrade being beaten to death. Keeling, however, refused to talk. For this action he was later awarded a DSO.

Ironically his life was probably saved when he, along with other officers, was transferred to the Kuching prison camp in Sarawak. Only four prisoners survived the notorious Sandakan Death Marches in the closing months of the war.

When Keeling returned to New Zealand in December 1945 he weighed five and a half stone.

Keeling was offered the possibility of a job in post-war Japan. It was to work as an investigator with the Second Australian War Crimes Section in Tokyo.

By all accounts, in the first year in the job he learnt the way the investigations worked and his superiors were pleased with him. It was as the Cold War intensified that Keeling came to have a different understanding of his role as war crimes investigator. Keeling concentrated on a case known as the Six Mile Road Incident. A Japanese officer, Lieutenant-Colonel Harimitsu Sugihara, allegedly ordered the massacre of 75 Australian and

Allied prisoners of war in Borneo, on 18 August 1945. Sugihara was hanged for the offence in one of the last war crimes trials of World War Two.

Doubts have subsequently surfaced as to whether Keeling, traumatised by his experiences as a prisoner of war, used his position to gather corroborating evidence that led to the wrong man being indicted for war crimes. There is evidence to suggest another officer, Captain Fukashi Hinokuma of the 124th Infantry Division, was present at the massacre and may have given the order to execute.

In this sense, Sugihara was a sacrifice.

Keeling is also rumoured to have brought back to New Zealand many files which he believed showed unresolved war crimes, or war crimes that the Allies, for reasons of political expediency, no longer had an interest in pursuing.

The documents to this day have never been found.

Keeling resigned from his commission on 8 February 1950.

On returning to New Zealand, Keeling married Olwyn Ruth Browning, whom he had met while working in Tokyo. They had a daughter, Alison June Keeling, in December 1950 and a son, Ross Caryl Keeling, in June 1953.

In 1961, Keeling and his wife separated.

Keeling never really settled down after the war. He worked initially as a deputy manager for Dominion Breweries. His jobs after this were numerous and usually terminated by excessive drinking. He was arrested, in 1974, for drunk driving. No charges were laid.

I laid the pages down and stared into space.

The chauffeur had come to the door and knocked. I told him I wasn't ready.

All these humiliating facts I hadn't known. His father living in Sydney. I'd seen a photo of an Edwardian man once – a portrait photo – but Dad had taken it off me and said it wasn't his father. It was an uncle. I was going to ask more, but Dad threw the photo into the fire: 'You don't want to bother yourself about all that rubbish.'

(At the time I tried to make his abrupt act seem logical – and a lot of my childhood was spent in this state: a good way to develop your speculative faculties, by the way.)

But of course it wasn't this that held me now. It was the business about the Six Mile Road Incident. Was this what I had been reading about? That excerpt like a glimpse into hell? Dad sending someone to his death. 'A sacrifice.' Dad, the war hero.

I cursed Ross at that moment.

I cursed him for sending me the document, knowing it would pull me back.

I cursed him for his abrupt, even contemptuous little butt-kick of a note.

I cursed him for reminding me of who I was.

Whose daughter.

I found myself murmuring, 'Dad. Dad.' And then, 'Why?'

A speculative brain has its uses.

*9

I rang Ross that night. Humiliatingly I had to ring directory services. Then it turned out he wasn't under his own name. He shared a phone with someone else. G. Henderson. I could imagine. I looked at my watch. It would be 9 a.m. there, Saturday morning. This act of imagining, of dissolving time, made me anxious. I had no wish, even theoretically, to go there.

Someone who stays away for a long time like me builds up a barrier, I realise now, which becomes in time almost impossible to climb. It was the site of all my anxieties. My neuroses, if you will. (I was honest enough to understand the weight of the past. I just had no desire to go back there. Investigation takes too much time. I was too busy going forward, putting space in between.)

A stranger answered.

Gary. I winced at his accent, at all it implied.

'It's Alison Burton here.'

There was a small pause of incomprehension, followed by a quick catch-up: 'Oh, His Majesty's royal sister.'

I didn't know what to make of this.

'Sorry, Alison,' the voice went on, impertinently personal, I thought. 'Here he is. Sparkle!'

I felt nauseous. I have·no wish, I said to myself in a bleakly Queen Elizabeth voice, to be introduced into the familiarity of your . . .

But the phone was snatched up –

'June?'

The bastard used my middle name, forbidden for over forty years. But it undid me. I felt tears spear through my lashes, coat my eyes so that, for a horrid second, I could not see clearly.

'My name is Alison and has been –' I struggled to assert myself by speaking tartly – 'for over forty years. Respect that.'

There was the suggestion of a breath expressed.

'Look Alison,' he said to me, 'This is too fucking important to be playing games. You got what I sent?'

I was amazed by his decisiveness. I felt affronted at the initiative being snapped away from me. *This isn't how it used to be*, I wanted to say. But perhaps, in this crisis, I was relieved. He was on the ground, after all. He was there.

'Yes, I did.' I said. 'Can you make sense of it?'

'No.'

'What . . . does Dad say?'

Ross let out another breath, but different this time in its nature. I smelt exhaustion.

'You have to see Dad, Alison. You have to come and see him.'

There it was. In my face. Immediately.

'I —' I tried to think quickly of reasons why I couldn't. 'I've got this big deal coming up. It's —'

'It's always crucial, Alison. It has been for the last, what, twenty years?'

Don't speak to me like that, you little twerp, I said to him silently, pouring all the scorn of my fifty-seven years down the line. Then I felt a kind of tidal tiredness pouring through my veins. I saw an unexpected vision of the tide coming in, creeping over Westmere mud, unstoppable.

I was hit by an exhaustion so complete I could hardly hold the phone. This surprised me so much that I stumbled.

'I will, Ross. Okay. I hear you.' How I despised this phrase. But it has its uses. Buys duplicitous time.

'Well, will you? *When*?' he said, suddenly expert at closing the deal.

I was on weak ground. 'I have to go to Basel next week. I'm contracted for a further month. Heavy penalty if I pull out. I can't —'

'All right,' Ross said, 'but come as quickly as you can. Dad's not in a very good state at the moment.'

'I hear you, Ross,' I said again, admitting defeat.

We didn't say goodbye.

It was an interrupted conversation.

I stumbled through the rest of the day, blank. I can't tell you what I said or did. I know at one point I saw a girl at a bus stop and I thought, she is the same age as Juliette. I found myself watching her in a trance. I was waiting to get home. Once I got in through the door, that blank wall of exhaustion hit me again. It took me all my strength to walk up the stairs, kick off my shoes. I fell on to the bed. I pulled up the duvet. I didn't have time to undress. And the hungry black took me into its arms and smothered me.

I was grateful.

That night I had a peculiar dream. Dad was throwing me into the water. Teaching me to swim. He always wore an old white shirt, like an office shirt, long sleeved. He used it to paint the kitchen, but this was really camouflage. It covered up the marks on his body. It took me a few summers to realise my father never swam in public.

Dad taught Ross and me to swim. We practised in the shallows to get the rudiments. Then, one day, he borrowed a dinghy and rowed us out. We thought it was for a treat. But once he'd got us out about two hundred yards, he told me to jump in.

I glanced at the shore. The houses, people appeared very small. I could even hear voices, and the sound came across the slick of water in a thin and watery echo. Looking down the side of the dinghy, I could see the depth of tide – glassy, welling – the mystery of its depth. Little frail sprats darted past. Vanished.

'Jump in, Alison,' he ordered me. I knew there was no brooking. 'Jump in, Ross.'

Ross, I saw, was clinging to his seat, his legs together, horror on his face.

I dived in elegantly, leaving behind a tiny spume of splash. Dad wiped it off his cheeks.

'Now you, Ross.'

'*Why*?'

It was always Ross's elemental defence: why?

'Because I bloody well tell you to. That's why,' Dad barked.

Ross quivered, shook. But his hands went down to the dinghy seat. He gripped on.

'Come on, scaredycat,' I called out. I was on my back, doing backstroke. I'd keep him company in the brine.

'I want you both to swim to shore,' Dad said. 'I'll follow behind at a safe distance.'

Such silence swallowed us. Ross said nothing. He lowered his face, looked down.

'Come on, lad, be brave. It won't hurt,' I heard Dad say in a confidential tone.

But Ross would have nothing of it.

'Stand up, Ross.'

Ross looked at Dad and said, 'Mum —'

'Mum's not here, is she.'

There was the faint grimace on Dad's unshaven face.

'Mum won't —'

'*I said stand up.*'

Once again, silence. I was enjoying myself, sinking back against the pillow of the waves. Saving my strength for the swim. I knew I'd collect Dad's medal on the shore.

Ross — ungainly, made nervous by his fear — wobbled up. Poor kid had pissed his togs. There it was, a stain all over his crotch. Dad looked down, then away.

'Jump in, lad, get yourself clean.'

'*I won't.*' Ross stood there. '*I won't. I won't. I won't.*'

He'd taken up his song.

Dad, in one movement, scooped him up in his arms and threw his sissy body into the water. Ross screamed, sank, rose up, his mouth wide open.

'Close your mouth, Ross,' I called out, but he sank again, then rose, his stick arms desperately holding on to the side of the boat. He was crying.

'Ross. Ross. Calm down, Ross,' Dad was saying.

I had the impression people were standing still on the shore. Listening.

'*Ross —*'

But all he would do was wail. As if Dad had been trying to drown him.

He wouldn't let go.

And that was how it was. Dad had to pull him on board. I swam to shore. It almost killed me. And behind me, just at the very last point of my hearing, I could hear the plash of Dad's oar, and I could see, as I turned my head with each stroke, Ross sitting there, stiff and still, shivering.

Much later, when I saw Jacques Louis David's pencil sketch of Marie-Antoinette on the tumbrel on her way to being guillotined, I recognised Ross's posture.

He would not give in. His father could humiliate him as much as he wanted. But he would not give in.

Things were different after that.

They always are.

Maiden Daughters
Sing the Blues

1

The second hand was sweeping towards the ashtray hour of 2 a.m. Alison's flight was more than ninety minutes late. But Alison had always been late. She'd mastered the art of disappointment, of not appearing when she should. Presents either did not arrive or arrived consummately late.

Ross was at an age when he should have been inured to disillusion. But he was a sucker for delight; that he was so frequently disappointed only prepared him for the next stage of disillusion.

Physically he was short. He carried before him a gut that expressed a glutton's appetite for comfort. It could easily have been for success, fame, approval — most of which expertly evaded him. He wore a fictitious wedding band on his fourth finger; a silver stud pierced his left ear. He was that dispiriting yet stoic vision: an aging gay man still game for triumph – a fool for love. He could talk up his best features. That he left empathy and insight out of the tally was typical of his almost radical lack of self-belief. He was nervous, reactive, as quick to take offence as to forgive. His life had not amounted to much. At the age of fifty-four, he was still a contract gardener.

Few people looked at him at Mangere airport at 2 a.m. Why would they? Everybody was gazing at the exit door from Customs. Like so much of contemporary life, it promised much but delivered little. The board had been announcing LANDED for over an hour.

Inside Customs, Alison did a most unaccustomed thing. She joined a queue. She checked her Cartier watch by reflex. This was as much to check her status as chronicle the lateness. With her, time was money. As a merchant banker, she was used to being ushered in and out of discreetly opened doors.

She prided herself on travelling light. Even crossing half the globe did not mean that she stooped to a large suitcase. She wasn't planning on staying.

At six foot tall, she was a commanding presence. Her expensively casual clothes could be read at a glance – the taupe linen slacks, the ethnic jewellery which, by rights, should have been in a museum. She wore little make-up. Another striking feature was proudly unplucked eyebrows. Her bob was Sassoon sharp, hair itself left a tasteful salt-and-pepper grey. Excellent cheekbones but in the fluorescent glare her skin looked jaundiced with exhaustion. It was hard, at fifty-seven, to mimic spring chicken, even if she wanted to. She didn't.

Only if you lifted away the wing of her hair might you

discover an ear shape similar to that of the brother who awaited her. Their noses too traced a similarly obstinate shape. Their blood type was identical. But apart from that, they differed in every particular.

Alison tapped her foot. She waited. She consulted, again, her Cartier.

She did not know what awaited her behind the doors. She had not been home for more than twenty years.

All her privileges – everything she had achieved – counted for nothing, dropped away, as she trundled her Louis Vuitton towards the exit.

Ross rustled aside his book (James MacKay's *Betrayal in High Places*) and stood up. But he had carefully chosen his ambush. He stood to the very back of the crowd where Alison would have trouble seeing him.

A Polynesian matron walked past with queenly bearing, eyebrows arched, her suitcase on wheels a deferential two paces behind her.

All around Ross, people were hugging and kissing. Here was the whole unexpectedness of the human race – unlikely couplings, combinations of hims and hers, of noses meeting noses, ear shape matching ear shape, male pattern baldness connected to sparse dome. Lovers, husbands, wives, children, grandparents were staging an impromptu group rally.

Ross stood alone at the back.

And suddenly there she was – his sister.

She stood in the blinding light, a tentative smile on her lips. Her eyes searched the hall. She suspected him of letting her down, not turning up. It was written all over her face. She glanced to the extreme left, the right. A look of panic advanced on her features, calcifying then settling into a prim defensive mask.

Stoically she lowered her head and began to pull her suitcase behind her.

'Alison. Here!'

A strange reaction was happening. Ross felt his face burning. Ross was grinning like a fool. He bustled forward, hesitating for an elderly couple trying to manoeuvre their trolley along.

Alison came closer. For a moment their faces glowed. It was indisputable, unanswerable, beyond logic. Like atoms calling to each other, all the neutrons of their past at that moment oscillated in wild confusion, in radical excitement, in a glow of genetic harmony: but what would they do? Hug like everyone around them? Grab hold of each other? Plant a big fat kiss?

Ross couldn't help himself. He reached out for her. She at the same time raised her arms. They leaned in together. But like so much about their family, the encounter was slightly mistimed. Both simultaneously turned a cheek to be kissed – and, instead of an embrace, each in that instant felt the slight thud of bone.

2

'I'm sorry I'm so late,' Alison was saying. 'You must have been waiting ages.'

Ross was having trouble with his contact lenses: his eyes kept watering. The fact he was crying quietly might also have had something to do with it.

Alison, in one sharp glance, saw this. She felt, though, surprisingly tender.

For Ross, it was in the unexpected reinvention of Alison as her father. Never before had the family likeness been so whittled, so sharpened, so driven to the point. It was as if Alison's whole adult life had had one object: to replace her father.

As for Alison, she was taking in a brother she had not seen for more than twenty years – not since that disastrous time in England when he'd turned up uninvited with a Pakistani boyfriend in tow. They'd made noisy love all night long on her living-room floor. But there was a new element about Ross: a self-possession. He was more masculine than she remembered: more *male*. He seemed focused, within his own skin, acquainted with all his failings and virtues – exactly what he was, no less, no more. Was this a failing?

She thought so, at ten to three in the morning.

The irritated way she looked, waiting for him to find his car, summed up her attitude. She did not suffer fools gladly, and there was the faintest air, as she glanced at her brother, of wondering just what species of incompetent he belonged to.

He took her, unerringly, with pleasure, to the oldest car in the car park. She had made an idiot of herself, she realised, when she had walked her suitcase to the Volvo stationwagon next door. But no, this was Ross's car – dented, dirty, exaggeratedly not cared for. An old-model Toyota, banana yellow, a wreck held together with bumper stickers promoting various forms of pious claptrap – whales, women and Maori.

'Sorry, Gary told me to clean it out. He wanted me to take his –'

His back was presented to her as he leaned in, burrowing out rubbish that had a suspicious smell: the paper bags looked like they might have once held meat pies. There were layers beneath scrumbled layerings of rubbish. But at that late hour, Alison just wanted to be taken to her hotel.

He turned back. 'You sure you don't want to stay with –?'

'No, no,' she said with what she hoped was not too unsubtle an emphasis – her voice, though, slid into a moderato of desperation. 'The hotel is fine till I find my feet. Perhaps next –'

'Gary wants you to come round tomorrow night for dinner.'

She left a small pause.

'Lovely –'

She felt exhausted to the bottom of her being. She desperately needed a shower. Even travelling first class had not shielded her from the damage of the flight – the long, long hours in suspension. Nor those strange moments, mid-flight, when she found herself staring at the innards of her life. She had felt moments of such nakedness, such isolation, she had wept. She wept for the wreckage in her life – her divorce and the abandonment of her daughter. She wept for her mother dying quietly and discreetly, so as not to bother her. She wept for the father she had left behind, and was now coming back to. Then, drying her eyes, she checked her eyeliner in a compact and told herself it was the usual potent effect of alcohol and altitude: you were guaranteed some kind of emotional crisis.

She had settled down to sleep.

The road was both spectacularly empty and overlit. Darkness bled to either side: Alison felt herself pitching, keeling, into a depthless vat of black.

Fucking bastards, Ross muttered.

In a quick, almost phosphorescent flash they passed a church. Its blankness, lack of poetry hit home. Her eyes welled: strobes of flax, then a strange kind of screen, temporary as a police site.

'Digging up the bodies,' Ross said. 'They're pulling it down just to straighten the road. Too much effort for people to turn a corner.' He snorted derisively.

They were driving on the straight. Lights illuminated the great hangars and sheds: it could have been anywhere.

She wasn't really listening. She was tired, too tired: hit, too, by something unexpected – the emotions of coming home. It was hitting her now, when she felt most vulnerable.

Suburbia took over: the great welling silence of an antipodean city by night. She felt it grab her by the throat. Fingers pincered in, claustrophobia almost overcame her. Then she relaxed. She glanced carefully across at Ross's profile.

He was looking straight ahead, frowning. She was struck by how much he now looked like their mother. At the same time there was a poignancy: Ross was aging; there was a faint stoop to his back, his neck was cross-hatched with wrinkles from the drenching sun. They were both getting older.

'So,' she ventured. 'What do we do about that historian sniffing around Dad?'

The car tyres made a slight whining sound on the road. They were on Mangere Bridge. Down there, to the left, a tanker lay at anchor, lights on. It was like a scene from a film – someone else's film.

'It costs about ten grand to hire a killer.'

They both burst out into a euphoria of laughter. Relaxed into the absurdity.

Then: 'But what shall we do?'

It was the surprise of Alison asking him.

'Fucked if I know,' Ross replied, keeping his eyes on the road. 'You should have a clue. After all, you're Big Sis.'

'Is Dad okay in the home?'

'What do you think?'

Silence a moment.

'I'll go and see him tomorrow.'

'Don't hurry.'

She looked at him again. He held the reins here and she didn't like it. 'What d'you mean?'

He turned and looked into her face. 'Alison. You have to prepare yourself. You've been away a long time. The chances of him knowing you are slight.'

He went on driving. Delivered his profile back to her. She hated him at that moment. He seemed to be saying to her that she was guilty: guilty of staying away, guilty of not being there.

But she was. She was.

She also felt dread – for what lay ahead. She resented the way Ross seemed to own the situation, yet she didn't want to become so involved she couldn't back out. There was an interesting opportunity in Berlin coming up in two weeks' time. She wanted to be back for it.

She resisted the neurotic urge she'd had ever since she'd left London, to get her air ticket out, to open it up, to make sure it existed. The ticket out of here.

I will never live here, she thought to herself, willing her muscles to relax as she looked with forensic interest out the window.

The late-night silence of the world crystallised around the car. A string of buildings, all one-storeyed: small factories and businesses. Streets empty, as if during a plague. It unsettled her. Then – and this was what she couldn't cope with – her perception of the place swung around, and she found she was looking out at what seemed a pleasant enough place, though rudimentary it was true.

Everything she saw was a remembrance of some forgotten domestic virtue, like kindness, or civility.

She reprimanded herself: it was the sentimentality of the morning hour.

'Thanks,' she said, as to a stranger, 'for coming and picking me up.'

'It was no trouble,' said Ross, mimicking her tone. They were both trying, she sensed, to locate the older note of kinship, of shared childhood, not trauma.

'I'll pick you up tomorrow, if you like. Take you out to Dad.'

She said nothing. She intended to hire her own car. She would find her own way. She wanted to see her father alone. She would make her own mind up. He would not drive her.

'Ross – don't you have work?' she said as he opened the boot.

He leaned in to take her luggage, but she beat him to it.

As she straightened up he said, half laughing – at her? Himself? She couldn't tell. 'Oh, I can take time off any time.'

She knew it was a reprimand.

'Don't worry.' She turned her back on him. 'I can find my own way, thanks.'

3

Alison woke with a headache. When she pulled the curtains back, the harbour – Aucklandness – rushed towards her. A bleakly brilliant light was shining on the waves. It offended her as much as it placated her.

The clichés were all there – the bridge, North Shore. Even some yachts out on the harbour, as if the working day was a charade – New Zealand was all *en fête*.

She felt homesick and alienated in precise measure.

Her room, in the Hilton, was luxurious in a honeymoon way – all tasteful comfort of a sort that could be conveniently cleansed.

She went to her handbag and got out her Panadol. Foreseeing the inevitability of a migraine, she had slit the cellophane with nail scissors in London: the kiddiproof seal was the thing that often deepened an impending headache into a pneumatic thud.

Two pills later, and a breakfast call from Ross. His New Zealand accent again assaulted her. The phone isolated the vowels and made them flatter or more U shaped. She shuddered, as if he were speaking South African.

'Gary wants you to come round for dinner tonight.'

She read the subtitles: *Not me*.

'That would be lovely.'

'He said round about seven.'

'Okay.'

'You all right, June? You don't sound –'

'I'm fine, thanks. *Caryl*.'

They were playing children's games. Using each other's forbidden and humiliating middle names. Each of them gasped a little, then burst out into a laugh.

It was the freshest moment since their meeting. Uneasily, Alison conceptualised the possibility – rare, novel – they might actually get on.

'You sure you don't want me to –'

'I'm used to finding my own way, Ross.'

'Okay. See you round seven then.'

He'd rung off before she could emolliate.

She wanted to wait for the pills to kick in before she faced her father. So she decided to maunder round the museum: a site of childhood. It would do to lose a few hours. Besides, the day was fresh, newly minted. A sharp wind came off the harbour. It bit into her face as she walked past Security – handsome Samoans tricked out in stylish suits – at the hotel entrance. They indicated to her the late-model BMW that had been delivered to the door. Metallic blue. Gleaming.

This was better. This was more like being in her own skin.

She turned the key and drove out into Auckland traffic.

This was where it started going wrong.

She had assumed, after London, Auckland would be very small beer, and she had assumed some familiarity. She had also studied the map the hotel supplied. But like all hotel maps, it was a piece of sophistry: a new city presented in a hologram, like a sauce artfully reduced by a duplicitous chef. Smaller side streets were left off as needless complications. And on-ramps to motorways weren't indicated: the motorway in Auckland simply was, as undeniable as night or day, or sea or land.

Besides, the city itself betrayed her. Or time did. Queen Street, which had been enormous and plush in her childhood, with department stores and banks, was now a shabby little alley in a gully. It could have been some small city in Asia, judging by the foot traffic.

Someone behind her parped their horn as if to awaken her.

She couldn't wind her window down and say: *I'm new here. I'm back after twenty-two years. I'm going to see my father. I don't know if he'll even recognise me. Give me a break.*

She couldn't say these things, because she didn't believe in excuses. Not even for herself.

She pulled over into a bus stop, studied the map in earnest. She could just work her way to the top of Queen Street, turn left into Karangahape, then slope over Grafton Bridge to the museum, and safety.

Outside the museum there were buses parked. Bevies of Asian people were getting off in loose formation. Alison walked up the steps, aerated by a sense of victory. She had found her way there and, even better, everything to do with getting to the museum, once she was on Grafton Bridge, had delivered her back to the Auckland of her childhood.

She was sideswiped by the power of reconnection. It was only when she saw Auckland as it had been that she realised, with piercing intensity, how much she missed it.

The beauty of the bridge, so long and narrow ('the biggest concrete single-span construction in the Southern Hemisphere' echoed in her brain); the delicate modesty of the khaki stone gates: the naked man, with his leg outstretched in an act of immodesty so at odds with everything you assumed about New Zealand – he was surely some sportsman? That must be the explanation.

As she'd driven down into the familiar beauty of the Domain, Alison had wanted to cry. The duck pond was still there. A memory stirred in her of Ross falling into the water while teetering on rocks to feed the ducks. Then, duplicitously, memory delivered a close-up. Her own hand nudging him over in the guise of steadying him. The anarchy of childhood flooded back, the barbaric search for the primacy of love. Her mother turning her face away, not looking. The carefully cut sandwiches, tomatoes bleeding, or really weeping, into white bread.

It was too much.

She accelerated past.

The steps of the museum delivered to her the altar-view of Auckland: the delicate beauty of its harbour, a soft thrush-egg blue, glinting in an autumnal sun. Behind it the deeply satisfying symmetry of Rangitoto – its Fuji calmness a seeming commentary on the restless disharmony, the competitive urge and squalor of the city facing it. A lawn spread away like a picnic blanket, pinned down by the elegant pohutukawa.

Here, ahead of her, was her past.

She pushed her way through the vast revolving door. A familiar hum came back to meet her: children's voices echoing in stony interstices; Maori guards at the door; the strange formality of the War Memorial Museum – mausoleum to the dead (and dying, she suddenly thought – the living dead) and, now, a site for tourism.

She paid. Of course she paid, it was user-pays, a slight shock it was true, a traducing of childhood. But Alison had no use for childhood, for looking back. So she told herself, even as her eyes searched for the oil painting of Sir Ed, Himalayas behind him. The Queen had already gone, in advance of the republic.

Sir Edmund was not there.

Some theoretically 'beautiful' or interesting piece of glasswork, kitsch as buggery, was in its place. Alison, who had no aptitude for art, but studied it seriously as a scientist studies phenomena, hesitated for a moment and paid duty by running her eyes over the mess of shininess. She supposed the fern and Maori motif meant something nationalistic: it didn't supply the key she needed.

And at exactly the same time she had a sense of being lost, she had a sense of knowing exactly where she was: the result of so many wet Sundays when her mother had given her two shillings while Ross went off on his car trips with Dad. Spending time with a male role model. Lodged in her brain for ever were the sites: the little Maori village with a pa made out of match sticks; the huge old stuffed elephant with its tiny glass eye staring down at you in impotent fury, its dust-flecked eyelashes so sadly human; and the longer halls, filled with old aircraft, uniforms and medals, which she always sped through, finding herself in the discreetly darkened uncertainty of the foreshortened colonial street. There she had spent hours trying to work out how she could reach around the plexi-glass to grab hold of one of those colonial cups and saucers. What she would have done with it, she now didn't know. Obscurely she felt she would have delivered it back to her mother, in fealty, or payback for all the wounds her mother suffered in silence.

All this was lodged in her backbrain.

But this museum was reformatted for the new century. The word 'War' had been dropped from the title for a start. The little ships, in satisfactory dissection, as if one could look within and see order and symmetry, had gone. A strange parade of pestilential animals introduced by the European replaced them.

Alison sensed racial reprimand.

The odour of Sunday school repelled her.

'Excuse me,' she asked someone in uniform: a pleasantly idle Maori man of indeterminate age. 'I'm trying to find the rooms to do with . . .' she hesitated here. The word seemed naked, obscene. 'War,' she breathed out, incapable of disguising its harsh simplicity.

'Up another floor,' he said to her with a smile that seemed unearned. 'You can't miss it.'

She walked through the exhibition once, getting her bearings.

Then she concentrated on the Pacific War. A tidy little thatched cottage of palm trees, all set in kiwi-dell darkness. The dimness made it illicit, the doings of war, the past. On a literal level Alison knew this was to do with light levels and conservation: but the crowded exhibit made it strangely claustrophobic. Or was it, Alison reasoned, the nature of war itself: you were delving in the devil's work, no matter how you saw it. It was noble, or ignoble, depending on which side you stood. But at its basis was butchery and killing. Death was at its core.

She read the captions numbly. She was searching, she knew inchoately, for some rationale to do with her father. Some explanation for what had animated him. Or even on a more basic level, of what lay behind his 'sacrifice'. Sacrifice was a big word in this place. Yet it had no contemporary meaning. People despised sacrifice. She despised sacrifice. Sacrifice was for losers. She thought of her mother's tomato sandwiches squashed and bleeding, a rug set out on the Domain. The grass was invariably damp and a soft chill always permeated the wool. This was the reward for sacrifice, as far as her mother was concerned.

And as for Dad. *Look at him.* Some part of her felt raw – unrewarded – spectacularly bitter. *What was his reward exactly?*

But then what had he done?

Fought, been imprisoned, tortured.

Not talked. The aura of 'not talking' had held her childhood in a brace as powerful as cement.

It was the box that talked. The box in the garage at Kiwitea Street. She hovered before this knowledge, deleting it.

She had had no use for the past. She had actively worked on erasing its painful side-effects all her adult life. She had needed to jettison, to move forward.

It was hard, now, to move in a reverse direction. All her instincts went against it.

But there the box was, a tea chest, artfully disguised by an old tarpaulin thrown over the top of it. Ross and she were caught, like in a camera flash, hesitating before it. She saw Ross's face, delicate, uncertain, keen.

Then a kind of ellipsis fell on memory, as abrupt as a guillotine.

She consciously focused on the exhibition.

She noted that in the big blow-ups of fascist war leaders, Emperor Hirohito had been tactfully replaced by Tojo: not good for tourism, she sensed, to insult a demi-deity.

She felt drawn to every exhibit but none of them precisely delivered to her what she wanted. Then she saw them: some earphones.

She put them on, and in this sealed, defenceless state – she could hear nothing of the contemporary museum – she heard the first, halting tones of an old New Zealand male. Recognition became a bodily fact. She felt her epidermis shrink, tighten like Gladwrap round her skull. Inward she went, disappearing like a spot of light on a computer shutting down. Only the old bloke's voice existed. And she was surprised to find her face damp. She was betrayed. She was crying quietly.

It was the modesty of the man's voice. He was talking about the most devastating pain and fright a human was capable of sustaining while staying alive. But with a asthmatic draw-in of breath, the old codger would only allow such modest phrases as, 'Yes, well, it got a bit rough round there' (his mates killed) and, for what sounded like a life ruined by post-traumatic stress syndrome, 'I don't know. I couldn't get it out of my head, you see. Silly what you think of. What you can't stop thinking about.' Long pause. 'But that's life, isn't it?'

She wrenched the earphones off. She was freely weeping. She had no tissue, naturally. She wiped her eyes against her elbow. She stood up. A young couple, a Japanese youth and his girlfriend, cut through the exhibition. They were lost. They had no interest in what they were passing through. The past – its sins, weight, horrors – meant nothing to them, had no grab. Casually dressed, oblivious, hungry to their own appetites, they disappeared.

Alison watched them go. She couldn't help but feel a spurt of antagonism. Their blitheness, their deliverance into a future that seemed to hold no guilt, perhaps not even memory, scorched her.

Then she felt ashamed of herself. Her rancour tasted of bile.

What did she mean?

Japan was one of the pivots of the contemporary world economy.

Yet as she left the museum she couldn't help noticing a Japanese man and woman of an older age laughing as they posed by the Cenotaph. Someone else was photographing them, and a congery of Japanese tourists, eagerly chatting and laughing, waited to get into the tourist coach.

Everybody was on holiday. Nobody had the gravitas of visiting a tomb or site of sacrifice. Except, she thought, with bleak resignation – touched with novelty – herself.

4

During the day Ross wondered about his sister. He had
rung the Arlington rest home and got through to Mrs
Stobbs, the matron.

'My sister'll be calling in today to see Dad.'

Why he was doing this, he didn't know. It amounted to
complicity. He wanted to make sure his father, or more to
the point the home was presented in the best of all possible
lights. He wanted to ensure that Alison comprehended the
energy he had expended on finding a reasonable place for
their father.

'She's here, is she?'

Mrs Stobbs couldn't keep a small frill of sarcasm out of
her voice. It was something they had in common.

'She'll pop in some time in the late morning, I guess.
Or early afternoon. She got in after midnight.'

He heard Mrs Stobbs answer some enquiry, her hand

over the receiver. Her tone was terse, direct.

'I'm sorry,' her voice came back on, swelling up like a bud fed on charm. 'I look forward to meeting . . .'

'Alison, her name is.'

'Alison.'

Ross chortled to himself as he pressed the off button on his cellphone. He could see that Alison was equal in steeliness to Mrs Stobbs. May the best wrestler win, he thought.

I am busy, Alison thought, as she backed the BMW into the car park. I have priorities, I do not have time to waste.

As she gathered herself together and walked up the wheelchair ramp to the main doors, she promised herself a ten-kilometre run once the ordeal was over. Alison liked to run. It cleared her head. She did her best thinking while she tested the limits of her body.

The smell immediately hit her. It must have been just after lunch. She knew she had mistimed it. Note to self: never come at lunchtime. The smell of cooked food – cabbage? – some sort of broiled meat underlaid by a sweetness, even a fugue of raspberry jam – merged with an indeterminate fug of fart, of released and liquid bowels, met the overheating and was converted into an insidious miasma.

With panic Alison heard the doors sliding shut behind her.

'Excuse me,' she said with a little too much crispness.

She heard her own English intonation and sensed heads turning to glance at her. A woman at a desk, and then the faces of the old people, sitting marooned in chairs. Even a cat, a fat tabby lying on its side, raised its head lethargically, looked at her, then, after a brush of interest, laid its head down slowly and closed its eyes.

'Excuse me, I'm Alison Burton.' Why did she say this? It meant nothing. 'I'm Eric Keeling's daughter.'

Her English accent didn't play here. What had once been the imprimatur of class now seemed to award only demerit points. Nobody spoke posh any more. The Queen was a tribe of one.

And here she was, in an old people's home.

A fleshly woman resisting early middle age popped out a door, glanced at Alison keenly, spoke to someone offstage, then came towards her at a fast tack. Her lipstick was fresh. What was surprising, given the environment, she wore markedly high heels.

'You're Alison, Eric's daughter, aren't you?' she said, smiling with a suspect joy. 'He's been looking forward to your coming. I know we all have.'

Alison nodded, smiled. She was aware of the other woman, Mrs Stobbs, quickly looking her over from top to tail. The flat shoes, the trousers, the enormous canary-yellow diamond not on her ring finger.

Alison cut to the chase. 'He's not in too good a state, I understand.'

Mrs Stobbs looked both ways for a moment.

'Come this way for a moment, dear,' she said as she ushered the returning daughter into her office. 'I think it's timely for us to have a nice wee chat.'

Alison read various things in Mrs Stobbs' face as she talked. She was running a business, obviously: she wanted to present as efficient, on the ball. But 'being human', 'empathetic' was also part of the job description. Her opening sally — 'You've had experience of Alzheimer's?'

– was a brilliant example of attack.

Alison found her eyes watering, unaccountably.

'What? Are you saying Dad has Alzheimer's?'

Mrs Stobbs looked up from a folder she had open on her lap.

'If I'd known precisely when you were coming I could have booked you in to see Dr Bateman. You know there's quite a margin of error sometimes with old people. Parkinson's, just geriatric deterioration . . . Tests so far have been inconclusive.'

Alison sensed reprimand.

'He presents well on good days, has reasonable locomotion skills. Of course it's best not to upset him too much by forcing him to remember. It's only the relatively recent past he can't recall. Short-term memory loss. Spotting. I imagine Ross has brought you up to date with his wandering off, getting lost?'

Alison nodded. He hadn't.

'Of course we encourage visits,' Mrs Stobbs leaned forward confidingly, fixing Alison uncomfortably in the eye. 'You have to understand that . . . after some time . . . many family members find –' she whispered this discreetly – 'the burden *too much*. But that's why we're here, Alison. To help *you*. Some people here are visited by their family members only on the statutories. But then we have one old dear who is visited every single day by her husband. The last time she recognised him was eight years ago. But he comes *every day* . . . takes her out for an ice cream, then returns her. Now, I know it's not a Hallmark card, but I call that *love*.'

A side door crashed open and someone barged in backwards carrying a tray on which Alison saw some jelly, custard and a half-masticated pudding – spat back into the bowl, it looked like. Milk was also spilt all over the tray.

'Oh. *Pardon.*'

The girl was in a smock. A candidate, Alison saw, for Weight Watchers. And flustered.

Mrs Stobbs glanced at her meaningfully.

'Yes, Bobbie?'

'I'm ever so sorry,' Bobbie said, her eyes going momentarily to Alison. 'But it's Room 17. He won't . . .' She lowered her voice just as she averted her flushed face.

Alison wondered how irregularly Bobbie washed her hair. It was a greasy mat attached to her skull. But her face, flushed with crisis, had the earnest simplicity of the well intentioned. Maybe homes like this couldn't be run without people, simple, like her?

Mrs Stobbs hurriedly stood up. 'I'll see to it. Bobbie, if you could take Alison down to see her father –' Was Alison imagining the word 'father' had the faintest admonition added to it?

Bobbie looked mystified.

'Room 14.'

Mrs Stobbs mimicked a sincere smile.

'These little emergencies are sent to challenge us.'

'We're all very fond of your poor old Dad,' said Bobbie with too much familiarity as they walked along a corridor. Alison felt herself more and more tense – less and less prepared.

'Some of them are nasty, you know. But not him. Not really. He's a real character, he is. Always going on about Shanghai.'

Alison just looked at her. She could hardly understand a word the girl was saying.

Then, as they got closer: 'So long as he's got the footie on the teev, he's a-okay.'

I had been away too long. I saw this instantly as a stranger, my Dad, turned to glance up at me from his easy chair. He had shrunk, all of him – chest fallen, jaws inward. His skull, naked of hair, had become adze-shaped. He was all Adam's apple and collar bone, with his hands, seemingly independent, vast as some kind of tropical crab. His legs pitifully thin. Even his skin seemed grey.

He was lost in a football match on television.

'Dad?' I found my lips betraying me.

Bobbie had already warned me not to stress him by pressuring him into memory. But I was reeling. I was frightened. I was coming to terms with the harsh clarity of that dreadful sentence: *I have been away too long.*

He looked behind me . . . his eyes sliding off me as they went to the clearly more familiar sight of Bobbie. His face lit up.

'Hello lass,' he said in a voice recalled: all boisterous charm, a thunderclap of good humour and warmth.

He looked at me courteously, with that curious body language I'd observed in him when I was younger and he was faced with a good-looking woman: he became alert, pert, one half of a vaudeville act awaiting his feed line. In time we would call this sexism. I think they used to call it gaiety.

He half saluted, struggling to stand up.

'No! No!' I advanced into his room: single bed, neatly made, and, more heartbreaking, a large photo of Elsie and behind that, a snap of myself and Ross. No photo of my mother.

'Please don't stand. Not for me.'

A metal potty under the bed.

He sank back, released from the effort.

'Eric likes going walkabout, doesn't he?'

Bobbie was talking to him like a derelict child. Dad's face lit up. He grinned pathetically. His toothless mouth. Repulsive.

'Doesn't he have teeth?'

I crushed this incriminating sentence. I didn't know how to act. I didn't know what my part was. His lack of memory, of connection, rendered me redundant. But my eyes had not finished their work: hungrily they drank in everything of him. Liverish spots on the top of his skull, the few stray hairs as wan as daddy-long-legs waving in the breeze. The large rivulets of veins on his wrists. The toe out of his slipper, a long yellow shield of toenail poking out.

I came towards him, knelt down and touched his hands. I couldn't help myself.

He shrank back, startled.

'It's me, Dad,' I murmured. 'Alison.'

He looked at me intently.

'Eric, this is your daughter, Alison. She's popped in to visit you.'

A quick look of suspicion passed over Dad's face. He glanced once, speedily, up at Bobbie. Then he looked at me intently. He said nothing. I plaited my fingers through his, but he left his fingers inert. He looked down at our hands, and I had the horrible sense he might withdraw his fingers. As it was, he left them with a childish lethargy. But his eyes moved again, questioningly, to Bobbie.

'It's all right, Eric,' she was saying soothingly. 'Everything's all right.'

I had a moment's inspiration.

My left hand felt out for the photograph. He watched me take it, his pupils enlarged. Once again there was a child's sense of enormity backed by a waiting, nervous passivity: as though I were about to smack him.

'Everything's okay, Eric . . .'

Bobbie went and turned the television up. The urgent tug of a football commentary surged into the room.

I held the snap of Dad, Ross and me. We were in the back yard, Kiwitea Street. Dad with the hose, Ross wet through, laughing. I'm standing, half turned, gazing into the camera. It was Mum who took the photo. As always she was the missing one.

My eyeline, now I looked at it, went straight towards the garage.

I held out the photo as some certificate of authenticity. I tapped myself, that shrunken little girl with her pert, unimpressed face.

'Dad,' I said. 'That's me. That's who –' and here I did a comic-book gesture to self – 'I am.'

Dad looked down at the photo for a long second, seemed about to speak. He cleared his throat, a big emphysemic rumble.

'That's me,' I said again, in a softer voice. I was kneeling. 'Me, Dad.'

'Photo,' he said. He spoke as if this act of identification in itself required a prize. Bobbie leaned forward expertly and handed him a pair of spectacles. They were from the 1980s, comically large, coloured a lurid green. I instantly thought of Mrs Thomson – Elsie. It was her favourite colour. Maybe they were even her glasses? Sellotape was yellowing on one of the hinges.

He placed his glasses on with the self-consciousness of a sportsman contaminated by the sissy business of words.

The glass magnified his pupils: I gazed into them — their unknowing hazelness, clouded, occluded — a Learish storm, a pencil point of dark.

He looked down at the photo for a long moment. Then a finger prodded the surface. The mismatch in space meant the photo buckled.

'That's the Captain,' he said to me, pride in his voice. 'She's a big noter over in London, she is. Could buy and sell the lot of you round here. Like this!'

And with this, he did an 'up-you.'

I went back to the hotel and pulled the curtains. My migraine had come back. I would not run that afternoon. I fell into a heavy, cumbersome sleep. I called it jetlag.

5

Alison's BMW nosed into the drive.

'She's here,' Gary murmured and I ran towards the hors d'oeuvres, which I'd spent a lurid hour preparing. I touched the parsley again, then nervously ground black pepper over them.

'Do you think there's enough?'

'Chill,' Gary said. He was standing there, with his washing. He was cracking towels stiff from the line. Folding neatly pairs of socks and underpants. It was his anti-formality device. I moved down the hall.

She looked smaller, I thought. Perhaps it was the strange perspective of a Victorian cottage hall. But she seemed slightly more tentative as each of us undertook the silent scrutiny of self as to how we would, henceforth, greet each other.

Solved, quickly, by a peckish, nervous kiss. I enlarged it

into an attempt at a hug, but her deceptively muscly body pushed past me.

This was an embrace too far.

'Pretty,' she offered by way of compliment as she advanced down the hall. I noted her taking in our separate bedrooms, Gary's bed neatly done, mine tumultuously undone, duvet raked back, socks all over the carpet like I was a hormonally imbalanced teenager. 'Central, too.'

'Gary, Alison.'

Gary came towards her, smiling. I saw him through her eyes. Overweight but carrying it well, with Polynesian aplomb. Unselfconscious – he was wearing old faded shorts that looked like they belonged on the beach, and Jandals. But his setting – the room, its classic modern furniture – all spoke of casual money. I saw her see this, as her eyes, nervously, came back to rest against mine.

Gary went to the bench and opened a Hawke's Bay wine.

Alison, dressed in an elegant minimalism of black, and low shoes of suspicious expensiveness, walked out on to the deck which led into the garden. The garden was all my work. It was, perhaps, overwrought with beauty: box hedges cut into a formal square, disguising the fact that a Freeman's Bay garden is always thimble sized. I had backed the hedge with scarlet hibiscus so we had a suspect seclusion.

'Oh. Lovely spot,' she said in real-estate speak. Her eyes would not look at mine. I gazed at her. Either she had been crying or the jetlag had made the skin round her eyes puffy. Her dramatic whiteness also made her look ill. That vein in her forehead, a ziggurat of nervous energy, pulsed.

'How did it go?'

'I have a migraine,' she said, shaking her head to the proffered hors d'oeuvres. 'I'm afraid I can only have – do you have water?'

Great, I thought, a party. Let's all relax.

Gary padded back in, calling over his shoulder. 'Migraine? Have you tried Nurofen? I can recommend it.'

She and he engaged in bonding conversation. I looked at her fingers, so thin, nervously shredding a paper napkin. She did this with remorseless, contained energy – almost fury. Catching me looking at it, she moved her hand away dramatically, then placed her ring hand over the nervous fingers.

She smiled at me coolly.

'I saw Dad this afternoon.'

I waited.

Gary brought her a glass of water, went back to folding washing.

'I want to find out if there's a better place for him.'

I felt an immediate and insensate rage, but disguised this by reaching for the hors d'oeuvres. I stuffed one, then two into my mouth. I suddenly felt very hungry. I might even get drunk tonight, I thought. Good occasion too. I feel like a fight.

'You're welcome to,' I said curtly, once I had room in my mouth to articulate. She looked at me vividly, tensely, her hand going back to the remains of the napkins.

'Look,' she said, 'have you considered that he might be better off in a smaller facility?'

I got up quickly and went up the hall. I didn't know what I was looking for. I needed to get away.

I heard Gary being polite. 'Sure I can't get you anything to nibble?'

'No. I can't really risk eating anything when I'm in this state.'

Oh joy, I thought.

The phone rang. I went to answer it as if it were deliverance.

For a moment there was a scramble of noise. Wrong number? In normal circumstances I'd have put the phone down, but the alternative – engagement with bitch sister – meant I hung on there.

A voice, male, came on.

'Sorry, mate.'

Hazeldean. Behind him a cross-hatching of other voices – it sounded like a woman? And perhaps a teenager groaning and talking back.

'Have you got a mo?' That suspect query.

'Yes.' Several hours actually.

'We're having a little . . .'

We?

'. . . shindig this coming Saturday. Spur of the moment. Wondered if you might like –'

'My sister's in town.'

This had a force I hadn't intended. It hinted at seclusion, even isolation in a necessary medical sense.

'Great! Great!' He held his hand over the phone so his words blurred. When he took it away I heard a teenage voice, hoarse with hormones, saying emphatically, 'But that just creeps me out.'

'*I don't care!*' a woman's voice said. '*All I want –*'

'Look,' Hazeldean said into my ear, 'I'd love it if you both could come. It's this Saturday, early evening, barbecue.

Twenty-six Wainui Ave, Point Chev. Okay?'

I wrote the address down, noting it was different from where I'd visited him.

It was several months since I'd seen him and I was suspicious about why he wanted to socialise. The fact was I still felt bruised by the way he seemed to know so much more about my father than I did. I didn't trust him – or rather I didn't trust myself, dealing with the situation. The cold-heartedness of history put me off. Chilled me. I lived with the reality of Dad, his moods, his neediness. It was I who'd had to clean out his place – wash the walls all around the floor of his old-man's stinking piss pot.

'Dad's in a home now,' I said, I wasn't sure why.

'Oh. Bummer. Is that so? Sorry, mate. Old age is a bastard.'

I left him with the clichés.

'Okay. See you. Bye.'

I went back to my sister with a bland face. I wouldn't ask her. Or I might. She was on parole.

A cat appeared. It was a long-haired thing, brindled a curious greyish pink colour. Its eyes, I noted, were a malignant yellow. Gary called to it overfondly. The cat glanced at him once, with calculation, then looked away.

'That's Tallulah,' Ross said, as though introducing a family member. He went towards it, picked it up. The cat, in his arms, turned to look down at me while Ross, the fool, cuddled it like a baby and kissed the top of its head.

This was all for my benefit, I knew.

'How's Juliette by the way?' he asked. As if this were a casual dart.

I tensed, even though my mind told my body to relax.

I saw Gary glance at me before he stood up to remove the hors d'oeuvres plates – mine untouched, Ross's like the site of a bloody skirmish. Gary helped himself to the last as his Jandals thwacked away.

'I haven't heard you mention her for quite some time.'

Ross was being an arch bitch. The cat tensed, pushed her back legs against his chest and leapt down on to the deck. She landed with a thud, stood there a moment. Assessing.

'We call her Tallulah after the actress,' Gary called from the kitchen. 'I think she's got the temperament.'

I liked Gary. He had a kindness, empathy.

'Juliette's all right,' I doorstopped. 'That is, she'll get in touch when she wants something.'

The cat was licking her coat. I thought: fleas, skin complaints. As if hearing my subliminal thought, she stopped, glanced at me. Right in my eyes. Her tail up in a flourish, she began to walk straight towards me. I felt a moment of panic. She hesitated for a moment then leapt, with astonishing deftness, on to my knees.

'. . . Oh!'

Ross came towards me, lifted the cat off.

'Alison hates cats.'

This was for Gary's benefit as he came back in. He was wearing a large apron which had the effect of making him ridiculous – Dadish. He laughed, I wasn't sure why. He was carrying a platter of meat. There was enough there for ten. In London, anyway.

I brushed the cat's hairs off my trousers. Then picked them off, one by one.

The cat squirmed against the forced regime of Ross's affection and, to my immense satisfaction, reached out with astonishing efficiency and traced a scarlet line against his arm.

Blood shone in the evening light.

Ross dropped the cat hard on the deck.

'Darling!' There was a reprimand in Gary's voice. Then the meat – pork? – hit the heated element and sizzle rose up. Ross blundered indoors, but as he passed I caught a glimpse of his face: a satisfactorily wounded look of betrayal.

Good, I thought. We understand each other.

When I got back to the hotel there was a light flashing on my phone. My migraine by then was coasting: I felt I was running ahead of it, outdistancing it, but I knew if anything untoward happened I'd be back there. I decided not to check the phone out till morning – then a half of me instantly asked if it might be Juliette. This made me hesitate. Then I wondered if it was Ross, ringing up to apologise. Neither option enticed me. Self-deliverance dictated I have a long hot shower, then crawl into bed, in the dark.

Stillness was what I needed.

The evening anyway had ended in tears. Metaphorically speaking, of course. Ross took it all ridiculously personally, every remark I made interpreted as a criticism. He'd burst out, at one point – four glasses of red wine in, à propos of nothing – 'Well, *you* try going round all the old folks' homes and looking at them. *You* try talking to social services and getting pushed on, from one person to another, all of them giving you assurances and every one of them doing fuck-all. It took me two *fucking* months of solid work – phone calls, meetings, appointments – as well as looking after

Dad – sleeping in his fucking nightmare unit, like being stuck in a dog kennel – to even get him *in* to Arlington House: so – *don't – tell – me – you – could – do – something – better.*'

We were sitting in darkness, outside. I watched the insects attack the lights, be repelled. I shivered. Gary cleared his throat nervously and poured a glass of water, first for himself, then, by extension, for Ross. Ross sat there and glared, not so much at me – he wouldn't meet my eye – but at the table. Then he stood up.

'I'm going to bed,' he said, and left.

Like a teenager he slammed his bedroom door.

After a tentative moment, Gary's eyes found mine and his face relaxed into an apologetic smile. He shrugged and said in a voice low enough for Ross not to hear, 'He's stressed out by it all. It hasn't been easy.'

I drew in a breath to speak, then decided it was better to wait. I had been away too long.

6

I had it all wrong. I saw that the moment we drove to the address Hazeldean had given me. The street was lined with cars. We had to park on the main road, walk back. The house was a '90s monstrosity, all faux plaster, probably rotting wood within. But on this late and becalmed evening, with the hint of chill in the air, it looked like a real-estate prospectus: all lit up, people crowding the outdoor patio area – indoor/outdoor flow incarnate.

A barrage of smart-arsed kids faced Gary and me at the door. Little tykes in war paint, running amok. The door was wide open; down below, a swarm of strangers. We walked in, placed our token bottle on a table on which there was a savaged ham, some European-style white bread and a selection of gourmet snacks bought from the supermarket.

Gary's eyes met my own. Our host was nowhere to be seen, so we both wore the superficial smiles that indicated 'friendly strangers'.

Down in the kitchen, on another level, a mini-party was happening. A woman in her early forties, athletic, harassed, was attempting to open a bottle of wine while someone was assaulting her with anecdote. Another woman, the antithesis of Alison, was putting some savouries into an oven. A nestle of people was talking drunkenly nearby. The party had settled into a mid-symphony overdrive.

'Ross!'

Hazeldean navigated his paunch across the floor. He was holding a glass of red wine, half empty, and talking over his shoulder to a circle of aging faces: I recognised some hitherto famous media people, journalists from the Springbok era, television producers who had, for unknown reasons, dimmed career prospects.

'Glad you came, mate.'

He shook my hand, his eyes turning with a silent query to take in Gary.

A little tribe of children whooped their way in between us. One of them, a pale-haired child, went up to an athletic-looking woman who had come towards Hazeldean. He had, instinctively, opened one arm into an embrace and placed it loosely on the woman's waist. The woman, who had a pleasantly lined face – I could have gone to school with her – smiled at me.

'Mum Mum, come and look at our face-painting!'

'In a moment,' the woman said, smiling apologetically but being jerked round physically by the child.

'Ross, I'd like you to meet my partner, Dotty,' he said. 'This is Ross, son of . . . you know –' and her face took on a cast of sudden interest. But the oedipal struggle would not give up.

'Mum!' The child bunted his head hard into her stomach. Her face spasmed in pain.

'Sorry,' she smiled as she was frogmarched away.

'I thought you lived down in that other house,' I said, I wasn't sure why.

'Fuck no,' he said, raising his eyebrows. 'Just minding the house for a mate whose marriage was in meltdown. Doing him a favour.'

I had it all wrong, I saw.

The party had developed into a steady drunken hum. Gary had separated himself from me and was talking animatedly to new-found friends, his back against the wall. I was on my own for a moment. Gaily I went into the kitchen in search of further alcohol. Parties are always like this – at a certain moment people stop drinking, but I want to go on. I fossicked among the empty bottles.

A woman was pouring tea down the sink and washing plates, stacking them. She was one of those women who looks ill at ease in a party situation. Her actions had the intensity of a kabuki actor. She eyed me suspiciously, then, sensing I offered no sexual vibe, relaxed. She shunted a boxed wine towards me – the dregs.

'Oh hello hangover,' I said, grinning as I turned the spigot.

She smiled wanly.

'Hi, my name's Anne. Anne Donaldson.'

We introduced ourselves, safe in the knowledge it didn't mean a thing.

I wondered for a moment what Alison might be doing. It was spiteful of me not to have asked her to come to the party. But I was fucked if I was going to have her big sister act in my downtime. I repressed the impulse that whispered to me I was being needlessly self-destructive just when we needed to share information. She had the rare family ability to inflict maximum damage on points of greatest weakness. She knew how hard it was for me to look after Dad. But in one phrase, 'I think we should look at better facilities', she had unhooked all my vulnerabilities.

The rest of the dinner that night had been a disaster. She nursed the remains of her migraine. I nursed my offended sensibilities. Gary talked and ate his way through the cannibal buffet as if he noticed nothing. He and she talked about business prospects in an open economy. Tallulah and I made peace with each other. I fed her scraps off my plate. At one point I'd had enough and went and had a lie-down in my room. But I got up to say goodbye when I heard Alison and Gary in the corridor.

Alison and I said a tense goodnight to each other. She hesitated on the doorstep, clearly anxious to make further plans. But I wanted to punish her. She had hurt me. It's like that in families, slash for slash, wound for wound: an answering silence is the best salve.

But standing there at the party I felt an irresistible, drunken urge to ring her.

I went to use the toilet. It was occupied. I came out and the woman at the sink told me where the children's toilet was.

Accepting that I had passed the ped. test, I went into a children's loo. Squatted on the dwarfish throne, glanced once at mawkish watercolours – one which I diagnosed as Hazeldean, a bearded giant with enormous hollow legs – then I rang through to Alison.

She answered immediately.

'It's me,' I said.

'I know –'

'Look –'

'Yes?'

'Look. We mustn't argue.'

She listened, I thought, to the thickened syllables of a sentimental drunk. She left a careful space for me to hear and appreciate the fatuousness of my gesture. But then she surprised me.

'You wouldn't guess what I'm doing?'

I didn't say: you've got your legs up by your ears being ploughed by a red-hot Maori tane.

'I'm driving round Westmere. In the middle of the night.'

'Jesus,' I said, and laughed. 'What's it like?'

'Well – kind of lunar,' she said in a small voice. 'I went and looked at Kiwitea Street.'

I was hit by her loneliness.

'Alison, come to the party,' I said. 'Hazeldean wants to meet you.'

'The guy who did the bio?'

'Mmm.'

Someone rattled on the doorknob. I prayed it wasn't a vigilante kid. 'It's busy. Won't be a moment,' I called.

I gave Alison the address. I sensed her immense relief. I flushed the toilet and came out to face the accusing eyes of an eight-year-old girl consciously holding on.

It was not the time or place. But the Dionysian sparkle, or looseness, made it easy.

'Why are you so interested in Dad?'

Alison asked it. Perhaps seeing her in the normality of

a Kiwi social setting humanised her. She wasn't dressed for a party – I was surprised to see she had on heavy running shoes, as if she might, at any moment, ditch the BMW and – what? Run for her life? The unexpectedness of it – the invitation, her presence – delivered a kind of vulnerability to her performance, usually so immaculate and sealed.

Her question, so direct, made Hazeldean reel. Or at least, in an advanced stage of drunkenness, he performed the art of ricocheting back.

'How many New Zealanders are ever involved in arbitrating, in any sense, on war crimes?'

Neither Alison nor I could supply the answer.

'It's a rare conjunction. And you see, justice is a difficult thing in a post-war situation. Can there really be such a thing as justice for a defeated enemy? When your own behaviour isn't under scrutiny?'

'But how did you get so much information about Dad?'

Alison would have made a good lawyer. She kept her eye on the main ball. I glanced down at my glass. Conspiratorially it was empty. I underwent an intense philosophical debate over the importance of staying to hear what was being discussed versus the importance of getting blotto.

I looked down at my feet as they tracked across the trodden grass. I smelt mud. An ADD kid by my side bounced up and down on a trampoline, face formed into a rictus of glee.

I walked past a woman whose face was familiar but whose name slipped my mind.

I nodded, smiled and said hello.

As I left her behind in my slipstream her name radiated

with the force of a pop-up neon. She was Rebecca Bright, investigative reporter, familiar because I had seen her on television for the past decade. She specialised in foot-in-the-door journalism. I glanced back quickly, checking out the effect of my gaffe.

And in that second everything about her seemed to be transformed. Her most casual gesture became hierarchical. The way her hand brushed away a lock of her hair, or she leaned back against the table, casually pushing away the empty glasses, became symbolic actions of a celebrity acting out the abnormality of 'being ordinary'. Catching my eye, she looked at me for a moment, then turned her back, as though sensing the danger of a photograph. She ignored me.

A lull seemed to have hit the conversation between Alison and Hazeldean when I came back. There was almost an eroticism in the silence, as they eyed each other.

'So you're not going to say?' Alison said at last, fiddling with her empty wine glass.

'It's not for me to say. Is it?'

'Some people would say it was.'

'An historian's responsibility is to tell the truth as he or she sees it,' he said. 'But you have to pick your moment.'

'Truth,' said Alison lightly. 'You've got a monopoly on it?'

'Mmm,' he said throatily. 'Depends.'

There was a little pause.

'What's this?' I said with the furtive edge of someone breaking into a two-person conversation. Alison shifted her eyeline to take me in. She didn't say anything for a moment and Hazeldean glanced at me once. But I knew, with a woman nearby, I was invisible.

'Frank here —' (Frank: I registered, subliminally, the slip into intimacy) — 'Frank is saying that he isn't ready yet to divulge his sources about that incident he talks about in the bio.'

I gaped at Alison.

'The Six Mile Incident,' Frank filled in.

'Oh. Yes.'

'The one,' Alison said, 'where you seem to suggest that Dad may have done something wrong. Perhaps sent someone to their death incorrectly. Isn't that what you're suggesting?'

Hazeldean blinked once, twice and looked uneasy. He looked round the party, as if for someone to save him.

But Alison was remorseless. '*Sacrifice*. That's a pretty big word, in the circumstances.'

But Frank wasn't giving anything away. Though he was getting off on looking at Alison who, I noted, also emitted a quiet, determined sexual vibe.

He just raised his eyebrows once, in an unreadable gesture. 'As I said, victor's justice is always highly debatable. What chance do the defeated actually have?'

Inside the house a kid screamed out. A door slammed. Someone hammered on the door.

'We know Robert McNamara best for the escalation of the Vietnam War,' Hazeldean went on. 'Remember Agent Orange? But he was also in charge of the fire-bombing of Tokyo. It was the first time napalm had been dropped on a civilian population. He himself said, just recently, if the Second World War had ended differently, he would have been put on trial as a war criminal. His exact words: what makes something moral if you win but criminal if you lose?'

Neither Alison nor I could think how to reply. It needed time. Thought.

'The strangest thing happened to me this morning,' Alison said, deciding to change topics. Or emotion. 'Some papers were delivered to me at the hotel. No note. Nothing.'

'What were they?'

'I don't know precisely. I just glanced at them.'

'*And*?'

I had borrowed Alison's prosecutorial tone.

She looked at me for a second, doubtfully – or doubting herself?

Frank, I could see, was fascinated.

'I don't know yet.'

'Who's it from?' he asked.

'No name attached.'

'Really?' Hazeldean's interest was piqued.

'For a while now I've been getting odd things in the mail. To do with that incident you mention, I think. At least brutal war crimes.'

'Really?' His tone this time was blatantly fascinated.

'Frank!' Dotty, his partner, beckoned Hazeldean to come over. She was standing with Rebecca Bright, reporter.

He raised a hand up to indicate he wanted her to wait. But Alison just smiled at him. She was enjoying being enigmatic. Or rather, it was her turn to hold the bargaining counters.

'Of course I have to wait for the right moment to talk to you about it,' she said.

He laughed and walked to join his partner and Rebecca Bright.

Bright, I noted, was looking directly at us.

Rather scarily, she smiled.

'What was that all about?' I asked Alison.

My eyes searched the depleted throng for Gary. He was leaning against a wall, talking to a liquored-up couple. His laugh, so fiercely joyful and anarchic, lit out.

'I've got to go,' I said to Alison, like we were old friends.

But I hesitated, waiting to hear what she and Hazeldean had been sharing.

'Oh, we were talking about Dad, of course. That case Dad investigated —'

I looked over at Hazeldean. He was talking to Rebecca Bright intently. Occasionally the journalist glanced our way. I had the sensation she might even walk towards us if we waited. But I wanted to go. Flight or fight, I guess.

'Time to go,' I said to Alison again, drunkenly leaning towards her on impulse. I planted a big fat kiss on her cheek. She turned to me a mask of a face out of which glittered two inscrutable eyes. I leaned in and repeated the kiss. My lips registered the coolness of her skin.

It was getting cold out there.

'We can only do this together,' I said to her in one of those sublime gifts of drunkenness — the permission to speak your innermost thoughts. 'You know that, don't you, June?'

She laughed. 'You're drunk, Ross,' she said, pushing me away lightly with her fingertips. 'You remind me of Dad.'

7

Alison called Ross punishingly early the following morning. She cut straight to the chase. She said she'd been reading the business section and spotted a small ad.

'It's Hazeldean, Ross. At the museum. Tonight. Talking about the Pacific War. Can you make it?'

'I don't know.'

'It's important, Ross. We've got to keep an eye on that bastard.'

They came in late to a mausoleum-like room at the back of the museum. Fifty seats had seemingly been hurriedly arranged. There was a small podium, a screen, a microphone.

'There's our bloke,' whispered Ross.

Alison surveyed Hazeldean on show. There was something Falstaffian about him. His tie was too tight. It seemed to be throttling him so his face had a congested, unhealthy, pre-heart-attack tinge. But he'd dressed up to present himself to the public: an academic-looking tweed jacket, some sort of discreetly armorial tie. He was laughing tensely like an actor warming up in a green room.

The organiser, Miss Martin, was engaging him in a difficult conversation.

The other 'contestant' was a cooler picture, a young woman who used elegance to twist her looks into *jolie laide*. She wore a startlingly red velvet coat from the 1960s, emphatic lipstick like a banner unfurled against a dramatically white face. Black hair cut sharply. Only when she looked up from her laptop and smiled at another young woman in the room did her eyes – dark, sparkling – express the adrenaline of someone about to give a performance.

This was Jules Harris, University of Otago, MA (Hons).

Hazeldean's eyes moved along the rows as he talked.

His gestures were senatorial, as if – this was emphasised by his portliness – he saw himself within some imaginary Roman setting. It gave the unfortunate sense of a prepared performance, possibly even done in front of a bathroom mirror smeared with toothpaste.

Ross suppressed a snigger.

Alison shifted on her seat. Men like this, pompous pricks, were exactly the sort of men she disdained. They'd stood in her way all through her career but were laughably easy to dismantle. As easy a target as the warship Hazeldean was talking about: the *Prince of Wales*, pride of the Royal Navy, sent out to Singapore to reinforce the impregnability of the British race. Sunk within minutes when attacked by the Japanese from the air. Welcome to the modern world.

'My point,' Hazeldean said with dramatic emphasis, sensing he was losing his audience, improvising. Ross began to pity him.

'My point is this: the Pacific War has historically been regarded as a much less important part of World War Two. In part this was because Europe was in the very last and most self-destructive phase of dominating the discourse of power. Yet standing from the vantage point of the present: what do we see? China rising to become inevitably a greater power than a chronically overextended United States; India also becoming a major world power. The vista we have been used to is breaking up.'

He held his audience now.

'In time we may see that the way we've perceived the dominance of Europe was a momentary, or millennium-long interruption – a blip compared with the longer-term powers, the Chinese and the Japanese empires of antiquity. Let us also not forget the more rational Arab cultures, which in fact preserved Aristotelean thought at a time when Europe itself slumped into the Dark Ages. Dark Ages may return to swamp *us*.'

The room was pin-drop silent.

'Seen in this context, the Pacific War, rather than a secondary theatre of less importance, becomes a hologram of our future. The Pacific War offers us the closest information of what might happen if the United States attempted to engage in military conflict with its Asian competitors. Think of the terms of the Japanese wartime empire: "The East Asian Co-Prosperity Sphere". Do we not live within it already? Let me ask you another question:

did not the Japanese military exploits of 1942 summarily end European colonialism for ever in the Asia–Pacific region?'

There was an uneasy rustling towards the back. Ross glanced at an elderly woman in a raincoat who clenched, as though in sudden pain.

'So what I am arguing is that the inevitable rise to dominance, to world power status, of the once great nations of the East – China, India, Japan – was presaged by events which now stand immediately behind us. The Pacific War, its events, atrocities, victories and defeats, are a signpost pointing to our future. As the *tangata whenua* tell us – we the short-sighted Pakeha obsessed with the materiality of evidence – the past is indeed ahead of us!'

With this passionate statement he paused dramatically, looked up into the audience. When no immediate storm of applause greeted him, he nodded and said a curt, 'Thank you.'

A spurt of applause by the organiser was overtaken by a more lethargic, even grudging sound: an audience stirred to a perfunctory performance of politesse.

Hazeldean looked harassed. This was not what he was used to. But enough of his followers – students awaiting marks for theses, camp followers, friends – were there to mask the somnolence and provide the camouflage by which he could slide back to the safety of his seat. He nodded once, twice, then, abruptly as a light going off, he lost all connection with the audience.

The organiser rose to her feet. 'Let us now welcome our second speaker, Dr Harris. Recently awarded a hundred-thousand-dollar grant from the Marsden Fund to look at the influence of Louise Brooks' bob on Katherine

Mansfield's modernism, she has her own website and blog. Her subject this evening is: "Bushido and the choreography of sado-masochism".'

Dr Harris was heard in silence. Possibly this was because her talk was pitched towards an audience familiar with – if not in bed with on a nightly basis – Baudrillard, Foucault and the rest. Or could it have been because she talked of ritualistic beheadings from such a distanced position that it seemed human nature was reduced in size to something like a miniaturised golf course – convincing at first glance, until you shifted your gaze and took in its shrunken scale. She talked about 'strategies', 'choreographies of sado-masochistic ballets, a dance in which the victim cooperates'.

'My point –' she gently closed the lid of her computer, so it seemed at that moment like the artful reduction, pleat by pleat, of a fan – 'is that the "war crimes" of the Pacific need to be and can only be seen from within the context of a complex Japanese code which dates back many centuries. It is not reducible to crude notions of barbarism, cruelty or hatred. It was in many ways a code of honour, at least as old and as honourable as chivalry in Europe.'

This was heard in profound silence.

'Do we have any questions?'

Miss Martin, the organiser, seemed a little nervous.

An elderly man stood up. His English was not good and his plastic raincoat rustled as he turned and addressed the others in the auditorium. He completely ignored the speakers on the platform.

'I am here because my family suffered 1942 to 1945. We lived in Dutch Borneo. My father was deputy manager of a rubber plantation. We were imprisoned by the Japanese from July 1942 till we were freed by the Australians on September 31st 1945. At 2.30 on a Wednesday afternoon. They gave us lollies . . . the first lollies I had seen in over three years . . .' His voice faltered, grew reedy and thin.

What he said next had the effect of being a recital. 'The Japanese came and got us when we were eating our lunch. We knew they were coming. My father told us to go to our room and collect the suitcases we had packed. My sister was crying, as was my mother. We lost everything. My mother tried to keep her spirits up but as the years passed she got thinner and thinner, and more silent. My father was tortured. They gave him rice, then they forced water in a hose into his stomach. His stomach grew in size. He was in terrible pain. They jumped on his stomach. He never recovered. He was a broken man. My sister who was twelve when we went into the camp has never been able to have children. We have never been given compensation. Thank you. I just had to tell someone.'

He sat down, trembling. The elderly woman whom Ross had seen wince reached forward to him and held his hand. She nodded at him. A ripple of consternation ran through the audience.

The two historians, for a moment, glanced at one another. Miss Martin looked increasingly nervous.

An elderly woman rose to her feet.

'I need to tell my story.'

She told the story of her husband who had come home from the prison camps and suffered a life of chronic ill health. He was in hospital with steroid-treated poliomyelitis when he died. The cause was given as pneumonia – until his autopsy revealed larvae inside his body.

'The nematode worm,' she said, 'had been living in my husband's body quietly since 1945. It was in every tissue. We did not know. Nobody told us. Until he was dead. This larvae came from the camps. Thank you for listening.'

She sat down.

And so it went on. Nobody talked about Baudrillard or Bushido or how the Pacific War presaged the future. In their ravaged faces, the dumpiness and dowdiness of their punchbag figures – the haunted quality of their faces, their inability to keep away from their obsessions – the old people spoke out. They had not come to listen: they had come to bear witness.

The final speaker, an old Dutch woman, seemed deranged. She spoke of loss of dignity, of loss of money: of loss.

'And still the Japanese deny it. And our own government, the British and American, all do nothing.'

A profound silence fell.

The organiser rose to her feet. She looked ashen.

'Thank you for sharing your . . . stories with us. I think we have all listened – and learnt a lot this evening. Now,' she hurriedly went on, 'please join with me in thanking our speakers in the customary manner. A cup of tea and biscuits will be served in the lobby. If you could make a gold coin contribution . . .'

Outside, it was a still night. Auckland had converted itself into a mantle of beauty. The container wharf took on all the irradiated brilliance of a cocaine high. Somewhere a ship horn sounded and a sudden spurt of stars seemed to open like flowers all over a darkling sky.

'Well,' said Ross. 'We sure got our money's worth.'

'I'll say.' Alison let out a sigh. 'Those poor old bastards.'

It was hard not to feel haunted by the stories – their pathos, truth.

There were footsteps behind them. It was Hazeldean making a getaway. But seeing a possible alliance, he tacked towards them.

'Phew. Tough audience.'

'It was certainly educational,' Alison's voice was cool.

Their eyes met.

'Can I ask you something?' Hazeldean asked. Ross was suddenly invisible. 'Weren't you in the varsity tramping club? Round '68?'

'Yes.'

'So was I. I'm sure I remember you.'

Alison managed a smile.

'And you're back here –?' Hazeldean stood quite close.

'To see Dad.'

They looked at each other intently.

Hazeldean was the first to look away. 'Well, good luck,' he said. 'Remember, if you want any help deciphering those strange documents you said you were getting, give me a –' and he did a phone gesture to his ear.

'Which documents are those?' Ross's voice took on the unfortunate whine of the perennially excluded child.

Alison ignored him.

A paper slipped out from Hazeldean's grasp and they watched as it wavered, then, in a sluice, disappeared under a car into a puddle.

The paper blackened.

8

I was suspicious. The envelope had no return name attached, and the label was typed, not handwritten like the other anonymous missives I'd been sent. A yellow envelope, my name and hotel. This worried me. The other envelopes had all been sent to my London address, but this new one implied surveillance. I took the envelope with me as I breakfasted. I left it by my plate, untouched.

I breakfasted slowly. I had already been for my run. I covered five kilometres, past the Parnell Baths and as far as Mission Bay. It was a day of choked cloud yet glaring light. Traffic hurtled over the harbour bridge and the sea itself was pale in colour, muddy around the shoreline.

As I ran, my thoughts reformulated into some sort of order. Like a jigsaw, at first all jumbled, then, as I ran along – the jigsaw started to fit together till, by the end of my run, the picture was more complete. But this picture – Dad

– the danger of Hazeldean – the nature of his enquiry – the sacrifice? – made no sense. There were Dad's eyes looking at me, bruised, fearful, frightened. Ross's eyes angry, accusing, then unfocused and sentimentally drunk: Hazeldean was different. He appreciated me as a woman, but I sensed he also carried some information he was withholding. He was dangerous.

As I finished my breakfast and wiped my lips, I reflected how this glaring whiteness of light seemed to be characteristic of my teenage years in Auckland. It was as if my early childhood took place under vividly coloured skies, whereas during adolescence the temperatures changed and Auckland became a world of concrete, grey skies and buildings defiant in their ugliness. I knew there had to be somewhere better elsewhere.

Strange to be back. It's never neutral coming home.

I had played with taking the envelope to the police. But what could I really say? I risked being ridiculous. I knew enough from coping with Juliette's brushes with the law that police work was based on nuts-and-bolts stuff: who did what, who hit whom, who stole what. This was different. Odd.

I took the envelope back to my room. I put it down. I thought I'd go to the library and look at some books. I knew almost nothing about the Pacific War. I'd take Hazeldean's potted bio of Dad and see if I could find out more about Dad's war. Also – I needed to read up on gerontology. I could have done this on the web but I wanted an outing. I wanted to experience, even revel in, all the feelings of being back.

Instead of which I found myself tackling the envelope, opening it with urgent fingers and sitting down.

It began with something strange about a fingerprint.

After half an hour, hearing the distant thunder of Hoovers in the hall, I stumbled to the door and put out the sign. 'Do Not Disturb.'

I had made a decision I would tell her nothing. After all, Alison had never shared anything with me. She had taken off as soon as she could. She had turned her back on me. And when I went to London on my big OE she'd shacked up with this English prick. I only ever stayed with her one night. It didn't work out. She married the English prick in the end. I remember getting her letter in Sydney where I was living. I read it tripping. There were photos. She was in a dreadful hat. Gloves. Her English relatives arranged round her like a back-up chorus. A ghastly assemblage of teeth. Eyes watchful of dropped hints as to social background. Alison already talked posh. In the photos she looked unreal, both beautiful, I realised, or at least very attractive – but there's something not there. It's us, of course, the flawed family.

I had gone to Sydney to make up a life for myself. I had come out to Mum by letter. She'd written back about her fears of my being condemned 'to a tragic end and lonely life'. This was my mother talking, living on her own, making a life of going to church, doing the flowers. Waiting for Dad to call her when he was pissed.

Dad was living with Elsie by then. Mum pleaded with me not to get in touch with him. Not to tell him. But I was enjoying myself. I had a lot of friends. I was reinventing my life. I felt I had a lot of time. And as I looked around myself, I wondered what loneliness Mum was talking of. Then one night, very late, I got a phone call. I was sleeping with my boyfriend of the time, Kevin. I'd fallen into the most beautiful swoon of sleep – one of those times when you're released into a being who has all the potentiality of a fully functioning human: the person I might one day be.

Then that phone rang. Naked, gummy, I ran to pick it up. There was that sound that used to be part of an overseas phone call. I stood there, looking out into the paradisial Sydney night – the sound of bats, and somewhere a car misfiring; across the street, in a lit window, someone was sitting over a mug of coffee. I listened to the sound of the line in my ear, imagining you could travel under the ocean, beneath all the waves, distance made sonic, and I would pop up right inside Dad's ear.

'Dad?' I said. 'Is that you, Dad?'

There was a whimper or a moan.

The phone was placed down, awkwardly, in the manner of a drunk.

Alison and I did not correspond. We lost touch. When Mum died I had to find Alison's address among Mum's belongings. Pitifully sorted out before her death. These for the Red Cross. These clothes for the Salvation Army. Her good winter coat, which she wore to church: 'Offer this to Mrs Jones. It still has good wear in it.' And when I called Alison her accent was so sharp it cut me. She said she'd come back for the funeral. She just had to shift some meetings. As it was, she never made it.

She never made it.

The story of her life.

And now, here she was, back in my life, as bossy as ever. As silently contemptuous. Do you think I couldn't scent the pity in her glance when she peered into the innards of my life? I was nothing to her. My life didn't amount to a tin of beans. I knew that. Of course I had my secret life. I don't mean sexually. I mean my other life, as a thinking sentient person. But let's not go into that.

As for Dad, he was never really interested in who I was. Probably when I started becoming political he sensed I was using politics against him. I went on Ban the Bomb marches as soon as I was old enough. We did school projects on the effects of Hiroshima. Dad laughed greyly and asked me what I knew about the Japanese prisoner of war camps. I wasn't listening. I wanted peace. That is, Peace. Dad was part of a discredited war. He was always boozed and angry, vindictive. I didn't want to know. Vietnam protests only widened the wedge between us. I wore my anti-war badges proudly. I grew my hair long.

'What are you, a girl?'

Coming out as gay was only part of the whole politicised process.

One I couldn't share with Dad.

Our antipathy hardened. In mutual absence. And then I came home to New Zealand. The Springbok tour was the final coup de grâce. Dad, lover of football, wouldn't talk to me. Poor old Elsie became the bridge between us. I rang her occasionally and she'd talk to me. It was through her I heard any news of Dad. I didn't see him for over four years.

And then finally Elsie rang me and asked me out – well, to be honest, she begged me to come and visit. 'Your father misses you. He's too proud to admit it but he talks about you all the time. You and Alison. Please come, Ross. I need you.'

It was this last sentence that won me over.

'I'll come if Gary can come.'

There was a pause. Elsie's breath was flecked with panic.

'Who's Gary?'

'He's my —' I made an instant decision not to say lover, which he was. 'He's my partner.' I dressed his naked heat in a more presentable garb.

'You're both very welcome.'

This was Elsie's statement of principle. Elsie the smoker of Craven A, Elsie of the plucked eyebrows. Elsie the codependent alcoholic, as social workers would put it. Elsie who kept Dad company through all his scraps. Elsie who took Dad to Mum's funeral, even though Mum'd specifically asked, as the one thing she wanted, for Elsie not to come. She wanted the dignity of being buried without scandal. But I understood instantly that Elsie was there so Dad didn't get out of control. Fat chance. Dad was tanked. Dad made a scene. It was grotesque. But at least Elsie was there to pick up the pieces.

But all this was behind us on that first nervous meeting. It was Easter time. Gary was at his diplomatic best. He and Dad hit it off from the first. Bloke to bloke. Talking about cars. I was left to confer with Elsie in their tiny kitchen.

'He's not too hot,' Elsie told me.

I knew that anyway. Dad had aged in the years since I'd seen him. This most of all dictated to me my future course. It was my first intimation he wouldn't be around for ever — primal knowledge that hit me in the plexus. I was winded by it. I could forgive him his yelled instructions to me on how to improve my life.

'Still working in the gardens, son?'

'Have you ever thought of going to university?'

'Do you blokes own that place?'

'Must be nice to have a cobber.'

'Keeps you company, does he?'

That was as far as it got. At times I'd catch his eyes moving from Gary to me, making up his own story. He never would admit we were lovers. That we were fucking each other. He deleted that.

'Any tasty girls there?'

'Isn't it time you thought of settling down? Marrying?'

But he was grateful I'd come back. His hands trembled when he shook my hand. His grip was less punishing. His eyes watered, though it could just have been old age.

I could see his deterioration. His lack of concentration. Failing memory.

At times Elsie would catch my eye and she would just shake her head, slightly, very slightly.

We didn't say anything.

'Don't forget us, Ross,' she'd say at the end of these visits.

'Don't forget us, son,' Dad would say.

When he said the word 'son', it always touched me. Of course it wasn't the honorific 'Captain', which he saved for Alison. Just as her photo had pride of place on their cocktail cabinet. But every time he called me 'son' I felt the weight. Also the honour. Direct. Terse.

That is who I am, I thought, in the end.

His son.

As for Alison: brother and sister is a less direct link. She'd been hauled back into my life, but she was there on sufferance. I didn't know how she'd jump.

As for me sharing my life or what I thought with her, I felt best protected by being less frontal or face to face. At times it's easier to talk that way.

When you have a history of damage between you, it's helpful to talk with a wall in between. Or a screen at least.

Being indirect can be the only way.

9

There was a knock on the hotel door, tentative but firm.

Alison, splayed out on the bed, waited. The knock repeated itself. She got up, sighed, stretched – was amazed to see an hour had vanished.

Without being precisely sure of why she did it, she flicked a pillow over the papers she'd been reading.

'I don't want the room serviced,' she was about to snap at the inevitably apologetic but implacable cleaner standing there. (Subconsciously she had heard them approaching room by room, the warning drone of the cleaner, doors opening and closing. And now this –)

She peeled the door back, angry.

Ross was standing there. Looking uncomfortable. But there was something in his face – bright, apprehensive. His eyes travelled beyond her, into the room.

She stood aside.

He walked inside and whistled.

'Très *chi chi*,' he said rolling his r's.

She shrugged. Noted his eyes surveying the rucked-up bed, pillow flung across the counterpane.

'Getting some shut-eye?'

The curtains were half-pulled against the glare. But now, needing light, or difference, Alison walked towards the ranchslider doors and slid them open.

A gull outside screeched, car horns peeped – a mat of sound, pressing. Ross glanced at the 'million-dollar view'. The room had a westerly aspect and the sun hadn't come round yet, so it was chilly. Several floors down below some people were working on yachts.

They retreated to the sealed silence.

'You'll never guess what!'

This was a slightly tiresome game Ross had played ever since childhood. If ever he gave her a present – be it a chocolate fish or Jaffa – the act of giving had to be ceremoniously underlined by him hiding the gift behind his back and asking her to choose 'which hand'.

She had forgotten all this gratefully, but now it came back, first of all faintly, like a faded photograph rushing back to mint condition.

'What?'

But her mind wasn't on him. Her mind was coiled, tight, somewhere else.

She noticed various things about him her consciousness hadn't earlier supplied: the grey hairs at the back of his neck, the deep lines on his forehead. But his urgency was making him boyish.

'Don't you have work today?'

'I work my own hours, Alison,' he said to her in a voice

which threatened to return to an older adversity. Wrong move.

'Well?'

'Someone's rung from *60 Seconds*.'

Alison waited.

'You know, a TV show like *20/20*, *Current Affair* and all the rest. What passes for current affairs,' he said with a snort. 'You know – five minutes' promo, two minutes' content, three minutes' wrap-up.'

'What about?'

'They're trying to get in touch with Dad.'

Brother and sister eyed each other. Alison, involuntarily sat down. The armchairs were deep, absurdly deep, a statement of luxury. Ross also sat, or rather squatted on the front of his armchair ready to leap up at any moment.

'Why?'

'I asked that. The person said she was just making enquiries about availability at this stage.'

Again they eyed each other's faces, in that second seeking some portent within the familiarity of features. Or was it comfort they were after?

Outside a sudden wind took up and a faint, even dismal drone could be heard – the peculiarities of bad architecture.

'Did you say Dad wasn't –'

'I said I'd have to "consult with my whanau".' Ross laughed a little. The absurdity. A whanau of two. 'I said the whanau would decide what was "appropriate".'

Alison, despite herself, was impressed.

'What did the person say?'

'She lost her grip for a moment. Then asked me where she could find him.'

'You didn't —'

'What do you think?'

'. . . Some tea?'

'Mm . . . okay. Yes.'

A pause.

'Why? Why now? I don't understand.'

This would take time.

'We've got to be really careful here.'

'I think,' said Ross, 'it's that fucking journalist. At Hazeldean's party. Rebecca Bright. They're always sniffing out a story.'

'But what's the story, Ross? I don't understand.'

Alison's eyes went to the pillow. Instead of ringing for tea straight away, she went to the phone by the bed and, as if casually, threw some more pillows over the manuscript.

Ross stood up and roamed about her room, looking at the prints on the wall — not bad, given the usual blandness of hotel art — then he went and stood outlined against the ranchsliders. He appeared to be thinking.

'It's obviously about that last trial Dad was involved in. Don't you think?'

'Or it could be — well, it could be his war record. He did win a DSO, after all. When's Anzac Day again?'

'Late April.' He paused. 'Do you think they're rounding up a few wrinklies for the kiddies to worship? Anzac Day's a growing franchise.'

'Could be.'

The tea came with surprising speed. A commercially handsome youth introduced himself, and then the tray. Ross eyed his pert behind as he bent over to put down the tray. The youth smoothly allowed a pause, and Alison slipped him a tip. His eyes blandly took in Ross salivating.

He wished them both a good day.

The door closed with ostentatious discretion.

They were silent as Alison poured.

'School project ahoy or . . .'

The piddling sound ceased.

They sat back.

'Um,' said Ross.

Once again Alison sped back to childhood. It amazed her the way the signals stayed the same. And how, after more than twenty years' separation, when nearly every cell in their respective bodies had been renewed, the signals remained unchanged.

'Um' had always been prelude to an awkward confession.

'I said she could meet me,' Ross said in a small voice, looking down.

She saw him as a nine-year-old, swinging his legs, saying he had spent the afternoon alone with 'Elsie', as he duplicitously called his father's mistress.

'She's a researcher. Anne Donaldson. You probably didn't meet her. She was doing the dishes at Hazeldean's party.'

'When?'

'Tomorrow.'

'What time?'

'Two.'

'Can I be there?'

The slightest mutiny of a pause. 'Yes.'

She could barely wait for Ross to go. He lingered, luxuriating in the time he had taken off work. Pathetically he liked being in the luxury of the Hilton. He wanted to know more about her life. What did she do exactly? What was her house like? Did she have photos? Did she live alone? Was there a garden? Did she like reading? Who was her favourite author? Was she in a book club?

In the end she had briskly put on her windbreaker and said she'd walk him back to his car.

'I bussed in,' he said. 'You don't park in the city. Too expensive. Unless of course –' he glanced at her – 'you're loaded.'

'I'll walk with you to the bus stop.'

'Don't bother, Alison. I'm over sixteen. See you tomorrow.'

She waited for the sound of the lift doors closing before she went back to the bed. She lifted away the pillows. Then she made a decision. She would take the papers with her. She bundled them into a bag, caught the lift downstairs and went to a café.

10

'Do you think Dad had a secret life, Ross?'

'We've all got secrets, Alison.'

They were sitting, waiting for Anne Donaldson, the researcher.

Alison had said nothing about the papers and, more peculiarly still, Ross had asked her nothing. She put this down to his self-obsession and incurable narcissism: she noted he'd had his hair cut. He was also clean shaven and wearing more than usually presentable clothes. There was a palpable sense of excitement in the way he jumped up when he heard car doors slamming outside. He went to the front of the house, looked out windows. He came back checking his watch.

'She's late.'

'By three minutes —'

Alison lifted up the newspaper cutting her mother

had saved. Dad getting his gong at Government House. A drunk's consciousness of imitating normality. His back so straight, saluting. Freyberg half-smiling, looking down.

The paper had yellowed, lost its elasticity. It felt light as a cobweb. So few relics left, so potent.

'Are we going to . . . agree . . . on what we . . . don't say?'

'What? I think we let her do the talking. Don't you think? Find out what she wants to know?'

'No interviews with Dad.'

'Of course not. That's impossible.'

'She'll probably realise that without that it's a no-brainer. I mean, without Dad –'

A knock on the door.

Ross jumped up, glanced at Alison, she thought wildly but with a shine of victory, and went to let her in.

Their voices came down the hall.

'I'm so sorry I'm a bit late . . .'

'You're not late at all . . .'

'I couldn't find a park . . .'

'Parking round here's a nightmare. They're thinking of introducing permits but locals don't want it. Most of them have off-street parking . . .' Ross was running away at the mouth.

The twosome walked into the living room. As with all renovated villas, it was at the back of the house, opening out into the garden.

'Oh –' the woman paused, spotting Alison. 'What a beautiful room.'

Alison saw a compact woman entering the uncharted waters of early middle age. Her hair was cut in a long fringe over a forehead Alison immediately knew to be sun damaged. She wore artful clothes that suggested Isadora Duncan with a more contemporary cut. *Mode à la Ponsonby.*

'What a gorgeous garden!' She went straight to the windows, looked out. Then, as if suddenly remembering, with a laugh she handed over a cardboard box.

Ross read the name of an expensive local cake shop.

'Oh, you shouldn't have —'

He had already prepared a miniature feast for morning tea — slices of ginger and raisin cake that Gary had baked; crackers, and hummus Gary had also made.

'This is my sister, Alison.'

'Anne Donaldson —'

The two women confronted each other, smiling. They shook hands.

'Oh, and look at that gorgeous cat!'

Tallulah, sitting on the outdoor table, formed a perfect obelisk, her face gazing into the garden. Sensing attention, she glanced into the room for a moment, assessed the potential for food and attention, then removed her gaze.

Anne Donaldson felt a moment's relief. She was asthmatic.

'Thanks so much for seeing me at such short notice.'

She had slid a number of folders down on to the table. Coffee was brewed and the three made all the adjustments necessary for comfort.

'You sure you wouldn't like some hummus?'

Ross pushed the plate forward.

'Thank you, I'd love to,' Anne said, knowing the hummus would be left untouched after a ritual bite. 'How delicious! Did you make it? So much nicer than supermarket hummus. I must get the recipe.'

She was aware of Alison's eyes boring into her. So she stopped stonewalling.

'How is your Dad?'

'Oh, he's –'

This was Ross, who needed another coffee.

'You know he's in a home now?'

'He's ninety,' Alison said quickly, 'and he's had a hard life.'

'That generation,' Anne said sympathetically. 'I don't think we understood, our generation, exactly what they'd been through. Especially the men. My Dad – he's passed on now – was in Egypt and then Italy. He took a bullet at Cassino and you know, he never said –'

'They never said –'

'He never said so much as a word about it. I had to find out after he died.'

'How did you find out?'

Alison was determined to get something useful out of this encounter.

'Oh –' Anne leaned forward and began thumbing through her folders. She did this for a concentrated moment. 'I can give you all the contacts if you want. One of the most interesting things is to get their medical records. They list exactly where they went, you know, in the war –'

'If they were in prison camps?'

Anne stopped her search.

'How stupid of me. Of course. I'm sorry.' She laid her folders down. 'I do apologise,' she said with the hint of a flush on her face. She noted the cat had got down from its perch – probably on the scent of food – and was now sitting, its rather stupid face staring through the French doors. 'My father died just a year ago. It's still rather raw.'

'Dad isn't in a fit state to be interviewed.'

Alison cursed Ross, his gabbiness – something else she remembered from childhood. You could find out anything from Ross by just letting him talk. He always incriminated himself, and now he'd given away this major bargaining chip.

Anne paused. 'Oh, I *am* sorry. Is he not in a good way?'

'Some more coffee?' Alison said quickly. 'Or cake?'

Ross, agitated, got up and let the cat in through the door.

'This is Tallulah.' He picked her up and cradled her. 'Say hello to the lady, Tallulah.'

Alison felt a vindictive streak of hatred for her brother. Had he no understanding of how he was portraying himself? Or was it his ploy – to present himself as a ludicrous cat-fixated homosexual who was suffering cradle anxiety?

'Hello Tallulah!' Anne called gaily. To Alison: 'I suppose your father suffers long-term effects from his captivity?' She picked up her folders again and thumbed through. 'I have a very interesting article here, off the internet, on the effects of overmedicalisation used to offset traumatic stress syndrome.'

She slid out a printout on 'Protracted Benzodiazepine Withdrawal Symptoms'.

'It was the drug they used most commonly after the war. To allay symptoms. But it brought its own problems –'

'Which were?'

Alison's voice had a sexy lower register at these moments of interrogation. Her intelligence shone.

'Loss of cognitive function, muscle pains, gastrointestinal disturbances.'

'Sounds like Dad,' Ross said. 'To be frank, he's a bit of a mess.'

'I know how hard it is find suitable places for returned soldiers. With Dad I put his name down for Ranfurly, but when a space came up he refused to go – he was doing okay so I let it slide, then came the crisis –'

'Same,' said Ross, not daring to look at Alison. 'It's been a right bugger.'

'More hummus?'

'No. No, thanks.' Anne shot a glance at Alison, whose hostility was palpable. 'I had to work hard to find a home nearby mine. I wanted him as close as possible to me and the kids –' this to Alison, with a smile. 'They say contact is important. And my kids – well, they were fond of Gamps.'

The childish nickname floated in the air.

The cat, sensing a deprivation of attention, struggled lethargically in Ross's arms. Carefully, very carefully, he put her down on the floor on all fours.

Anne began to feel an asthmatic tightening in her throat. Her eyes began to water. Skin itched. She got up and went towards the French doors.

'Your beautiful garden,' she said. 'Do you mind? If I look?'

Alison followed their conversation outdoors. When they got to the far end of the garden – a mere eight metres away – their voices became indistinct for a brief period. Alison thought of going out to supervise Ross's undoubtedly random, anarchic utterances, but she hesitated.

The cat had followed them out but sat a distance away.

There was a hint of malice in her eyes.

When they returned to the living room, Anne got out a small reporter's notebook and began her questioning. Alison was fascinated to see how Anne kept eye contact with whoever she was talking to, even as she kept writing – shorthand surely? – the pages scurfing over and over. Alison frankly admired Anne's centripetal approach. She started with the obvious, working always towards the enigma. What did they know of their father's war service? Where had he served? For how long? His captivity. His becoming a war crimes investigator. What had he investigated?

Since neither Alison nor Ross answered these questions with any precision, the process faltered.

Ross recommended she contact Frank Hazeldean.

Since Anne had been at Frank's party, there was every likelihood she had.

'I'm interested,' she said, 'in what *you* know.'

'Or don't know,' Alison replied coolly.

Ross repeated the line about neither of them knowing much. He then went off on a jag about his father – the way he never spoke, his PTS. Anne's pen stopped but her eyes glistened. She was all empathy as they exchanged emotional fluids about the silence of returned soldiers. The drinking, the occasional outbursts of violence.

Alison cringed as Ross retold the story of their father dropping to the ground at the sound of a car exhaust. He told it like it was a wry joke.

Anne scribbled industriously. She looked quietly thrilled. The jackpot.

'I don't think this is what you want to know about.'

Alison put her foot against the door.

'I mean. It's not about war trauma, is it? Or is it?'

'Just getting the background,' Anne replied, after a second's disquiet. 'Okay, so let's retrace where we've been.' She glanced down at her notebook, but Alison felt this was purely for effect.

'I'm interested in one particular case for which your father gathered the evidence.'

Alison and Ross were silent.

'It's the last case he investigated. The defendant was a Lieutenant-Colonel Sugihara. He was charged with the unlawful execution of seventy-five prisoners of war, many of them Australian.'

'Where do you get your information from?'

This was Alison.

The power balance had changed. It was Anne who was prevaricating. But she, glancing at the two, said, 'Frank has given me some pointers. It's in the Archives. I'm sorry, I don't have all the details with me. It was one of the last cases of the war. Your father's gathering of evidence was key.'

They had come close to the enigma. Neither Alison nor Ross said a word.

'Let me ask you something else — a tea chest. A box of documents. Were you aware of the existence of such a thing?'

Immediately, Anne Donaldson knew she had struck gold.

This was because the brother and sister exchanged looks, and Alison said, 'There was a box, yes. I seem to recall it was in the garage at Kiwitea Street?'

'Did you ever see what was inside it?'

Another quick, descending depth of pause.

Anne Donaldson was an astute judge of silences. As

a researcher she always knew the moment she had that sensation of a lift in freefall that she was near the truth.

'You have to remember Dad left home when I was twelve and Ross was nine. We were kids.'

'So you never saw inside?'

'The tea chest you mention . . . I seem to recall it disappeared after a while.'

'When?'

'I'm not really sure.'

Anne noted that neither brother nor sister exchanged any eye contact: the sure sign of a lie.

'And when do you think it disappeared?'

'Well, you know, children's sense of time –'

Ross broke in, 'I was in Standard Three, I think. That made me eight.'

Anne looked at him. She smiled. She would ring him back in the early evening when, she was sure, he'd had a few. She'd done a bit of detective work outside: the recycling bin was filled to overflowing with empties. There was no one so indiscreet as a lush.

'What's this for anyway?' This was Alison.

'We're thinking of doing a piece on victor's justice. But really we're just feeling around to see if there's a story.'

Anne closed her notebook, slipped it into her handbag.

As she retreated up the hall, she shook hands with Alison. 'You're over here for long?'

'Just to see Dad, really.'

'Where do you live in London?'

'Islington.'

'Can I be so rude as to ask what you do?'

'Banker,' Alison replied.

'Oh goodness. Gosh. You would be excellent for our association, which often has talkers who are executive women who have made it overseas –'

'I kind of like my privacy,' Alison replied too quickly. She wore an insincere, saccharine smile to match Anne's.

'It's been so nice to meet you.'

'And you.'

As Ross said goodbye at the door, Alison overheard Anne say, 'Oh, by the way – I forgot – what's the name of the home your father's in?'

Ross, like a fool, provided it.

11

'I'm afraid your Dad's not too hot today.'

Mrs Stobbs was nowhere to be seen, though her office had the smell of a powerful scent she seemed to favour. Bobbie was holding the fort, watering some African violets.

'Mrs Stobbs had to step out to do the banking.'

Alison and Ross stood there. They'd gone straight out to Arlington.

'We've changed his medication and it's having some adverse effects. Short term –'

'What to?' Alison said.

'Well, we started off with rivastigmine, which was to quieten him down a little and offset his anxiety state –'

'Anxiety?'

'He's worried about something. Shanghai. He keeps banging on about it.'

'Changi.'

Bobbie just looked at them.

'But he seems to be reacting badly to Nivaline. Shaking, diarrhoea – weak stool, constant . . .' Bobbie maintained eye contact. 'He's also sleeping too much. As if he's depressed. It's dangerous.'

'We have concerns –'

All three of them were standing like intruders in Mrs Stobbs' domain. The side door was open and out of it Ross saw an elderly woman in a nylon dressing gown standing very close to a window, looking out. But there was no view – just an enclosed courtyard, windows running with condensation.

In the middle of pebbles stood a yellowing bromeliad.

'We have concerns,' Alison was saying, 'about people or persons unknown trying to contact Dad.'

To Bobbie this sounded like extra-sensory perception. She swallowed a giggle. A sense of humour was what saved her sanity.

'Pardon,' she said. She sensed a tetchiness between brother and sister. But since this was by no means unusual among the heirs of a person in an old people's home, she generously overlooked it. She was off in forty minutes anyway. (She planned a trip to the movies, a seat on her own: the indulgence of a chocolate-dipped ice cream accompanied by a pack of crisps – her own version of sweet 'n' sour.)

She suddenly knew what to call the pair in front of her – Sweet 'n' Sour.

'The media want to get hold of Dad.'

This was more interesting. 'We're up to date here on all our provisions and bylaws,' said Bobbie. 'Anyway, this is something you should talk to Mrs Stobbs about. Not me.'

'No,' Sour said, aging herself with a frown. 'It's like this. Dad was a returned serviceman in World War Two. He did quite notable service.'

Bobbie nodded. She knew that. Old Eric had told her a thing or two. Families had no idea of the confidences traded late at night. Confessions of lonely souls accompanied by bodily evacuations, both of them at times involuntary – and equals in mess, she thought.

'Television might be wanting to contact Dad to talk about some aspects of his war service . . .'

Bobbie noted how Sour skipped over the last sentence – the guts. She'd be no good down on her hands and knees wiping up stool.

'. . . and naturally we want to protect him.'

But not yourselves. Bobbie understood perfectly.

'I'll tell Matron when she comes in.'

But Bobbie had her own mission.

'Look, I think it's best if you taiho about seeing him just at the mo.'

Neither of them moved.

'We know you're doing your best by him,' said Sweet.

'It's just the new medication . . . Sometimes it can be disturbing for family members . . . who don't understand what's a momentary side-effect.'

She looked at Sweet, so gullible, so eager to be divested of responsibility. Running home to Mummy, looking for the tit.

Sour. Implacable. 'I'd still like to look at him.'

Bobbie sighed inwardly. So be it.

He was slumped back on his chair, motionless. His head was thrown back, jaw yawning open, and he presented a frightening vision of what he might look like dead.

'Oh God,' Ross murmured.

The television was playing. Footie. Australian rules. A rising crescendo of a goal.

'Can't you turn that blasted thing off?'

'He gets upset if he wakes up and it's not on. It's like a baby minder.'

They were all whispering.

Bobbie skilfully extricated the remote off Eric's lap. She muted it.

Suddenly Eric's breathing stopped. His index finger twitched. It jerked again and, as if in syncopated sequence, his Adam's apple rose up and down, his mouth clapped shut with an audible wallop, fell open again as dramatically. Various gagging sounds rose in sequence up the tunnel of his throat. His tongue – furred and snot-yellow on its pelt – lolled out, slithered back, tried to liquor up his parched lips. His head shot up with a terrific force and finally he was sitting there, stunned, looking directly into the eyes of his daughter.

He stared at her for a moment of shocked silence.

'Cap . . . than,' he croaked thickly.

Even Ross could hear a thrill of joy.

Bobbie came towards him smoothly with a glass of water.

'Here, old chap.'

She bent his hands around the glass. She guided his hand up to his mouth. She tilted the glass to his lips. All this was done quickly, efficiently, matter-of-factly. Yet it had the effect of making his own children bystanders.

Eric's pupils, vast in his eyes, meanwhile took in the presence of his son.

When the glass was removed, he concentrated on the bulky business of swallowing. The moment he could get his breath, he yelled out, 'It's the Captain, Ross. She's come for me!'

He tried to stand up, his hands grabbing hold of the sides of the chair, but his legs, shrunken inside their trousers, his withered arms, could not provide the leverage. He sank back again, letting out an appalled whinny.

'Who's a frisky boy today!'

With a stage wink, Bobbie went to help him. But he pushed her aside, out of his view and stayed seated. He blinked twice in rapid succession and a strange look came over his face.

'I was having the strangest dream. I was back in Tokyo. Trying to contact a mate of mine.' His eye fell on Ross. 'Come here, son.'

Ross twitched and went closer. He bent down on his knees to his father's eye level.

Remarkably the old man shot his hand out and grabbed Ross's wrist in a pincer hold.

'You forgive me, don't you, lad?'

The pitiful clarity of the sentence – its emotional challenge – hung in the air.

'Yes. Why?'

His father tugged Ross's hand so violently, his shoulder jerked.

'Don't fool with me, boy.'

He seemed disgusted by his son's easy acceptance of something that was clearly troubling him. It was everything that was wrong with the modern age: emotional cowardice, easy acceptance of things that should be doubted.

His voice, now reedy and thin, could no longer command the parade-ground shout. But its eerie quality, its plangent need, was more powerful. Eric thrust his son's hand away from him.

'I don't want your pity.'

Alison burst out into a laugh. Clapped her hand over her lips as her father turned his eye to her – rheumy, vindictive, angry.

'What's so funny, girlie?'

She came closer. It was her turn. She squatted down before him.

'It's you, Daddy. If you could see yourself.'

The remains of his hair standing up. Potty by his feet. Big yellow toenail poking out of his slippers. He looked like an angry tot awoken and keening on the side of his cot.

'You remind me of Juliette when she was a child.'

What was she saying – babbling? In front of the nurse, eyewitness to their private rites of humiliation and need for absolution.

'Son,' Eric pulled his son by the shoulder now. Yet in that moment something happened to Ross. His face became blank, and sank back into an older unhappiness. His father was mishandling him, pushing him, pulling him towards his sister.

'Look who's here, son. It's your sister.'

He pushed Ross's face close to Alison's. They looked at each other – it couldn't be avoided – and each of them broke out into a sweat.

'She'll take me out of this place.'

'It's the meds,' murmured Bobbie loudly.

'You're going to take me out of here, aren't you, Captain?'

Eric released Ross's shoulder and for one moment Alison took in her brother's expression – humiliated, unloved, spurned. It was her father's love, she knew in that instant, that had set her on her way. Just as her brother was and would always be discarded. Worthless. Bargain basement.

The worst thing was that he knew it.

Alison could read it in his face. And there was nothing she could do about this almost feudal inequality of love.

'Here, Eric, take this.'

Bobbie held in her palm a single pill.

He glanced down at it. Looked around wildly. With one jab he knocked the pill out of Bobbie's hand.

'You're going to make me angry, Eric.' Bobbie felt around the floor, located the pill. 'And you don't want that, do you, Eric.' She rose up before him.

He looked up at her. There was something new in his glance – something troubling. He looked abject. He shrank down in his seat and then reached out in an equally desperate jab and grabbed hold of Alison's arm.

'*Get – me – out – of – here.*'

'Not today.'

Alison was surprised to hear the iron in her voice. She was deserting him. Betraying him. Ross was already at the door.

'Tomorrow. I'll be ready tomorrow. I don't have much to pack.'

'We'll have to see about that,' Bobbie said. She was talking to him like a child. Without his noticing it, she popped the pill into his mouth. She handed him the glass of water.

He drank, his eyes, enormous, looking over the glass at his children.

Who were deserting him.

When Bobbie took the glass away, both Ross and Alison were at the door.

'Ross, your sister is going to get me out of here.'

'Yes, Dad,' Ross lied, as usual.

12

I had suffered enough. I had gone through enough. I had paid my dues. I knew I'd never be loved as Alison would be. But where was the news in that?

As we walked away, neither of us risked speaking. We just wanted to get away — echoing, I guess, the primal rush of all living beings approaching the smell of death. But I was more overwrought than this. I wanted to talk to Alison. I thought of that period after Hazeldean had told me all that stuff about Dad. I'd gone off on a jag, learning everything I could. Desperately. I wanted to know this man who seemed to be disappearing before my very eyes. We had our lifetime's silence between us. I wanted to catch up. While I still could. So I read all the books I could lay my hands on.

It was a strange education. I found myself weeping, weeping all the time as I read. The tears just coursed down my cheeks. It wasn't so much the horror of what I was reading – though there was that. It was the fact I hadn't known. I had chosen not to know. I had been arrogant. I had been proud. I had marched against the Bomb, luxuriating in all the horrors of bodies burnt by the nuclear blast. I had turned my face away from everything that had happened to Dad. No wonder we'd never worked out a way to be. Until it was almost too late. Or was too late.

As this afternoon in the hospital proved.

But it still hurt. It still rankled that he loved Alison more than me. I admit this.

So you ask me why I never told Alison I knew a lot more about Dad's past than I let on. You ask?

I'd got used to presenting myself as an idiot in Alison's eyes. I knew how she saw me. I felt the breath of her contempt on my back every time I turned away. She was successful, no matter how you looked at it. I had no career. I had a partner, it was true, whereas she was lonely as fuck. But every time I talked to Alison I reverted to the way we'd always been. I was the stupid hopeless younger brother.

It became my camouflage. Or, if you like, the end result of a life of chronic low self-esteem. I couldn't help seeing myself as Dad saw me – this man whose approval I secretly wanted more than anything in the world. It was the same with Alison. I wanted her to say she thought I was okay.

At the same time I knew she never would. Like Dad, she'd rather die than say it.

Strange how long the reach of childhood is.

The fact is certain plants grow best in the shade. I had cultivated secrecy as a survival art in my childhood. It was difficult, as an adult, to know when to let it go. I lost myself in research. Call it a distracting activity. It kept me alive.

I went online. I turned to libraries where, unread, there were faintly soiled books on prison camps and torture. So many of them. I looked around at the happy-faced Asian students: eager to create a future as far away as possible from that dark labyrinth. I entered the labyrinth. I went in search of Dad. I wanted to know that secret being: the man who could love.

Yet on the evidence of that afternoon, the chances were slight. There was a gleeful destructiveness in Dad's behaviour.

'Jesus wept. It was tough in there.'

I glanced at Ross. We were in my car. He left an *I-told-you-so* silence for me to appreciate but terminated it by saying, 'The old bastard sure knows how to manipulate.'

I laughed. It felt good to laugh.

'With the bedpan at his feet. Like King bloody Canute.'

'If he could have got to his belt he would have wielded it.'

I was busy indicating right. I turned into a more major road. I didn't immediately respond.

'So where in this hell-forsaken burg do we find a reasonable place to have lunch?'

I didn't want to be on my own. I couldn't have borne it.

'Oh really? You want to?'

Ross showed a touching disbelief that I might want to spend time in his company.

But he was unsettled too, I could see. He needed me just as much as I needed him. He was unhappy.

We were learning awkward things, like how to be a

brother and sister again. As adults.

'You were going to show me the sights.' I said, consciously trying to lighten the atmosphere. I didn't really care the direction we went in.

'Is that okay? Can you spare the time?'

'Well . . .' He hadn't had time even to put his seatbelt on.

I was always a fast mover when I wanted to be.

'Yes, sure, sis. I'd love it.'

The remains of lunch were being taken away. I toyed with my water glass while Ross helped himself to another glass of Oyster Bay Sauvignon Blanc.

For a moment we relaxed into the delinquency of people evading time. It was a pretty, sunny afternoon and something dormant within me stretched. Perhaps, looking around the café – overcrowded, noisy – I comprehended I could have been anywhere. Or was it that I understood, with the force of a tumultuous argument, this was no longer the Auckland of my childhood? That persistent greyness of vision had evaporated to be replaced by this eager over-consumption, this hunger for pleasure. Nearly all the women, I saw, were blonde and over-made-up – but this was no different from London. What was different was a kind of note – an unheard musical note – which was a frankness about pleasure. Poor darlings, so naïve.

But nice to drop in on, for a moment. Especially to escape that vision: Dad with his head thrown back. Those gaping jaws.

'I'll risk a glass of wine, thanks.'

Ross poured – too full a glass, naturally. I sipped. It was surprisingly good.

'What shall we do about Dad?'

Both of us had deliberately left it till the end of the lunch to approach the thorny question.

'What can we do?'

I noticed Ross wasn't paying attention. He was looking very directly over my left shoulder. I glanced around quickly and saw a once-handsome man, like a league footballer run to seed. He was sun-tanned and reckless with alcohol. He was sitting, his fingers entwined with those of a woman miles too young to be his wife.

'Are you not telling me something, Ross?' I said.

He jumped. 'What?'

'Him. Do you *know* him?'

I indicated the bloke.

Ross blushed and mumbled, 'I wish.'

It felt good to be doing dish together. I wanted to prove I could connect.

'I don't trust that woman who came around sniffing for trouble.'

'Anne Donaldson?' Ross shrugged. 'A woman who does the dishes at parties can't be all bad.'

'But what about this case she wants to know about?'

Ross looked into my eyes.

I blinked and looked down. I played with the napkin, pleating and unpleating it.

'I'm terrified she'll try and get in and see Dad in the home. He's in such a weird state anything could happen.'

Ross opened his mouth and was about to speak. But I cut him off.

'We're not talking ordinary things here, Ross. Executions, massacres. It's explosive.'

I had lowered my voice, I wasn't sure why. In this

bright haven, what was the meaning, the precise weight, of such things as biological warfare, incinerating people alive? I found myself shivering.

'And all that stuff about Dad in that bio. Stuff I really didn't know about. I'm having trouble assimilating it all, Ross. I feel so . . . humiliated . . . I know so little about . . .'

I couldn't finish the sentence. To my horror, a tear rolled down my cheek.

Ross put his hand out. Touched mine. I left it there for a moment, then began to feel its meaty weight. I hated it. Pretending I needed another glass of wine − or did I? − I reached over for the bottle. It was empty.

Ross asked the waitress for another.

'A glass will do.'

'You're driving. I've got the afternoon off − I can have another glass or three.' He settled back. 'We can go up to look at Mickey Savage, maybe tool round Parasite Drive.'

I squirmed to hear his old lefty phrases. But I needed him, I realised.

'Well, Dad was hardly a person for telling us things,' Ross said. 'He made a virtue of silence.'

I wanted to say that holding things in had its point. But Ross was looking at me with that strange manner of his, dying to spill the beans. About what?

'What do you know about Unit 731?'

He blinked.

'It's something that has come up quite recently,' he said, blushing. 'I guess with 9/11. Anthrax makes a come-back.'

The waitress had returned with a bottle, uncapped, in the fraction of a second. Smilingly she poured.

'A lovely afternoon, isn't it? Dessert?'

I waited till she fucked off.

'It's clear Anne Donaldson is sniffing round that Six Mile Road Incident. Hazeldean seems to be interested in it too.'

To my immense annoyance, Ross shrugged. 'What can we do exactly?'

'Protect Dad.'

'I'm trying to, Alison. That's what I've been trying to do all along.'

I took the stroke but pushed on. 'You know I told you about the documents I've been getting?'

'Yes.'

'Parts of documents or the whole. But the latest one was different. I noticed the address wasn't handwritten for a start. All the others were. This one was typed out.' I searched for words. 'It was some strange kind of novel. With Dad as the central character, Ross.'

He blinked again and glanced behind my shoulder to the rugby player. My gormless brother was cruising when I wanted to talk turkey.

'What sort of character was he?'

I thought for a moment. 'Haunted, I'd guess you'd say. It was when he was in Tokyo. It seemed to hint – well, it was pretty explicit – that he had another whole life.' I looked down. I was uncertain how much I could trust Ross – how much I wanted to. 'It had the strangest title.'

Ross said nothing but watched me carefully.

'Lucky Bastard.'

His face flooded with blood. It was the wine. He opened his mouth, a little like someone drowning. But I got in first.

'Well, it's only fiction, Ross. Something made up. Why should we bother taking something untrue seriously?'

It was really time for us to go.

But we lingered on this neutral ground.

'Ross,' I said, carefully rinsing my tongue, no more, in the glass of wine. I placed it down, consciously, a distance away from me. 'Can I ask you something about – well, bisexuality.'

He raised his eyebrows. 'Yeah, check him out.'

I raised my eyebrows in turn.

Ross made a facial gesture to two tables over. At the man I'd noticed earlier. He was listening to the woman who was talking to him in a heart-to-heart way, her head down, fingers tracing a pattern on the table. But even as she talked his eyes lifted for a moment and checked out Ross. There was a frank stab of desire there.

'He's bifocal.'

'Oh God,' I laughed, or was it sniggered? It sounded horribly like the latter, and I felt a little dirty, aged about thirteen. I sat up straighter. Was I pissed?

'Can you . . . tell me . . . something about it?'

'Well,' said Ross, laughing at me. I coloured. 'There's a view that there's no such thing as a bisexual. Or, alternatively, we're all a little bisexual ourselves –'

I made an impatient gesture with my hand, wiping crumbs off the table on to the floor.

The waitress was back, like an evil accomplice, filling our glasses to max.

I put my hand over my glass quickly. 'No thanks,' I said, my voice a little too crisp.

Ross breathed out and murmured. 'He's on his way

to the loo. Significant look to me as he goes. What's the betting he's in there waiting for me?'

'And –?'

Ross shrugged. 'A bit of frottage . . . a mutual display . . . maybe exchange of phone numbers for a later fuckn'suck sesh.'

'I don't want details,' I said with distaste.

Ross sighed. I was surprised at the depth of his sigh. He was perhaps more exhausted than I thought.

The visit to the home had taken it out of him too.

'It's like this, Alison. I come into this restaurant with you and I'm read as heterosexual. Even if I'm as camp as a row of tents, I'm allowed to pass. But if I come in here with Gary, there'd be no hassle, nothing even remotely uncool or hostile. But you feel – inside yourself, you feel this little blip. This resistance. You're read instantly in a certain way, and you have to live with all the possibilities of that reading – obscene, hostile, cartoonish, absurd. You have to wear it. Think of how much more convenient it is to just . . . pass all the time. You can marry, have children – grandchildren. You still pursue cock on the side.'

I blinked. Left a thoughtful silence.

'Why?' Ross asked. 'Are you thinking you might . . .'

I looked at him aghast.

'No,' I said, conscious of the indignant note in my voice and how this betrayed me.

Ross whinnied away with his stupid laugh. He laughed and laughed and laughed.

'You don't think Dad ever –?'

'Whatever made you think that?'

The wine went down the wrong way and Ross started coughing loudly, his face red. People at the next table paused, then smiled companionably.

'Shall I pound your back?'

'No. No,' he said, reaching for the glass of water I proffered. He drank it in silence. His colour slowly returned to normal.

'I'm sorry,' I said, signalling for the bill. 'It's too ridiculous.'

'All sorts of things happen in war,' Ross said. 'I don't think we can understand what happens . . . when people are facing – well – death. I think all sorts of barriers go down.'

I paused. 'But why would he always be on your case?'

Ross shrugged. 'Who knows. He probably hated himself. It's not unusual,' he said wryly.

I comprehended suddenly how Ross might have lived with self-hate. But then, I understood, so had I. It wasn't difficult, after all. Dad had been pretty expert in passing on his low self-esteem to us. Turning us against each other.

We could all do with a little kindness, I guess, though I winced inwardly at the concept.

I paid the bill with my credit card, computing dollars into pounds. And experienced the satisfaction of all returned sons and daughters: a first-rate cheap lunch.

On the way home I couldn't stop myself. Or else it was the wine.

'What happened to that box, Ross?'

'What box?'

'You know the one. The garage.'

He looked at me swiftly. 'Oh.'

You stupid little clot, I thought. You've been on the ground all these years and you didn't keep track of the one thing Dad thought was sacred.

But his eyes said something as harsh back to me: you've been living overseas all these years, happy not to do the hard yakker. Who are you to make a point?

It was curious how quickly our animosity could be reanimated.

But I was beginning to understand how Dad had set both of us up. To fight. Even distrust each other.

'There was no box by the time I came to take Dad to the home.' Ross sighed — it could have been with defeat. He looked out the side window for a long moment. He seemed to harbour a grudge. And the odd thing was — I didn't blame him either.

'What happened to it, d'you think?' My voice was carefully neutral this time.

'Dunno,' Ross said, looking a little guilty. 'You know, by the time I realised he was so bad it turned out he'd been giving things away. Lucky he gave Mum his war medals really. Otherwise they'd have gone the same way.'

I looked at him, shocked. But what would I have done with them? Framed them? Juliette wouldn't want them. Or she'd want them for smack to go up her arm.

'As for the box, there was no sign of that.'

We drove on through the changed landscape of our childhood.

'What do you think happened to it after Kiwitea Street?'

'I did find a tag for a luggage repository,' Ross said, looking ahead. 'But when I got there they said the payments hadn't been kept up.'

'*And?*'

'I asked what had happened to the stuff. They sent it off to George Walkers. The auctioneers. I rang them.

They said their records only went back five years. I tried to describe it but the man said, "Mate, we have over three hundred lots in a weekly auction, you're asking me to identify a box. What was in it?"'

'What did you say?'

'Documents, I said. "Things my father brought back – Dad was a war crimes investigator in Tokyo – "

'"Japs eh?" the bloke said. "Right nasty cunts from what I heard. Pardon my French. Well," he said, "it all depends if someone sat down and read them. Most people have a small attention span – hate to tell you this, mate. If something came up, maybe it got sold on. Otherwise, sorry, mate. Can't help you. Probably went out to the tip."'

Neither of us said anything for a long moment.

'But you remember what was in the box, don't you, Ross?'

He looked at me. 'How could I forget? I had nightmares about it every fucking night for about three years.'

'So did I.'

He looked impressed. I was at the confessional.

'I didn't know that.'

'There are lots of things you don't know about me, Ross,' I said a little too smugly.

As Ross got out of the car he suddenly leaned back in and said to me, his face flushed with wine, 'You know that novel thing you mentioned?'

I gunned the motor. I wanted to clear my head. Go for a long run. It had been a long – too long – afternoon. The fact was I disliked the treacly business of confession. Its self-absorption appalled me. How did anyone get ahead when they spent their life looking backward? It was the stance of losers.

'Give me non-fiction any day of the week,' I said. 'Stick to the facts is what I say.'

Ross's face had flushed an even more unpleasant colour. I wondered if he might have a bad heart. Or was his drinking even worse than I suspected it to be?

'Whatever.'

He slammed the door with more than necessary vehemence.

13

'Look this way, please.'

The make-up woman hovered, her brush an inch away from my eyes.

'It just knocks the shine off –' the brush tickled its way across my forehead.

'Cover me in make-up,' I lied. 'Just make me beautiful.'

Trish half smiled. She'd probably heard it all before.

Gary's and my sitting room had been dismantled. The big leather couch was pulled away from the wall. Someone was adjusting lights.

There was a scurf of dust underneath the couch. I could see a dead match. I felt an urge to go and get the Hoover, then thought, What the fuck. It's too late now. Relax.

The cameraman, wearing board shorts, Jandals and a faded Hawaiian shirt, was looking through the camera.

'Trish. Can you sit in?'

'Be one tick,' she murmured, concentrating on my nose.

'Oh, and sign this,' she said as she clicked shut her box. She placed down a piece of paper. 'Release form. You sign down there.'

I made an attempt to read the verbiage. But the print was too tiny and I didn't want to appear uncool. She had kindly supplied a pen, so I splurged a Hollywoodish signature of the kind a silent film star might make when he hoped to graduate to sound.

'Trish, raise your face and we'll get an eyeline.'

She looked over at me, winked.

'When's Madame arriving?'

'Due in five.'

'Okay everybody, let's move it along a bit. Madame doesn't like to be kept waiting.'

The director, a thoughtful-looking young man, picked up the release form as though he were tidying things away and handed it to Anne Donaldson.

I was pleased she was there. She'd already coached me through my questions.

I thought for a moment about Alison. She hadn't shown. She said if I wanted to go ahead and make a fool of myself on nationwide television, it was my business but I shouldn't forget I was representing Dad.

'Come on, Alison,' I'd said, 'it's a once-in-a-lifetime.'

She just looked at me as if I were mad.

We were by the lifts at the Hilton. I'd gone in to ask her if she'd be in the programme. We'd already let the doors judder shut twice.

'We have to stand up for Dad.'

'I don't trust the whole thing. It doesn't smell right.'

I looked at her, and felt a sense of disappointment.

'I'm doing it,' I said.

She stepped into the lift and looked back at me.

'Don't fuck it up, Ross.'

Her lack of confidence bit. 'Alison,' I said as the lift doors slid shut. 'Please?'

I waited in case she decided to come down.

She didn't.

Don't fuck it up, Ross.

Thanks Older Sister.

My front door opened and I heard high heels coming down the hall. Instinctively everybody in the room looked busy. It was as if a timeframe had been subtly sped up.

Rebecca Bright walked into the room, talking on her cellphone.

'I'm not interested in that. No. It's not our audience demographic. We need —'

Although she was smaller, much smaller than she seemed on screen, she radiated a kind of energy. She sat down in one of the armchairs and Trish stood by. Abruptly Rebecca nodded, indicating Trish could begin.

'Yeah. Find me a kid mums 'n' dads can relate to.' Rebecca laughed with a surprising belly laugh. 'Right. Not that little munchkin killer on P. Get rid of him.'

She clicked her phone off and raised her face. The make-up woman began her serious work, covering The Face in a strangely orange foundation.

'All right?' the director said to me. 'We're about two away. If you just stay there in position. Alan, lower the blonde a little, it's hitting the side of his cheek.'

Alan adjusted one of the light stands.

I was tingling all over. I felt like someone about to go on stage for the first time. I was acting as myself, but the make-up, the strange artifice of the camera crew, all made me feel I was in the theatre.

I had smelt the limelight.

I worried too about whether I'd recall my lines – Dad's war service, how he was when he came back. Even who I was seemed questionable. Anne had said there'd be other questions. 'Beccy likes to throw in a few curlies, to spice things up.'

She didn't say what they'd be.

'Ross. This is Rebecca Bright.'

'Don't stand up, don't stand up!'

She held her hand out: a small hand with expensive nails. Tanned. She was unnaturally tanned all over, like someone on a perpetual holiday. Her trademark streak, in the helmet of brunette hair, identified her as much as her lustrous eyes. Her head seemed too big for her body.

'Ross, isn't it? Thanks so much for speaking with us about your dad. Nervous?'

She didn't wait for a reply. Anne handed her the questions, which she studied, intently.

Lights were altered, sound levels taken, then she looked up brightly and, at the nod of the director, said, 'Okay folks. Let's roll.'

'Ross. That was fantastic. Can you just go again, but maybe boil it down to two sentences max?'

I blinked. But I was professional.

'I'll throw you the question again,' Rebecca said.

With the instantaneous intimacy of film crews she had

become my new best friend. 'You're doing beautifully by
the way.'

She altered her tone to one of caring-and-sharing.

'Ross, what are your memories of how your father was
after the war?'

'I was, well, he was . . . volatile, he flew off the handle
very easily. His nerves were bad.'

'And did he react in any way – to loud noises for
instance?'

'Oh. Right.'

I understood. I repeated the story of Dad hitting the
ground every time a car exhaust popped. Yet as I said it
something strange seemed to happen. It died on my
lips, became less and less true. In making it public, I was
losing ownership of it. Exclusive ownership. But wasn't
this 'sharing', 'letting go'? I couldn't escape a backbeat of
treachery.

Don't fuck it up, Ross.

Rebecca's eyes had enlarged in sympathy. She was
nodding, nodding.

'It must have been tough . . . on all of you.'

'We coped.'

I was aware my voice had become dredged in sentiment.
I felt tears mist over my eyes. A great, expectant hush fell in
the room. But I couldn't cry.

Was I stupid to feel that there was an abrupt drop into
disappointment? Rebecca even looked miffed.

'And your Dad. He weighed what when he came back
from Borneo?'

'Five –'

'No. Ross.' This was the director sounding just a little
bit tetchy. 'Sorry to break in, mate. Remember you start

each sentence with a statement.'

He waited for a nod from the soundman.

'Okay. Rolling.'

'Dad was five and a half stone when he came back from the Borneo prison camps.'

It was strange how artificial the taste was in my mouth. Even something certifiably true became inauthentic. What was I doing exactly? Trying to give Dad's side of the story, that's what.

'And how is your father now?'

'Dad's not too good, actually.' I heard my voice spark up into spontaneity. We were almost in the open. 'He's in a home. He has memory lapses, and his old wounds, you see, from the beatings he got in the camps, have come back to . . . haunt him.'

Haunt was not a word I'd normally use but it seemed right for the dramatic space we were in.

'Okay,' Rebecca said, her normal no-nonsense voice returning. 'I think we got that. Turn the lights off for a mo, let's have a breather.'

The lights pinged off round us. The room fled back into its normal colourings, which seemed dismal. Most of the crew went outside to the back veranda where Trish had set up a table with coffee, snacks. People rolled cigarettes and stood about, yakking about families, partners, last night's television.

I was pinioned to my sound thing. I wasn't sure if I could stand up.

Anne brought me a coffee. 'You're doing beautifully,' she told me. 'I hope it's not all too painful for you?'

'No,' I said, startled. I was about to ask, Why? Should it be? 'No. Well, I think it's important to speak up for men who were in Japanese prisoner-of-war camps.'

But I wasn't being honest.

Telling about Dad and the exhaust had not been painful. It had become frighteningly meaningless.

'There's not too much more,' Anne said, nodding to me as she got up and went to join the people outside.

'I s'pose this is all news to you?' Rebecca looked at me with an even gaze. 'That your father illegally removed documents from the Australian War Crimes Tribunal?'

Don't fuck it up, Ross.

'I'd never heard of it – until comparatively recently.'

I was aware my face was taut.

'You see, there's evidence your father took certain documents. Documents to do with war crimes . . .'

'Why would Dad –'

'I'm asking you.'

I said nothing.

The camera rolled on.

'There was a case, you see, a final case – right at the very end of the period when war crimes could be looked into.'

I just looked at her, aware I was sweating. For some unknown reason I began to feel guilty. Guilty by association.

'These papers relate to the execution of a Lieutenant-Colonel Sugihara.' The way she said execution slowed it all down so each syllable carried a weight.

I shook my head. The lights were piercing bright inside my skull. I felt the beginning pincer of a headache – tentative, a little incandescent worm feeling its way through the nerve-endings in my skull.

'You never saw these papers?'

'I don't know what happened to them.'

'So you did see them?'

'I'm saying if they did exist I don't know where they are today.'

I felt Alison close to me as I spoke.

'You know what Lieutenant-Colonel Sugihara was accused of?'

'A massacre.'

'He was accused — and found guilty — of the massacre of seventy-five Australian and other prisoners of war in the last days of the conflict. In Borneo.'

'I don't know any details about that.'

'The question is, Ross,' Rebecca Bright asked, 'did your father who, as you've told us suffered dreadfully in the Japanese prison camps, *deliberately* alter evidence in order to obtain the conviction of a man who may have been — *may have been* — innocent?'

'Rebecca, Dad never talked about anything like that.'

'He never talked about it!'

'No, he didn't. And he's not in a fit state any more to answer questions. I don't see your point.'

'My point, Ross, is this: an innocent man may have been sent to his death by your father as an act of revenge. Your father won a medal and has been praised as a hero. War is messy, we know that, but we have to fight through the murk of the past — to find the truth.' She left an eloquent silence for a moment, then turned straight to the camera. 'Never forget this, folks. *If there's a story, we'll find it!*'

'I understand that,' I said, furious. 'But maybe you —'

The cameraman took his head away from the camera.

'— maybe you should think of doing a programme on the psychological and physical after-effects of imprisonment by the Japanese on prisoners of war.'

'Oh we did that ages ago. Didn't we, Anne?'

Rebecca was taking her sound mike off. All around us other lights were pinging off. For a moment everything appeared dark.

'Yes,' Anne's voice replied, 'we did that years ago. That lovely old man – what was his name? We flew him to the Burma railway and he broke down and wept.'

'He popped his clogs soon after,' Rebecca said, handing her mike over. 'Rated through the roof, though.'

I was an outsider in my own house. I couldn't wait for them to go. It was like casual sex, post-orgasm. But Rebecca was doing the 'noddies'. I was sent out into the garden. Anne, who was beginning to seriously annoy me, talked to me about cuttings she wanted. Garden advice on the cheap. My headache was starting to blossom. To the rest of the crew I had become, briskly, invisible. The gaffer was on his mobile, arranging the shoot at the next location. The cameraman was arguing with his partner about who would pick up the kids from school.

I needed to go to the toilet desperately. But as I came to the doors of the sitting room the director held his hand up, stopping me from entering.

I stood there, waiting.

'And so your father was what weight when he came back from the war?'

Rebecca was repeating the questions, but this time with the camera on her. She spoke to a vacant space with deep empathy.

'Okay. Come through.'

When I came back from the loo she was sitting there,

performing a dumbshow of empathetic nods, amazed reactions, thoughtful facial expressions. Her final tic was more unusual: an expression of doubt.

14

'So what did she ask?'

We had arranged to meet down at the ferry buildings at four. We were halfway to Devonport – midsea.

'She asked me about that fucking box. I don't know why they want to know all about it.'

Alison said nothing, looked into the distance.

'What did you say?'

We exchanged looks.

'I said I didn't know anything. Or rather, if the papers did exist, I had no idea what happened to them.'

We were silent a while.

'Well,' Alison said slowly, 'I can't see the point in us talking about them. The box has disappeared. They were Dad's papers. They were his business.'

'But don't you think it weird that someone's obviously got them? And keeps sending them to you?

'I find it odd that it's to me they're sent. Not you.'

'Maybe if it was sent to the tip, someone did get hold of it?'

I looked back at Auckland: from the water it took on a lying enchantment – it looked like a city.

'But why me, Ross? Why me? Who knows my address? And, what's even weirder, knows that I'm here?'

I shrugged.

A container ship was going out to sea, and behind it rose the vivid expanse of Rangitoto Island. Its darkness, at that second, seemed comforting, a giant sock of bush covering its form from tip to toe.

A place where no humans lived, so close to the city.

'We should go there one day. While you're here. It's worth it,' I said, knowing we never would.

'I'd like to.'

We were both thinking about the implications of the questions surrounding Dad. Had he held papers that might have explained the evidence that sent a man – possibly innocent – to his death? The issues were so enormous it was hard to know how to approach them.

I looked at Alison's profile. There was a small frown between her brows. She was holding up extraordinarily well physically, but today, the ordinariness of the day, the way she was plunged into thought, humanised her: we were both in our fifties, after all. She turned round and looked into my eyes for a moment.

'You remember what was in the papers?'

'I remember the insects eating into them . . . and some sort of massacre? Bodies burning?'

It seemed odd, out on the harbour, in the silvery light, talking of this. A toddler walked past, a mother running behind. Two German tourists sat against the wall, studying a map intently, ignoring the view.

'Should we fess up?'

We both looked at each other.

'Ross, I think I remember seeing the box. Later.'

'*Really*? Where?'

'In the shed at the back of Dr Saddler's place.'

The ferry arrived, braking with a spume of water and, with disorienting movement, drawing parallel to the wharf. People around us prepared to make a move. The Germans' backpacks whacked into me as they stood up, bent down to pick up plastic shopping bags and turned themselves to the exit. They nodded, smiled.

'*Entschuldige bitte.*'

'Saddler's?'

We were walking through the decay of an ugly terminal: it was like a bad mall.

'Remember Dad used to go there, to watch his mate building a boat?'

I nodded. I recalled the boredom of those visits. Men talking together about a boat. I sat in the car reading for as long as I could, burying myself under the skirts of Georgette Heyer. When I couldn't bear it any longer I'd go in. Dad and other men would be standing around, exchanging laconic comments in some sort of eviscerating short-hand.

Nobody was smart enough, or knowledgeable enough.

They knew it all.

Football, the war. Politics.

I hated interrupting them. There was always a moment of disquiet as they adjusted their sarcasm to take in the hopeless sissy Eric had for a son.

I never stayed there long.

In my mind's eye, though, I travelled around the shed – another male preserve. I saw an old pastel calendar of a beauty, red-cheeked, black-haired, saucily eyeing the viewer. The calendar, I remember, was April 1958. Nothing else stood out.

'I'm sure I saw it there, up near the rafters,' Alison was saying. 'It was an ordinary-enough-looking tea chest, except it had those stamps on it, and Dad's name.'

I recalled that Alison had played tennis with the Saddler daughter, Susan.

'Do you know what happened to Dr Saddler?' she asked.

I shrugged.

'He probably turned into a barbiturate. He sure gave Dad enough.'

'I went there today,' Alison said, suddenly confessional. 'I wanted to go out and have a look. Confirm in my mind that it was the place.'

'And?'

'It was empty. That is, they'd gone long ago. But the moment I saw the shed it came back. The box was up on the right-hand wall, just above the door when you came in. You didn't tend to notice it, because it was against the light. But one day Dad asked me out there and they all got lost in talk about the boat. I was standing there, doing homework. When I looked up, I saw it.'

'Did Dad see you –?'

'Don't think so. You know him. Once he goes off on a tangent it's goodbye Daddy.'

We were walking up the main street. I glanced over at the war memorial. I was looking at war memorials more these days, was struck by the fact there were so many of them. And if you looked at them in any detail, the number of names on them – the dead – was often staggering. What made it melancholy was that these statues were usually, probably necessarily, ignored by the living. They were invisible as that box had been to me.

We went into some second-hand bookshops, separating by silent consent. But we met, after a while, at the books on the Second World War. Alison was standing there, quietly yet intensely reading.

'I'll buy it,' she said, flicking the book's cover back to show me. *Prisoners of the Japanese.* 'I find it a little humiliating – how little I know.'

When we were on the boat back, after a lunch at the Esplanade, Alison asked me casually, 'So did they say when the show's going on TV?'

'It's going to air,' I said proudly, copying the lingo, 'next Sunday.'

15

As I came into the corridor I overheard a modern-day miracle. Dad talking.

'See, it was so hot the flesh just fell off you. No medicine. Hardly even salt. Once a bloke got the squitters, he was a goner. Like that.' Click of fingers.

Dad's voice was expansive and seemed to be luxuriating in detail. I paused. Who could he be talking to?

'I knew a bloke, his balls blew up to the size of a watermelon. Couldn't walk. Took him days to die. The worst of it was, you didn't take much notice. Fought for his bed things or plate. Sometimes we'd bet on how long it'd take. Mostly though we just sat. Sat there like we were fucking lizards.'

For a moment I imagined he was talking to Anne Donaldson. I was horrified. Or was the whole film crew in there?

'There was one chap in there used to be a chef for Queen Mary. The old tart back in London. He used to entertain us by describing all the meals. Go into real detail – so many asparagus, a sauce of this, so many quail. We'd lie there and picture it in our heads, and d'you know what? The strange thing was you could almost taste it. Till you woke up. And then it was worse. But we'd still egg him on. "Tell us about the dinner of two hundred dishes," we'd say. "Which one?" he'd say. We'd say, "You know. When the Czar came to visit." Or the blimming Kaiser and fifteen German princelings.'

I pushed the door back with the full impetus of ownership that comes from being family.

Bobbie was there. She was sponging his back. She looked up and smiled sunnily.

'Hello, matey,' she said. 'Your Dad's in a nattering mood today.'

Dad looked up at me through half-lowered lids.

'How'd you be, son?'

He seemed fully online.

'I'm okay, Dad. How are you?'

The exaggeration of his toothless mouth took on the shape not of tragedy but of a grin.

'I've got my wee girlie looking after me.'

Bobbie showed no sign of paying attention. She had that marvellous ability to concentrate on immediate care, which struck me at that moment as only one step away from saintly. I felt a warm rush of gratitude towards her.

'Told you,' she murmured to me, 'he'd settle into the new meds.'

'Dad?'

He was no longer looking at me. Bobbie had finished

sponging him and she was helping fit the awkward meccano of his lanky arms into his shirt. The wounds on his shoulders and neck. That strange lump on the back of his spine, like an island. I'd gone out of my way in the past not to look closely at Dad's body but, as with a lot of things now, I was paying more attention.

'You all right, son?'

'You seem chirpy today, Dad.'

'Why? Who said?'

Bobbie walked out past me, raising her eyebrows in a look which said, 'Good luck'.

'Dad –' I came closer to him and sat down on his bed. He looked at me, but with doubting eyes. 'Dad, you know the trials you –'

His eyes were darting. His old tongue came out and licked over his lips. He reached for the buzzer beside his bed and pressed it. He pressed it twice.

I stood up. I felt unquiet panic backed up by an eerie hilarity. The infantile and cruel within me wanted to poke at him and laugh.

Footsteps came down the corridor. It was Peka, a wardsmaid. She was big as a Sumo wrestler, with glossy black hair pulled into a roll on the top of her head. She looked from Dad to me, in arbitration.

'What you want? Why for you ringing me?'

Dad sat there, silent.

'You making me the pest.'

She straightened out the bed vehemently.

'I think we're okay, thanks Peka.'

She looked again, as if she had missed something – perhaps parental abuse. I felt a twinge of guilt.

'You good son for bad father.' She laughed merrily.

The size of her hands. She went forward and punched the pillows behind Dad into life. Dad, I noticed, cringed away from her. For one moment Peka's eyes caught mine.

Dad sat there, his head looking down, his hands shaking. I felt a spasm of empathy for him: he was gently shaking all over, his body subtly vibrating. He fled a look up at me, and I was taken aback to see his eyeballs pleading, his mouth ajar and his tongue darting out, again and again.

'What is it, Dad?'

He lowered his head and looked down. He stayed obstinately mute.

'You buzz me anytime you feel, Mr Eric,' Peka said, accompanying this with a laugh.

She left the door slightly ajar and I listened to the scuff of her shoes as they moved down the corridor. Dad seemed to be listening too. And as they died away, his hand came out and grabbed my own.

'Don't leave me, son. Take me home.' Then he said a word he'd never said to me in his whole life. '*Please.*'

I sat with him for a while, holding hands, thinking to myself with a sinking heart it was strange what life did to you.

When I felt the grip of his hand lessen, I waited a little, listening to his breathing: he had fallen into a light snooze. Every so often his throat caught, and he cleared it with a series of subterranean clicks and gasps. But when I finally slid my hand away his eyes opened immediately and he looked straight at me.

'I'm off now, Dad.'

He just looked at me. Then he mumbled in a low voice, but I couldn't hear what.

'Promise me, Ross.'

'Promise what?'

'*Promise.*'

I had no idea what he was talking about.

'Okay, Dad. I promise.'

16

A bandage is best pulled off fast. I had awoken and gone for my usual run. The morning was celestial. The light over the harbour was brilliant, rinsed in a purity that seemed to be Antarctic. The smallest tuft of a mist-like cloud lay horizontal on Rangitoto, as if placed there by a considerate master painter.

I ran my usual fifteen kilometres, then realised today was the day I could extend it. I ran up to Michael Joseph Savage Memorial, ran through the gardens and looked up the harbour.

I'd be going back soon.

I looked around me, my consciousness surging with adrenaline. It was beautiful, I had to admit it.

I began my run back to the hotel at the slower pace of a champion doing her lap of honour. Of course it all fell into squalor as I came back down Quay Street. I couldn't imagine what graft lay behind the hideous mess of McDonald's and crap apartments. It felt like Mexico.

I showered, dressed then grabbed the Sunday paper, which I'd not even glanced at when I went out running.

And you could say my life stopped.

There was a full-page advertisement for that night's *60 Seconds*. Its headline read 'Villain or Victim?' Below it was a photo of Dad as a handsome young man in uniform. It bled into a telephoto-lens snap of Dad in Arlington – confused, his hair standing up.

'We bring the story of a Case of Misjustice – the Case of the Hero Who Wasn't . . .'

I knew in that second I wasn't going home any time soon.

I had let Dad down nearly all my adult life. I knew in my heart – I could face it now I was thinking of making amends – I had turned away from him as soon as I could. But now I had to be the daughter he had always hoped I would be.

I had to live up to being 'Captain'.

I rang Ross.

A bandage is, as I said, best ripped off fast, so I blamed him. He had precipitated the whole thing. His stupid, stupid vanity. The vanity of an insecure ego.

He cut me off.

Touché.

Until now, I had cut him off – cut Dad off – so effectively it was perhaps time they returned the compliment.

I was not going home.

Home.

I was going to hang around. I would see Dad – and if necessary, my errant brother Ross – through.

A captain is the last to leave a sinking ship, I recall.

'Hello. Don't hang up. Listen. I know I spoke before in anger. I was angry. But listen to me. We have to hang together. We have to *be* together. What time is that show?'

As if I didn't know.

'Seven thirty,' Ross said.

'What are you doing today?'

'Ga and I –' how I hated that word, but I accepted now I'd have to get used to it – 'Ga and I were going to go over to Waiheke to a vineyard for a late lunch. '

'We have to go and see Dad.'

Ross said nothing.

'Have you rung Arlington?'

'No.'

'Shouldn't you?'

'They don't get Sunday papers. Only the *Herald* during the week.'

'That's not the point, Ross. I'll ring. We have to make sure nobody gets to Dad.'

Nobody gets to Dad. How strangely dramatic that sounded.

'What do you mean?'

'This is called a media event, Ross. It's open slather. Every crackpot radio station, every loser with a theory –'

'It doesn't say which home he's in.'

'That's never stopped the paranoid.'

'Okay then, I'll come and get you at the Hilton. We can go together.'

I didn't answer.

When I got downstairs, I felt a pulse of animosity

towards Gary, who was sitting in the driver's seat. I wanted to keep this private, inside the family.

Then I saw there was no point. It had broken all the bounds.

We drove in silence. At one point, while we waited for the lights to change to green, Ross's cellphone went. I jumped and realised how nervy I was.

'Hello?'

The lights changed to green but Gary stalled. He cursed, fumbled with the keys, someone behind us tooting loudly.

'No! No! No comment.'

'Who was that?'

'Newstalk ZB. "Is your father a war criminal?"'

Ross clicked his phone off.

'Also, "Where is he in hiding?"'

'Keep your fun-wig on!' Gary yelled to the car that had pulled out from behind us with a screech of rubber.

The driver, a young mother, gave us the middle finger.

I looked out the side window. Auckland had never looked more repellently ugly: a loose collection of factories set under a concrete sky.

'Fuck,' said Ross, though his voice was wan.

We pulled into Arlington. The car park was empty apart from a police car parked just to the right of the wheelchair access ramp. Its windows were wound down. Empty.

'Fuck,' said Ross again.

Inside two policemen were standing in the corridor by the reception desk. Mrs Stobbs was there. She was talking and looking distinctly worried. When she saw us, her face flickered: discomfort deepening into panic. But the look was quickly cancelled out by one of professional coping.

The two policemen – one beefy, with hairy forearms in shirt sleeves, the other younger, paler, slightly more eager – turned to glance at us.

Mrs Stobbs came down towards us. I noted she wore heels, even on a Sunday. Had she been called in from elsewhere?

'I'm sorry, I've got bad news.' She spoke to me rather than Ross.

Ross groaned. Gary slid his arm up on to his shoulder. I saw the policemen read the relationship.

'What?'

'Your father's missing.'

'What do you mean missing?'

'He's not in the laundry or the kitchen.'

Bobbie had come up behind Mrs Stobbs, puffing. She seemed genuinely worried.

'He was last seen at 2 a.m. Peka went into his room, checked he was okay. He appeared fast asleep. He'd been given his night meds.'

'Did you see him take them?' This was me, the inquisitor.

'He put his hand up to his mouth. When Bobbie came in this morning, his bed was empty.'

'He'll probably be somewhere close by – gone walkabout.' This was Bobbie, who seemed more in charge of the situation.

Mrs Stobbs fingered an earring nervously. 'I don't want the media . . .'

'He may have gone down to the local shop for sweets. Lots of them go down there. It's a magnet.'

The walkie-talkie on the shoulder of the younger cop

crackled into life. He suddenly looked alert. Perhaps it offered something more exciting than old folk gone walkabout.

The elder policeman said to Mrs Stobbs, 'When was the last sighting?'

The younger cop leaned forward.

'Boss, it's an armed assault.' There was eagerness in his voice.

'Sorry, we gotta go,' the elder man said. He put his notebook in his back pocket. 'Ring Central for follow-up.'

They walked quickly; then, their walkie-talkies bristling with info, began to run out the door.

Their car roared away, the wash of the flashing light coming in through the door. We listened to the siren as it rose up, then grew fainter.

We all looked at each other. It was hard to know what to do.

Bobbie shrugged.

'Can I offer you a cup of tea?' Mrs Stobbs said, directing a glance at Bobbie. 'I think I can set your mind at rest. This isn't, unfortunately, an unusual occurrence, and nine times out of ten they're found in surrounding streets. We call the police because it's the most efficient way of putting the word out. Please don't worry too much. The situation is completely under control.'

Gary and Ross were having an argument about which was the best way to get back to Ponsonby. We'd been cruising around the streets of Panmure for an hour or more. It seemed pointless as each fresh street, ugly as the next, seemed to offer the possibility of revealing Dad. Then we got lost. And now they were going at each other hammer and tongs, releasing all the pent-up emotion.

'You've turned down the wrong street. It's that way!'

'Listen, you two,' I said from the back seat.

The back seat. Me.

I leaned forward. 'There's no point —'

'You keep out of it!'

Ross didn't turn round but I read from the ruddiness of his neck how dire the situation was.

'I said. *Turn left.*'

Gary kept driving.

Nobody said a word, and suddenly there he was. Dad. Sitting on a bus seat. Drinking from a container wrapped in a brown paper bag. Gary accelerated, but as we got closer the person went from being Dad to not being Dad at all: it was a street person, nowhere near as old as Dad, but thin, desiccated, mumbling to himself in an endless stream of internal argument. For one second his eyes brushed past ours, but then he snapped off the connection angrily and raised the bottle to his lips. This was so eerie, so like Dad yet so unlike Dad, that it broke the mood in the car.

'Oh shit,' Ross said in an entirely different voice. 'I thought it was him.'

'Me too.'

'Do you think he knew about the thing on TV tonight?'

'How could he?'

Gary said, 'Let's go somewhere for coffee. There's no point us driving endlessly round here.'

He found the motorway entrance soon after, and we left the world of Panmure behind us. Gratefully.

Ga cooked us a quick and efficient evening meal. He and Alison chatted sporadically about kitchen equipment

– stoves, fridges, blenders. I was restless. I couldn't settle. We were all on tenterhooks about Dad. Ga had given the police and Arlington his cellphone number. At times I glanced at it, sitting on the divide by the bench. It looked so inanimate – dead. I wondered where Dad was. He'd gone walkabout before, but had been quickly located. He'd never gone during night or early morning. Had he heard about the television programme that night? Was I responsible?

It seemed strange that he was nowhere local. We'd even driven down to the boat ramp near a mangrove inlet, but the question that faced us – acres of mud while the tide was out – was too harsh.

'Do you think –?'

'Maybe not immediately –'

'We should tell the police –'

'I'm sure they're thinking –'

'Gary, I want the police to know what we're thinking. It's important. At least it is for me. And Alison.'

Silence.

We ate our dinner with the sparse hilarity which must accompany last rites. I supped too much wine. Ga, I noticed, didn't rise to get another bottle when the first bottle revealed itself as empty with remarkable speed. He pushed the bottle of Aquavit towards me with a glance.

Alison ate carefully, sparingly, her face distant. As if she were listening for the cellphone. I noticed how slowly she chewed each mouthful. Not like me, the bolter. I eyed the blank eye of the television. It reflected back, in its treacly depths, three middle-aged people having an awkward supper.

But then the door opened and down the hall came an unwanted presence: Banquo's ghost, or rather Jasper,

Gary's son. He stayed with us every third weekend. Jasper was six foot three, and sixteen. If his face could have had any expression he might have been handsome, but there was something inert, miserly and inward about the boy: he struggled to string together a sentence. He still couldn't drive and had to be ferried around door to door by parents. Or taxis. He only came alive before a game console: he lived for Xbox. We got Sky Sports for the weekends he stayed with us.

I could see Alison's eyes grow more intense as she looked at the easy kiss on the lips Gary exchanged with his son – I couldn't recall whether I'd told her Gary had been married, had a son. Withholding information was a family trait, I guess – a way of leverage or holding on to power. But the way she busied herself with her fork and napkin told me she was uncomfortable – very. I let her think Gary had a teenage sex slave on the side for another few seconds, then I introduced them.

'Alison, this is Jasper. Ga's son.'

Jasper raised his eyebrows to me by way of greeting.

We'd reached a plateau of subtle enmity disguised as neutral friendship. It might have been my relationship with Alison, in better circumstances. Yet a glance from her eyes, into mine – sharp, interrogative – told me she, just as I, did not welcome this witness at such a vulnerable hour.

'Jasper, shake Alison's hand.'

This was Ga trying to get the boy to act semi-human.

With a lumbering surliness that was quite touching, he held out his hand.

'Hey.'

17

They were sitting, in a blitzed, expectant silence, through a spume of ads.

Alison shifted her gaze to take in her brother.

Unexpectedly she felt a swoop of tenderness for him. In his excitement, the way he folded his body into itself, leg around leg, arms embracing his upper chest, he was so like the child she had known: about to get a prize – a booby prize, she felt certain.

The noisome cacophony of soap powder, its redemptive qualities, died away. There was a second's quiet. Alison felt her heartbeat lurch violently.

The well-known sound of a ticking clock . . .

Rebecca Bright, in the kabuki style of television, introduced herself, shifting her gaze from off screen till she – somewhat unnervingly – made eye contact with the viewer.

'Tonight,' she said in her pleasantly conversational voice, 'the story of a tot with Zellweger Syndrome who braved two years of invasive surgery to emerge –' a slight emotional pause – 'as a fully functioning child. We follow her bravery – her pain, and, yes, the tears which precede the triumph.'

A quick series of images, each one a winning cliché.

'*Also*: everybody collects something! Tonight we bring you the story of eighty-four-year-old Arthur Callendar, a West Coast character who collects stuffed possums – and dresses them up in ante-bellum ball gowns!'

'*But first –*' Rebecca Bright's voice settled into the timbre everyone recognised as 'doing business': the tone that unerringly allowed her to ask the first men with Aids exactly what it was like when their parents turned their backs on them; the raped women guided to describe the number and location of penetrations under the guise of exploring the full depths of victimhood. Bright could be guaranteed, as her byline said, to ask the questions you were afraid to ask.

'Tonight we bring you the story of a New Zealand *war hero*, a man who survived the *Japanese death camps* . . . a man who became the *judge* in his turn of the men who had held him *captive* . . .'

'That's not right,' said Alison.

'Shhhhh!' spat Ross.

'Children,' said Gary.

Jasper looked bemused.

Footage came on of Eric as an old man at the home.

Rebecca Bright's voice-over: 'Today he's a broken man. Suffering from memory loss, lonely and forgotten . . . Eric Keeling lives out his life in an institutional setting . . .'

Off-camera voice: 'Mr Keeling! Mr Keeling!'

Bobbie came out and led him indoors.

Zoom in to a blank window. A hand adjusts a curtain over a window.

Ross's voice came on: '. . . he's not too good . . . he's haunted.'

Bright's voice-over followed, as Ross's face faded into the screen.

'Today Eric Keeling's son tells us what it was like growing up with a father – who had been through the Japanese death camps.'

Ross groaned out loud and put his hands over his face. He felt his skin burning – he was blushing – but he still couldn't resist looking through his fingers.

Gary said, 'You look good, Sparkle.' He reached out and placed a hand, a warm steadying hand, on Ross's knee.

Alison pursed her lips.

Ross implored silence, deletion, as he listened to himself whittering on about his father's reaction to hearing a car backfire.

He betrayed his father. He knew it. He betrayed Alison. He betrayed his childhood.

He wanted to die.

He heard, as if in stereo, Alison let out a long low exhalation of breath through her teeth. She murmured, 'Fuck!' in a soft voice that, for some surreal reason, Ross thought might be how she'd sound during sex. It was all wrong – everything was wrong.

The camera crawled into his face, his identity. Like a worm it ate into him, consuming everything human about him but leaving behind this weird – lying – replica. It was identifiable as Ross by the chipped bottom tooth, the lines by the side of his lips. But these things went from being human defects into things more symbolic of his fallen state – his cravenness, his traducing of everything private and decent.

Yet Ross felt something contradictory. He realised another version of himself was being born on live television. He became the poignant, suffering and sensitive son. Son of the terrible father, the *abusive father*, as Rebecca Bright hurried to call Eric Keeling.

Alison could not bear to look at him. She kept her gaze manically on the screen. She blitzed out all the horror around her – her homosexual brother being comforted by his lover, the lout on the seat right beside her glugging away on his metal teat. Instead she felt the fury inside her concentrate, fume up. She wanted, needed, to listen to everything false and untrue being said about her father on television.

She'd sue the bastards if necessary.

A photo of their father came on, spruce in his uniform, when he signed up.

'Where did they get that?' she called out, outraged.

Ross put a hand over his face protectively.

Voice-over: 'This is how Eric Keeling looked when he signed up – a brave young Kiwi off to fight for his country . . .'

Then footage cut in of soldiers released from Japanese prisoner-of-war camps.

'But this is what he looked like when he came back . . .'

It was a shock to think of the prisoners as men, as Europeans. They were slaves, they were *untermenschen*, they were humans whose dignity had been stripped off them, and even this parade in front of the cameras was part of their shamelessness: the exhibition of their rickety limbs, distended stomachs, the obscenity of the small cloths covering their genitalia, their vacant eyes. It was as obscene as it was horrific.

Alison felt a spurt of anger.

'They're trying to say one of these men is Dad.'

The footage was slowed down.

Ross was sitting there, a hand half over his face. Immobile.

'Why do they look like that?' Jasper stirred and asked his father in a low voice.

'They've been starved in a prison camp,' Gary answered, as to a child of ten.

'Why?' Jasper whispered.

Ross stood up. 'Cunts,' he yelled at the television. 'Cunts!'

Jasper looked intrigued. What was happening in the room was more interesting than the spooky old horror film on TV.

'Sparkle. Calm down. It's –' Gary had stood up too.

'Shut up, the pair of you,' said Alison. 'We need to listen.'

Chastened, the two grown men sank down.

Jasper smirked to himself. Dad being pussy-whipped. Choice. What a ball-buster. But you wouldn't want to meet her on a dark and stormy night.

The ads came on.

Brother and sister did not risk eye contact. Ross reached over and found his glass was empty. He lumbered up and found a bottle of red in the cupboard.

'Not that!' Gary cried from the sofa. He jumped up. 'That's got to sit for at least five years.'

One of his fucking precious vintages. Ross hated Gary with a vicious jag of bile.

'Well, what then?!'

Gary thrust a cheaper bottle at him. 'Take this.'

'Thanks, *mate*.'

Alison heard Jasper whispering to Gary. 'What war was that?'

'Second World War,' Gary said.

Jasper awaited further information.

'More than twenty million people died.'

'Eeeew. *Gross*.'

60 Seconds came back on.

Shots of a paddy field, green and dank. A low, oppressively grey sky. Palms still in the heat. The camera drifted to the left and disclosed a track through the paddy field . . .

'It was on this lonely road,' a voice started up. The camera moved forward to show Rebecca Bright. She was wearing tropical clothing ('disaster casual') and her skin looked damp. As she spoke she waved away insects invisible to the camera.

'It was on this lonely road, in the late afternoon of Thursday 18 August 1945, that a local man was walking home . . . He came across a line of what looked like walking skeletons . . . many of them naked.'

(Double exposure of prisoner-of-war skeletons shuffling along in present-day jungle.)

'They were Australian prisoners of war. Guarding them were twenty-five Japanese, armed with bayonets and parangs, a kind of local slasher. If the prisoners were starving, by this time the Japanese were hungry too. There hadn't been a shipment of food or supplies for more than seven months. The Japanese airstrips had been bombed into oblivion. The war seemed over except the Japanese, isolated and still fighting hard, would not accept it.

'It had arrived at end-times. The Japanese had shot those prisoners too sick to be taken. The other prisoners of war they used as beasts of burden, carrying their supplies. They were heading for the hills.

'The local man noticed there were two Japanese officers. Their names were Lieutenant-Colonel Harimitsu Sugihara and Captain Hinokuma.

'The prisoners were squatting down, waiting, as were the Japanese guards.

'That afternoon, as it slid into darkness, our eyewitness was told to go home. He was told the road was blocked a quarter of a mile in both directions . . . but our eyewitness did not do that . . . he did something more human.

'He walked a certain distance, then he climbed a tree . . .'

The camera located a palm tree, zoomed up to the foliage, then lost focus. The light quickly advanced into gloom, then night . . .

Lighten and reveal interior. A large-screen television is playing in the background and there are various consumer items placed around. But the room is poor. The door is a cavern of blistering light; small children, semi-naked and with protuberant stomachs, stand by the door jamb, looking in. Beyond can be seen puddles, mud, chickens and wet washing.

Rebecca says in voice-over: 'The name of our eyewitness was Ng Lim Koo . . .'

A brief shot of a photo of Ng Lim Koo as a young man.

Rebecca: '. . . This is his son, Ng Lo Hing.'

He is a man in his fifties. He shows a marked similarity in his features, but he is plumper. He is sweating, though by no means uncomfortable. He looks directly into the lens for a long moment.

Voice off, Rebecca: 'What did your father see that long-ago afternoon as it darkened down to night?'

'He saw nothing. He had climbed the tree. The field was full of long grass. But after a while he saw all. Everyone sitting in silence. Then one prisoner, young man, Australian, make a run for it.'

'What happened then?'

'He was shot in back.'

He looks into the camera, no expression on his face but clearly waiting or thinking something through.

Rebecca: 'And what happened next?'

'The prisoners were killed.'

'How?'

'Some were shot. Some bayoneted to death. Others hacked to death by parang.' The man shrugged. 'My father also see heads cut off.' Here he did a swiping, beheading gesture and made a whisssshing sound.

'Nobody tried to escape?'

'No. They all stand up and die in relay. Go to death in silence.'

The camera just hangs on the man's face as he looks into the lens. An elongated moment of silence . . .

'So nobody fought or cried out or tried to run away?'

'No.'

'And then?'

The man shrugs; this movement is instinctual, a kind of shrugging off of horror.

'He waited up tree, too frighten to come down. He see in distance a fire. Much drunkenness. He would never tell me what happen next.'

'He never told you?'

'No.'

The man looks sad. He glances down.

'Bad time,' he says. 'Much unhappiness. For all.'

'Did he see or hear who gave the order for execution?'

Lo Hing looks as if he is thinking, though there is a momentary sense of disbelief that he is being asked the question. He shrugs. 'I was not there that day.'

'Did your father go back to the field later?'

He looks down and is silent a long moment. 'Bad things happen. Things everywhere.'

'What kind of things?'

Lo Hing moves and reveals in his hand a pair of spectacles. They are old-fashioned round glasses. One of the lenses is fractured but still holding together. He holds them up to the camera, as evidence.

His face is unsettled, deeply ambivalent but proud to be holding something that is historic.

The camera zooms in to the cracked lens which, for a moment, vibrates, catches the light, dances like a thread of fire.

We fade out to black.

Iris up on words that read: 'To the World he was Just One. To us, All the World.'

It is a tombstone. The words are cast in bronze.

1821793 L.Bdr.

E.J. Keller

Royal Australian Artillery

18 August 1945

Age 19

Greatly missed by Mum, Dad, Sid, Ruby, Gran
and his beloved fiancée Gladys.

A flower trembles in the light.

The shot widens out and discloses one hundred graves, one thousand graves, two thousand . . .

Rebecca Bright stands there.

'This is the grave of one of the brave young Aussie boys killed on that lonely road as the day fell into darkness. Ted Keller was just nineteen. Nobody knows if these are his bones in the grave. You see, animals from the jungle have no respect for soldiers dying bravely in the defence of their country . . . In the last days of a war most of us in time will forget . . . The animals of the jungle drag the bones away . . . the bones themselves disappear . . . but the pain remains . . .'

Rebecca is serious, tense. She looks into the camera for a long moment.

'Eric Keeling thought he found the man responsible for this horrible *atrocity*.' She gave the word atrocity a special emotional punch. 'Eric Keeling, war crime investigator, thought he had traced the man who gave the order to kill. But did he?'

Cut to Associate Professor Hazeldean. He is sitting in a book-lined study, wearing the tweed jacket and tie he wore to his talk at the museum. He's talking at speed and a sense of adrenalised enjoyment emerges from his mastery of his subject.

'The complication was there were two officers present that day. Lieutenant-Colonel Sugihara and Captain Hinokuma. By right, Sugihara was the more senior officer. But by this time cracks had developed in discipline, as well as in overall approaches to what was clearly becoming the end-game of the war.

'There is some evidence to suggest that the two officers argued about what to do. There is a possibility that Captain Hinokuma decided to go ahead with the execution despite what Sugihara thought. Our problem is this: when Captain Keeling left Tokyo he took a certain number of documents with him. Without these documents we may never know who gave the order for the massacre.'

Hazeldean shifts in his chair, takes off his glasses and looks into the camera.

'Butchery is inseparable from war, particularly the end-game of wars when acts of retribution swing into force. We enter a world without morality – one very close to insanity. Possibly the Japanese officers thought it wise to kill all possible witnesses. Probably none of the men present that day thought they would ever face any questioning about what went on in an obscure field off a road which was hardly even on a map. But after the war, Captain Keeling – himself tortured by the Japanese in Borneo – came to look at this very case. Payback time, you might think.'

A shot of Rebecca Bright nodding thoughtfully.

'By this time, though, there was a problem. A big problem. The Cold War was happening by the late 1940s. The Soviet Union and China were the new enemies. The

Americans were desperate to have the Japanese as friends. Not enemies. The word had come down the wire that all prosecution of Japanese war criminals must cease. It was Keeling's last chance to get a prosecution.'

Rebecca Bright: 'So what happened?'

'Hinokuma had vanished into the Japanese underground by this time. He couldn't be found. However, Sugihara was found. He was in a prison in Singapore. It looks like Keeling "found" Japanese eyewitnesses present at the massacre who said Sugihara, not Hinokuma, gave the order to execute. Strangely enough, all their reports are so remarkably similar in detail they look like they've been written by the one hand.'

Rebecca: 'And whose hand would that be?'

Hazeldean: 'I think it's obvious, isn't it?'

Shot of Rebecca Bright waiting for a response.

'Captain Eric Keeling, DSO.'

Rebecca Bright is back standing in the killing field. It is now in early darkness and a strange, flickering light is on her face.

Rebecca Bright: 'It's an open question to this day whether Eric Keeling, suffering painful memories of his own victimisation, set Sugihara up. What we do know . . .'

A trap door springs open.

A weighted body falls.

'Lieutenant-Colonel Sugihara was hanged by the neck like a common criminal. He was found guilty of the execution of seventy-five prisoners of war, even though he denied it to the end. He left behind him a wife and three small children.'

As the camera moves back . . . from the body, which

jerks, twirls, then falls still . . . a photo fades up of a Japanese family from before the war. A keen-looking professional soldier in martial uniform, a wife in kimono, smiling slightly, with two small boys in shorts by her feet. A little girl holds a doll. It is a studio portrait and they all look immaculate, prosperous and confident of their future.

Zoom in to children's faces.

'They will never know whether their father was a criminal or an innocent man . . . set up by an investigator over-eager to get a conviction. A real case, one might think, of victor's justice.'

The camera cuts to Ross.

He looks shifty, uncomfortable, and there is a long pause.

Rebecca Bright in voice-over: 'When Keeling eventually resigned in disgust at the way the investigations were being curtailed, he departed – with a box full of documents. In this box was evidence which might show *once and for all* – whether Eric Keeling was a Kiwi war hero, or a war criminal himself . . .'

Cut to Rebecca Bright in Gary and Ross's living room.

'I s'pose this is all news to you?'

Ross: 'I'd never heard of it – until comparatively recently.'

The camera has crept up to Ross's face. The slightest twitch in an eye muscle seems to message guilt.

'You see, there's evidence your father took certain documents. Documents to do with war crimes . . .'

'Why would Dad –'

'I'm asking you.'

The camera has crept in ever closer. Sweat limns his face. He looks panicked, defensive.

'I know nothing about it.'

'You never saw these papers?'

'I don't know what happened to them.'

'So you did see them?

'I'm saying if they did exist I don't know where they are today.'

Obviously as guilty as hell.

'Rebecca, Dad never talked about it –'

'He never talked about it?'

'No, he didn't and he's not in a fit state any more to answer questions. I don't see your point.'

Now he's completely lost it.

'My point, Ross, is this: an innocent man may have been sent to his death by your father as an act of revenge. Your father won a medal and has been praised as a hero. War is messy, we know that, but we have to fight through the murk of the past – to find the truth.'

Rebecca Bright turns straight to the camera and looks down the barrel triumphantly.

'Just remember this, folks ... If there's a story, we'll find it.'

Tick tick tick ... tick.

18

None of us moved. Gary muted the sound. He got up, it seemed with conscious effort, and said, 'Well!'

Ross just said in a faint voice, 'Jesus wept.'

I couldn't look at him.

I watched Gary go and check his phone. He picked it up, peered at it and placed it down again. No message.

'I think we all deserve a good stiff drink.'

He leaned down into a cupboard that I saw was full of spirit bottles. Dishearteningly full. I had no intention of taking part in a wake.

'Oh Alison. How ghastly.' Ross stood up. 'I never thought —'

You never thought. The story of your fucking life.

'It made us seem —'

It was a time of unfinished sentences. I stood up myself. I felt if I didn't move I'd lock into position.

Jasper got up and drifted towards his father. Gave him a big hug. I felt a savage bleakness. *Juliette*.

I couldn't go there. Not now.

'I'm going to ring Arlington, see if there's any news.'

I stood up to use the landline.

Gary held out his mobile as I walked past – top shelf, minute, glinting with expense. I preferred the connection, at this moment, of phone to wall. Besides, I needed a moment of darkness.

I didn't turn the light on as I walked down the hall. I felt something raw, horrible within me. I had just seen my father humiliated. Life in one way or another, since the war, had been one long unrolling of humiliations for the poor old bastard. And now this, at the very end of his life, a cruel unmasking.

I needed time. I needed a lawyer. I wanted to ask whether we could sue for the filming of Dad unawares. No permission had been given. I didn't give a fuck, in a way, about the other issues. Those men were dead. Dad wasn't.

I leaned my head, my forehead, against the wall. The wall was pleasingly cool.

'I didn't look too bad, did I?'

Ross's voice, in the kitchen, was vulnerable. I felt myself flushing.

'I mean – I didn't look too haggard?'

They were canoodling. It was sick-making.

You looked like someone who betrayed his father.

I dialled through to Arlington. I got someone new who didn't know who I was. She refused to give any information about Dad. She said she had strict orders. When I tried to explain who I was, she left an unimpressed pause and said

I was the third person claiming to be his daughter that night.

I rang the police. This took quite some time.

Gary came down the hall, opening the door into my personal darkness. As if I'd left the lights off by mistake, he turned them on; then, seeing my startled look, he wound the dimmer back to a crepuscular softness. He left whisky for me: a small glass almost full. I lifted it to my lips but the smell discouraged me. Reminded me ironically of Dad.

A voice, male, came on and asked me what was the nature of my enquiry.

'Concerning the disappearance of Eric Keeling from the Arlington rest home.'

'Case number?'

There was a pause while he presumably checked a computer. I heard the click of keys.

'Nothing new,' he said, 'I'm sorry. We'll let you know as soon as we have anything. We have your contact details on record.'

'Thanks,' I said, and put down the phone. I felt a kind of dread. I looked at the door at the end of the hall, the light blooming against the glass.

I took my untouched scotch back down the hall and set it down, ostentatiously.

'I'm going out to Panmure,' I said. 'I'm going to look for Dad.'

My eyes never for one moment came near to Ross.

He had become invisible to me.

'I'm coming too.'

As soon as I said it, it reminded me of how it used to be when we were kids. Alison always that little bit older, more knowledgeable. Her disdain for me had resurfaced.

'I'd rather go on my own.'

I hated the way she wouldn't look at me. It was so wounding. I felt I had undressed on nationwide television – or rather that a manikin purporting to be me had come to volatile life on screen, had said certain things –

'Alison. You have to understand. The way that thing was edited.'

'You mean you never said it?'

She was already outside, waiting for a taxi. I could tell she regretted my picking her up earlier and bringing her to our place.

Gary offered, of course, to drive her back but she said, a curl on her lip, she preferred to make her own way. And the way her eyes went to me, then swerved away, indicated she thought Gary had his hands full looking after me. (Jasper, anyway, said his father had to drive him to his next destination.)

'Don't go, Alison,' I said to her. 'Please. I think we need –'

'I want to look for Dad,' she said, her words spaced apart by all that couldn't be said. She could have slapped me hard in the face.

'*You* wouldn't come forward and defend Dad.'

'You call that defending?'

'He can't speak for himself any more, Alison. I've been speaking for him all the time you were so fucking busy in London.'

'You always were a chatty Kathy, Ross.'

We hated each other genially then.

I wanted to answer her back: *You ice queen. No wonder your fucken daughter –*

But a beaten-up old Honda pulled up. A light clicked on inside and I saw an elderly African man, his face a mask of exhaustion. He glanced at us.

We both straightened.

'I want to come with you, Alison,' I said as I walked down the path behind her.

She didn't answer. She got in the back of the taxi. The driver looked over at her. It must have been towards the end of his working day.

I opened the door to the front passenger seat. Got in.

Gary called out, 'Ross, you need something warm to put on.'

I closed my door, furious.

Alison leaned forward and delivered little sharp punches to my shoulder.

'Get out! Get out!'

'I won't. I will not.'

The driver's look was cautious.

I sat there looking straight ahead.

'I'm not getting out.'

Gary ran down the path with a jersey.

It's not a polar mission I'm going on, my sluttish inner voice said. But fortunately I didn't speak out loud, because I felt numbly grateful. He leaned in, kissed me – hard – on the lips.

The driver suddenly looked wise. His eyes rose to the rear-vision mirror to check out the 'lady' in the back. She kicked the back of my seat hard.

'Fuck you, you little cunt.'

I put my seat belt on.

As the taxi took off, Gary made frantic 'ring me' actions with his fingers. Jasper stood there wolfing down some slices of bread, unconcerned.

We drove in spectral silence to the Hilton.

It gave me time to appreciate the extent of the disaster.

'What are we going to do?'

Alison had driven dangerously fast over the motorway to the Ellerslie-Panmure exit. Since it was Sunday night and 9.15 the lanes were relatively busy. I glanced inside each car, noting the little theatres of isolation, frenetic comedy, meditation, blankness and exhaustion. I never once turned my face to look at Alison's mask of scorn. She had not said a word to me since she swore.

She had let me into her car, or at least not physically fought to keep me out. I was an invisible space all around her. I didn't exist.

Since this wasn't so very different from how it had been when I was growing up, I fitted back within the carapace. I was, to some degree, merely at home. It isn't hard for a homosexual to feel at home with guilt. You could say, alongside effrontery and escape into the weightlessness of sex, it's a major musical motif. But it also pulled me back to some adolescent, pre-articulate state of self-pity. I loathed myself in an eviscerating way.

We coasted along the Ellerslie-Panmure Highway. It was the old southern exit from Auckland from when we were kids, but these days it had a ghostly, vaguely criminal silence. Every car seemed on the way to a tinny house.

'Alison. What are we going to do? Just drive round all night?'

She didn't answer for a long time, but kept driving slowly along the dreary back streets of Panmure. The sublunar lighting made everything both stark and tawdry. Most houses had a light on, indicating television. The few people out walking were all young, furtive. Their faces turned to look at our cruising car with suspicion.

'We should go and check out where Dad and Elsie lived.'

This broke something. Alison had to accept my directions and working in tandem softened the distance between us, or at least allowed me to talk.

We drew up before Dad and Elsie's little unit. A party was happening. The place had changed hands and everything about it was different: cars parked, some in a random way which seemed to indicate haste. People on the doorstep, glow of cigarettes. Reek of marijuana. No sign of Dad.

We tooled round outside till it began to look suspicious. Besides, a car like that – a BMW without mags and conspicuous bling – was such an unusual sight it begged a question as to the occupants. Neither of us was up to protecting ourselves against more than curiosity. When we sensed the shadowy figures outside the door were looking towards us, Alison released the clutch and took off.

As we drove away, I glimpsed the humped-up shape of Gringo the cat sitting vigilant on the next-door neighbour's letterbox, awaiting dawn.

We drove around an endless sequence of streets till it became apparent that in the whole ziggurat there was no sign of Dad. Neither of our mobiles went, though Gary texted me continually.

I had left the phone on silent, so it was only when I saw the glow I knew I had a message. It had the subliminal warmth of a heartbeat.

*R u Ok?/ Wen you cum hm?/I go to bed now/Gnight drlng
don worry too much he be ok.*

I answered him discreetly but it was impossible for
Alison not to get the message that, whereas she was on her
own – there was nobody to care whether she was up all
night or not – I had someone to whom I was connected on
a moment-by-moment basis. I caught her glance towards
me as I deleted Ga's last message.

The scorn which had made all her features rigid had
lessened over the evening. Seeing an all-night petrol
station, she swerved and drove in, got out and, seemingly
at the last moment, asked me if I wanted anything.

I asked for a Coke, no sugar.

I watched this intrepid figure negotiating the low-rent
atmos. Her car was a liability here. Several faces inside low-
slung cars dense with marijuana looked at us with disdain
melded into curiosity. I considered what I'd do if the
situation got difficult.

It was all ridiculous, out of control, surreal.

I felt as I had when I was teenager out late. Escaped into
the anarchy of the night-time world of New Zealand when
the demons come awake.

She came back, triumphantly, with low-sugar Coke
for me, some water for herself, and some salt and vinegar
crisps. This last was a humanising gesture. Surely a woman
who could run fifteen kilometres didn't stoop to comfort
food. Or did the fact she could run so far mean precisely
that she could afford cholesterol?

'I think we should check out the estuary,' she said to me
in an ordinary voice, or at least a voice no longer suffused
with anger.

She drove along, one hand on the steering wheel, while we sucked and chomped. The bag lay open between us. It was inevitable our hands would collide.

'Sorry,' I said, taking my hand away.

She put her hand in, took out a handful. Crammed them in her mouth. There was something touchingly teenage about this: no longer the cool, svelte Londoner.

'I'm sorry, Alison.'

She glanced at me. Sighed.

'It's a bit late, Ross, don't you think?'

I shrugged, put my hand in the bag. There weren't many crisps left and it suddenly became important to get my share. I took a generous grab. I watched her eyes register this.

'You toad.' She snatched out a handful, then I put my own hand in the moment she took hers out and grabbed the rest. I opened the packet upside down and ate all the crumbs.

'Yum yum yum,' I said.

We were back to being kids together.

She didn't say anything but found her way, miraculously, down the side streets to the estuary.

She always had a better sense of direction than me.

Ross and I sat there a long time, the car pointing its nose at the water. The tide was coming in slowly, you could see it. I had turned the engine off and we just sat there, like a couple who had come to some resolution not to argue. Or more like lovers who had reached a point of irreconcilable difference.

We got out after a while and walked round. I called out: 'Dad! Dad are you there? It's me, Alison. Dad?'

I heard the desolation in my voice. It was wretched. I walked down on to a clay bank, which fell away sharply. All around me the strange, surreptitious sounds of a tidal estuary by night: little prickings and pickings – crab sounds, creaking of mangroves, the distant thrum of car tyres on the motorway.

I called out again.

'Dad? Dad!'

Ross came and got me after a while.

'It's no use, June. No use. We might as well go home and wait. He's not here.'

I waited. I couldn't give in. He stood beside me. 'Alison?'

'Okay,' I said, for once accepting he was right.

But before I clicked on the car key, I hesitated. 'Ross,' I said, looking straight ahead, out to the perspective of a channel winding itself through mangroves. 'What do you honestly make of what they're saying about Dad?'

I turned to glance at him and his face looked odd. Softened with emotion. I looked away quickly. I thought, God, he's going to get sentimental on me. Just when reason is most required.

He sighed. 'I don't know. I just don't know at all. It could be possible.'

I clicked on the ignition, flicked on the lights. They must have been on full beam because they blasted out two columns of light, blue tinged, as if smoke were running through it. It cut the night in two and lit up, in ghostly shape, the contorted limbs on distant mangroves. The tide turned liquorice, glinting with malice.

I felt my skin tighten.

'I don't know what decisions Dad did or didn't

make with that trial they keep banging on about,' I said. 'But I don't think it's right for Dad to be called a "war criminal".'

I put the car into reverse and took my foot off the clutch. The car rocketed back. I grappled with the lights, turning them off forensic. They were lighting up a weatherboard house opposite as though we were a police sting.

'God, no!' Ross cried out. 'Even though he was an A-grade arsehole as a father. That doesn't mean the poor old cunt has to be insulted.'

I eased my foot away, and the car leapt forward.

'What do we do?'

This proposition – me asking younger brother – was so unusual, he seemed to be half grinning when I glanced at him.

'Fucked if I know.'

It was as we were driving along that I found myself saying to Ross in the kind of voice that intimated I'd made up my mind, 'Ross, I'm not going back to London immediately.'

He looked at me in blank silence. Then he let out a whistle, less like a tyre going down than a small firework of celebration.

19

Let this be my confession.

Everything I say here is true.

One day Dad took me into the garage at Kiwitea Street. I must have been round about eleven. Ross was going on nine.

Dad said to me, 'See this.'

It was the tea chest – an ordinary-enough-looking tea chest, except on its side there were some words stencilled in blue-black paint:

CPT E KEELING
2ND AUST. WAR CRIMES SECT.
SCAP

Dad had prised the top open with the claws of a hammer.

'I want you to look after this, Alison.'

I can't trust Ross, he might have been telling me.

'What's in it?' I asked.

'Documents which show what really happened,' he said. 'The war.'

This took me quite a while to comprehend.

It was dark in the garage.

He took another sip. He was drinking his home brew.

I waited. I was always a cool customer – or, rather, I found it was best to wait for other people to make remarks, mistakes.

'What do you mean?'

He didn't reply.

'Dad?'

'Well,' he said. 'It's like this, Captain. It got to the end of the war and terrible, terrible things had happened –' the way he said it froze me – 'I can't ever tell you – I don't want you ever to experience – but to *know* – we all have to *know*. Otherwise it all meant nothing – sweetfuckall –'

This was so unusual it arrested me.

'Can I look now?'

He wanted to say no. Instead he looked at me a long time and sighed, and then he said, 'You have to promise.'

'Promise what?'

'That when I'm gone –'

'Dad,' I said.

'No, lass,' he said, 'one day, I'll be gone. It's the law of nature.'

At the time it seemed a form of lunacy. He was probably only in his early forties.

'I have to rely on one of you two. I've told Ross already, but I wasn't too sure he was listening.'

'No,' I said, smiling (Dad grinned back), 'he's not the

listening type, is he, Dad?'

'Too bloody busy nattering,' said Dad. 'But you, I know you, lass, you're a chip off the old block.'

I blinked. I could feel tears, but I knew I mustn't. He hated emotions.

'Okay, Dad,' I said in as flat a voice as possible. 'Hit me with one.'

What he showed me that day was a strange document; I couldn't understand it. The smell of the paper was dank, as if recovered from the bottom of a creek. The look of it. And then the words.

```
              Keeling Capt
          Investigating Officer.
```

'That's me,' he said. 'I was asking one of those crooked bastards —'

I looked down the words.

'But he says he doesn't know —'

'They all said that. They disappeared into the fucking smoke.'

Then, seeing me there, he went red.

'Lass, you have to forgive me. I get carried away.'

I could see he didn't think he was being manly. His hands were shaking. The smell of beer was on his breath. I pitied him. But I had to be careful he couldn't see, scent, my pity.

'What do you want me to do with this, Dad? Hunt him down? I'd wring his neck with my bare hands if I could.'

Dad looked at me, then he smiled bleakly.

'Lass,' he said. 'There's been enough of that.' Then:

'It's not that I'm asking –'

I waited. And waited.

I saw his lips forming, but it was like the words wouldn't come out. I looked at his eyes. They were focused on something I couldn't see – something he was frightened of yet that also made him angry.

Then he took the paper off me and put it back in the tea chest and closed the lid.

When he turned around, he seemed surprised at finding me there.

'Go on,' he said to me, shooing me out. 'You scoot outside and play in the fresh air.'

Of course I was fascinated, horrified. I told Ross. All right, I boasted about what I'd seen. Kids are always looking to have the upper hand, it doesn't really matter what in.

I said to Ross, 'Dad showed me what's in the box.'

He looked kind of sick. He was a little short-sighted, and his hazel eyes made this strange sort of movement round our back yard. He always suspected me of knowing more than him, getting more of everything, which was right. The oldest always does. More hidings, more restrictions. It's given to the oldest to break the parents in.

'What . . . when did he?'

It was so easy to gull Ross. He always wanted to believe. I made it as ghoulish as possible. But my telling stilled me too. An aura of death drifted over our back yard. I felt myself grow serious and slow.

Ross didn't know whether to believe me. I could see him looking at me sideways.

'Yuck,' he said. 'That's horrible.'

'It's what our dad investigated,' I said, urgent to back

up Dad's credentials. His falling flat on his face with each car exhaust had withered his standing.

'Can I see too?'

'No.'

'Why not?'

'You're not old enough.'

This brought him to a stop. He looked at me craftily.

'But you looked.'

'Dad showed me. It was special.'

'I want to see,' Ross said flatly.

Then, raising his face in rebellion, so I looked down all across the flat disc of his face – freckles blanched, brownish lashes, blister by his chapped lips, a faint bubble blowing at the corner of his mouth – he said: 'I don't believe you. You made it all up. You seen it at the pictures.' He lowered his face then, smiling softly, convinced.

I pinched him hard, in that spot I'd worked on since age three. Right in under the ribs, at that nice piece of flesh by his waist. He skewered away from me, screamed.

Mum came out.

'What's going on?' she said. She was washing down the kitchen ceiling. Hair in an old camisole, sweating.

'Nothing,' I said blandly. 'Ross is just being silly.'

He swept a resentful look past me, then towards our mother.

But he knew he couldn't betray me. Otherwise I'd never show him our treasure.

'Why don't you both go up to the library and choose a new lot of books. Or there's that garden that needs weeding.'

We both simultaneously appeared busy.

Inside the shed we approached it as a mission. Pincering

towards it, on tiptoes. I enjoyed my self-importance. Ross was always a scaredy-cat, terrified by nightmares, dreams – all the things that aren't there. I was never frightened of anything – at least I never let on. I didn't want to lose face. Ross never cared. It was like he never had a face to lose.

We crept round the borders of the garage, all the time poised for a surprise entrance by Dad himself. He'd have had no compunction in strapping both of us. Me around the legs; Ross on the hand – occasionally, I have to admit it, on the body. Ross's muteness used to drive Dad into a frenzy. 'It's as if he's encouraging me,' I once heard Dad say later. When he was disgusted with himself. Looking down at his shaking hands. 'I had to do it, Olwyn,' he said to Mum. 'I have to make a man out of him.' Mum said nothing. Then, when Dad had calmed down, she'd say, 'But he's only a boy, Eric. He's only seven. Do you want to scar him for ever?' Dad answered back with a queer smile: 'It never hurt me.' At which Mum just looked at him, eloquently.

I later learnt the art of placing a comment when a man can hear it. I sometimes think this is the nature of marriage: knowing when a sentence can implode. Knowing when to keep silent. And also, as far as I am concerned, when to speak. When they can or will hear you. There is nothing as obstinate as a man who will not hear.

That afternoon we crept around. Almost screamed out when the tin roof pinged.

I shifted off the canvas, which smelled of summer holidays and grass.

'You stand watch,' I said.

I didn't want him to see how I opened the tea chest. I

wanted him only to know what I could tell. I pulled the lid off it, slid it aside and was immediately attacked by . . . guilt, I suppose. Dad had trusted me. I was older. Ross was a cry-baby. I didn't know what it might lead to. But also I wanted to lord it over my baby brother. I wanted to show him conclusively that it was me our father loved and trusted. That Ross would only ever know the world through me. He was my one-person gang, my underling.

But I almost jumped out of my skin when I felt a faint fan of air on my neck. It was Ross, standing right behind me.

'Stand back, you pig,' I said, giving him a push.

'I wanner see,' he whined. 'I gotta see, June.'

'Stand back over there, by the wall,' I said. 'I'll pass you something. And keep your eyes closed. Hold your hands out. If you peep once I'm not going to tell you what will happen to you.'

He did as he was told. I looked at him standing there. A skinny blind kid, his hands reaching out. I despised him.

'Keep your eyes closed!' I ordered.

His lashes stayed low.

I placed the snail I'd found on the side of the chest right in the soft pink of his palm. I watched as the snail unfurled itself, antennae wavering.

Ross's lids pricked open.

He dashed the snail hard against the wall. I watched it slide downwards, broken, slime oozing out, bubbling. I went over to it and picked up a piece of wood. I bashed the snail again and again.

'You Nip bastard,' I said. 'That'll teach you to be so cruel.'

I kept on hitting it for it so long I didn't notice Ross

was already in the box.

He was sitting there daintily, in his girlie way, a leg crossed over. Papers resting on his lap.

He didn't raise his head to look at me.

'I didn't say!' I yelled out. I wanted to hit him.

He glanced up at me, but as if he didn't quite see me.

'What you looking at?' I asked. I made to grab the page. But he easily shifted it away.

'Get your own,' he said.

I'd never known him so independent. He glanced at me once, a curious, adult look in his eyes, then lowered his head.

Ross was always good at reading out loud. He read out the piece which I remember to this day. The one Dad had shown me.

It was in a field somewhere – a paddy field. Six Mile Road.

Later we played our games. I was in two minds about which one to be. It seemed to me I should be one of the Australians being shot, then roasted. But I had no taste for victimhood, even then. I understood it was noble, and that your soul went straight to heaven. I even understood that our dad was going to get justice for you. But you were dead. You'd died horribly, shamefully.

It was much better suited to Ross, who always did a good dying swan. Besides, I enjoyed torturing him. Well, not torturing him exactly, but the odd rope burn didn't go amiss in making our games more real.

I poured the petrol on (cold water from our hose). He screamed like a girl. I grinned as I watered him all over. He was meant to be dead, anyway, but being Ross he managed to stay alive, to enjoy the pain more deeply. He groaned and moaned, his lids half open, begging me to finish him off. But it was my delight to imagine striking a match.

'BOOM!' I yelled as the flames flickered all over his body. I watched, between half-closed lids, as his flesh fell off, in flakes, straight from the bone. And it was me who ate him. He was tasty, that kid.

The only trouble was he sat beside me, feasting too. We let the fat ooze down our mouths, got it on our arms; we fought over the last juicy bit – the liver. It was our speciality. We'd read about it in Dad's box. We never ate liver at home, had no idea of what it tasted like. But we'd worked out that was the real treat.

Only when Mum came out and said, 'What's all the noise about?' in her when-will-the-school-holidays-end sort of voice did we look at her, startled to see another living human.

'It's nothing,' piped up Ross the quisling. 'We're just playing war games,' said he.

Our Mum looked at us, and then came down the steps and walked up the path, under the clothesline. Her shadow quivered, touched us.

'What war games are those?' she asked.

'Nothing,' I said quickly. 'Just something made up.'

She wasn't convinced.

'Look,' she said to me, 'you've got that nice cardy all covered in mud. Besides, look at you, Ross. You're all wet. It's winter, for heaven's sake. You're both acting like animals. Not children. Come inside. Ross, you go into the bathroom, clean yourself up. Get into something dry. Alison. I want a word with you.'

She ticked me off to a standstill. Once she found out I'd got into Dad's box she looked seriously worried.

'I have never seen what's in there,' she said to me. 'It's your father's private business.'

'He showed me.'

She looked startled then. 'Showed you what?'

'Something in there. It's nothing much,' I said, with the professional coolness of a child who knows nothing. 'Just old bits of paper. They stink. There's weevils in there, and paper mites eating them up.'

She looked at me sceptically.

'Old things to do with the war,' I said. 'You know. Dad, in Tokyo.'

She stood up. 'You must never –' she said. Then stopped.

'Never what?'

'What was that game you were playing?'

'Oh, just kids' stuff, to keep Ross entertained.'

'What kids' stuff?'

I felt embarrassed to be caught out.

'He's burning to death. I've shot him, then I set him on fire. He tries to drag himself away, see, he's only been shot through the leg, he's still alive, and he's trying to drag himself away . . .'

'Stop,' my mother cried, putting her hand out. She looked upset. I heard the tap in the bathroom stop. We had old plumbing in that house. She looked over at me in the silence, judging, I see now, whether it was better to let things pass, accept I saw with a child's eyes. If she made more of it, it might only register more deeply.

'But he's getting away, Mum. Don't you see it?' I cried. 'He's crawling away from the burning bodies. I see him, I bayonet him, stick it in good —' and here I made a mistake by acting out the enjoyable jab of the bayonet, the judder as it hits the flesh, the splintering of the bone — 'but he crawls away into the bushes, there's so many of them, Mum, all dying —'

'How many?' she asks, suddenly caught.

'Well at least seventy-five, according to the documents.'

She sat down. She was still.

'But don't you see, Mum,' I said, grabbing hold of her hands and trying to squeeze them so she'd see, 'that's the good thing, Dad'll catch the Nip bastards who are feasting —'

It was my use of bad language. She reached across and placed her cold hands on my forehead — her hands were always cold to the touch, even though soft and kind, and at this moment trembling.

'Darling,' she said to me, pulling me into her embrace. I fought her, I hated to be touched by her; I loathed, even then, the compromises of her life with Dad. 'Darling,' she said to me, 'don't use that word. Don't say those things. Don't think about it. It's all over now . . .'

Just then Ross came in, pink from the warm water in the bathroom. He liked walking round naked at that age. 'What's all over?' he asked, hating to miss out on anything.

'Go and put some clothes on immediately, young man,' Mum said to him. 'Aren't you cold?'

'I don't have anything to wear.'

When he'd left, Mum said to me, 'Don't ever let your father catch you. If he does, then there'll be real trouble.'

I knew she meant the strap.

Alison has forgotten. She had nightmares. She joined Dad in her caterwauling. I haven't forgotten that. Alison always wanted to make out she was the ultimate tomboy, but because I studied her in miniature, so to speak, I saw behind the mask. She wasn't even really brave, she just managed to pretend. I didn't understand then that pretending was half of what growing up was all about. Pretending not to feel things. Hiding feelings. She couldn't hide her nightmares.

They began about a week after our game. I can't date it too precisely. But I woke up and thought I was still alive, trying to get out from under all the other burning bodies. Instead it was Alison. She hated the nakedness of it. Mum got up, of course. Dad refused to do anything. 'Bloody kids,' he mumbled. As if he hadn't woken us in his own time. Alison felt mortified. She said she'd seen a man out the window. Mum believed her. There was a man looking in windows at that time.

So Mum got Dad up and forced him, in his dressing gown and torch, to walk around the outside of our house. The following day, Dad put screws on Alison's window, so it couldn't be opened from the outside. But in a way he was only locking her in. She woke every night from then on, at a quarter past three exactly. She was screaming and wetting the bed. It was one up for me, I thought. She caught me looking at her when Mum took out her bed sheets one morning. There was such a look of sour hate I felt taken aback. It had gone beyond a game. I felt oddly ashamed, for her.

And of myself, for seeing.

Mum never told Dad. I mean his responses were always so difficult to guess. I did overhear her once say to him, 'Why did you show Alison what was inside the box?' He denied it, but in that voice that had enough doubt in it for him to wonder whether, in a moment of lachrymose drunkenness, he might have.

'What's in that box anyway?' my mother asked.

They were sitting up late and my bedroom was right by the kitchen.

'Nothing to do with you,' he said.

'But it's in my house.'

'*Our* house,' he said.

'Our house.'

'It's not in *our* house, it's in the bloody garage,' he said, his voice slurred by drink.

I could sense my mother working out how safe it was to go further.

'But what is it? Why is it so top secret?'

'There are things you don't want to know,' he said.

It must have been frustrating for my mother. Besides, she knew if she pressed it any further he'd explode.

There were all sorts of things you couldn't ask or say or do.

A lot of them had to do with the box.

Within a week it had gone for ever.

20

I woke up in the dark, palpitating. There was that horrible lurch as I tried to work out where I was. The room, artfully darkened by double-strength curtains, returned no clues. I'd taken a tablet, an indulgence, no doubt – but I was taking no chances. I wanted to escape consciousness.

A tablet is necessary after an evening in hell.

I thought – this all happened in a flash – that I might be back in London, in my house. Then this certainty destabilised and I was uncertain of my actual age – I felt my skin, its looseness, the sliding weight of flesh – I'd returned for a second to the horror of being thirteen – trying to be brave as a way of not showing how shit-scared I was.

I fumbled round for the light switch, knocked something over: wet spread against me. My rational mind knew it was water – but, vividly, at that second, it was blood. Warm, sticky – staining.

I cried out. Felt, at last, with infinite relief, the little plastic shaft that flicked on the grand urn shape of the bedside lamp. All the luxury sped in around me. Pampered me with this version of my reality, of who I was, or might be pretending to be.

I felt miserable even as I laughed out loud at the ludicrous nature of my nightmare. It was my old nightmare from childhood, immaculately reintroduced after forty years.

I lay awake for a long time, not exactly thinking but taking courage from the fact there were curtains, a carpet, chairs and, on the bedside table, that strange story someone had sent to me.

I touched it contemplatively. In some strange way it comforted me. It helped me understand the enigma that was Dad.

Then I heard a delicate, very light tapping. I got up and went to the curtains. When I pulled them aside I saw it was raining. Dawn had come, and it was as if the sky were a piece of lunch paper and someone had taken a sharp pencil then drawn zigzags all over the dirty grey.

On the balcony something dripped monotonously. I shuddered to think where Dad was. I dropped the curtain back, returned to bed.

I was just drifting into a dream. The phone rang and I instantly came awake.

It was a male voice, a policeman.

'Is this Alison June Burton?'

'Yes.'

'This is Constable Renfrew of the Otahuhu Police Station. We'd like you to come down to the station.'

'Yes, of course. Have you found him?'

The smallest, most damaging pause.

'It's not good news, I'm afraid.'

I didn't know what to say, and what I said was stupid.

'Okay.'

Just that – flat, no hysterics, nothing. Business as usual. Some people might admire this, but to me, at that second, it seemed the dryness of a bankrupt soul.

'Okay,' I repeated it more thoughtfully.

'You can take your time.'

'I'd like to bring my brother. Is that okay?'

I seemed wedded to the banality – the safety? – of this word.

'Yep. That's okay, Mrs Burton,' the constable said, ringing off.

I got up. I was uncertain of the time. Out on the harbour the rain had set in. It was a dirty day. I watched a ferry lift up on a wave, crash down. The spume looked icy. I could hear voices down below. People running past.

It was 10.20 a.m. by the clock. I felt disoriented.

I rang through to Ross on his mobile. It was turned off. I rang through to his house. It was on answerphone. I felt a bleak implosion within.

Okay, I thought, I'll do all this myself.

I rang back to Ross's cell and left a message.

'Look Ross, it's bad news about Dad. I'm off to the Otahuhu Police Station. I'm not sure why, but it doesn't sound good. If you get this, call me.'

I went and showered. I intended to shower quickly, but in the end I felt there was no point in hurrying. Bad news waits. I took my time. I dressed with care. I blow-dried my hair. I looked at myself in the mirror.

So this, I thought, smoothing over my stomach, is what an orphan looks like. You are on your own now, kid. Finally.

But then I realised that's what I'd always been.

I had a hangover, a terrible nag of pain. Sometimes hangovers can seem like old friends, familiar as an argument you know every part of. But this one felt rough, abrupt. It hadn't been a good idea to switch to scotch from red wine.

Gary was still up – that is, he'd fallen asleep in front of the TV. I looked at him, his legs awkwardly astride, his ludicrously small dressing-gown coming to the top of his knees. It had fallen open and I gazed at his genitalia dispassionately. For some reason – perhaps my latent hysteria – I thought of Dad's cock: a strange thing, I admit, to think about at such a moment. Cocks all have their individuality and perhaps it is only a homosexual who can hymn the minute differences in texture, volume, shape, elasticity. Gary's cock was comfortably thick, as was my father's. I can still remember as a small boy seeing Dad's for the first time: it seemed elephant-trunk like, destabilisingly huge, emerging from its monstrous rough of hair. I thought it was some carbuncle, a distortion, even an illness. By extension it seemed part of Dad's weirdness – his tensions, the cicatrising marks all over his back, the aches in his knees, his stiff neck. Dad caught me looking at it and covered himself up with his towel.

They say fathers turn against their homosexual sons when they realise their sons are looking at them with desire. They douche this with the coldest plash of water they can manage. Yet I have no recall of desire at all. None.

They say – 'they say' – this happens before you're properly conscious of what you're feeling or saying. So perhaps my awareness of desire is obliterated.

I came towards Gary and kissed him lightly on the forehead. He jumped.

'Jesus –' he said, blinking.

I neutered the television. 'Sorry darling, didn't mean to frighten you.'

He glared at me, got up, ruffled. He took two steps away, paused. 'No luck?'

I shook my head. I was about to open my mouth but Gary betrayed me. He began walking like an automaton to bed.

'Got an early morning meeting. Must sleep. Don't disturb.'

I heard his light ping off. A moment later I heard his bodyweight hit the bed. I was alone. Spectacularly abandoned was how I felt. I slid the DVD in and sat back to watch the recording of the show. This was a deeply illicit pleasure. I wound the sound down so it was barely a whisper. I inspected my own performance in the safety of isolation. And I drank. First of all I poured a finger of scotch, but as the night wore on I splashed whisky in the glass recklessly. I slowed myself down, re-watched the DVD endlessly. I didn't like what I saw. I'd been placed in an impossible situation. But then I'd placed myself there.

But something else happened as I steadily drank myself into a stupor. The story within the piece – the massacre – lifted itself out of the surrounding context and pushed itself forward. It stared at me with startling clarity.

Had Dad provided eyewitness accounts to ensure that the wrong man was hanged? Did he unscrupulously revenge himself? Provide a 'sacrifice'?

I heard a noise outside. Then I realised it was water falling on concrete. There was that hole in the spouting I kept meaning to get fixed. The sound took up, grew steady, then intense.

I passed out.

Dad was lying on a table. He looked exhausted. He had no trousers on, and his legs looked like they'd been caked in mud.

A blue hand towel, worn and dirty, was laid over his private parts.

I stopped at the door and Constable Renfrew behind me had to nudge me forward.

'I know this is difficult for you, Miss –'

'Mrs,' I said on automatic, shocked at how literal I was being. But if there was ever an occasion to be literal, this was it. 'When did you find him?'

'About five o'clock. Some kids were going out floundering. Seems to have got caught in mangroves.'

'What was he doing there?'

'Anybody's guess.' A pause, then: 'It's not unusual, Mrs . . . Mrs . . .'

'Burton.'

'. . . for old folks to go walkabout from Arlington. Strange how many of them end up in the tide.'

'Why didn't you deploy people to look there last night?'

'I'm sorry, Mrs Burton. You have to understand police resources. We had multiple emergencies last night. Attempted murder. A rape. He was low down on our priorities. I can get the list.'

'No,' I said. 'No. I don't need it.'

We paused.

'You'll want to spend some time alone?'

I wasn't sure if I did. I didn't know what I wanted. I wanted Ross to be there, sharing this solitude – this responsibility towards manufacturing feeling.

I wanted to feel something – a lot. But I was all hollowed out. I went towards Dad – or, more correctly, his physical remains. Already his face had that curious yellowy whiteness of the dead. There was a residue of mud on his eyelashes, and I realised that the – police? the undertaker? – had already bathed his face to make him presentable.

'Oh Dad,' I found myself saying.

I couldn't think of anything else.

At this point my phone went.

I contemplated not answering it – in the circumstances I could easily have let it ring. But I grabbed, ignobly, at anything that would take me away from the situation.

I didn't want to be there, facing myself.

'Alison.'

'Ross. I'm here with Dad now. They found him. This morning. He's dead, Ross. Dead.'

I don't know what it was. Saying that word. I broke down.

'I'm at the Otahuhu Police Station.'

'I'll come. Stay there. I'll be there. I'm on my way.'

He clicked off.

I cried for a while. I cried for Juliette and my hopeless fucking marriage; for the way I didn't get on with Ross; for Dad slipping out of my life like this.

The door opened a crack and an apologetic male voice said, 'Mrs Burton, would you like me to send in a bereavement counsellor?'

'No,' I sobbed. 'No. Thanks. Everything is okay.'

There was a crash on the Southern Motorway. Cars were backed up, their brake lights trickling red down the windscreen. This is where I spent the next forty minutes. Windows steamed up, an occasional flare of red and blue indicating a cop car edging its way through gridlock. The radio informed me there was a 'fatality' ahead.

I pushed my horn in frustration and inched towards the nearest off-ramp. It seemed terribly important that I get to the police station as soon as possible, though the rational part of my brain knew this was a fiction. Why the emergency? It was all over. There was no hurry. But I kept up my adrenaline, fuelled by a hangover. Under my breath I kept saying, *The bastard, the bastard.* Then, the closer I got to the station, I changed it to, *The poor old bastard, the poor old bastard.* I felt something else break in me. Perhaps it was relief. Perhaps I was thrilled that the responsibility was being taken away from me. That it was over.

I couldn't find a park near the doorway – I saw Alison's Beamer was there. The rain had intensified, was drumming on the roof. Lights were turned on inside shops and houses. There was nobody on the street. I looked around the car. On the back seat there was a pathetic little collapsible umbrella – and even then, two sides of it had broken. It would be useless in the rain.

I decided to make a run for it, and the wet immediately pasted itself all over me.

I burst in the doors, I suppose, like a lunatic. There was a stillness, a silted-up silence inside. Perhaps there was no crime that morning, or else the police had processed everyone efficiently. There was only an abashed Polynesian mother sitting there, watching the scene as if it were TV.

I trailed my wet to the counter.

'Excuse me, I'm Eric Keeling's son.'

There was a moment's pause, not of recognition but suspicion. The constable just looked at me: the fluorescent lighting overhead did him no favours. He looked like an out-of-condition wrestler with a taste for Danish pastries. And he had the irritated air of someone who'd just been interrupted.

'Dad – he went AWOL,' I said, then a heave of emotion escaped my body. It was totally involuntary and it came out in a hiccough.

The constable turned to the side and called out, into a room I couldn't see: '– Jason. Son.'

That basic descriptor.

He went back to what he was doing.

I turned to the Polynesian woman. She looked at me and I looked at her.

A side door opened and a young constable came towards me. His face was decently cast into empathy. He glanced into my face for a moment, then nodded.

'Sorry, mate. He's through here.'

His voice was like a high school student's, rough textured from lack of use.

He walked in front of me and – God forgive me, but I wondered as I looked down at his pert little arse what he'd be like in the sack. I tried not to gaze hungrily, aware of what a sick fuck I was to be thinking of sex at such a moment. Maybe I was clinging to it – the familiarity of cruising, its automatic gesture – or maybe I was clinging to the idea of life, enjoyment, pleasure at such a bleak moment.

'Wait a moment,' I said to him. 'I need to –'

He turned round and looked at me.

'Toilet?'

'Through there.'

In the toilet I wiped the rain off me. The mirror was brutally honest. I wasn't the handsome thirty-year-old I saw in my mind's eye, about to fuck a cop. I was more like an escaped loon. Hair plastered to my head. I remade myself, cast myself back into being more human.

When I came out, the constable had gone. But the furthest door was ajar, and through it I saw Dad's feet.

There was a small tag attached to the big toe. And I saw Alison's body slide in between me and my father.

Ross came in as he normally did, a little shamefaced. He went towards Dad and stood looking down at him for a long moment. Then, for whatever reason, he laughed.

'Poor old bastard.' He looked down his legs. 'Where's his pants? His belt?'

'They found him like that.'

I couldn't help the aggrieved tone in my voice.

Ross sighed heavily – it was a heave of emotion followed by – oh God, a sob. Tears began to course down his slightly foolish face. In a speeded-up second I debated with myself what my responsibilities were. He took them from me. He came towards me and, horrifyingly, opened his arms wide. And, as if I were Gary, his lover, enveloped me in them. He began to bawl.

I smelt his wet clothes, the wool of that repulsive red pullover he still had on, the particular scent of his hair – the last remnants of a child smell deepened into something arid and dry: the cardboardy smell of age and decay. I had another awareness, of the unfortunate proximity of his crotch to my pelvis. Delicately I turned my lower body away. His crying deepened in fury.

This really is too much, a voice in my head said. You never even liked him. I was the person Dad liked. Loved.

This gave me courage.

I was aware the constable had looked in. I tried to raise my eyebrows sardonically, as a message of complicity between two outsiders. Instead he looked down quickly, discreet before such raw emotion. Yet he must witness emotional carnage all the time. Might it even have been an illicit attraction of the job?

Ross's keening wound back a couple of decibels. I felt his cleaving to me lessen.

You can imagine my chagrin when the bastard, after leaking his emotional excess all over my neck and shoulder, wound down to silence but still held me in a rictus of an embrace. (I have to be honest and say I surprised myself by holding him as sternly.) He let out a small, babyish gurgle, then pulled himself away. There was a slight suctioning sound as our skins came apart.

'I feel better now I've got that off my chest,' he said, as though congratulating himself.

Why did I feel betrayed? Short-changed? Once again he had messily taken up all the emotional space, apportioning a pauper's banquet to me, his older sister. A statue is given more permission to mourn.

'They have to have a post-mortem.'

This was Alison. Mumbling, which was strange for her. She was looking down, keeping her face obscured. Her hair swung forward and acted as a shield. It reminded me of her as a teenage girl, oddly touching. She seemed vulnerable and I longed to hug her again. We'd done this instinctively at the police station, our bodies unselfconscious with grief. Her fingers had even spasmed some message into mine – harsh, desperate: the fingers of a drowning man, I thought. For one rare moment I conceived the possibility that I loved Alison. Then she dropped my hand quickly.

I'd persuaded her to have a cup of tea. She was all for returning to the city. Going ahead with funeral arrangements. Notices in the *Herald*.

But I said to her, 'Alison. You don't know Auckland. In situations like this, the city goes into total gridlock. From Waiwera to the Bombays cars are stalled. It's better to stay where we are.'

We were standing under a shop veranda, rain whipping in to the pavement. An elderly Indian woman, her sari tight about her body, was wheeling a barrow of taro indoors. The sky had darkened and in the distance was an ominous roar of stalled traffic. A wailing ambulance sprinkled through the air.

'We need to sit down, June,' I said, unaware I was even using her childhood name.

She looked at me palely. She was exhausted, I saw. Bitten down to the quick.

She just shrugged. As if, at this point, she understood the practicality of ceding control.

'There's a good Vietnamese restaurant somewhere round here. I've read about it in the *Herald*.'

So there we sat, our fingers on the oily plastic tablecloth, gazing at the pictures of food. It was a working man's place, the tables occupied by a mixture of office workers on a lunch break and local Vietnamese.

Eventually a waitress came over.

We ordered. I wasn't hungry till I looked at the menu in detail. Suddenly, at the thought of food I was ravenous.

'They said he was probably just wandering along,' she said.

'Do you think he knew?' I looked into Alison's eyes. 'About the TV programme?'

She shrugged, devolving responsibility off herself – to me, I felt. I frowned.

'I asked Mrs Stobbs and she said, no, nobody contacted him that she knows of –'

I didn't say anything.

Our food came and I ate with a singular concentration. After a while Alison said, 'Actually, it's quite good.'

'Yes, well, the colonies do food quite well these days. So I've heard.' I hooked up a noodle on my chopstick and heaved it around.

She flashed me a quick smile before hiding it behind something more austere. She sighed deeply.

'I don't know what to do, Ross.'

This was so astonishing my chopstick stayed in the air. But then it went back in, trying to pick up a strand that would lift out in bulk.

'What about?'

'The crap they're talking about Dad. Do we just let it sink without trace? Go cold? These media sensations often just run out of steam after a while.'

We looked at each other.

She reached down to the teapot and turned it around thoughtfully.

I shrugged. 'Hard to know. Probably better.'

I made a face, caught somewhere between apologetic

and pragmatic, and went back to the conundrum of my noodles. Yet as I gazed down into them, I heard just a very light word, like a wing brushing past my ear.

It was Dad's voice.

Promise.

We had the lucky sense of being people indoors. Once or twice someone soaked would walk by. Then a young woman came by in bare feet, proudly wet, laughing as she shook the water out of her curls.

'You know you said before . . . that you weren't going back for a while . . .'

Alison's mouth opened slowly, suggesting she might recant. But she looked at me, waiting, tentative.

'. . . I'd like to – help. I mean, I don't know what Dad did in that case – whether he cooked the books – but I –'

I found I couldn't go on. I was breathless. It was too soon. I found tears scalding my lids. Before I could stop them, they started running down my face.

Alison's hand leapt forward quickly, and she squeezed my hand. But once again she did this so fiercely it hurt. I tried to pretend I liked it, but I didn't. It stopped the tears though. Double-quick. Perhaps she knew it as a technique. But I doubt it. She looked to me as she'd never looked before – worn out, no longer having any techniques of prevarication or defence. Or attack.

'I don't know much of anything any more.'

'You remember that afternoon Dad tried to get you to swim?'

We were waiting for the rain to lessen.

'No.'

'When Dad . . . threw you into the water?'

'No. No. I learnt to swim at the Teps,' I said. 'I caught the bus in from Westmere every Wednesday.'

Alison looked unconvinced.

'There was such a handsome boy there,' I said. 'Once I touched him, just lightly, almost accidentally. On the thigh.'

'And?'

'He grabbed hold of me. Hard. I was frightened. Fool that I was. I was so madly obsessed with him. The fact of sex – the ugly practicality of it – seemed to not . . . connect, at that stage.'

'You were lucky not to be interfered with. It might have had long-term effects.'

'It's not good living with regrets,' I said.

'Better than living with trauma, surely?'

I looked at Alison levelly. Wasn't it about time I introduced her to the reality of who I was? 'I wanted him to hammer out everything that was pansy-like and pathetic in me. I wanted him to infuse his maleness into me. With the end of his cock, if need be.'

Alison looked shocked at my explicitness.

'Wasn't it –' she risked empathy for a moment – 'the things maybe Dad didn't . . . couldn't provide?'

'But it never happened,' I said lightly. Letting her off the hook. 'I got – or didn't get – my maleness from other sources.'

'You hated Dad.'

'He beat the shit out of me, Alison, you know that.'

She shook her head.

'He did not!'

'The plastic strap. Yellowy with age. The metal buckle.' I watched her blink. 'Dad never did.'

'He was trying to strap the pansiness out of me.'

'He did not, Ross. At least – not that I remember.'

She paused.

'He did, Alison,' I said flatly. 'He did. I don't . . . exactly blame him. In fact now, as an adult, he gave me something he probably never thought of.' I laughed ruefully. 'I've got quite a taste for spanking – being spanked. Hurt me, Daddy. Make love to me. Thanks, Big Daddy.'

'Please.'

'Well, this is how it interweaves and works itself out, Alison. It's not all just done and finished in the past. It lives on. In me. And you.'

This abrasive honesty was too much.

I thought about my father and how his experiences of the prison camps had lived on inside him. How these experiences had expressed themselves continuously. It had corroded him. The unsaid, the unspoken. The silence within.

'I don't know about that, Ross. There are some things – well, it's better not to remember.'

Then, seeing what she'd said, she stopped.

Some images flooded back into my brain.

Dad. Kiwitea Street. The hall. Dad crouched down in the corner. Ross in another room. His crying had stopped. He had no further tears to cry. He was just drizzling out his despair.

Mum was in there too, with Ross.

I got up, closed the door on it all. I put a record on.

'It's My Party and I'll Cry if I Want to'.

I turned it up as loud as it would go.

Mum came in and wrenched the record off. It was one

of her few moments of action, when I think of it – probably an indication of the desperation of the situation. Then, even more amazing, she smashed the record. Which wasn't easily done. They were nuggety, those little 45s.

Maybe she was indicating something else had broken.

Mum and Dad separated not long after.

I pretended I didn't feel a thing. It seemed safer, or really, practically, the only way to survive.

Strange to be sitting in a Vietnamese café in Otahuhu, waiting for the rain to lessen, your dad just dead. You find something out about yourself.

I thought: perhaps that's where my coldness of heart comes from. Call it toughness. Self-protection.

This came at me with the abrupt force of an electric shock. My arm jerked out. Knocked over Ross's cup of jasmine tea. It leaked through the detritus of a meal, over the plastic cloth.

The waitress came along with tissues, began mopping it.

'No harm done.'

She laughed, with tired grace, and walked away.

21

Alison took a lift up to the third floor. The doors opened into a fluorescent-lit corridor of mean proportions. There was an office opposite. A secretary sat behind a computer.

'Excuse me, I'm looking for Associate-Professor Hazeldean.'

'Third door down the corridor to the left,' the secretary said, not removing her gaze from the screen.

Alison found the door slightly ajar, knocked.

'Come in.'

Hazeldean's expression tightened. He stood up, seemed about to offer his hand.

Alison ignored all pleasantries and kept eye contact. She looked into the back of his head.

'Sit down. Please.'

She sat.

'I . . . I was very sorry to hear about your father.'

She left a beat.

'To hear what?' Her voice was cold.

'That he had . . . passed on.'

'I'm not here to listen to your . . . regrets, Professor Hazeldean. I want information. I want to get a handle on the – alleged – evidence that my father took part in some war crime.'

He started. 'Oh, that's the language of a television programme, of smear and innuendo. Your father took part in no war crime. I can assure you of that.'

'You took part in the programme. In fact, the programme couldn't have existed without you.'

She had cornered him. He smiled ingratiatingly, lifted his hands in a small gesture that said, I give up, but also segued into, not so fast.

'I think we could talk about this over coffee,' he said.

'I'd prefer, if you had the time, to talk to you now.'

'What do you want to know – specifically?'

She was silent a moment and Hazeldean admired her. Shame about the tightness round the mouth, the drawn look that gave her flesh a strange, luminescent quality. She wasn't wearing lipstick. Hazeldean got the idea it was a code of mourning.

'For quite some time I've been receiving . . . documents.'

'I remember you telling me this at the party. What sort of documents?'

'I wasn't sure at first. They were parts of larger documents – pages – usually signed off by Dad as investigator. They seemed to be part of his investigations into various . . . atrocities.'

Hazeldean's breathing had quickened. He felt his heart lurch. Primary material. He nodded.

'Like –?'

'Beheadings. Biological experiments on people. Implanting plague in humans.'

He nodded impartially.

'One of them seemed to be an eyewitness account of the Six Mile Road Incident. Possibly.'

He whistled.

'They upset me, perhaps deliberately. Made me think of my father. Then, when I got back here to New Zealand I received a story. A kind of novel, I guess.'

Hazeldean's eyebrows went up.

'A strange sort of sub-Graham Greene story. Fiction. Yet with Dad as the central character.'

'What was it about?'

'It was about . . . his mood, I suppose, or everything that led him up to the point of making a decision –'

'About Sugihara?'

'No.'

'What about, then?'

'About the psychological state of mind, I guess, which would lead him to make this . . . what would you call it? *Transgression*.' She looked at him. 'I believe the word you used was sacrifice.'

She was whipping him. He reddened. 'Well, the media requires a certain crudity. To get a point across.'

She ignored him.

'I want to know more about this case – Six Mile – that you've based your case on. I'd like to look at the material with my own eyes.'

He looked surprised.

'I thought you were only here –'

'I'm around. For a while. I'm taking some time off.'

This explained, perhaps, the difference in her. She seemed less tightly coiled.

Alison meanwhile glanced at the books on his desk: *The Intimate History of Killing*, *Forgotten Armies*, *On the Most Prominent Form of Degradation in Erotic Life*.

'How long have you got?' he asked, stretching his legs out and putting his hands behind his head. He felt a pleasurable gush of anticipation. The pedagogue in him came out. Along with it some other feeling, more distinctly physical.

'You have to understand that the Japanese saw capture and defeat in different cultural terms from the West. The cult of Bushido dictated that capture rendered the person a non-human. Death was preferable –'

'I'm not one of your students, Frank. I'm not here doing Extermination and Extenuating Circumstances 101.'

He barked out a laugh, and glanced at the open slit of door.

'So the point is, in a massacre, to make sure nobody survives? No eyewitness?'

'You could say that.' He looked at her shrewdly. 'Or if there are eyewitnesses they all tell the same story.'

'You have these eyewitness accounts?'

'No. That's the thing. A lot of the paperwork disappeared with your father.'

Alison looked directly at him. 'You mean, the box?'

He nodded.

'What would you say if I said I have distinct memories of what papers were in that box?'

He sat up. 'I'd say I was very interested.'

She was silent.

'Well?'

'I remember them very clearly.'

'Aren't you going to tell me?'

'No. Why should I? You're willing to ruin my father's reputation, disturb me and my brother deeply. For what?'

'Historical accuracy – it's my job.'

'Dad's life was fucked up by war, and now you want to fuck up his reputation. What's left of it.'

'I'm sorry. It's not that. It isn't.'

'What is it then?'

'Victor's justice is a very hot issue right now. You saw the phone images of Saddam Hussein being hanged? It's not so very different.'

'It is when my father's concerned.'

'I said I'm sorry, but the issue is bigger than your father.'

'You do this for a living. Do you?'

His flush had deepened. 'What was it Martin Luther said? "Every lie must beget seven more lies if it is to resemble the truth and adopt truth's aura."'

Alison thought, Truth's aura. And then she thought, Seven more lies.

She hated him genially.

He found her sexually exciting.

She stood up and he stood up, too quickly, and came around the side of his desk.

'I'm sorry,' he said, opening the door. They were standing very close, eye to eye. She gazed into his eyes as if she were standing on a platform, in a darkened room, and out there was a limitless space that she was scrutinising minutely, every detail.

'I have to defend Dad. You know that.'

'Yes.'

He felt his cock tingle and, like a plant in animated germination, jerk alive. The air was exciting, anarchic. He came closer to her.

'I'll give you any help I can,' he said. 'Information. Whatever documents I have. You might have better luck. Sometimes the talented amateur –'

'The talented amateur?'

'Let's say, then,' he said, blushing, 'the non-professional historian . . . can find out things . . . stumble on things. There's a lot of ambiguity in the case – I'll help you all I can. I'll send you all my references.'

She paused.

'Let's make a date,' he said, his face crimsoning further.

At this point the secretary walked by. She glanced in and Hazeldean, a little startled, called out a too ebullient, 'Good afternoon!'

The secretary didn't reply.

Alison's face was all doubt, all scorn.

'I mean . . . if you want to meet up again, I can organise my papers – give you what I've –'

She had gone.

After a moment he heard the lift doors close, then there was silence.

22

When I got back to the hotel there was an envelope under my door.

I really couldn't stand it. Not anything more.

I noted it had arrived at the hotel two days earlier. For whatever reason — my being so busy? — the staff hadn't delivered it.

A kind of elemental deafness had descended. I didn't know what to make of anything. I felt deep guilt for what Dad had done, might have done. Yet the terrible thing was I, like Ross, knew nothing about the incident, apart from what memory provided: our childhood game. That was startlingly specific.

Was it a false memory? I had based my life on fact, on prosaic figures, on daylight. I did not feel at home in the shady nimbus of 'truth's aura'. I despised half-shades. I liked things plain. Yet there was no plainness here.

Nothing straightforward.

I also felt attacked by remorse for what had happened to Dad. I had surgically removed myself from the mess of his life. One voice within me – the voice of reason – asked, what could I have done? Stayed at home? Been one of those tortured maiden daughters, the sort you don't see any more? (Like integrity or honour, maiden daughters as a concept have gone out of fashion. Time has proven them redundant.) If I had stayed at home with Dad, would it all have turned out any better?

As it was, Ross had played the maiden daughter – maiden daughter in hell, I was tempted to think. It hadn't made it any better. All three of us – Dad, Ross and I – had perhaps adopted the seven lies as a stratagem, had unknowingly learnt the art of silence. We were tutored in it and adopted it as our natural language. The painful thing in this situation was to learn how to undo. To penetrate the core of silence. To feel the articulation of a limb that had atrophied.

I lay down on the bed. I glanced at the envelope unwillingly.

Once again it had no return address, no name. But unlike that strange piece of fiction, my name and address were handwritten on the outside. In that strange awkward hand, as if the person had barely made School Cert. It was like all the others.

I slit the envelope open.

What could be worse news?

Inside was a document. It was handwritten, like a preliminary report. The paper was old, the ink faded. I recognised Dad's writing.

I am a lowly soldier but a hungry one. We are all starving now. Some days we have a little rice, other days nothing. It is a much harder war than it was in 1942, when we won such glorious victories for our Emperor. Now all is slow, very slow. We have no strength left and all around us we can hear sounds. People are moving about, saying things. I hear whispers in the grass, in the palm trees. I start to feel a great sadness.

We are marching into the hills.

We do not have many bullets, and the prisoners, they sit down too. It is a field off Six Mile Road. Some look at us, deep into the eyes so we look away.

They have brought their possessions with them, scraps.

They think they are shifting to another camp.

Perhaps.

The evening is darkening all around us and Lieutenant-Colonel Sugihara will not listen to Captain Hinokuma. I have heard them argue before, back in camp. Lieutenant-Colonel Sugihara says war is nearing end and we must prepare for what comes later. Captain Hinokuma says he does not believe this. He says it is American propaganda and even if the homeland is invaded we have enough soldiers in Asian empire to keep fighting. For ever.

If necessary, Captain Hinokuma say, we must release ourselves of the burden of these prisoners.

But I hear Lieutenant-Colonel Sugihara. He says that he thinks it has reached a time when it is better to be slow in making rash decisions.

We must cleanse these people, get rid of waste, say Captain Hinokuma.

The Lieutenant-Colonel is silent a while and he picks up a piece of grass.

If this insect here is to die, does that make our lives better?

If the insect is eating the grass that I need to eat, yes, replies Captain Hinokuma. He takes a blade of grass and puts it in his mouth.

He spit it out, not taste good.

The soldiers are getting restless and the prisoners themselves are like drowsy men coming awake.

Then a bad thing happens. One young Australian, he crawls away into the darkness.

He is shot.

See, cries Captain Hinokuma, this is what we are facing. It is life and death here.

It has been life and death for too long time, answers Lieutenant-Colonel Sugihara. Too much death.

You are having treasonous thoughts.

I am having the thought of a man.

You are soldier, not man.

The Lieutenant-Colonel is silent and looks into the field.

Remorse is for women, says Captain Hinokuma, taking out his sword.

'Let us end this discussion in the right manner.'

With that, Captain Hinokuma walked away.

It is strictly not correct, as he is inferior officer.

Hinokuma gives the order shobun. Prisoners to stand. They do so in great tiredness. Some can hardly stand. Their friends help them to their feet. Very silent. So silent I can hear my own blood rushing through body for I know what is to come. We all know what is to come. Captain Hinokuma nod and say it is time.

The prisoners are shot in relays.

Nobody says anything, neither Japanese nor Australian.

Nobody tries to escape.

We are ordered to burn the bodies.

What happens next is not in the rule book. The soldiers lack discipline. But we are forgotten and nobody can see us or what we do. Afterwards all feel only one thing: tiredness. The war goes on too long.

I think of how things used to be. Sitting at desk. Running for train. Meeting sweetheart. Even being bored with old relatives is so far away as to seem a dream. That night most of us get very drunk. But the more we drink the more we become sober. The remembering follows me wherever I go. It awakens me every night and asks me: did this terrible thing happen? I am telling you now so I can escape the remembering.

Private Sono Miyake, 124 Infantry.

23

It was on the tip of my lips to tell Ross about the document when we were clearing out Arlington. But I didn't. I just couldn't. I didn't want to believe what it was saying. About Dad.

It was too much.

But then I decided I couldn't live with not being truthful. If I had learnt anything from being with Ross, it was that we had to share everything. The burden.

So I decided I'd give it to him when he got home from work. He'd asked me out there to have dinner with him. Gary was working late. He'd told me where he hid a key in case I got there before him.

I felt an interloper when I let myself in. In the living room a clothes horse was up and selected underpants of an expensive sort were drying. There was a single slipper, which looked like it had been abandoned in haste, on the edge of a rug. And documents – rates notices, an overdue library book – placed face-down close to the front door.

I walked down the hall. Ross's bedroom door was open and I glanced in at its state of chaos. It was a picture of his mind – unkempt, underwear scattered everywhere, dirty clothes which never quite made it to the washing machine. Gary's bedroom, by contrast, was a chapel of order and decency.

I went and sat in their living room and waited.

I got out the envelope with the last testimony in it. Checked I still had it. Put it away again.

I lost focus.

There was a curious sound behind me.

It was the cat flap.

Tallulah came through, stalking straight towards me. There was a magnificent pace to her stride. Her tail was up and I witnessed every muscle beneath her fur articulating: in her mouth a sparrow.

The cat's eyes were enlarged, glossy black. She glanced up at me, right into my eyes. I could read the message: Look at how I am alive. I am at the centre of all creation, the harbinger of life and death. I am altering the order of nature. Or: I am fulfilling nature's design.

She was the perfect killing machine at that moment.

I noticed her fangs puncturing the breast of the bird. The bird's eye was glassy. It seemed to entrap me in its drama.

I stood up.

'Oh fuck.'

She laid the bird down not far from me. The bird lay there, its left wing at a strange angle. It was hyperventilating, its small breast rising, falling. Beak open.

Its eye begged.

'Take it outside!'

Stupidly I indicated the door. I went over and unlocked the French door, widened it back.

'Outside, Tallulah!'

The cat did not even glance at me. It was trapped in its own drama, the vivid scent of death upon it.

A paw went out to nudge the sparrow. The bird lay still. The cat moved away, half a metre, and sat obliquely to it. The cat began to lick its coat, but in such a way it seemed superb, full of contempt.

The sparrow suddenly came to life. Its wings beat desperately and its claws contracted as it pivoted round on the carpet.

I saw a drop of blood.

The cat leapt back. With a paw, she threw it up into the air.

The sparrow landed on the wooden floor. The cat came over to it. Nudged it into play. She batted it along the floorboards, towering over it, prodding it into life.

The cat seemed to be grinning.

The sparrow's feathers had become fluffed up. Its claws were spasming in pain.

It was sickening.

'Finish the poor thing off! Kill it!'

I grabbed a newspaper and went towards the bird. I scooped it up. The sparrow rocked, then rolled over on to its back.

'I'm sorry,' I said to the bird. 'I'm sorry, I'm sorry, I'm sorry.'

I didn't know what I was saying sorry about. My failure with Juliette? Not getting back for Mum's funeral? The way

Ross and I didn't get on? The mess of Dad's life? Strange how things can telescope back.

I walked out with the bird into the garden.

Its eye kept gazing up at me. Into me.

For a moment the cat sat looking around, as if suspecting the bird was still there. This interested the cat more, this development in its play.

I went and got a spade. I would decapitate the bird. Bury it. End this indecency.

But the second I turned my back away to lift the spade the cat had the bird in its mouth. In fact all I saw was the tail of the cat as it romped away. Like a champ, I thought. Round a circuit.

It disappeared round the corner of the house for a more leisurely kill.

I felt unsettled. I found myself walking back up the hall to leave. Instead I walked into Ross's bedroom. I took an older sister's privilege, felt a kind of hunger to understand him. To be inside his world.

There was the bed, king-sized, sheets dragged on to the floor. Some local art that didn't interest me on the walls. A computer on a table, and a nestle of papers. This seemed the one zone of order in the mess. A pile of papers was neatly laid face-down, a red pencil on the top. Underneath was a sheet from Auckland University. It was a night class: 'Creative Writing'.

He'd always had this thing about 'being creative'. Poor sap. Dreamer. Hider from reality.

Very quickly I lifted up one of the sheets. So I was a spy. Strange what you do while you wait for your life to take form.

The paper shivered in my hand. I felt electrified.

It was the first page of *Lucky Bastard*.

There were red marks, like slashes of blood, all down the page. Corrections.

It said clearly at the top: 'By Ross Keeling'.

I dropped the page back. I walked away.

Outside on the front step were a small liver and a claw. The merest smear of blood indicated where there had once been a living bird.

I stepped over it, avoiding the carnage.

I didn't leave a message.

Good things can wait. As can revenge.

24

What can I say of the funeral? That Alison and Gary and I were there, with Jasper to swell the crowd. Bobbie put in a surprise appearance. She was the most vocal mourner. At times her little half-suppressed sobs and mewings acted as a reprimand for our seeming lack of feeling. Two elderly men arrived late. Reg and Len were from the RSA. I had the feeling they were drunk.

All Pakeha men of a certain age seem like brothers. Perhaps it was the diet, or the tough upbringing or genetic position in relation to forebears: large ears, clumsy noses, awkward hands; a kind of genuineness amid the loss. Loss of hearing, loss of mobility: loss of contact.

I kept thinking of Dad's autopsy report: not the lungs filled with seawater but the other things – the fractured tibia, the back bones smashed, the kneecaps, the vertebrae fused together. It was a map of his war: the injuries he'd got as a young man, present like a ghost in his skeleton, telling me his stories, urging me on.

Promise.

'Dust to dust . . .'

The two old geezers had brought a little tape machine with them. The technology seemed heartbreakingly old. You only ever saw these things in second-hand shops. You couldn't give them away. They plugged it in. And when the moment for 'The Last Post' came, Len came forward with a ceremonious air, inclined his head at Dad's casket and indented the button.

For a moment we whirled in a state of suspension – a few crackles of sound, then it came on: a recording both tinny and real. Only the most hard-hearted could not be moved. Dad's casket juddered slightly – the minister had obviously pressed a button. The casket began to lower. But just at that point the tape must have become stretched, because the trumpet, reaching its most plangent note, wobbled, rose into a higher note than ever, and then became subverted into a Jimi Hendrix version of 'The Last Post'. Reg lurched towards the tape deck. Jasper smirked audibly. Bobbie sobbed. I laughed – I laughed out loud, indecently yet joyfully. Alison's eyes, pained and sorrowful, swept by mine. I felt Dad would have laughed. But then the tape fell back into its rhythm and Dad's casket stopped its fall.

'You may gather round and pay your last respects,' said the undertaker, urging us forward so that the next funeral could get into the crematorium on the tidy half-hour.

I was drunk. I don't know how it happened. It's more Ross's department than mine. But Gary had laid on a royal wake: there was enough food there for a crowd of forty, and the over-abundance made its own silent comment.

Mrs Stobbs arrived 'unavoidably late', held up by a crisis at Arlington. She had sent a showily expensive wreath, with a card peppered with the semi-legible signatures of 'all the girls from Arlington'. *In Our Hearts and Thoughts Forever*, read the printed words.

Crap, I thought, then I wondered what it was that made me always so hard on everyone. Because I'd always been hard on myself? I reached and filled my glass again.

The two old soldiers had come back for a feed. Len and Reg. Jasper seemed unaccountably spellbound by them: he stretched his long legs out as he leaned against the railing on the deck and frankly gawked.

They were spinning tales.

I had my own fish to fry.

I made a beeline for my brother.

Ross had been crying, I could see that. He and Gary did one of those ostentatious gay embraces that are meant to show us the meaning of true feeling. I have to admit I was touched – or suddenly lonely. I was on my own. Except the Stobbs woman had chosen me as a likely victim for conversation. I eluded her with a frankly glassy smile.

'My brother,' I murmured.

I went up to him and touched him lightly on the back with my finger pads.

'Ross, why aren't you drinking?'

'Don't know. Giving it a rest.' His eyes went down to my glass. 'Can I get you some more?'

I nodded. Some strange muteness had overtaken me. When he came back I said, 'I don't know what to think any more. There seems to be falsehood and treachery everywhere.'

He just looked into the back of my eyes. I had the eerie feeling he was seeing through my defences. I was unused to this – the X-ray penetration of family. Perhaps this was why I had run away?

Hold it. Where did that come from? Run away. I'd never admitted it to myself before, but now, here at my father's wake, my face unaccountably hot, I saw myself for what I was: I had avoided nearly everything I humanly could. Juliette suddenly came to me, her accusing, viperish face, hungry, pale – hurt. I raised my cool hands up to my cheeks. Ross, fuck him, was looking at me, a weird smile on his lips.

'What?' I said to him accusingly. 'What!'

'Nothing.'

He looked down.

I was finding him unreadable: Ross, who was normally as transparent as cellophane.

'You know those papers,' I said, incapable of not raising it. Going straight for the heart. The point. To meddle. Soothe. Or pinprick.

'Which papers?'

He seemed dangerously quiet. He had gone pale. Still.

'That thing someone dropped off at the hotel. For me to read.'

He nodded. Or really, his head just slightly dipped.

My tongue had injudiciously chosen the word 'thing'.

'*Lucky Bastard.*'

'Yes.'

'Who wrote that – we should sue –'

I was babbling, I knew it.

'I did.'

'You've sued? How did you find out who wrote –'

'I wrote it,' he said.

He was looking at me with that strange, back-of-your-skull look again.

'What do you mean?' I blustered. 'You wrote it?' I wanted him to spell it out. Confess.

'I – wrote – it.' He looked down, then up again. 'I've always wanted to be . . . a writer, Alison. Always. That's what I wanted to do . . . be. I wanted to understand Dad. Walk in his shoes.'

'Well,' I fired back. I hated myself for what I was about to say, but I couldn't help myself. 'You have it all wrong. The background details of Tokyo's palace, for example. Completely wrong. Did you do research? You didn't go to Tokyo, did you?'

'*Stop treating me like I'm your fucking perennial kid brother.*' His voice was tart – raw with hurt.

Heads turned. Mrs Stobbs looked interested.

I blushed. 'Dad wasn't gay.' I couldn't stop myself. 'I don't know why you had to pervert him –'

Ross bubbled up into laughter. 'In the book he isn't gay, he's bi.'

'Whatever,' I said, my lips toxic. 'It's a lie, whatever you've written.'

'It's fiction,' he said, 'it's an imagination. I tried to imagine being straight, but do you know what, Alison, it's a bit like you. I couldn't imagine the alternative . . . So, I made him bi . . . to put myself in his shoes, if you see . . .'

I primly shut my lips.

'Why didn't you tell me?'

He looked at me, not speaking.

'Well, I guess at least you finished something,' I said,

distancing myself from the book. 'Congratulations. You won't publish it, will you? I mean –'

His face was white and I thought, again, of Juliette and how I effortlessly, and really without meaning to, hurt her. Wounded her with my assumptions. I wondered what had made me so armoured, so deflective – so aggressive.

I put my hand down on the table, touching his. By accident. He jumped, coloured and slid his hand away.

He walked off, leaving me there.

I was alone.

I got as far away from Alison as I could. I went into the garden and looked down at the plants. I practised breathing through my nose. Tallulah, with that empathy of cats, came towards me, and very delicately leaned her body into my leg. She looked up at me, her eyes huge. I picked her up, cuddled her, kissed the flat top of her head.

'At least you understand me.'

The moment I put her down, she headed off to the barbeque quick smart.

I felt numb. Hurt. But I'd decided – for once in my life – not to drink. I'd stay stone cold sober.

An odd decision, you'll agree, on an occasion when by rights you have permission to get totally wasted. But I couldn't go there. Risk it.

I drifted towards the old bastards, who were still holding court on the back deck, Jasper providing them with endless tots of whisky. They had the recklessness of children on a spree. Determined to enjoy themselves.

I looked at them. My feelings were so complicated. They were the ones who'd always sneered at me. Called me a pouf, if not to my face then in the way they looked at me. The ones I hated by return post. They were Dad's tribe, Rob's mob, a monstrous crew of eviscerating drunks. Right wing, RSA. But on this day of days I decided it was time to lay down my arms.

Declare peace. With the world. As I knew it.

I was numb, was what it was. I was tired.

Reg reached down for his glass on my approach, raised it in salute and said, 'Your Dad. God bless him. Poor old bastard.'

And he sipped injudiciously and deep. Smacked his lips on coming up for air.

I took in his large ears, broken nose, veins clotted all over his face. Large pores on the nose too. Those vehement eyes of men of that generation. Men who had seen too much – and kept quiet. For too long.

'We were talking of your Dad's mate. In the camp.'

'Ross was his name.' This was Len, the smaller of the two. He had the lightweight body of the perpetual drunk – desiccated.

I blinked. One more thing I'd never known about.

'They was like two peas in a pod.'

'Brothers.'

'Nothing queer.'

'But then we had a shakedown one night. The radio was discovered.'

'Your father's mate got beaten up.'

'And your Dad . . .'

'Steady now, Len, steady.'

'We all of us knew it was no fucking use.'

'You only get beaten up.'

'But your father couldn't hack it. Not watching his

mate getting done over.'

'He went berserk.'

'Trying to stop them.'

'We all of us knew it was no fucking use.'

'That's when . . .'

'It wasn't good.'

'What'd they do?' Bobbie's voice cut in. She had come and stood by the French doors.

'They put him in the pen.'

'That's what we called it.'

'It was this high.' Reg indicated chest height.

'You couldn't stand, you couldn't lie down.'

'They took you out each day and bashed the living daylights out of you.'

'You had to try and stand.'

'Once you fell over, you were a goner. They'd kick you to death.'

'We had to line up and watch.'

There was a moment's silence, brooding.

Len pushed his empty glass forward, accusing.

What oblivion could ever be enough? What recompense?

Jasper, a beat too late, glugged it full.

Len took it straight to his mouth, drank.

'He was in there for five days.'

'Outside. In the full sun. Ninety degrees.'

'We had to line up and watch. Not move. Not say a thing.'

'Blokes stood there, tears streaming down their faces. Others didn't move a muscle.'

'It was best to store it up. File it. Keep it.'

A silence fell.

Len's voice when he spoke was lower, quieter, more reflective. 'It isn't good what you were forced to do.'

'It's the hardest part afterwards.'

'What you found yourself doing. Just to stay alive. You never knew you had it in you.'

Silence again.

Jasper leaned forward and refreshed Reg's glass. But Reg, perhaps surprisingly, swerved his glass away. 'Enough, lad,' he said.

Len sniffed his drink and looked into the darkening garden. He was silent a while. Then he shook himself.

'Better take a slash.'

Bobbie got up and started collecting dirty dishes. Noisily.

Jasper drifted to the computer.

Reg and I were left alone.

Reg said to me conversationally, 'I don't know what all the fuss was in that television thing the other night. We made sure we killed every last Nip we found. Didn't matter if they were prisoners or not. Wounded or not. A Nip was better off dead.' He drank soberly now, with a kind of processional slowness. 'It was kill or be killed, son. That's how it was. And I pray to God that none of you —' his eyes swept by the stripling Jasper, his voice rough and coruscating with anger, hurts, resentments — 'have to do what we found ourselves doing. It's fine at the time, you think you're young and tough . . .'

I escaped into the kitchen. The lights hadn't been turned on yet and the room had a pleasing kindness. Bobbie touched me on the arm.

'I'd like a word with you, Ross, when you've got a

mo. I wouldn't want you to think I was up to anything underhand.'

I looked towards her blindly. I was still thinking of what the old blokes had been saying. I was thinking of Dad and his nightmares, crying out.

So that was what Dad was always fending off.

His cries of *stop stop stop* cut fresh into the room.

I felt very old as I thought back to the child I had been, the resentful young man so intolerant of his father. How we had misunderstood each other, looked past each other and seen only demons whereas there might have been harmonious parallels.

In some ways I knew I was still that age, arrested and terrified.

Dad coming at me with the strap.

Dad escaping from the cage.

Explaining things doesn't always unlock a situation. If you've been locked into a position and you've got older that's the way your bones have set.

I guess that's what happened with Dad and, by extension, to Alison and myself.

I glanced at Alison and saw she looked fragile. She kept gesturing with her shapely hands – imploring, wringing gestures – placating? Soothing? I wasn't sure. She had lost colour in her face – her skin looked like ivory tissue paper that had got wet. She had lost her pep.

As had I.

'Ross, you've got a mo, eh, mate?'

'What?' I said with a swing of annoyance, as if swatting away a fly.

And then I saw in Bobbie's face a lifetime of rebuffs. I instantly regretted the way I'd spoken. She turned away.

'Please. I want to know. What did you want to tell me?'

'Those papers,' she said fiercely and loud in the silent room. Gary had come in and with frightening synchronicity turned on a lamp. The light did no favour to all our old faces. I looked into Bobbie's hazel eyes. They were vehement.

'It was me who bunged those documents in the post to your high and mighty sister.'

Alison stood there, silent.

'Under strict instructions from your Dad. He asked me. Yours Truly.'

'*Why*?' This was Alison.

'We got to go.'

It was the old bastards, Len and Reg, going off duty. They all but saluted as they stood there. Pissed as farts. Len's hands kept straying out as he stuffed peanuts into the pocket of his suit.

'Good to meet you, son.'

Len stood forward with the familiar fierceness of that generation. He stared hard into my eyes. A mariner divining storms at sea or currents leading to shipwreck or safety would not have looked more closely.

'I can see him in your eyes.'

I felt walloped with emotion. My eyes watered. I saw a wince cross the old man's face. Dealing with a nance. Yet he held his hand out – an old man's hand, carbuncular yet oddly soft on the palm. He gripped my own and wrung it mercilessly. He poured into it all his feelings – confused, ambivalent.

'I fucking loved your father,' he whispered.

I grimaced.

Reg was easier. He danced back from me, shaking his hands.

'Got the old rheumatiz, son.'

I hesitated. Should I hug him? I saw the alarm in his face. The abject fear.

I kept my distance.

'Thanks so much for coming . . .'

Alison took on the job of getting the old codgers outside. Gary and Jasper were driving them back to the Ranfurly. But as she went out the door she flashed me a look which swept past Bobbie. It said: *Stall her.*

I looked at Bobbie. Her face was neutral. I guessed she wanted, in particular, for Alison to 'share' her tale.

But old people take so long to do anything, perhaps conscious of how little time they have left. Alison was away a long time.

'You were always the apple of his eye,' I overheard.

'The way he kept us up to date with your career.'

'He'd be proud of you.'

(But not of you, Ross, you tosser.)

Finally the door closed.

Alison came back. She sat down and poured herself a large scotch.

'Oi, I thought scotch gave you a headache.'

'What the heck,' she said, using an old-fashioned term whose primness charmed me.

I poured Bobbie one too.

I had a glass — oh joy — of carbonated water.

I was going to stay sober if it killed me.

Bobbie raised up her glass.

'He was a good bloke, your Dad. Decent.'

Neither Alison nor I knew how to counter-offer.

She glanced at Alison. 'Every so often he'd give me an envelope and ask me to post it off to you.'

'But did he say why?'

'I never asked what was inside. It wasn't my place.'

'But *why*?' This was Alison again.

'Maybe he wanted to get in touch. Keep in touch, say?'

Alison's face saddened.

'Maybe he was trying to tell us – let us know –' this was me, mediating – 'what was troubling him.'

'Nah.' There was some elemental scorn in Bobbie's voice. 'Don't kid yourself.'

Her lips twitched. 'It was to put the boot up ya crack good and hard.'

And she laughed.

Her laugh was scornful: scornful of our deliberations, of Alison's accent, of the top-end dishwasher, of Gary and me with our feline baby, of the wealth she saw around her that she would probably never have: she who stooped and wiped the faeces off the arses of old men and women, parents unwanted by their own children, or children incapable of doing these intimate tasks. All this was in her laugh.

Alison and I glanced at each other. Was this Dad's last malicious act? His final attempt at cutting us down to size?

Or had he been trying to say something else? Something more important?

It was hard not to believe the latter, even though we were freighted with the anxieties and emotions of the 'bereaved': sad, glad to be rid of the nuisance, suddenly aware of the vast gap that had opened up before us. All of it, at once, in perpetual noisy revolve, like a dishwasher that takes for ever to go through a single cycle.

It was hard to hear – to make sense of anything – above this internal noise.

'But where were they kept? Ross, he didn't have them with him when he shifted in, did he?' This was Alison the public prosecutor.

I shook my head.

Bobbie looked from one to the other of us. She took her time.

'There was a box. In storage. A kind of tea chest. I had my eye on it. Thought it'd come in useful if I ever shifted.'

'Do you know where it is?'

It was her turn to enjoy her power. She sipped her scotch. 'What sort is this? How much it cost?' Then she went off on a segue about her plans to go to Brisbane for a break, and how she always made sure to treat herself well, once a year.

'It can get you down, looking after all the old folks. Not that I mind. Someone's got to do it.' She was running off at the mouth.

Alison looked exhausted.

'The box,' I broke in. 'You know where it is?'

Bobbie stopped mid-sentence and a look slid over her features again. A reprimand to our human gracelessness. She would not give in easily. She sat in sulky silence. We listened to the glass being turned round and round.

I noticed Tallulah at the French door, signalling to me that she needed a human to let her in so she could make her customary entrance to huzzas.

I angled my gaze away.

'Listen,' I said. 'Maybe we should have a coffee somewhere and then I can drive you home.'

This led to a nightmare at Valentines. It was worth the price to see Alison squirm at the plate Bobbie brought back from the buffet: cream jelly, fruit sprinkled all over with hundreds and thousands and chocolate chips – a nine-year-old's idea of heaven.

I saw Alison's silent query: is she all there?

We heard about her life. Grew up on a dirt-poor farm. Sister pregnant at thirteen. Kept the baby who was Bobbie's favourite niece and heir.

As she chatted away artlessly she seemed to reveal some essential goodness. Which neither Alison nor I possessed.

She was kind. That was what she was. Yet appalling, too.

Finally we drove her back to her unit out the back of Mt Albert. It was dark. Had the closed-up smell of a small place without ventilation. It was an unwanted insight into the barrenness of her life. Panties – large and plain – drying, a flat-screen state-of-the-art television and, naturally, no books. Microwave and a packet of Cheezels left open, stale. There was a budgie in a cage, hopping frantically back and forth. Its excrement lent a high, unpleasant odour to the air.

I could see Alison checking to see if she could open any of the windows.

'I'm only renting till I get my own place. I've saved up a deposit. Got my eye on some flats, see, out in Papatoetoe.'

Alison provided the right sounds, commending Bobbie's grasp of the market economy.

I was struck by a photo of Dad pinned to the fridge

with a magnet. It had been cut out of the *60 Seconds* ad in the newspaper. Dad as a young man.

'He was good-looking once,' I said by way of conversation.

'Yep,' she said. 'A real hottie.'

She led us through a door to the left. The second bedroom. No light in the socket. Only a spear of light from the door.

There was the box.

I went towards it.

'Yeah, have a gander. I'll pop on an instant.'

Alison and I glanced at each other. Like children again, we hesitated then went forward.

Alison slipped off the rug that covered the top. Removed the lid.

In the darkness, its emptiness gleamed.

'It's got nothing in it,' Alison said.

'Hold on.'

She felt down and then, with a shudder, withdrew. 'Ugh!' she said.

Was it all a joke? Had Dad – or Bobbie – purposely put something revolting in it?

She thrust her hand down again. Lucky dip.

She pulled something out.

Out in the kitchen I heard a microwave ping.

Alison was holding a sheet of paper, folded. She unfolded it.

    Q You were in the Six Mile Road
    field on the evening of 18 August
    1945?

A So far as I can be sure of time so long ago.

Q You were a soldier in the Division at that time?

A I was.

Q You said last October to Captain KEELING it was LIEUTENANT-COLONEL SUGIHARA who gave the order shobun, execute these men.

A I thought I heard LIEUTENANT-COLONEL SUGIHARA say the word shobun.

Q Was there any doubt in your mind this meant execution?

A It can mean many things.

Q For example?

A It can mean move the prisoners to the rear.

Q But the prisoners were starving men, many of them naked. Do you seriously suggest they were marched out into a field, the field was then sealed off and yet the prisoners were being 'moved to the rear'?

A I do not remember that.

Q But you are sure you heard LIEUTENANT-COLONEL SUGIHARA say shobun?

A I am no longer sure.

Q But you told Captain KEELING that you were sure and put it in your statement last October?

A I just imagined it might be so and I stated it.

Q Have you any regard for the sanctity of the oath you swore before making your statement?

A Yes, I have.

Q Why put in something in answer to a request which only might be true?

A I said so because I believed so at the time.

Q Why did you believe so at the time?

A I was repeating what I heard.

Q Was this your unaided recollection or had you been prompted, or was it suggested to you by the Interrogator?

A The Interrogator told me he had other witnesses who said it was so.

Q Do you mean, at the suggestion of the Interrogator Captain KEELING, you put into your statement that which was not true or matters over which you had no clear recollection?

A Yes, I do.

Q Where was this statement taken from you?

A In Tokyo.

Q Yes, but where, what building?

A The Meiji Building.

Q That is not a prison. It is a block of offices, is it not?

A Yes, it is an office.

Q With many people in it? People walking up and down the corridor outside?

A Yes.

Q. The door to the room was not locked?

A The door was not locked.

Q So any senior officers or members of the public could walk by.

A It is possible.

Q Was there any reason for you to fear for your safety while you were in the office?

A I was a little shaky as there were so many foreigners there.

Q At any time were threats of violence offered towards you?

A Nobody gave me either torture or bad use of language.

Q Or threats?

A No physical threats were used.

Q But now you say you wish to make corrections to your past statements because in the past you answered to certain matters suggested by the Interrogating

Officer which were not strictly true.

A I found myself too eager to listen to suggestions which caused my errors.

Q Was it out of politeness or a wish to please Captain KEELING?

A Yes. But he was also quite angry at times. He shouted at me. He came very close to my face. I wished to keep my job as a cleaner of the Australian barracks.

Q You realise the importance of these matters?

A I did not dream that I would one day be here standing in a court.

Q But now you say you do not believe it was LIEUTENANT-COLONEL SUGIHARA who gave the order?

A That is the part I now wish to be corrected.

Q That you heard CAPTAIN HINOKUMA give the order shobun?

A: That is correct. I am saying that now. I stand here wishing to make these corrections. It is good to be in such a free court as this.

It was late by the time Ross dropped me off. The city was deserted. The lift was empty. The doors opened to reveal a bed big enough for three but in which I would, of course, sleep alone.

I didn't mind this. I needed time to think things through.

I turned on the lamps and went to the windows. The harbour out there was spuriously glamorous: waves tipped barley-sugar orange from the lights across the bridge.

I opened the door a little and went and stood outside. There was a cool wind but I let it bathe my skin, my eyes.

I could see down below a young woman sitting on a ledge, talking on a cellphone. She was hunched into it in a way that recalled Juliette. She even had her long hair, her concentration. Her other hand meanwhile worked in counterpoise, ashing a cigarette, drawing phantom shapes – the large space of her dreams, desires, undercut by something more basic.

She was arranging a deal of some sort.

I felt an ache in the back of my throat. I knew it wasn't Juliette yet I felt that unless I took the lift downstairs and checked her out I might lose her for ever. It was like a test. I was acting like someone slightly insane, yet I felt compelled. My breathing had become fast. I felt my skin tighten. I caught the lift downstairs, cursing its slowness. I ran outside. But the girl had gone.

25

'What does it mean?'

Ross let the papers fall on to his lap. It was the following morning. He picked them up again and did exactly as I had done. Read them again, closely.

'It means, I think, that Dad . . . well, bullied witnesses. Stacked the evidence. As that bastard Hazeldean said.'

I found it strange to be indicting him. My father.

I'd had more time than Ross to assimilate the fact. I'd read the papers once at breakneck speed, then more slowly this morning, parsing them for sense – for flaws. I couldn't see any. Then I'd gone and had a hot shower. I let it run for a long time, thinking of nothing. Trying to. I washed my hair. I took my time drying myself. Then I cleansed and moisturised. I realised I was evading my own glance before the mirror.

So I looked.

What are you doing here? my eyes said back. *Your vigil is almost over.*

I'd deliberately withheld the other documents from Ross. I wanted to punish him for the trick he'd played on me. He would pay, compound interest.

But after the disaster of the funeral I thought I should come clean. We needed each other.

'I don't know what to say,' Ross said.

He put the papers down on the coffee table as if they might contaminate him.

'I kept hoping throughout the night I'd dreamt it.'

'I do have a thought.'

I teetered there, uncertain of what I was doing. Ross's claim that he no longer remembered being thrown in the drink by Dad, his counter-memory of the strap, made me hesitate. I knew memory was of course subjective: but Ross and I shared it at points. This after all is the basis of family and friendship, all relationships.

But I still had to trust Ross. Could I? Or more to the point, could I trust myself? My own feelings?

Of late I'd become more tentative. In fact I found myself becoming more and more uncertain about a lot of things. Cracks had appeared in everything I thought – about Dad, his heroism, his behaviour during the war. Ross, my idiot kid brother. Tosspot. Me, the tough survivor.

I also realised truth leaked out through these cracks. You had to look closely. Very closely.

Perhaps it was time to cut myself some slack?

'Ross, you remember the papers we looked at in the box when we were kids?'

My voice was oddly tentative.

He was depressed, looking into space, frowning.

He made a vestigial sound – it could have been yes or no.

'*What* d'you remember?'

I decided it was best to leave it open.

After all, it was a long time ago. I didn't want to prompt him.

He looked back at me, his eyes reading my face.

It occurred to me we'd slipped back into that family way of knowing things intuitively – beyond words.

'Livers,' he said after a while. Recalling. It was as if he were ventriloquised and his lips, of their own volition, were talking. 'I remember us pretending to eat livers.'

I waited.

'Bodies burning . . . and . . . men –' his eyes checked mine out – '. . . men eating flesh. Bodies.'

'Cannibalism,' I said. 'That man up the tree. What he saw was cannibalism.'

I flashed back to our childhood games: how we'd dumb-acted the whole thing out.

'Can't you see that's why nobody wanted to talk about this case? Why nobody wanted to accept responsibility – Sugihara or Hinokuma? It was what happened after the massacre that made everyone duck for cover . . .'

We looked at each other.

'Those were the bones Rebecca Bright said the "animals" dragged away.'

We looked at each other.

'Do you think this is why Dad insisted on this case going through?'

It was an enticing thought. And something that it would be healing to believe. It sparkled before us, the alluring possibility.

An escape clause.

Like family members throughout time we could accept this interpretation, even live with it, live by it. Plenty of people in Germany, in Japan, did . . .

Ross was frowning. He looked uncomfortable. He shrugged.

'What!' I cried, like someone having something precious snatched away. Which I had. 'Why don't you think it's possible?'

He was back to being obstinate. I flashed back to that memory: Ross sitting upright in the dinghy, refuting Dad's scorn, proudly refusing to jump into the sea.

Ross and Dad hating each other viscerally.

I saw this doubt, the last remnants of this hatred, in Ross's face. He looked bruised, and obstinate, and ugly.

He shook his head slowly. 'It's too easy, June.'

'Don't call me that!' I cried out, scalded. 'Don't! I've spent all my adult life becoming who I am. I left that shit behind.' I took a deep breath. 'My name is Alison Burton. In fact people back home call me Ali.'

He did nothing but produce the ghost of a smile.

'Don't be so fucking superior with me, mate.'

His smile froze. His eyes found mine. He shrugged again.

'You think you can leave things behind?'

'If you try hard enough,' I snapped, knowing at the same time it was crap. You could walk away but it walked with you. The past. It stood ahead of you smiling, waiting for you to catch up.

Like Dad . . . like . . .

'I don't know.'

Ross had stood up. He was walking round my room.

'Maybe cannibalism in Japanese culture is like it was in *Maori* culture.'

His face had adopted the pious look of a Pakeha explicating Maori.

'To Maori it was giving wairua – spirit, strength. Or absorbing the strength of the enemy eaten.'

'Ross darling, we're talking about starvation here.'

He just looked at me unconvinced.

'Why do you think they kept so quiet about it?' Besides, I wanted to say: we acted it out, you and I together. The innocence of children.

He looked at me neither convinced nor unconvinced.

'You do remember, don't you?' I challenged him. 'We ate the flesh off the bone. Our special treat was the livers. Even when we didn't know what they tasted like. We left them till last. Yum yum yum. You remember that?'

Even I could hear the pleading tone in my voice.

He looked at me, pale, fascinated. Or was it repulsed?

'I've spent a long time forgetting. Certain things.'

'But you remember that?'

'I remember a game we played, Alison. A game.'

'Don't help me then.'

'There are some things it's better to forget,' Ross said.

'But isn't that what you've always railed against? Isn't it memory – of certain things – you've always clung to?'

'Not that.'

The repulsiveness of the subject matter was wearying on the spirit. It tended to darken everything till you felt unsubtly depressed by it all. By thinking of it you carried the weight.

It was a weight I realised Dad had carried.

It could corrode, maybe even corrupt, in the end.

You'd do anything to get out from under it.

The men who did it, those who watched, those who stood by. Everyone implicated in the aroma of death that drifts downwind from war. Until it seemed to reach us two, sitting in a hotel room, not moving.

'Strange what you remember,' I said.

'And what you choose to forget.'

Ross had got up to go. He was unconvinced. Refusing my escape clause. Leaving me with it, a liability.

'Alison, you're forgetting what Dad was like. Could be like. Or maybe you've forgotten. Or never knew.'

I knew he was talking about that crap about the belt. Dad as bully.

Why did he harp on about trivialities, I wondered. Kids in the '50s were all belted. That was how we grew up. Maybe it was what put the boom into baby boomers. It was the slackers who came after.

'I'm off tomorrow,' I snapped at him. 'Back home.'

I had my own escape clause.

26

I went to say goodbye the following day.

Alison opened the door and I saw, in one sensation, like a dying fall, she felt the same: bruised, betrayed. Uncertain.

Yet her physicality softened me: she was my sister, with her long-legged thighs so like Dad's, the persistent obstinacy of Dad's nose, his height, and then the small fracture of Mum's looks. They could have been Mum's eyes looking at me. Wounded, sore, tired from trying to understand what probably couldn't be understood.

This was new. Perhaps she felt the same on seeing me.

She left the door open and walked wanly back into the room. I saw her suitcase on the bed, open and half-packed. Unusually for her, stuff was just chucked in, pell-mell. I looked round for my novel but couldn't see it. The bin was empty.

I flicked my gaze away.

'Well?' she said, turning to the window. The clear light from the sea below showed a tear-tired face.

'Well?' I echoed, and we looked at each other, waiting.

She drifted to the kettle for something to do. I noticed her hands shaking. Was she frightened of me?

'Did you sleep all right?'

I was grappling for the right tone. I didn't want to talk about that other stuff. Maybe the fact was it was impossible to come to a decision. About what had happened or not happened off Six Mile Road.

The kettle's bubbling rose up. She kept her back to me.

She poured out the water.

'No wonder he was so tortured.'

She carried the cup to me, her eyes looking down.

We sat there.

'You're happy to be going back?'

'Yes,' she said. 'Yes.'

'I'm sorry.'

'I'm sorry too.'

Silence.

Outside the tackle on a mast kept up a frenetic, neurotic sound.

'I've got so much work waiting for me. They'll only hold my job for so long. Besides –' She took a sip, then winced. The tea was still burningly hot. 'I'm eager to get back.'

The transparent falseness lay between us.

I knew I should stand up and wish her good luck. Did she need a lift to the airport, etcetera. Except I didn't. I took the right of family to be clumsy – obdurate, immovable.

Her eyes flickered towards me. She looked nervous.

'Would you like a biscuit?'

She got up and went to the little repository.

I noticed the label at the back of her top was sticking up. On impulse I got up and tucked it back inside.

I felt her body shudder, and she whipped round, I thought, to turn on me.

Except tears were welling up under her lids, cascading downwards as if there were no end to them.

I didn't know what to do. She was a proud woman.

I came closer to her.

I went straight up to Ross. I couldn't hold it in. I didn't know what was happening. I began to cry. Before I knew it, I was sobbing. Ross was crying too. We were holding on to each other and crying our hearts out.

The loss of control felt exhilarating.

'Juliette's a user, Ross.'

This came out. I didn't know where from. It was like it had been waiting there all along.

Ross's eyes said: Go on. I want to hear.

'I've done everything, all I could . . . all I could humanly do.'

And then it tumbled out, roared out: a bloody awful birth. I found tears streaming down my cheeks and I was blubbering, saying, 'I don't know where she is, how she is, I don't know – *anything*.'

This exposition of the female art of emotional abandonment appalled me. Ross, however – forever the chump – seemed moved. He put his arms around me. And I surrendered.

I surrendered. I would like this notified and written

down somewhere. Then thrown away.

But I'm honest enough to write it down here.

Like the British at Singapore, the Japanese at Tokyo Bay in 1945, I endured the unendurable.

I surrendered.

'I must look a mess,' I said.

Ross was filching out a tissue. His face was reddened, nose running. (The village idiot in person, I thought.) He grinned at me. Took a few dozen tissues and hooted.

'What a fucked-up family,' he said with, I thought, a note of self-congratulation. I was about to reprimand him, then I bit my tongue. Painfully. I would need to change the way I did things. I saw that.

It would not be easy.

I went and sat down. I put my hands between my knees and shut them there. Some strange mood had overtaken me.

'Caryl?'

'Yes, June.'

'You remember you said to me ... you wanted to imagine your way into how Dad felt?'

This was raising a most tender subject.

He blinked and looked back at me, apprehensive, perhaps, of my aptitude for surprise attack.

But I had nothing left.

Nothing.

I needed to show Ross this.

'I understand that now. I do ... I want to go ... to where Dad was imprisoned. Kuching. And on the way go to that Six Mile Field. I mean,' I said quickly, 'I don't know what he did or didn't do – that last case – whether he cooked the books – it looks like he did –'

Ross waited.

'I want to see for myself. With my own eyes. Go there.'

Ross stood up.

'Not that . . . there's probably anything left . . . but . . .'

For once in my life, courage seemed to fail me.

I couldn't look up.

Then I raised my eyes and looked straight into Ross's.

He was waiting.

I was blushing.

'I wondered if you might like to come with me?'

A Greater Silence

Protests spread across China against the visit of the Japanese Prime Minister to the Yasukuni Shrine, which commemorates Japanese war criminals. Crowds, estimated at 400,000 in Beijing, called on Japan to apologise for Second World War crimes against humanity. Protests also ignited in neighbouring South Korea and provincial cities across China. The Japanese Prime Minister issued no statement. An aide said the Prime Minister intended visiting the Yasukuni Shrine as it honoured Japan's 2.5 million war dead. It had nothing to do with war crimes, the aide said.

— *New York Times*, 2005.

'Let's have a slow morning?'

They had awoken to the child-dream strangeness of both of them in beds in the same room. It had been Ross's suggestion that they share a room in Kuching. Alison naturally preferred a room on her own. But then, in a flash — a flash that illuminated the space between their finances — she understood. Ross could not afford a single. And naturally, as naturally as they had been contestants for the miserly love of their father, he would not accept her generous offer of paying for his room.

'But I have the money!'

'No doubt.'

It would not do, would be painfully awkward. It was more natural they undergo the awkwardness of negotiating a shared space. Times of waking, sleeping, amount of time spent in the shared bathroom. Precedence. The realities of how their aging bodies worked. How many times in the night each of them might pad to use the toilet.

The first night, a remarkable transition, had worked out well enough. They had slept fitfully, excited as children in a holiday camp.

Only late at night, both of them wide awake, Ross had said, 'It's true, isn't it?'

'What?'

She lay there reading the unfamiliar patternings of net curtains on a textured ceiling: it was a broad sweep of pattern, a cluster of detail like a small army waiting — poised for a surprise attack.

'That Dad — that he . . . more than likely . . . did falsify evidence —'

'To get that man hung?'

It seemed important, in that darkened room in a hotel in a foreign city, to speak plainly.

The darkness helped.

Ross sighed and changed his position in the bed so he

lay on his side looking at her.

'Yes. To get . . . not revenge, I don't think it was revenge –'

'It was revenge,' Alison said flatly.

'Justice. As he saw it.'

There was a moment's pause, for consideration.

'I wish these places had windows that opened. Air conditioning always makes me feel embalmed. Or part of some kind of all-American embalming process.'

'Welcome to a twenty-first-century nightmare.'

Alison got up and went to the fridge. The light of the opened door revealed her body – the slight stoop of age, the thinning shanks, small compact stomach even on a woman so athletic. He looked away.

'Water?'

'Mmm.'

Like children they enjoyed their treats.

'What time is it?'

Ross felt round for his watch.

'Two minutes past two, here. Eight o'clock in the morning in Auckland.'

'Shall we go to Six Mile Road tomorrow?' This was Ross.

'Yes.'

'I think we need to . . . get that out of the way first. Then we can –'

'Relax?'

Like an elderly couple they had taken to completing each other's sentences.

'I don't blame Dad,' Ross said.

Alison was quiet.

'We don't know what he went through. Not really.'

'I feel let down. Betrayed.' Alison's voice was cool. 'I loved Dad. Admired him.'

Ross said nothing for a minute. He had lived with his father's failings more intimately.

'I just feel sad. Very sad.'

'Me too,' Alison said at last.

They listened to the silence which lay between them, warm.

'You know that story you wrote?'

'Yes.' A little terse.

'Why? Why did you do it? To trick me?'

'*No.*'

'Well, why then? I believed it.'

'I wanted to . . . try and understand him. Why he might have . . . acted as he did.'

'But there was no male lover?'

Ross was silent.

'There was no male lover, Ross?'

'In my book there was.'

Alison said nothing for a moment.

Then Ross spoke carefully. 'I wanted your approval, Alison. I wanted you to say for once in your life that I had done something good. I wanted you to understand.'

Alison sighed. 'I think I understand.'

The silence extended, grew.

Ross yawned, a deep, long yawn.

'We should go to sleep,' Alison said. 'We've got a big day tomorrow.'

Ross and Alison breakfasted at leisure.

They deserved time and space. They needed the softness of different circumstances to expand in. The dark coil of the mystery must elude them, or they must elude it – for moments, days, weeks – if they were to humanly survive.

'Salamat pagi.'

'Say that again for me, if you please.'

Alison observed Ross's use, even brand, of antique charm. She felt a fondness for him, as for a developing or even undeveloped child. She recognised the charm. It was their father at his best – wry, intuitive, marvelling at the world. Amid the breakfast debris – eggshells, tea, toast crusts – she felt the sickening lurch of pathos.

She thought for a moment of the flight from KL. They had already been travelling for over seven hours before they took the flight to Kuching – a step down, off the main branch line to Europe, America, the world. They seemed to be flying into darkness.

The plane was largely empty. Opposite them, sitting on her own, was an exhausted-looking housewife, nodding off to sleep, her burqa touching an opened magazine that showed Posh Spice.

Later still, when the taxi drew up before the hotel, Alison had seen, ghostly as a dream, an emaciated transsexual walking off at speed, as if to an assignation.

The transsexual had glanced at her, at Ross, assessingly.

It was another world.

They had arrived.

Watching the husband and wife come towards him, the guide saw them as curiously mismatched in the perfect symmetry of unhappy couples everywhere. She – tall, thin, unattractively muscly for a woman; the husband dazed, off-centre, smiling.

The wife nodded, as brusque as the wife of a magistrate inspecting local troops.

The husband came towards him, saying, 'Good morning or – how do you say – wait! Wait? I have it here –' and here he stumbled through, like a learning child – 'Salamat pagi.'

'Salamat pagi,' Donny replied, awarding the Australian a dazzling smile, such as a prince might give to a favourite pupil at a prizegiving. To the wife he awarded a curt nod.

'We are brother and sister.' The wife disassembled herself in a slow and carefully segmented sentence.

'Ah! Brother and sister! Ah!'

Amid a festive jollity they shook hands.

'From New Zealand.'

'My name is Donny and I am your guide to Six Mile Field.' There was a faint American burr to his English. He was Chinese-Malay – plump as an only son.

'Your English is good.'

Ross was flirting with Donny, Alison could tell. As the car backed out, he'd checked out Donny's marital status: his hands, soft and plump, had a pinky ring, and his nails were beautifully manicured, each nail brought to a strangely feminine point. The name – Donny – seemed so fake, more American than from Sarawak. But Donny, checking out the rear-vision mirror, was professional. He brought Alison into the conversation.

'My sister is at Wisconsin College studying Business Studies. I go visit her whenever I can.'

They were driving away from the centre of Kuching.

Donny took them to a raw subdivision on the furthest

outskirts of the city. The heat of the day had risen. Palms hung still in the heat. A kind of pearlene haze covered the sky. Ross and Alison dripped sweat. They were two degrees away from the Equator.

The earth's surface had been scraped back to clay. Apartments two storeys tall were being thrown up. Prosperity as a paper-thin illusion.

They were in the wrong place, surely?

'This isn't it,' Alison said.

'No,' Ross echoed, thinking of *60 Seconds*.

Donny's eyes behind the sunglasses checked out the recalcitrant foreigners.

'Yes, this is Six Mile Field.'

He nosed the car forward. And braked gently, as if to pierce an illusion.

Ross glanced out and saw on a mound a small concrete stump, a marker.

Donny hopped out and courteously peeled back Alison's door. It could have been a subliminal order to exit. Face facts.

'Memorial for Six Mile Massacre,' Donny said with practised tact.

Ross got out. The moment Alison emerged she lost vision, felt a moment of utter panic – blindness. Then realised it was condensation on her sunglasses.

Donny stood to the side, taking the hands-behind-back stance of a discreet undertaker.

A lorry lumbered by.

The small stump was heartbreakingly crude. Knee height. And with a bronze plaque.

Here on 18 August 1945,
75 Allied servicemen gave their lives
for the cause of Freedom.
We remember them.

In smaller lettering it said, 'Provided by the charitable donations from the St Kilda RSL, Victoria, Australia.'

Somewhere a radio was playing loudly. Robbie Williams.

Behind the memorial was a wreath discarded from some earlier ceremony. All that was left was its bamboo outline held together by green plastic twine. Ants moved over it in a demented fury.

'But this doesn't look like the place where *60 Seconds* was filmed.' Ross spoke in disbelief.

Donny came closer. 'I was also guide for NZ TV crew.' He nodded, smiling. 'Rebecca Bright —' he slid his wallet out and looked through a sizeable collection of cards. 'She a very positive personality.'

He held the card out as evidence.

Alison read the card: 'Investigative journalist.'

'Miss Bright decide this not look enough like Six Mile. Like it might have looked at time of unfortunate event. They ask for advice on finding field. Many others look just like. I advise.' He sounded proud.

Alison's eyes found Ross's.

'All the same, look all the same,' Donny said, catching some inflection in their gaze.

'But not the same,' Ross said lightly.

'Not the same but the same.'

Ross and Alison turned away to look at the memorial. Their backs turned to him. Faces hidden.

What could they do? They had not brought flowers. Neither of them was Christian, so they did not pray. Or the prayer they said was internal, silent.

The heat was uncomfortable yet the occasion seemed to demand some form of ceremony. Ross slid his camera out.

'Will you take our photo please?'

They did not smile, Donny noticed. They stood tensely together, staring into the too bright light, their faces scrunched up. He had taken Japanese to sites of horror. Australians. He was impartial as his grandfather, who became an 'interpreter' to the Kempetai, the Japanese secret police.

'Sunglasses off please,' he called out.

They obeyed.

Now the light swept into their faces, revealing them in all the damage of middle age: they clung together, wrecks, flotsam carried to that point – clinging, not drowning.

'Smile!'

The day was weaning towards a high, almost unbearable humidity. Sweat beaded and slid down Ross and Alison's faces, necks, backs, under their arms. They were pits of moistness, pale as paper, unacclimatised.

They were lunching at a Lebanese restaurant. Ross had found a plaque that said the building had been the HQ for the Japanese army during the war. It had a high second storey: you climbed a sharp ascent of stairs and there, on an open veranda, lay some hastily prepared tables. The place was deserted. Perhaps the climb put people off. No service was visible.

Alison tapped the table nervously. She needed

rehydration. Ross jumped up and went to locate the owner. They ordered a meal and waited.

'Dad was probably part of the slave labour who built this building,' Ross said.

Alison looked at him.

'I read about it doing my research. Prisoners of war were marched in each day, four miles. Hard, I guess, when you're suffering malnutrition and malaria.'

While she waited, Alison looked around. From the height of the second floor it all made sense. It was architecture as paranoia. It was a sniper's view, if worst came to worst. People down below were miniaturised, made subtly less human, more like targets: the detail of their faces was lost, but the blank of their bodies remained visible, vulnerable. She shivered.

Her hands were stickily placed on the plastic cloth. She thought about the way history resided invisibly in buildings. Was it there as a resonance? A ghostly litmus, a sort of inner click that only certain individuals were attuned to – could hear. Survivors were like this: capable of tuning things out but at the same time tuning in to one particular sound, a kind of echo, a vibration left over from pain and horror.

Yet it was a burden bordering on mania. She had no wish, no wish at all, to be one of those survivors, or children of survivors, the point of whose life is to recreate a privileged victimhood. This she despised.

She shivered. Why was she here? Was it for a rest on her way home to England – or was she seeking her father still? Elusive Eric, as distant in death as he had been in life?

The food arrived. Alison drank three cups of milkless

tea. She chose her moment carefully.

'Ross,' she said, dangling her hand over the balcony, as if to bathe in air, 'I've booked us into an eco-lodge. A surprise gift. We may as well enjoy ourselves,' she added with a hint of what Ross thought of as Helen Clarkish steel in her voice.

Ross was fanning himself with a map. 'Oh darling, I don't think eco-lodges are quite me.'

Alison looked sour. Then, when the hint of a smile flitted over Ross's face, she allowed herself to smile.

'It'll do you good.'

'As Dad used to say. And look what happened there.'

They flew to Sandakan. There was a sense of penetrating ever deeper into the mystery that was Borneo. A boat took them up a river for two hours. The river was mile-wide and brown. Palm forests gradually gave way to a riverine forest. The boat stopped every so often the further they got up the river. A guide pointed out orangutans dangling from trees.

The animals gazed down at the interlopers, visitors who once would have come hunting with guns. Now they carried cameras. An image was what was captured. It was a national park, a remnant left over to remind humans of what had once been everywhere. The haze from burning forests grew clearer.

The eco-lodge was less stringent than Ross had feared. There were separate toilets, even showers. It was more like a luxury tramping lodge where penitents of the coming ecological catastrophe came to take rest, relax, rest their fears.

They went out that night and looked at birds by

torchlight. The following morning, they were invited to board longboats, powered by outboard motors.

Ross was being surprisingly amenable. There were twenty-five of us, all strangers. In time these people would become clearly divisible: the honeymoon couple in their late thirties; a spooning couple from the Nordic states, like an earlier version; a family from the Benelux states with beautiful unburnt skin – a sprinkling of Australians.

The exception was a Japanese man, neat and clean. He appeared to be on his own. In his early forties, a creamy skin and full-moon face with observant eyes. He was dressed in a preppy fashion. But what struck me immediately was his sense of containment: the white flannel he used to wipe the back of his neck; his socks, I noticed that first morning, were pastel yellow, an unusual colour for a man.

He kept a kind of Zen-like space around himself.

The boats were lined up before the jetty and people were getting on: honeymooners clinging together, the slight or even pronounced shyness of strangers before intimacy. Ross had leapt into a boat beside an Australian queen of stately mien. Somehow the Japanese man and I ended up together. Two oddballs.

I looked at him and he creased out a smile, half bowed in the boat. I was aware, overaware, of his superb cleanliness. Beside him I felt like a hairy, sweating barbarian, even though I'd put on clean clothes that morning.

'Good morning, my name is Hakyo Matsumoto.'

I found myself trying to bow in reply, a difficult process in a rocking longboat. I could not manage the art so seamlessly. Found myself grabbing the side of the boat as it pitched.

He laughed, though regretfully, and reached forward to steady me.

'It does not do to rock the boat.'

His touch did something to me. He took his hand away.

'And your name?'

In the uncharacteristic confusion I had not said who I was. This was so unlike me, this ludicrous maidenliness, I found myself blushing. What could be more absurd, a fifty-seven-year-old virgin?

Well, not quite.

At that moment he said to me quickly, as though supplying a line.

'You are hoping to see the orange orangutan? Maybe the proboscis monkey? The last on our disappearing planet?'

He took up his camera and raised it to his eye.

Everyone else sat with cameras ready on their laps.

'Yes,' I said as to a child. 'Yes, I'm hoping to spot an orangutan.'

At that moment the outboard motor started up. In the racket I saw his eyes look into mine: a dark, unreadable glance.

'You are sightseeing here in Borneo?' He asked me when the noise took up.

'I can't hear,' I yelled back. I glanced back at Ross. He was sitting behind me. He was beaming like a child on a school trip. Nattering with his new friend.

I turned back to Hakyo. I made an executive decision. I would not hide my wounds.

'My father was here in the war.'

We were threading up a tributary – the water brackish, the river narrowing. Petrol fumes bloomed blue over the surface of the water.

Hakyo looked at me, then inclined his head.

Brad, another improbably named guide, in Reebok vest, scarlet cap and sunnies, cut off the outboard motor. Silence packed in around us.

Hakyo raised his camera and began an efficient inventory of the wildlife. The purple-throated sunbird. The little spiderhunter. The dusky munia. But they were sparce attendees at this end of the world rite. This didn't put anyone off. We wanted value for money. All around us were the click and whirr of cameras. Like an old-fashioned adding machine in a bank.

The boat drifted. Our guide got out an oar, anchored us. He eloquently pointed out wildlife we otherwise might not see. It was only after a good fifteen minutes that he turned on the motor.

Under the veil of noise, Hakyo said to me, as if our conversation was merely interrupted, 'And was your father here? On this flood plain?'

I decided to forge ahead. I would not prevaricate or hide as though I were ashamed of him. 'He was captured at Singapore. In the Australian army. Was put in Changi Prison, then moved to Sandakan, and later to Kuching.'

He lowered his head in acknowledgement. I sensed he knew, understood the dread meaning behind these names.

I looked deep into his eyes. The sun overhead, so high in the sky now, pierced the globe of his retina and for one moment appeared amber.

'Later he investigated war crimes. A famous case,' I said boldly. 'The Six Mile Road Incident.'

The motor had cut off so my last few words were shouted out. The indecency stared me in the face. Fortunately, Ross was gabbing away to his new Australian friend. Hakyo gave away nothing to indicate he had heard.

Instead he lost himself in inventorying another vanishing species. When my eyes caught his, he nodded, as if we had come to some understanding.

'I too have been to Six Mile Road,' he said.

We did not speak for the rest of the trip.

I came across him later that evening. It was getting dark and he was leaning on the balcony of the dinner-house, a kind of elegant pavilion built out over the river. The last rinse of sunset held in the sky. But the jungle was dark and a great quietness seemed to have overtaken the world.

I came and stood beside him. He glanced at me once intently and then, looking out to the river, said, 'It is a peaceful place to come?'

'It's good to relax for a moment.'

'Peace is the best,' he said. 'These are the words on the Japanese Memorial Park on Labuan Island. Placed there by the Asia–Pacific Friendship Association. You have seen?'

I said I hadn't.

'There was a battle there at the end of hostilities. Japanese soldiers hid in caves. Buried alive. On the list, if you look, there are no injured. That is because nobody survived.'

I wasn't sure what to say.

'Peace is the best,' he said again. He seemed to be brooding. Uneasy. Then he burst out. 'I am sorry to be giving you disturbing news. I am an historian. Your father's innocence – or guilt – concerns me.'

Somewhere, across the darkness of the river, birds began to caw in panic. Thrashing of wings. Desperate. It sounded like a crocodile had snatched a bird. Then, as suddenly, the noise ceased. An oppressive silence rolled across the surface of the river. It was getting darker by the moment.

I felt a spurt of fury. At being cornered. This was a private mission, almost a pilgrimage. The last thing I wanted was someone to prod at our wounds. We needed silence, space, distance. How had Hakyo found us, that's what I wanted to know. But I would bide my time.

I felt a tear of sweat roll down my spine.

'I was alerted to your father's case by Professor Hazeldean. It is quite a hot debate at the moment. Is there such a thing as justice when a people are conquered? Or only theatre pieces in which the victor enacts rituals of revenge thinly disguised as justice? You know?' he said. 'Like the Americans hanging Saddam Hussein.'

The look of horror must have registered on my face. I did not know what to do. Or say. My heart was beating painfully.

I thought to myself: wouldn't it be a trick to have a heart attack? In a jungle lodge two degrees away from the Equator.

At this moment a crowd of people entered the dining room. A young woman on the staff came forward with an oil lamp and placed it down nearby. The fumes flittered across the surface of the table. It was this that made tears force their way out of my eyes. I swear this to you.

I could see Alison was upset about something. We were

seated at dinner. It was a convention of the place that people were separated from partners. She had her back to me, was talking to the family from the Benelux countries. Every so often she turned around to glance at me, and I could see something had gone wrong, sensed it was the unhappy coincidence of her being approached by the good-looking Jap. I myself wouldn't have minded placing my thigh, artlessly, against his. I tried to send Alison a message the one moment our eyes connected. She looked dismal, frightened. I couldn't work out what had gone wrong.

I wanted to shift beside her but we were trapped. It was impossible.

When dinner ended I noticed the Japanese man going over to Alison and speaking to her quietly. She looked stricken.

They shook hands. There was some kind of strange electricity in their grasp, even I could see this.

'La!' called Suzie, an Australian matron. 'It's strange what happens in the tropics-la!'

But when I went towards Alison she flashed me a warning glance I hadn't seen for many years. It reminded me most of when she was a teenager. I would knock on her door. There would be a long wounded silence. Finally I would yell out, 'June, open the door.' But when she peeled the door back the blast she sent me – silently – through her eyes: it was as if the typhoon inside her soul roared out and swept everything away before it.

She lay down on her bed in our shared room.

'I have a headache.'

'It's the fumes,' I said. 'Those bloody outdoor motors. Talk about fucking ecology.'

She didn't reply.

'Can I get you anything?'

'I need to be on my own for a while.'

On the longboat it was established, in one of those patterns that emerge so seemingly spontaneously yet which quickly have the force of iron, that Alison always sat with 'The Jap'. Hakyo Matsumoto, she told me his name was. He had a wife back in Japan, she said. I rolled my eyes.

It took me a while to notice that they only spoke when the outboard motor started up. Then they seemed to be involved in some intense conversation.

'Oi,' I said to her when we were dressing for dinner that night. 'He's good-looking, that bloke.'

'Who?' she said.

'Oh, come on now. Doesn't he get you hot?'

She said nothing.

'He does me,' I said. 'I wouldn't mind sinking between his thighs.'

'You're being pathetic, Ross.'

'No, sexually frustrated. Foreign travel always makes me horny –'

'Shut up,' she cried then. 'Don't you ever think of anything else?'

'Well,' I said, a little wounded. 'It helps to fill in time . . .'

'What does?'

'Sex. Sexual curiosity.'

She said nothing. Turned her back on me.

2

I couldn't sleep that night. The following morning we were to be woken at 4.30, have a scratch breakfast, then go for a walk in the jungle. 'A walk in the jungle' – how odd that sounds. We had paid for leech-socks, that is, socks that covered the top of your gumboots so blood-sucking leeches couldn't penetrate. Basically, the less revealed flesh, the fewer opportunities for the leeches to attach: a general rule in life, I would have thought.

Why did I not tell Ross about the Japanese historian? I hesitated – I wanted so much to confide in Ross. But I knew it was key that I manage the situation. I'd leave it to the right moment. I told myself it was because Ross was so unpredictable you never knew what way he'd play it. Whether he'd want to barge in and accuse Hakyo of being unethical. Or try to sleep with him. But none of this was true. I had to acknowledge it as I lay there. The bitter fact was I still resented the trick he'd played on me with that book.

Revenge can take many forms. Strange, though, to find yourself siding with a stranger against your own brother.

The blood bond is a noose as often as it's a golden chain.

We stumbled through breakfast in that tepid silence of people awoken too early. We got into the boats. The first light was touching up the gunmetal sky with oddly effeminate wisps of chiffon. The great grey-black mass of jungle revealed itself in duplicate on the river. Everything was still.

We put-putted off, then accelerated.

Neither Hakyo nor I spoke.

The boat dug its prow into mud. Our guide, Brad, jumped off and helped us disembark one by one. This was a dank world we were entering, surfaces glaucous with rain and shade. But there was a track. Armed defensively with cameras, we set out, all of us silent, a little apprehensive about what lay ahead.

Hakyo and I found ourselves separating out. The others vanished, though we could hear their voices disembodied behind the mat of leaves and trees. I kept my eyes on the ground – gumboots suctioning in and out of grey-black mud. When once I raised my head and glanced around I saw a world in which it would be difficult to survive if lost. I thought of the soldiers, on either side really, and how they must have felt that whatever they did there would remain unseen. Neither of us spoke for a while, then Hakyo began talking as I expected he would.

'I was told two New Zealanders had visited Six Mile

Road Memorial the day before I did.'

I had allowed him to take the lead, perhaps uncharacteristically. He turned and looked back at me.

'Naturally I asked who you were. Donny told me your names.'

I didn't know what to say, so I said nothing.

'By coincidence I found myself here. I saw two people who were pointed out to me as New Zealanders. I checked your names in the visitors' book here. I decided I would get to know you.'

Again I said nothing. Then, pulling my gumboot out of the mire, I made my move.

'What right have you to harass us?'

He looked taken aback.

'Do you know what we've been through?'

'Professor Hazeldean did me the kindness to tell me there was a television programme. I have not had the privilege of seeing it.'

'My father was called a war criminal.' There was a thin, strident note in my voice. Defiant. Bleak.

We had halted in the jungle, letting the others get ahead. I could no longer hear their voices. For a half-second I sped through the mad thought that I was alone in this place with someone I really didn't know. He could be a psychopath.

I couldn't read the expression on his face. Was he half-smiling in sympathy? Compassion? Was he enjoying my pain? My perplexity.

'You people all right?'

It was Brad calling out. Brad with sunnies on the top of his cap, just as you might see on Ponsonby Road.

'Yes.'

I was the one who called back. But I felt a heaviness in my heart. I was always the person who called back. *Yes.*

Yes, everything is all right. Keep walking. Keep moving forward.

Except now I wanted to be still. I could not move.

I looked at Hakyo. 'My father was tortured by the Japanese,' I said. 'He was only a young man. He lost his youth here – *here* – in these swamps. One part of him never came back. He got to be a bitter old man. Our lives were affected by it. There was no support. The government he'd fought for couldn't care less. So what did it all mean? What was it all for?'

We were surrounded by the monstrous silence of the jungle – something I had never thought about before. I had imagined it might be noisy with birds, or with distant crashes of larger animals moving about, or fighting. Instead, silence. Utter stillness.

Was it a sign of depletion? Of the coming great silence, when the world settled into oblivion?

Or were there other silences all around us?

A silence of unanswered questions.

How could this have happened?

What did happen?

Would it happen again? When? To whom?

The silence of those men going to their execution.

The silence of the executioners, and those who came after.

A depthless silence. Unending as a void.

I made a move to go, but Hakyo stopped me.

'Please, one moment more. I have a sad story you must hear. It may help you to understand.'

I found myself trembling.

'Lieutenant-Colonel Sugihara. In Singapore. Earlier. He was involved in *Sook Ching*.'

I looked at him. I had no idea what he was saying.

'You have not heard?'

My silence betrayed my perplexity.

'It is translated: purification by elimination.'

Its Nazi emphasis was unmistakable.

'The Chinese were tied together by wire, back to back. Like fire crackers, you know? And then they were thrown into the sea. Shot. It is efficient of course. One body leads to the next. They drown each other. Very efficient. Sugihara was only carrying out an order. But . . . such an order.'

He sighed.

'A man can be too long at war. War is bad. Peace is the best.'

There was nothing more to say.

'I'm sorry,' I fumbled.

'I too am sorry.'

We started walking back.

'You okay?'

We'd made it back to the lodge and were about to have a late and celebratory brunch. Everyone had gone back to their rooms to shower and get changed.

Alison looked at me glassily. Didn't reply.

'Do you want to lie down?'

'No, no. I . . . just let me get through brunch, then I'll lie down and have a sleep.'

She came to the brunch conspicuously soiled. Everyone else was dressed in fresh outfits, as if for elevenses. I had never seen her so distressed. The others looked at her and kept their distance. A jollity had come over them, as though they'd passed some primordial test. I didn't at first notice that the Japanese man wasn't there.

'How was your walk?'

'Fine.'

'You seemed to get lost at one point.'

'Lost or found.'

'You and the good-looking Jap.'

She didn't rise to my innuendo.

It was towards the end of brunch that Alison turned to me, her eyes weird.

'What's that?'

She pointed down to something at her feet. At first I thought it was an earring. Then it flexed slightly.

'It's a leech, I think,' I said, just as she turned her wrist over. Her shirt sleeve was dappled all over with spots of blood. Even as we looked at it the blood blossomed – scarlet on white – her shirt changing into a thousand rising suns.

'Oh God!'

She stood up.

The amount of blood was incredible.

With brittle hilarity, she called out, 'It's me the blood leech got, everyone!'

People applauded sardonically, with a touch of concern, but it added to their holiday – a neat little incident, a further jungle tale.

Alison raced away. I followed behind her.

'Alison, are you all right?' I asked when I got to the room.

She was in the bathroom being not very conservation-minded with the water. When I touched her on the shoulder she was just standing there, very still.

We sat side by side.

'Could we get away?'

'I want to speak to him.'

I felt resentful. This, of all things, was the most perfidious big sister act.

'Why couldn't you have told me?'

'Do you think it's only about you?'

'Well, Dad was my father too.'

She didn't speak. She seemed stunned.

'But you should have – you could have trusted me. Tried to.'

'Like you trusted me – with your book?'

'Is that what this is about?'

She didn't reply.

'Can't you give it up? Can't you see what I was wanting, trying to do? I wanted you to understand . . . Dad . . . how he might have been. What he'd been through. I wanted you to understand *me*. What I want to do most in the world.'

'You could have told me.'

'You could have told *me*.'

She glanced at me once, a brilliantly wounded look. I had the feeling we were looking at each other for the first time in our lives. Looking deep into our real selves. Naked.

'I know,' she said in a very worn-out voice. 'I couldn't tell you, Ross, because I couldn't trust myself. Not you.' She took my hand. 'I'm sorry, Ross. I'm sorry.'

She gave a laugh, dismissive, pleading. It was so unlike

her that I found it disarming. I wanted to hug her, but I knew she'd hate that. So we sat there, holding hands.

'I've reached the end of the road,' she said, less to me than to herself. 'I'm going home – to what? I'm bone tired. I don't know . . . any more. All sorts of things.'

Her fingers spasmed a message into my hands. I surged a feeling back. Then she did something unusual: she sighed deeply and slumped her body against mine. We sat there holding one another.

'Poor old Dad,' I said for no particular reason.

'Yes,' she said. 'Poor Dad.'

We sat like that for a long moment.

One part of me was dying to run out and find the Japanese historian. But I knew I had to stay with my sister. Then Alison resolved the situation. She shifted away from me and looked directly into my eyes.

'Ross . . . you know what you wrote?'

'. . . Yes?' I braced myself for another douche of acid.

'I believed it. I bought it. I think you should . . . well, it's better than being a gardener!'

She laughed again, a tender, uncertain laugh. I laughed along with her.

'Forgive me.'

I suddenly comprehended that the whole coming home to New Zealand had been like a slow-motion breakdown for her. She was like a hard-boiled egg rolled remorselessly along a hard bench: her shell was crazed all over. As was mine. Perhaps that's age, in the end. Getting old. Being covered all over by the tiniest haircracks. Our wrinkles are merely metaphors – or mirror images for all the tiny breakdowns involved in being human. In matching idea to reality. In reality instructing us again and again how our ideas failed, or are in vain, or not good enough – real enough.

We learn our inner ugliness, and failures lurk like some essential skeleton. All the rest is flesh which fades away. But then there's your self-knowledge, the things you learn painfully, through falling. And blissfully, in those rare moments of human flight.

I went in search of him.

'He's down there. Leaving.'

I ran down the boardwalk, to the jetty. Hakyo had just stepped on to the boat. His luggage was thrown in. The outboard motor started up.

We looked at each other in silence.

And then he did something that perhaps only his culture could do.

He bowed.

I – foolish barbarian – sodomite bound for the flames of hell, according to some – inclined my own waist and returned the compliment.

'La!' Suzie the Australian cried. 'Two weeks in the tropics and we're all Asian now-la?'

The boat turned. Water separated us.

I stood there a long while and watched the boat getting smaller. And smaller.

I put my hand in the air and waved.

There was nothing for a moment.

Then he waved back.

On the launch back to Sandakan, Alison slept. She looked exhausted. When she woke up, she was disoriented for a moment, then she saw me looking down at her.

I grinned. 'You forgot it was the fag who won on *Survivor*?'

'Fuck off. Don't be so banal, Ross,' she said. However, she was smiling greyly.

We'd got to know each other again. Even our weak points we could negotiate.

It's called family.

3

We parted at KL airport. At one of those weird crossroads where you go off to different parts of the globe.

We pulled our luggage over to some chairs. Alison still had her tiny Louis Vuitton. She opened it up, got out her computer and checked her emails. She was busy for twenty minutes. Then she closed the computer lid. She had a strange look on her face.

I guessed it was business. Some opportunity. She seemed excited, or disturbed.

'Guess what?'

Our childhood game, except the roles were reversed.

'I don't know. What?'

'Juliette.'

I tried to read her face. But I couldn't.

'She wants to see me.'

I carefully judged what to say.

'That's all?'

'That's all.'

'Good,' I said.

'We'll see.'

I checked my ticket, my passport. I was really fumbling before the big goodbye.

'Come and visit me in London, Ross.'

We hesitated.

We both stood up.

Would we hug and kiss? Had we learnt anything about the art of being kin?

But it happened easily this time. We melded together as if we fitted. As we drew apart, my hair caught in Alison's earring. I winced. She laughed. We tugged and pulled, then carefully extricated ourselves from the tiny web of pain and connection.

She flicked away a white hair from my head, plucked so fresh the end had a small stamen of scalp attached to it.

'Steady on,' I said. 'I haven't got so many of those.'

She laughed.

We held there, incapable of parting.

I said, burbling really, 'It's good we at least didn't have to go to war, Alison. Not like poor old Dad. Our lives haven't been so fucked up.'

'Not by that.'

'I'll see you soon,' I said.

She nodded.

'I'll be there.'

I waved, but she had already turned and gone.

The Pacific War is often called 'the forgotten war'. Perhaps because of this many of the wounds remain unhealed to this day. My own father, Gordon, fought in the Egyptian and Italian campaigns, as was common with many New Zealand men. Like many of his contemporaries, he never talked of the war. This novel is dedicated to him, and to the men who carried the burden of things done, things seen, and things left unsaid.

— *Peter Wells*

There's fuck-all left of me
of what there used to be.
— *song from Changi Prison,
Singapore.*

Lucky Bastard